PRAISE FOR

"Fast-paced, action-packed, and full of laughs." —Nerdist.com

"Enthralling and pure magic, Grey's debut is delightful!"
—*Romantic Times*

★ "Sparks fly. . . . Will please fans of Cassandra Clare and *Game of Thrones* watchers with its remarkable world building, richly developed characters . . . [and] a breathtaking climax that . . . cannot come soon enough!" —*Booklist,* Starred

"A feisty heroine, fun supporting characters, a mission to save the world, and some seriously spicy romance." —*SLJ*

"A page-turner—I was hooked from start to finish."
—*Latina*

"Sharp drama that leads to a conclusion begging for a sequel." —*The Bulletin*

BOOKS BY MELISSA GREY

The Girl at Midnight

The Shadow Hour

The Savage Dawn

The Shadow Hour

MELISSA GREY

EMBER

YA
GREY

9.99

TO BUMBLE, FOR KEEPING ME COMPANY

This is a work of fiction. Names, characters, places, and incidents either are the product of the author's imagination or are used fictitiously. Any resemblance to actual persons, living or dead, events, or locales is entirely coincidental.

Originally published in hardcover in the United States by Delacorte Press, an imprint of Random House Children's Books, New York, in 2016.

Visit us on the Web! randomhouseteens.com

Educators and librarians, for a variety of teaching tools,
visit us at RHTeachersLibrarians.com

The Library of Congress has cataloged the hardcover edition of this work as follows:
Grey, Melissa, author.
The shadow hour / Melissa Grey. — First edition.
Summary: "With the firebird awakened, the war has become even more dangerous for Echo and her friends. There is a darkness spreading too and staying in hiding might not be enough to keep them alive"—Provided by publisher.
ISBN 978-0-385-74467-6 (hc) |
ISBN 978-0-385-39100-9 (ebook) | ISBN 978-0-375-99180-6 (glb)
[1. Fantasy.] [BISAC: JUVENILE FICTION / Action & Adventure / General. | JUVENILE FICTION / Love & Romance.
| JUVENILE FICTION / Legends, Myths, Fables / Other.]
PZ7.1.G75 Sh 2016
[Fic]—dc23
2015040916

ISBN 978-0-385-74468-3 (trade pbk.)

Printed in the United States of America
10 9 8 7 6 5 4 3 2 1
First Ember Edition 2017

PROLOGUE

Rowan could pinpoint the exact moment he fell in love. It would take him ten years to admit it to himself, to gather the vocabulary necessary to encompass the complexity of his emotion, but he experienced the first stirrings of affection the second Echo stepped into his life.

That day, Rowan's mother had sent him, armed with a basketful of freshly baked cupcakes, to play with the Ala's orphans. The cupcakes had gone fast, and Rowan was lucky to have been able to snag the last one, a fluffy concoction of red velvet cake and cream cheese frosting.

When the human girl entered the room a hush fell over the children. Her uncombed brown hair made her look like a wild thing, and she clung to the Ala like an anchor. She had no feathers. Her bare arms looked almost obscene compared with the down that covered Rowan's skin. Her big brown eyes zeroed in on the cupcake in his hand as if she were a hawk hunting for her next kill. She was so skinny, so pale.

He extended his hand, the half-eaten cupcake cradled in his palm as if it were something precious. And to the girl, it was. Even if he had licked off most of the frosting already.

She took it from him with a look of such awestruck gratitude that Rowan had promised himself, at the tender age of seven, that he would devote the rest of his life to conjuring forth that smile. It was a beautiful smile, and he wanted to preserve it. He wanted to preserve *her,* just as she was at that moment. Happy.

During the decade that followed, he succeeded in making Echo smile like that more often than not, and she opened his eyes to a part of the world he had never before been able to see. He wasn't good with words—they didn't always make sense on the page—so Echo read to him. They would spend afternoons in the library on Fifth Avenue, his head resting on her lap, her hands carding through the feathers on his head as she read aloud from Dickens and Vonnegut and Rowling. He fell in love with those stories the same way he fell in love with her. A little grudgingly at first, but eventually with complete abandon. He tried to return the favor by teaching her how to draw, but Echo was hopeless. The poor girl couldn't draw a straight line to save her life. Their love was as sweet as red velvet, as fluffy as cream cheese frosting.

Now, looking at the girl who stood before him in the Black Forest, framed by a halo of fire, he could hardly remember that person. She was a great and terrible thing, a being of pure magic, raining destruction down upon them.

Until that moment, Rowan had never seen battle, had never smelled the sharp coppery scent of blood in the air, had never heard tortured shrieks rise above a cacophony of death. The flames that engulfed the forest—devouring trees in a violent cascade of unearthly crimson and gold—licked at his feet, seared the exposed skin of his hands. The only battles Rowan had ever known were two-dimensional renderings of wars gone by, immortalized as massive paintings lining the walls of museums. He'd studied them for hours, head bent over his sketchbook, fingers blackened from smudging charcoal across the page. The imagining of chaos was quite different from the reality of it.

Echo stood by a weeping willow, silhouetted by the orange flames behind her, arms extended low, palms facing up. Their eyes met across the field, and Rowan called to her, even though he knew she couldn't hear him.

The sights and sounds of the battle raging around him fell away. Echo raised her arms, as if she were about to ward off a blow, but what happened next defied explanation. Fire poured from her palms, unlike any fire Rowan had ever seen. The flames were as black as coal and as blindingly white as the sun. They were so bright, his eyes watered, and he had to look away.

Echo had told him that she was hunting for the firebird, that she had a map that would lead her to it. But the results of her search weren't anything Rowan had expected.

The girl he'd fallen in love with over cupcakes and stories had evolved. Now she was something savage and fierce, a celestial beast framed by a blaze of her own creation.

Echo hadn't just found the firebird.

She *was* the firebird.

Holy. Shit.

CHAPTER ONE

Who are you?

The question soared across the scorched sky, spoken by a chorus of voices that seeped through the cracks in the rocks that glowed like coals, that oozed from the pulsing hot brightness of the magma inching down, down, down to swallow all life in its path.

Lava ran over Echo's boots. She looked at her feet, dispassionate, divorced from the sight of the rubber and leather bubbling and melting. Her shoelaces caught fire, but she did not feel them burn. Soot coated her skin, clung to her hair, her eyelashes, her clothes. The blue had been burned out of the sky by the eruption, and darkness descended, called forth by a veil of ash.

Who are you?

"This isn't real," Echo said.

And that isn't an answer.

This was a dream. And in this dream, she was burning.

Her skin blistered in the heat. Magma rushed around her ankles. It didn't scare her, though it had the first time she'd had this dream. And the second. And the third. But by now, she'd lived through this scenario so many times, it was beginning to feel routine. All she had to do was endure it. Soon enough, she would wake up. She could do that. If there was anything at which Echo excelled, it was surviving.

She ignored the question—she'd yet to answer it in any of her dreams—and looked toward the gaping maw of the volcano. She stood at its base, watching it belch fire and smoke and ash into the heavens. Screams rose from the village below. That was the worst part. She could ignore her burning body, but she could never tune out the screams. Every night, without fail, from the first night. The night she had opened a door into the world and let the firebird enter. She could feel it now, its wings fluttering inside her as if testing the limits of its mortal cage.

Every night, the same question was posed to her, asked by a speaker with a thousand voices ringing as one: *Who are you?*

I am Echo, she thought. She didn't speak the words aloud. She knew the answer wasn't correct. Or perhaps the answer was simply not complete.

Lava crawled up her legs, past her knees, her thighs, her waist, consuming her inch by inch. In seconds, or perhaps minutes—time was so hard to track in dreams—it would rush into her mouth, her nostrils. It would seal her eyes shut. Soon, her entire body would be trapped on the side of the mountain, glued to the spot like a fly in amber.

All she had to do was survive. Dying in dreams wasn't

the worst part. Waking from them with more questions than answers was. *This* was her fault. The eruption. The fire bursting from the earth. The darkness eating the sky. The screams of people caught in the middle of a cosmic dance that had begun eons before they'd been born. Soon, Echo would wake up and start a new day. But soon never felt soon enough when she was trapped in this dream.

Who are you? The question was clear, even over the anguished wails of the people below.

I am their end, Echo thought. *I am their destruction. I couldn't shield them from something I caused. I opened a door I shouldn't have opened and now I don't know what to do about it. I am alone in this.*

Then the voices asked, as they did whenever she dared consider her solitude: *Are you?*

Echo had opened a door to let the firebird in. But she couldn't help wondering what she'd let out.

CHAPTER TWO

Friday night in London's Camden Market was a sight to behold. Stalls were tightly packed into the space, each vying to be louder and more eye-catching than the next. Rugs of dubious Persian origin swayed gently in the wind, and the brash yellow of streetlights sparkled over an array of glass pipes on a nearby table. The July air wasn't exactly what Echo would call balmy, but it amplified the scents lingering about the market. Her stomach grumbled as she caught a whiff of what smelled a lot like kebab. Maybe she'd grab some on the way back. Maybe she'd even pay for it. Last night's dream weighed on her, but the weight had grown so constant she could ignore it if she tried hard enough. *Compartmentalization,* she mused. It was a hell of a skill. And if any city in the world could help her forget her troubles, it was this one.

She elbowed her way past London's bright young eccentrics, searching for the stall Jasper had sent her to find. She didn't need to look behind her to know that Caius was right on her heels, shadowing her with unwavering focus. When she'd told him that she was making a supply run, he hadn't even given her the chance to ask to go alone. He hadn't wanted her to go at all, insisting that it was safer in the East London hideout they were holed up in—an abandoned warehouse registered under one of Jasper's many aliases—but Echo needed to breathe something besides the stale air she'd been sharing with him, Dorian, Jasper, and Ivy since abandoning Jasper's Strasbourg home and going on the run three months ago.

With Jasper's injuries, they couldn't go very far. Ivy had done her best to heal the wound he'd received taking a blow meant for Dorian, but even she needed supplies. The second Ivy had mentioned she was running low on the herbs for the poultice she'd been using on Jasper, Echo had jumped at the chance to restock. If she spent one more minute in that warehouse, she'd lose her mind. She needed distance. From the others, from her bed, from the water-stained ceiling she stared at every night when she finally woke from her tortured slumber. Luckily, Jasper knew of a warlock who'd set up shop in London selling goods to anyone with enough of an eye for magic to find his stall.

She scanned the area, letting her gaze roam over the organized chaos of Camden Market. Magic didn't like to be looked at head-on. It preferred to twinkle in one's peripheral vision, teasing with a hint of its presence. Since that moment in the Black Forest, when she'd welcomed the power of the firebird into her body, becoming its vessel, Echo found that she was more attuned to the subtle hint of magic in the air. From the corner of her eye, she caught a shimmer around a stall, not fifteen feet from where she stood. Before, she would have noticed only the faintest haze in the air around the stall, but now the warlock's magic gleamed in the artificial twilight of the market. When she turned to look straight at it, the shimmer disappeared. *Found you.*

She cast a look over her shoulder, meeting Caius's green eyes across the crowd. He kept close to her, but not so close that it would look like they were together. His idea. The baseball cap perched on his freshly shorn brown hair and the thickly applied foundation that hid the delicate scales on his cheekbones had been Echo's idea. He'd squirmed in the chair as she piled on the makeup, unaccustomed to the sensation of goop on his face, but if she had to wear a disguise, so did he.

Echo reached up to adjust the blond wig she'd pulled on before leaving the warehouse, and nodded, just enough for Caius to see it. The oversized sunglasses and newsboy cap she'd swiped from a dozing East London hipster on the tube added an extra layer of anonymity, but Caius remained on guard. They were still being hunted, by the Avicen, the people Echo had come to think of as family. By the Drakharin, led by Caius's own sister. By pretty much anyone with even a passing interest in the firebird. Never before had Echo felt quite so popular.

The corner of Caius's lip turned up ever so slightly, and Echo let herself smile back in response. It hadn't occurred to her to object when he'd insisted on accompanying her to the warlock's shop. Caius had proved himself an exceptional companion. Sometimes, they would go up to the roof of the warehouse and he would point out constellations to her, regaling her with the Drakharin stories behind the stars. She knew the human tales and the Avicen ones, but these were new to her, and precious. Caius never wanted to stay out for long—again, safety first—but those moments were special.

When she was leaning against the roof's cold concrete with Caius just inches from her, she didn't feel like a person of interest, or a chess piece in the war between the Avicen and the Drakharin. She didn't feel like the firebird, the one tool that both sides desperately wanted to control in the hopes of ending their centuries-old conflict. She was just a girl, lying next to a boy, gazing up at the stars.

"Looking for something?"

The voice pulled Echo back, reminding her of where she was and why she was here. She broke eye contact with Caius, who was now leaning against a streetlamp two stalls down, examining his fingernails, the epitome of nonchalance, and turned to face the man who'd spoken.

If oatmeal were to take a human form, it would manifest itself as this guy. Light brown cardigan. Stained white T-shirt. Beat-up cargo pants. Converse All-Stars that had once been white but had darkened to a sad gray. Sandy hair that was neither brown nor blond. Everything about him screamed beige. The only thing that seemed off was the pair of retro Ray-Bans hiding his eyes. But since Echo was also wearing sunglasses at night, she was fresh out of stones to throw. Rolling a cigarette as he looked up at her, the man sat by his stall in a metal folding chair, legs crossed at the ankles and raised to rest on the table beside him.

"Can I help you?" His Cockney accent was thick. He brought the cigarette up to his lips and licked an exaggerated line along the top edge of the paper to seal it. The cheap silver jewelry on his table was laid out haphazardly, as if he wasn't interested in selling it. That suited Echo as she wasn't interested in buying it.

She fished a small slip of paper out of her pocket. Jasper

had scribbled a symbol on it—an equal-armed cross, with a diamond at the center and small triangles capping each arm—and told her to present it to the man. It was the international symbol for "Here there be warlocks." Under the sigil, Ivy had added a list of ingredients.

"Yeah," she said, "I'm in the market for some hard-to-find goods."

The man leaned forward, dropping his feet to the ground as if movement was a chore. He took the paper from Echo, bringing it up close to his nose to examine it. Seconds ticked by. Echo fought the urge to bounce on the balls of her feet or anxiously drum her fingers against her thigh or reach up to scratch at the wig's netting, which had been irritating her all night. Traveling incognito had been fun for the first five minutes, but the novelty had worn off, just as her patience was now wearing thin with Wonder Bread the Warlock.

The warlock peered at Echo over his sunglasses, giving her the chance to see the one thing that marked him as no longer human. His eyes were entirely white, as though the pupils had been swallowed whole. The sight of them was enough to make Echo's fingers itch for a weapon. Warlocks were bad news. She longed to reach for the dagger tucked into her boot. A nearby radio crackled with static as the announcer read off the hour's headlines. A plane crash a few kilometers outside Sydney. The upcoming presidential election in the United States. The cloud of volcanic ash clogging the sky over New Zealand after an unexpected earthquake had caused an inactive volcano to erupt three months ago; apparently, it was still rumbling, still smoking. Bits of Echo's dream flitted through her mind, but she pushed them down, as deep as they would go.

"These are some pretty serious healing supplies," the warlock said. He handed the paper back, rising to his feet. "You in trouble?"

"Perpetually."

"My kind of girl." The warlock stepped around the table, into his stall, and began rummaging through the boxes beneath the table. He took his sweet time. He glanced up at Echo, a little too keenly, and asked, "Come here often?"

"Nope."

She willed herself not to look back at Caius. The last thing she needed was to engage in a rousing bout of chitchat with the warlock. The more he kept talking, the more likely it was that he would ask questions Echo couldn't or wouldn't answer. She was beginning to think that maybe she should have listened to Caius and stayed at the warehouse, hidden behind the layers of wards that protected them.

With a shrug, the warlock said, "Most people who come to me are looking for something a little less . . . benevolent." He popped to his feet, holding several ziplock bags full of herbs. He offered them to Echo, but when she reached out to take them, he yanked them back. "Payment up front, love. That'll be five hundred."

Highway freakin' robbery, Echo thought, even as she swung her backpack from her shoulder to retrieve the wad of cash she'd taken from Jasper's stash. Though the warehouse wasn't the most welcoming place—the ceiling leaked, the pipes were rusty, and the heating was more hypothetical than real—it was remarkably well stocked with a variety of currencies. She slapped the money down on the table. "There. Gimme the stuff, and I'll be out of your hair."

"Ooh, feisty." The warlock slid the ziplock bags across the

table to her, but kept his hands on them. "I think I'd like to get to know you a bit better."

Echo took the bags, ignoring the way his pinkie finger briefly stroked the side of her hand. "The feeling is *not* mutual." She dropped the bags into her backpack, then zipped it back up and slung it over her shoulders. "I'd say it was a pleasure doing business with you, but that would be a lie."

She turned, heading for the market's entrance, the warlock's bark of laughter ringing in her ears. Her skin felt slimy where he'd touched her. She rubbed her palm on her jeans as if that could erase the sensation.

A hand slid into hers, and she jumped, instinctively trying to pull away.

"Relax," Caius whispered, breath warm against the shell of her ear. "It's just me."

Tension drained from Echo's body, replaced with a tingly feeling in her gut that was a close relative of contentment. She liked the way his hand felt in hers. She liked the rough texture of his calluses combined with the softness of his skin. They'd grown closer over the past several weeks, though they hadn't progressed any further than cuddling. A presence tickled at the back of her mind. She ignored it. It was getting easier to silence Rose, but whenever Caius touched her, that voice had a habit of piping up as if his proximity were a summons.

She tightened her hold on Caius's hand, relishing the tiny smile that graced his lips. They walked toward the Camden Town tube station, where they could catch a train back to the warehouse. Completely non-magical travel had been another one of Caius's ideas. That would make it harder for people to track them, if they were looking for signs of magic or the residue left behind by shadow dust. Echo couldn't argue with the wisdom behind the idea, but she missed the convenience of traveling through the in-between, of walking through a door in one city and exiting into a completely different country.

She bumped her shoulder into Caius's arm. "I thought we weren't supposed to look like we were together. Isn't this breaking the rules?"

Caius smiled again, looking down at their joined hands. He ran a thumb along her knuckles, right where the warlock had caressed her, as though he were erasing the last trace of that unwelcome contact. "If there's anything I've learned from spending time with you," he said, leaning down so she could hear his quiet words, "it's that some rules were meant to be broken."

The lights of Camden High Street twinkled behind his head, casting a soft golden glow on the strands of hair that escaped his baseball cap. Echo wished that he didn't need to hide his scales; she wanted to watch the light dance along his cheekbones, catching the scales' slight texture and shine. He looked at her expectantly, waiting for her to respond. His eyes were a brighter shade of emerald than human green, almost as though they were lit from within.

He's beautiful, isn't he? said the voice inside Echo's head.

Shut up, Rose. To Echo's eternal surprise, Rose complied, but not without a flutter of sensation in Echo's mind that felt suspiciously like ghostly laughter. It sent a tremor through her body.

Caius gave her hand a quick squeeze. "Echo? Are you all right?"

She cleared her throat and looked away from him. Rose's thoughts may have been unwanted, but Echo couldn't exactly argue with her. Caius was lovely to the point of distraction. But he didn't know that Rose had felt the need to point it out. He knew Rose was there, buried deep somewhere inside Echo's head, her soul inextricably linked to the firebird's energy, but the extent to which Rose had made herself at home wasn't something Echo was prepared to share. She had power now, responsibilities. There were people depending on her, and hearing voices wasn't a character trait that screamed dependable. And so she kept Rose's comments to herself. Maybe there would come a day when old ghosts kept their silence and left Echo alone in her own head. A girl could dream. But until that day, the fewer people who knew, the better.

They were nearly at the tube station. They'd hop on the Northern line and be home in less than half an hour, but the thought of going back to the warehouse, of returning to those too-familiar walls and too-thin mattresses strewn across the floor, was suffocating. Echo needed more time away, more time to pretend that the weight of the world wasn't resting squarely on her shoulders. Her stomach rumbled again, and she had an idea.

"Yeah." She squeezed Caius's hand back, eliciting another small grin from him. He smiled more these days, though it wasn't quite the same as the unguarded smiles she knew from Rose's memories.

Mágoa, Echo thought. *Portuguese. The residue left behind by sorrow.*

The traces of long-ago grief clung to Caius, affecting every gesture, influencing every detail of his behavior, however minor. Rose's Caius had been a different person, though Echo found that she liked this version of him just fine. But even then, questions still plagued her. She wanted to ask if what he felt for her was real. If all he saw when he looked at her was a dead girl. If she was insane to think that a history as tangled as theirs—hers, Caius's, Rose's—could ever have a happy ending. But all she managed to ask was "You hungry?"

Caius's smile wilted, turning down at the edges. "We really should get back."

Echo skipped ahead, using her hold on his hand to guide him toward the kebab place on the corner. London was riddled with them, and the quality was always a bit hit-or-miss, but she was willing to take the risk. "Oh, c'mon. A wise man once said some rules were meant to be broken."

With a quiet chuckle, Caius said, "He doesn't sound very wise to me."

But he didn't fight as she tugged him along, leading him toward the siren song of kebab. Strolling down the street looking like a couple was most certainly against the rules, but the night was young, and so was she. This moment was hers, and she would cherish it, even if—or maybe because—she knew it wouldn't last.

CHAPTER THREE

When they returned to the warehouse, bellies full of greasy kebab, it was almost exactly as they'd left it. Candles sitting in puddles of wax were scattered about the large room on the top floor, illuminating the space with a soft yellow glow that reflected off the black-painted windowpanes. On the ancient television in the corner, a BBC host interviewed an expert on climate change, their voices overpowered by the occasional rumble of a passing train. Half a dozen mattresses had been pushed to the corners of the room and were surrounded by piles of clothing in varied states of disarray, from absolute chaos (Echo's) to military neatness (Dorian's). Jasper's clothes fit Dorian and Caius, though the latter's broad shoulders meant the borrowed shirts stretched across his chest in a way that was impossible not to notice. Echo had lasted two days living in Jasper's oversized sweats before she couldn't handle it anymore and snuck out in the night. She'd broken into a vintage boutique—they were all over East London—and absconded with an assortment of clothes for herself and Ivy. The talking-to she'd received from both Caius and Ivy for going out alone had been worth it. You never quite appreciated the fit of a decent pair of jeans until you didn't have any that weren't bloodstained or ripped.

Jasper lay on his mattress, one hand dangling over the side, the other draped dramatically across his forehead. The vibrant colors of the feathers on his head, cropped short enough to look almost like hair, were dark in the candlelight, but their deep purples, velvety blues, and speckles of warm gold were still visible.

Echo riffled through her mental lexicon for the right word to describe Jasper. "Pavonine." That was it. "Of or resembling a peacock."

Dorian sat cross-legged on the floor by the mattress, running a rag over the steel of his sword. His silvery bangs fell across his eye patch as he tilted his head toward Jasper so he could hear whatever the Avicen was saying. Echo had come to realize that Dorian cleaned weapons the way some people bit their nails: absently, when there was nothing better to do. The blade hadn't seen action for months, but Dorian polished it daily, keeping it pristine.

Caius locked the door behind them and started checking the wards around it, testing them for weaknesses. It was the only entrance to the hideout. One way in, one way out. Caius had insisted it was safer that way, and when he *insisted,* it had the tendency to feel more like a royal edict than mere suggestion. If their little group were found, he could whisk them away through the in-between. Caius was one of the few people Echo knew who didn't need to bother with shadow dust or thresholds to access the in-between, though the effort it would take to transport four other people would cost him dearly. All magic came with a cost, no matter how powerful you were. As far as emergency plans went, it wasn't the absolute worst, but Echo hoped they'd never have to use it.

She dumped her backpack on the floor beside the door. "Children," she called, "I'm home."

Ivy popped her head out of the bathroom door on the opposite side of the room, long, snowy hair-feathers gleaming in the dim light. "Oh, thank the gods," she answered, wiping her hands on a washcloth as she walked over to Echo. "If I had to listen to Jasper whine about his poultice one more time, I was going to gag him."

"Excuse me, young lady, I do not *whine,*" Jasper said, angling his head to glare at Ivy. "I *lament.*"

Ivy rolled her eyes. "You're nineteen, Jasper. Don't you 'young lady' me."

Echo knelt down, fished the bags of herbs out of her backpack, and handed them to Ivy. "No bickering. This is a bicker-free zone. Bickering is an offense punishable by death."

"Don't mind, Ivy," said Jasper. "She's still mad I bought Park Place right out from under her nose."

"And here I was thinking that what happened in Monopoly stayed in Monopoly," Echo said. The board game had lasted only a week before Caius had confiscated it and hidden it somewhere deep in the bowels of the warehouse. Their last game had nearly come to blows.

Jasper exhaled a pained laugh. "Oh, you sweet little fool." He struggled to sit up, succeeding only when Dorian slipped a hand underneath his shoulder to help prop him against the wall. Ivy went over to his bedside, laying out the ziplock bags in the order she needed them. "And honestly, Ivy, can't you fix me any faster? I'm sick of lying around like a lump on a log." Jasper winked at Dorian. "Though at least the nurses are cute."

Pink suffused Dorian's fair skin, inching past the eye patch all the way up to the dusting of scales on his temples. A tiny smile teased at his lips. Jasper had taken to showering Dorian with compliments the same way Dorian cleaned his sword and Caius checked the wards. Habitually.

Ivy was less amused. She ripped open one of the bags so forcefully that dried green herbs scattered across the floor. "I'm a healer," she said through clenched teeth. "Not a wizard." She shoved the herbs at Dorian. "Grind these."

Dorian accepted the herbs because when Ivy told you to do something in that tone of voice, you did it. Catching Echo's gaze, Ivy said, "Can we talk?"

Echo nodded, not liking the sound of it. Whenever someone said "Can we talk?" it was always followed by something deeply unpleasant. That was a universal truth.

They made their way to a corner of the loft, as far from the others as they could go. Caius shot Echo a concerned glance, but she waved him away. Ivy pitched her voice low so she wouldn't be overheard. "Jasper's not healing."

And there was the deeply unpleasant something.

"Well," Echo said. "It was a really bad wound, right? It's going to take a while."

Ivy shook her head. "I mean, it's not healing. At all. The herbs I'm using are fighting infection and keeping it from getting worse, but it's just *not* healing. I think there might be some bad magic involved, but I don't know how or why or what. I haven't reached that part of my training yet." Ivy rubbed her arms as if fighting a chill. "I was sort of distracted by getting kidnapped, then rescued, then whisked away on a globe-trotting adventure with our merry band of misfits."

Caius drifted to their corner, despite Echo's silent instruction that he leave them be. "Is this about Jasper's injury?" he asked.

"Yeah," Echo said. "It's not healing. Ivy thinks there might be some bad mojo happening."

With a slow nod, Caius said, "I think our resident healer is right." He looked over his shoulder to where Dorian was grinding herbs while Jasper watched, naked adoration in his amber eyes. "It was a Firedrake sword that wounded him." He grimaced. "My sister—or should I say, the new Dragon Prince—once approached me with a plan for making her regiment even more lethal. Tanith wanted a warlock to curse their weapons so that even if a wound wasn't a killing blow, it would still kill its intended victim."

"Like a poison," Echo said.

Ivy let out a string of un-Ivy-like curses.

"Exactly like that," said Caius. "I forbade Tanith to do it. After my last few experiences with warlocks, I had little desire to involve myself with them."

"What happened to sour you on warlocks?" Echo asked. "Other than the fact that they're pretty much evil incarnate."

Caius's grimace deepened to a full frown. "I don't think they're particularly fond of me, as a matter of fact." He rubbed the nape of his neck, a gesture Echo had learned meant he was about to confess a truth he would rather keep to himself. "Shortly after my election to the throne, I called in a team of warlocks to strengthen the wards around Wyvern's Keep. Our mages were good, but there's nothing stronger than the type of dark magic warlocks traffic in. I promised them untold riches after they completed their task. I didn't exactly deliver on my promise."

"And what *did* you deliver?" Echo asked.

Caius met her eyes, his expression guarded. "Death. I couldn't have warlocks on the loose with detailed knowledge of the keep's fortifications."

"Christ," Echo said. She knew about Caius's past. He had done terrible things. That was not news. But it was easier to see him the way Rose had: as a person who wanted to use his power for good. Who didn't want to hurt people. He had changed in the century after her death, and the years since had seen his hands soaked in more blood than Echo could imagine.

As if he could read her thoughts, Caius said in a soft voice, "I never said I was a good person."

Ivy shifted uncomfortably beside Echo. "What happened to the warlocks who kidnapped me from the Agora?"

A moment passed in awkward silence before Caius said, "I killed them, too."

Echo watched the play of emotions on Ivy's face. She knew the abduction had been the most traumatic event in Ivy's life—up until the battle of the Black Forest—but Ivy was a gentle soul. Relief and guilt warred in her expression. "I see" was all she said.

This wasn't a conversation Echo wanted to have at that moment. Or ever. "So we can't go to those guys to ask for help," she said. "What are we going to do about Jasper? We can't just leave him like this."

"His wound will kill him," Ivy said. "Eventually."

Caius let out a wary breath. "If it's truly dark magic, then the only way we can fight back is with dark magic."

“And the only people who practice that are warlocks,” Echo said.

Caius nodded. “I’ll talk to Jasper. He might know one or two who would be willing to help for the right price.”

“Let’s try not to kill anyone this time,” Ivy said.

A line formed between Caius’s brows as his frown deepened. Echo was too tired to deal with this. She didn’t want to think about Caius murdering people—no matter how creepy and unethical those people were in their own right—and she didn’t want to watch Ivy judge him for it. Hell, Echo judged him for it. And somewhere in the back of Echo’s mind, Rose was probably forgiving him. The cognitive dissonance was a lot to handle. Their *lives* were a lot to handle.

“Great,” Echo said before the conversation could continue. “Now that that’s settled, I need to get some rest.”

She left them to their business and plopped down on her mattress, positioned farthest from the windows. With a single, unreadable backward glance at Echo, Caius returned to checking the wards. Ivy joined Dorian by Jasper’s bedside to continue preparing the herbs for a new poultice. The sound of their banter was a comforting white noise. They’d been holed up for months, but it was still strange to consider how unlikely their group was. Two Avicen, two Drakharin—once mortal enemies—and Echo, the lone human. She looked down at her hands, remembering the black and white fire that had burst from her palms. Maybe she wasn’t quite so human after all.

The mattress dipped beside her. She looked up to find Caius sitting next to her. “Wards okay?” she asked.

He nodded. “Solid as ever. We’re as safe as we’re ever going to be.” He ran a hand through his dark hair. A few days ago, Dorian had forced Caius into a chair, brandishing a pair of scissors. *This is getting out of hand,* Dorian had said. Echo, Ivy, and Jasper had shared a bag of microwave popcorn while they watched Caius stew in resentful silence as Dorian cut his hair. That was what passed for entertainment in the warehouse. Caius kept touching the back of his neck, like he wasn't quite used to the new length. He turned to Echo, eyes gone dark in the flickering candlelight. "How are you feeling?"

Her smile was small and tight, her jaw clenched. Now that she was back in the warehouse she felt strangled. Odd. Exposed. It was nothing like her home, the secret room in the New York Public Library, with its fairy lights and stolen treasures and mountains of books. The silence and solitude of that place had suited her. The image of that empty room, still shielded by its wards, made her chest ache. But thinking about the things she'd lost was infinitely easier than thinking about the people she'd left behind. *Like Rowan.* She pushed the thought down, deeper and deeper, as far as it would go.

"I'm fine," she lied.

Caius was not fooled. "You don't look fine."

A train rolled past, shaking the windows. Echo broke the hold his gaze had on her and focused on the television. On its screen was aerial footage of plumes of smoke, bellowing forth from the mouth of a volcano somewhere in the Pacific Ocean, miles off the coast of New Zealand. The flawlessly coiffed blonde behind the news desk relayed the baffled opinions of experts who had agreed en masse that the volcano was supposed to be dormant and that its recent activity was nothing short of a conundrum, as there was no logical explanation for the tectonic movement that had caused its eruption.

Something deep inside Echo tugged at her as she watched clouds of black ash and oozing rivers of bright magma flash across the screen. The feeling wasn't recognition, but a close cousin to it; it felt as though a force within her was trying to communicate in nonverbal sensations. The volcano had erupted the same day Echo had driven a dagger into her own heart, freeing the firebird from, as the prophecy put it, its cage of bones.

Caius was saying something, his voice low and distant, but Echo heard none of it as the image on the screen switched to the complete and utter ruin of a village, half-collapsed walls sticking up from the ash-covered ground like fractured, blackened teeth. It looked exactly like the village from her dream. She grabbed the remote to turn up the volume and shushed Caius.

"—the scene here is simply devastating," intoned the field reporter, his wool coat snapping in the wind, his hair fighting free of its pomade. Behind him, what looked like a rescue crew combed through debris, lifting fallen planks of wood and shuffling around jagged chunks of stone. The dark mass of the volcano was visible in the distance. "This entire area of land has just been destroyed. There's nothing—and no one—left."

"Is there any word on the ground as to what could have caused this?" asked the blonde in the studio, unruffled by the elements.

The field reporter ran a finger along a wooden stump beside him. His gloved hand came away covered in what looked like soot. "No idea yet, Sandra. But a member of the recovery team has told me that this"—he rubbed his fingers together, smearing the black soot—"residue doesn't appear to be volcanic in origin, despite the recent activity in the area. We're not quite sure what it is, but we're hoping to have answers soon."

"Thank you, George," the newscaster said. "And keep us posted. . . ."

Echo thumbed down the volume. The tugging in her gut intensified, as if the firebird were shouting at her without words, trying to force her to realize something that should have been obvious but wasn't. The volcanic eruption. A village swallowed by fire and ash. And all of it timed to neatly coincide with the firebird's appearance. With her dreams. With the sense of dread that had been building in her since she had sliced open not just her own body but the fabric of the world, letting in a cosmic force she didn't understand.

Caius pitched his voice low so only Echo could hear him. "Are you still having those nightmares?"

She nodded, still not looking at him. The muscles in her neck were taut enough to snap. The others knew about the dreams. It was hard to keep something like that a secret when you woke up screaming several nights in a row. But she didn't want to talk about them. They made her feel powerless. Confused. Consumed by questions and plagued by suspicions that she had done something terrible and irrevocable.

"It's connected," Echo said softly. "I started dreaming about the volcano before I heard about it on the news. It started that night." She gestured to the scar on her chest, which was only just visible over the collar of her T-shirt. "The night all *this* happened." She swallowed. The words were still strange on her tongue. "The night I unleashed the firebird. I let it into me, but I don't think it's the only thing I unleashed."

"Perhaps it's a coincidence," Caius said. "You went through

something extremely traumatic. Maybe your psyche latched on to the idea of the volcano and conflated the events in your mind."

She shook her head. "I dreamed about the volcano before I knew it had happened. We didn't have a TV at Jasper's loft in Strasbourg. I hadn't heard the news yet. And that village—I saw it, that exact one."

Caius reached for her, maybe to offer comfort, but she pulled away.

"It's not a coincidence," she said. "I know it. I *know*."

Echo couldn't believe in coincidences, not anymore, not when she lived in a world peopled by creatures that should be more at home in fairy tales than on the streets of major metropolises, not when she herself had become a thing of magic and myth. She could feel Caius's eyes on her, questioning, wondering, just as she was, what her role in all this was—what the *firebird's* role was.

The bird that sings at midnight from within its cage of bones, Echo remembered, eyes still trained on the now quiet television, riveted by the scene of destruction, *will rise from blood and ashes to greet the truth unknown.*

She'd often found herself mulling over the prophecy that had led her here, to this warehouse, to these people. The last line in particular. What truth? As the sensation that was not quite recognition strengthened, as the firebird pounded against the inside of her skull, demanding that she take notice, take action, do *something,* she thought that maybe she was about to find out.

CHAPTER FOUR

The night air rustled the short strands of Caius's hair, tickling the back of his neck. He stood on the roof of the warehouse, hands in his pockets, skin still warmed by the memory of Echo's body heat. He'd waited until she fell asleep, curled up on the mattress on her side, long brown hair spread out on the pillow like a dark cloud, her brow furrowed even in slumber. Caius had smoothed the wrinkle with a gentle touch, mesmerized by the way she'd turned toward his hand, mumbling something incoherent. People were supposed to look younger in their sleep, but Echo seemed older than her years, as if the weight that bore down on her was even heavier when she was most vulnerable. At night, Caius knew, she was plagued by the lives of the vessels that had come before her, memories that weren't her own crowding her head like unwelcome houseguests. And that was when she wasn't forced to live through an eruption, the lone witness to a cataclysmic event that claimed an island in a far-off sea. Eventually, she'd stilled, and Caius had come up to the roof, leaving the others to their nighttime rituals, seeking as much silence as one could find in a place as chronically boisterous as London.

He gazed at the city spread before him, the silhouettes of buildings dark against a sky so polluted by ambient light that the stars were all but invisible. He and Echo had spent many a night trying to pick out the brightest ones, though she occasionally mistook a passing plane for a shooting star. Even when the constellations weren't wholly visible, Caius still told her the stories he'd carried with him since childhood: tales of great dragons cutting through the sky, wings as black as the void of space, eyes glittering with the fire of stars. The sky, all Drakharin children were told, was the realm of the gods, where Dragon Princes of days gone by ascended when their reigns came to an end, destined to watch over their earthbound brethren for all eternity. Caius had believed those stories, as children so easily did, until the day of his coronation, when he'd knelt before the assembly of Drakharin nobles that had elected him, and swore that he would serve his people until his dying day. As the weight of the crown settled on his head, he knew that he'd given up the chance to live a long and happy life. Power corrupted, and those it didn't corrupt, it killed. He'd met his sister's eyes from across the room, burning as bright as rubies, speaking truth to the lie of her proud smile. He should have seen it then. The jealousy. The ambition. He should have known that his reign would end with Tanith. But love had blinded him, as it was wont to do, and he'd only seen the twin he entered this world with, not her potential for betrayal, and believed what he wanted to believe. That her love for her brother was greater than her aspirations.

Behind him, the hinges of the rooftop door squealed as it opened. Caius didn't need to turn around to see who had just come through it. He'd recognize Dorian's footsteps anywhere.

Dorian came to stand beside him, pale hair and even paler skin bright in the darkness. A coin appeared in his hand, as if from nowhere, and he proceeded to roll it over his knuckles, fingers moving with a practiced grace.

"Where'd you learn to do that?" Caius asked as he watched the effortless motion of Dorian's hands.

Dorian faltered, and the coin slipped from his grasp. He caught it with his other hand and slipped it into his pocket. "Jasper."

"An Avicen teaching you coin tricks." Caius let himself smile. "Now I really have seen everything."

Dorian chuckled softly. "If you look closely at the horizon, you can see pigs flying in the distance." He turned to Caius, single blue eye as focused as a hawk's. "Speaking of Jasper . . ."

"I know," Caius said. "He's not healing. Ivy told me. I think the blade that wounded him was cursed." He added, "By a warlock."

Dorian swore softly in Drakhar. "You never let Tanith off her leash to do as she wished, but now that she's Dragon Prince, there's no one to stop her. Without you there to hold her back, she's getting reckless." His hand drifted to his side, where his sword would be had he been wearing it. "I would sooner die than allow a warlock to touch my blade. Gods only know what magic they could work on weapons without you even knowing."

"I know," Caius said. "And that's why I never wanted her to do it. But it seems she has and now we have to deal with the consequences."

Beside him, Dorian shuffled, hands curling into fists and uncurling. "Jasper is the one dealing with the consequences. We have to help him, Caius. We have to do something. I can't just sit here and watch him die because he took a blow meant for me."

Dorian, pleading for the life of an Avicen. Caius stifled a smile. He turned back to survey the urban vista before them. It was so different from the world he'd known, but he was finding a kind of alien beauty in that difference. "If the blade was truly cursed by a warlock, then perhaps a warlock can remove the magic infecting his wound."

With a weary sigh, Dorian turned to rest against the parapet, arms crossed over his chest, back to the brightly colored lights shining through the windows of the warehouse across the way. There was a party in that warehouse every other day. Echo called it a rave. "Well, I'm fresh out of warlock friends after we killed the last batch we worked with. I'm afraid you and I are beginning to earn something of a reputation in that community. Those bridges are a little too burned for us to use."

Their eyes met, and for a brief moment, Caius caught the rawness, usually so well hidden, in Dorian's expression. Dorian turned away, breaking the connection.

"I have a plan," Caius said, "but I don't think you're going to like it."

"How many times do I have to say it?" Dorian asked. "I'd follow you anywhere, Caius. Prince or not."

"Well," Caius began. "We're going to make a new warlock friend. We just need *a* warlock. Any one will do. Jasper has mentioned before that he used to run with a band of warlocks in his"—Caius curled two fingers in the air, forming quotation marks, a gesture he'd picked up from Echo and Ivy—"'*wild and reckless youth.*' I'm going to see if one of them would be willing to help us."

Dorian opened his mouth to object, but Caius held up a hand. "I know what you're going to say and I don't want you to say it, because then we're just going to argue and you know I always win."

Dorian scowled. "Only because I let you."

"Be that as it may," said Caius. "Jasper's wound requires magic neither you nor I can counter. We need help, even if that help comes from a distasteful source."

"You're right," Dorian said, his words punctuated by a rapid exhalation. "But Jasper's in no condition to go anywhere," he added, all protective indignation. Caius sank his teeth into his lower lip to hold back a smile. After so many years of pining after his prince, it was nice to see Dorian's affection focused on someone else. He deserved to find love and to have that love returned.

"And that's why I'll be contacting the warlock of his choosing." Caius pushed himself away from the parapet, stretching his arms high above his head. It was getting late, even if the dull roar of the party across the way showed no signs of abating. He took one last look at the stars, dimmed by the noxious clouds that hung above the city. As prince, he'd done little to deserve his place in the heavens, but he'd meant every word of his vow. He'd protect his people and serve them, even if he had to do it from afar, without a title and with precious few allies. Even after they threw their support behind someone else.

He started toward the door, Dorian hot on his heels. "I take it you mean to go alone," Dorian said.

Caius pulled the door open, grimacing at the loud sound of the hinges complaining. They needed a good greasing. The staircase was dark, illuminated only by a single, flickering bulb hanging sadly from a rusty chain. "I need you here, Dorian. To protect the others." He winked at Dorian over his shoulder. "Besides, I doubt I could pull you away from Jasper even if I wanted to."

Dorian missed the top step. He grabbed the banister, catching himself. Caius laughed, then clapped a hand over his mouth when Dorian shot him a dark look. "Sorry," Caius said, words muffled by his palm. He lowered his hand. "But it's true. You're quite smitten."

It was hard to tell in the shadowy stairwell, but Caius was willing to bet that there was a pale pink blush painting Dorian's cheeks. With an indignant huff, Dorian headed down the stairs, brushing past Caius. Oh, yes, that was most certainly a blush, crawling all the way up to the silver hair.

"I don't know what you're talking about," said Dorian. He kept his back to Caius as he descended, rounded the bend, and then began making his way down the next staircase.

"Of course not," Caius said, taking hold of the banister and swinging himself down in front of Dorian. He bent his knees as he landed, silent as a cat. "I'm sure all those surreptitious glances mean absolutely nothing."

Caius was through the door before Dorian could muster a response. He felt lighter than he had in weeks. They had a plan to help Jasper—or at least the very beginnings of a plan. A plan in infancy. And it was probably a terrible plan, but it was better than nothing, and sometimes, that was all anyone could ask for.

CHAPTER FIVE

Echo woke to the rich, bitter scent of freshly brewed coffee. Her eyes flew open. The coffeemaker in the warehouse had broken two weeks ago, dripping its last forlorn drop of badly burnt coffee as she and Jasper looked on in sadness. Echo bolted upright, kicking off the sheets and pulling a hand through her sleep-tangled hair. In the corner of the room, where they'd arranged boxes of instant oatmeal, cups of ramen noodles, a microwave, a rickety table, and a kettle into a makeshift kitchenette, stood the Ala, greasy paper bag in one hand, and a cardboard tray holding four large cups of coffee in the other. Her expression was that of a disgusted parent walking into a child's messy bedroom.

"Honestly, when was the last time any of you ate something that couldn't be prepared in a microwave?"

"Ala!" Echo sprang to her feet, legs tangled in the sheets. The Ala was here. The Ala had brought food. The Ala was a goddess.

Echo's shout woke the others. On the mattress nearest her, Ivy grumbled, pulling the sheet higher above her head, while Caius rubbed a hand over his face, hiding a yawn. His dark hair was mussed from sleep, but it was an artful disarray, the kind that beckoned to be combed through with questing fingers. He met Echo's eyes and smiled a little wryly as his gaze dropped. Only then did Echo remember that she wasn't wearing any pants. Thankfully, the gray T-shirt she'd nipped from Jasper's stack of clothes hit her mid-thigh. She looked back at Caius and shrugged. Coffee and a hot breakfast were infinitely more important than sartorial modesty. She kicked the mess of blankets off and made her way to the Ala, who was setting the bag and coffee tray down on the table.

Echo threw her arms around the Ala and buried her face in the Avicen's shoulder, breathing in the familiar scent of honey and old books that clung to the Ala's raven feathers like perfume. The Ala hugged her back tightly, and over her shoulder, Echo caught sight of Dorian on the other side of the room, sword drawn, a frown frozen in place. Echo bit back a laugh. Dorian had been on watch during the night, standing guard to make sure no intruders made it past their wards. He looked absolutely stymied that the Ala had been able to do it, breakfast in hand, as though the wards were nothing. But the normal rules of in-between didn't apply to the Ala; she could navigate its darkness with an ease no living creature could hope to match, even Caius.

Echo pulled back, looking up into the Ala's onyx eyes. "I missed you."

The Ala smiled and smoothed down the unruly strands of Echo's hair. "I missed you, too, my little magpie." She gestured to the food on the table. "I brought your favorites.

Bacon, egg, and cheese on a bagel, and jelly doughnuts. I thought you might like something a touch more substantial after weeks of eating nothing but"—she picked up a box of Pop-Tarts, squinting at the label as she read the ingredients—"high-fructose corn syrup."

Echo yanked open the bag and drew in a deep breath. *Heavenly.* She grabbed a doughnut and bit into it, powdered sugar drifting down like snowflakes, savoring the taste of the jelly as it exploded on her tongue. It was bliss. Around a mouthful of doughnut, she said, "I love you."

"As I love you, little magpie," the Ala said. She turned and looked at Dorian's sword, lifting a single amused eyebrow. "Do you plan on using that, boy?"

Shamefaced, Dorian lowered the blade. "No."

"Then I suggest you put it away."

He did.

Caius drifted over to where Echo stood, clutching the bag of doughnuts. Now that he was close to her, she was more self-conscious about her state of undress and the powdered sugar on her face. One of his hands settled on her lower back briefly as he reached around her to claim a coffee, the warmth of his skin radiating through the thin cotton of her shirt. He brought the cup to his mouth and smiled at her over the lid. "Good morning," he said, voice rough from sleep, slightly deeper than normal. He took a sip, Adam's apple bobbing as he swallowed, the angle of his head highlighting the elegant line of his throat.

Echo rubbed at her sugar-coated lips with the back of her hand. "Morning." He knew what he was doing. He had to know. No one got to be two hundred fifty years old without learning how to make drinking coffee look pornographic.

Behind her, the Ala cleared her throat. Echo jumped, and Caius winked at her. Now he was just being unfair. Echo snagged a napkin from the depths of the paper bag and wrapped another doughnut in it to take to Ivy.

The Ala made her way to the bank of windows at the other end of the room, near Ivy's bed. "Come, Echo, I have something to discuss with you."

Echo followed, doughnuts in hand, and plopped down on the mattress. A wordless groan emerged from the Ivy-shaped pile of blankets. Echo poked at the center of the blanket lump until Ivy peeked out, delicate features pulled into a frown, white feathers sticking up at odd angles. Waving the doughnut under Ivy's nose, Echo said, "I got you a present."

Ivy snaked a hand out from under the covers, grabbed the doughnut, and retreated beneath the blankets.

Echo looked to the Ala, who was watching their exchange with a bemused expression. "So, what's the deal?" Echo asked. She took another bite of her doughnut. Jelly leaked around its edges. "How are things at the Nest? Is everyone okay?"

By everyone, she meant Rowan. Their relationship might have been burned to the ground in a firestorm of bad decisions and even worse luck, but she couldn't *not* care about him. Caring about Rowan was inherent to her being, ingrained in her DNA.

"Everyone is fine." The Ala's tone was all too knowing. "Including Rowan."

Echo breathed a small sigh of relief. There was a chance, one she was reluctant to acknowledge, that he would hate her for the things she'd done: siding with Drakharin or, at the very least, appearing to; running off with little explanation and leaving him to deal with a mess she'd helped create.

Killing his partner. But even if he hated her, she'd still care. She would always care, no matter what catastrophes she wrought.

The Ala leaned against the windowsill, hands resting by her sides. Stray bits of sunlight dappled the unevenly tinted panes, backlighting the Ala with a soft glow. "But that's not why I'm here." She glanced at the corner of the room, where the TV was sitting, dark and silent. "I assume you've kept abreast of recent events."

Echo ceased her chewing and the mouthful of doughnut slid down her throat like a heavy lump of clay. "If by recent events, you mean all this weirdness with an active inactive volcano, whole villages swallowed up by destruction, and recurring nightmares that seem to be pointing a finger directly at me, then, yeah. Kind of hard to tear my eyes away."

"These events are more than mere anomalies," said the Ala. "I can sense it."

From beneath her pile of blankets, Ivy asked, "Like a disturbance in the Force?"

The Ala nodded tightly. "In a manner of speaking."

From the corner of her eye, Echo saw Caius shift and set his cup of coffee on the table, only to pick it up and then put it down again. She turned just enough to see his face; he was looking at her, but he wore an odd expression, one she couldn't quite read.

An unfamiliar presence ghosted softly at the back of Echo's mind. She squeezed her eyes closed, letting it settle. If it had been Rose, she would have known. Occasionally, she felt the press of other souls—long-dead vessels—against the walls of her skull, but they were never as tangible as Rose. Sometimes, she would feel emotions that she knew were not her own: fear, regret, despair. When the presence stilled, Echo asked the Ala, "Okay, but what does any of it have to do with me?"

The Ala pushed away from the window, smoothing her hands over her long, gauzy skirt. The white linen was a stark contrast to the pure black of her skin and feathers. "I think these bizarre happenings have everything to do with you." At Echo's chagrined expression, she amended, "Everything to do with the firebird, that is. I'm sure you're familiar with Newton's third law of motion."

Echo's love affair with physics in her early teens had been brief and turbulent. "For every action, there's an equal and opposite reaction," she recited. The words were nothing new; she'd read them in a battered physics textbook fished out of the library's discard pile—out-of-date volumes were prime candidates for permanent relocation to Echo's private collection—but now they took on a new weight.

"When you awakened the firebird," said the Ala, "you created an imbalance. The universe detests an imbalance. You, my dear, are a creature of light. And where there is light, there must also be darkness. I do not believe your light came into this world alone."

A creature of light. It was a lovely way of putting it, Echo thought. It made her seem pure when she felt anything but. She felt crowded, her own mind polluted with everything that wasn't Echo. "So the dreams were true. The volcano, that village. That was me."

"No," the Ala said, voice strong with certainty. "But sometimes, when a door is opened, we cannot always control what comes through."

The Ala came over to Echo, dropping to a crouch by the

mattress. Ivy curled into a little ball, shins resting against Echo's thigh. It was a comforting pressure, a reminder that she wasn't alone, no matter how isolated being the firebird made her feel. "This is, of course, all speculation. There are certain . . . methods of accessing the information that might illuminate our situation, but they're far from pleasant."

Echo rubbed her mouth with the back of her hand, her appetite forgotten. "Whatever it is, I'll do it."

"This won't be easy." The Ala tucked a strand of messy hair behind Echo's ear. "I'll have to sort through the contents of your mind, to see if I can learn the firebird's secrets. But I can't choose what we unearth. The process is unpredictable at best, and traumatic at worst. You might see things that will frighten you."

A sudden flash of someone else's fear seized Echo. She closed her eyes, trying to block out the memory, but that just made it worse. Behind her lids, all she could see was the blinding brightness of flames. The smell of burning feathers, the sound of crackling wood, and the feel of her own skin blistering in a heat so powerful, Echo thought that if she opened her eyes just then, she would find herself in the inferno that had claimed Rose's life.

"Echo?" Ivy's voice was soft and a little unsure, but it anchored Echo. She opened her eyes, clinging to the sound of her friend's voice like a tether.

Echo had to clear her throat twice before she could speak. "I'm fine," she said, in a voice only the tiniest bit uneven. The others were all looking at her as though they expected her to break. Caius gravitated closer, coffee forgotten on the table. He paused halfway to the mattress on which Echo sat. She wondered if he felt like he couldn't intrude, not with Ivy on one side of her and the Ala on the other. She wanted to tell him that it was okay, that she wanted him near, but she couldn't find the words. And even if she could, she wasn't entirely certain she wanted to share them with a rapt audience.

She drew in a shaky breath. And then another. And another, each one slightly steadier than the last. Eventually, the phantom stench of acrid smoke cleared, and she felt like herself again.

The Ala was still crouched in front of her, dark eyes full of concern.

Echo smiled for everyone's benefit but her own. *Put on a happy face,* she told herself. *Be strong. For them.*

"But before we head through the looking glass," she said, reaching to confiscate the remainder of Ivy's doughnut. She pointedly ignored the halfhearted scowl her friend threw at her. Stealing food was normal. It was her thing. Not Rose's. Not the firebird's. Just hers. Echo nibbled on the edge of the pastry, focusing on the way the powdered sugar melted on her tongue. "I need to find some pants."

CHAPTER SIX

Echo closed her eyes, focusing on the sensation of the lumpy mattress beneath her and the warmth of the sun on her face as late-morning light filtered through the painted windows. She was lying in the corner of the room farthest from the door, hidden by bedsheets strung to the ceiling with twine, which doubled as privacy curtains. She heard the Ala's skirt whisper against the hardwood floor as she settled into a comfortable seated position. The Ala had warned Echo that the process of submerging deep enough into her subconscious to access the firebird's trove of repressed memories would be difficult and time-consuming.

With her eyes closed, Echo's other senses were heightened. The sheet-curtain may have provided the illusion of isolation, but she could still hear the sounds of the others quietly milling about the room. They were trying to be as unobtrusive as possible, but there was only so far they could go. Their voices were hushed, and though Echo couldn't understand their words, she found it hard to concentrate on her own psyche while they spoke. Even so, she didn't want to tell them to keep completely silent; a small part of her liked being able to hear them. The familiarity was comforting, like a crutch. Ivy's voice joined the quiet conversation, her tone inquisitive. Echo drew in a deep breath, let it out slowly. Focus, she told herself. *Eye of the tiger.*

"Are you ready?" the Ala asked.

"Not really," said Echo. Her nose was itchy, and she was suddenly aware of every uncomfortable spring digging into her back. When she reached up to scratch the bridge of her nose, the Ala tutted.

"You have to stay still for this to work, Echo."

"I know, I know." Echo opened her eyes to find the Ala looking at her, expression somehow both soft and stern. "It's just . . ." Echo folded her hands over her stomach and knotted her fingers together. They'd grown worryingly bony. Stress had done a number on her appetite in the past few weeks. She looked back at the Ala, not bothering to mask the fear in her eyes. "I'm scared."

The Ala's face softened, and she stroked Echo's hair back from her forehead. "It's all right to be scared. I'd be surprised if you weren't. You're about to delve into centuries' worth of memories, many of them unpleasant. Tragedy seems to have followed the firebird's vessels like a dark cloud, leaving wounds that have never quite healed. What we're about to do is equivalent to pulling out the sutures and forcing them to bleed anew."

"No offense, but this isn't your best pep talk."

Amusement tugged at the Ala's lips. "There's no sense in

lying to you with sugarcoated promises that everything will be fine. You're entirely too clever for that."

The words weren't comforting, but at least they were honest. Echo nodded, her hair rubbing against the thin pillow beneath her head and escaping the braid she'd quickly put it in. With more determination than she felt, she told the Ala, "All right. Let's get this show on the road, shall we?"

"Remember, I'm here with you," said the Ala. "If you become lost, simply call out for me, and I will find you." She placed a hand on Echo's forehead, her skin cool against Echo's. Her hand slowly descended, covering Echo's eyes inch by inch until all she could see was darkness. She closed her eyes, and when she felt the pressure of the Ala's hand lift, she was surprised that she couldn't see the light of the sun behind her lids. She cracked her eyes open and sucked in a gasp. The ceiling was gone.

Above her, the sky was a blanket of black velvet, punctured by a dense scattering of stars. The moon floated overhead, full and heavy, like a bright, ripe fruit. Instead of the warehouse's drab gray walls, large smooth stones surrounded her, arranged in a neat circle. In the distance, she saw a ring of trees and, behind them, a dense forest. Her hair caught on dry twigs and brittle leaves. She scrambled to her feet, but her body felt wrong, like her skin was stretched too tight over her bones. She stumbled; her center of gravity had shifted. She looked down. No wonder her body felt different. It wasn't hers.

It was dark, so she couldn't quite make out the color of the clothes she wore, but a brisk evening chill pricked at her bare upper arms. She brought her hands up to rub her forearms, and when she felt the slightly raised texture of her skin, she froze.

No way. No freaking way.

Holding her hands out, she wiggled her fingers, feeling unfamiliar muscles bunch and flex. Moonlight danced along the scales on her forearms, the glow making them shimmer.

She was a Drakharin. Well, she was in a Drakharin body, but after dealing with Rose, she was beginning to appreciate just how fuzzy the line between self and corporeality was. She brought her hands to her face, feeling for more scales. The skin there was smooth, though, and her cheekbones were sharp and prominent, so unlike her own face, which still clung to the softness of youth. Her fingers traced the curve of her cheek to her ear, running along the ridge of her jaw, up to the fullness of her mouth. She touched her nose; it was long and aquiline. When she felt the bridge, she smiled. A smattering of scales was peppered across the skin there, like freckles.

When she spoke, her voice was alien. "Where am I?"

The only answer the night offered was a resounding silence.

She peered up at the stars, trying to pick out constellations she might recognize. Her brief love affair with astronomy had left her with a rudimentary knowledge of the night sky, which had been refreshed by the time she'd spent on the warehouse roof with Caius, gazing up at the stars stubbornly shining through London's smog. If she could find Polaris, then maybe she could get her bearings. Scanning the sky for the familiar shape of Ursa Minor, Echo frowned.

The sky wasn't right.

Or maybe it was, but it wasn't the sky she knew. None of the constellations were where they were supposed to be.

And then it hit her. The alignment of the stars, when viewed from Earth, changed with the procession of the equinoxes. If she had been whisked away to a memory that took place thousands of years ago, the celestial pole wouldn't look the same. She craned her neck, even though she could feel it getting stiff, trying to find something she would recognize in the place where the North Star would be.

Slowly, the stars began to form shapes in her mind. She brought up a hand, tracing patterns in the sky.

There.

The constellation Draco. The dragon. How fitting. Caius had told her that it was considered the king of the sky in Drakharin mythology. And that four thousand years ago, one of its fainter stars had been the North Star.

Four thousand years.

She looked back down at her hands, at the strange body that she now inhabited. A chill raced along her spine, raising the fine hairs at the back of her neck.

A sound from the woods, like the snapping of twigs underfoot, made her jump. From the shadows among the trees emerged a group of hooded figures, chanting words in an unfamiliar language.

The unease in her gut blossomed into panic, heady and sharp.

"Who are you?" she asked, though she knew it was futile. If she couldn't understand them, they probably couldn't understand her. But, to her surprise, the words that came from her mouth weren't in English. Her lips and tongue moved in a way that felt completely foreign. It sounded like the Drakhar Caius and Dorian occasionally spoke, but the words had a different cadence to them. Four thousand years. It must have been some kind of proto-Drakhar.

The figures approached, closing in on her.

"What do you want?" It felt like her brain was on a time delay. She thought the words in one language and spoke them, a fraction of a second later, in another.

One of the hooded figures spoke, and Echo's mind raced to translate its speech. "You know what we want, Samira."

From the folds of the figure's robe, a hand emerged holding a long knife, the blade curved and wicked. "There is power in you," he said, never breaking stride as he approached. "A great and terrible power. You are both the key and the curse."

She turned to run, but there was nowhere to go. All around her, hooded figures closed in, long cloaks gliding across the grass with an audible hiss.

"No," she begged. "Please."

The man holding the knife was so close to her now, she could see the gleam of his eyes beneath the hood. The light caught the scales on the backs of his hands and scattered across his knuckles. The circle closed in around her. She took another step back, only to collide with the person behind her. Both of her arms were seized. She struggled, but no matter how hard she pulled, bare feet slipping on the grass, she couldn't break free.

"Why are you doing this?"

"The light has chosen you," said the man with the knife. Over his shoulder, she saw the shadows among the trees writhe as if they were alive. As if they were listening, eager to witness the macabre tableau unfolding within the circle of stones. "But so has the dark. We cannot let the kuçedra go free."

He raised the blade, holding it level with her throat, its steel shining in the moonlight.

Fear, both hers and Samira's, made Echo's heart pound wildly. It felt as though it would burst right out of her chest. "What are you talking about?" Echo asked. "What's a kuçedra?"

"There is no light without darkness," said the robed man. His voice had a distant quality, as if he wasn't quite talking *to* her so much as *about* her. The figures in the circle repeated the words after him, like some kind of prayer. "No life without death. No gain without loss. No savior without a destroyer." His hood angled toward her, as if he was studying her from its dark depths. "One cannot exist in this world without the other. The kuçedra," he added, pity slinking into his tone, "is your other half. Your mirror image. And we cannot let it free. You are a danger because of who you are. Of *what* you are."

Before she could react, the man drew the knife across her throat. A warm rush of blood flowed down her neck. Her knees buckled, and she sank to the ground. They lowered her gently, reverently. Her life bled out of her, hot and sticky. Blinking up at the stars, she tried to speak, but all that came out was a wet gurgle. It took a few seconds for the pain to register. It followed in the knife's wake, sharp and hot.

The light has chosen you. They thought—no, they *knew*—that she was the firebird. But the firebird was not what frightened them.

The hooded figure leaned over her, bringing up the knife to lick at the crimson slick of her blood along the blade. He passed the knife around the circle, and each member of the group cradled it as if her blood was something precious, something sacred. The man who killed her knelt beside her, cupping her cheek with cool fingers.

"Your sacrifice will be remembered," he said, lips stained cherry red with her blood.

Echo felt her heartbeat slowing, each agonized pump pushing forth less blood than the one before it. She should have passed out by now, but something in her fought for every scrap of consciousness she could hoard before it was stolen from her. She blinked up at the sky, taking in the stars that floated above, arranged in constellations of light that told stories to anyone willing to connect the dots. For a brief, disjointed moment, Echo was glad that Samira had at least had this—one final view of something beautiful—before her life was snuffed out.

Súton, Echo remembered suddenly. *Croatian. "The inexorable approach of the end."*

And then Samira's heart pounded its last beat, and together, they died.

CHAPTER SEVEN

With a gasp, Echo opened her eyes, fingers scrabbling at her throat. The memory of her blood—Samira's blood—spilling from the wound was so real that she could almost taste the coppery tang of it on her tongue. She pressed her hand into the skin of her neck, remembering the way she'd felt it split beneath the blade. The memory of pain remained even if the wound hadn't.

The Ala's hand hovered near Echo's shoulder, as though afraid to touch her. "Echo? Can you hear me?"

Chest heaving, Echo gulped down great lungfuls of air, relishing its staleness, so unlike the fresh scent of grass and woods in the memory. "I died," she said, voice breaking on each word. "I just had my throat cut. Well, I mean, not *my* throat, but . . ."

Echo's fingers lingered on her neck, feeling the rapid flutter of her pulse, reminding herself that she was whole and unharmed. But it had felt so real. Her gaze darted to the Ala. "You were right. We fucked up. *I* fucked up."

The Ala leaned forward, eyes ablaze with a mix of concern and curiosity. "What did you see?"

Before Echo could answer, Caius poked his head around the curtain. "Everything all right?" he asked, as if he knew everything was most assuredly not all right.

"No," Echo said. "Yes. I mean—I don't know."

He nodded slowly. "Anything I can help with?"

Echo shook her head rapidly. "No. I just . . ." She turned back to the Ala. "I saw a girl." She looked down at her hands, at the smooth, lightly tanned skin, devoid of scales, stretching across her knuckles. "I *was* a girl. She was Drakharin. Her name was Samira. And she was scared."

Caius came to sit next to her on the mattress, close but not touching. She wanted to throw herself at him, to feel his arms wrap around her and forget the death she'd just witnessed. The death she'd felt. His expression softened, and he offered her his hand. She took it, focusing on the feel of his skin against hers. This was real. Not the memory. He gave her hand a gentle squeeze and asked, "What happened?"

"They killed me. Her. They killed *her*." Again, the scent of blood filled her nostrils, sharp and metallic. Echo closed her eyes, but that only made it worse. She opened them, taking in her surroundings, grounding herself. She was with the Ala and Caius, in an abandoned warehouse in East London, sitting on a wildly uncomfortable mattress. She was here. Not there.

"They who?" asked the Ala.

"I don't know," Echo said. "A bunch of Drakharin in

hooded robes. I woke up in a circle of stones, and they came and killed me. They said that the light had chosen me but so had the dark." She touched her neck with her free hand. "And they mentioned something. Uh, a kushed . . . kuskera . . . I don't remember exactly, I was a little distracted by the awful, violent death."

Both Caius and the Ala went still as stone. "Kuçedra?" asked Caius.

Echo nodded. "Yeah. Why? What is it?"

He shook his head, one hand rising to rub at his temple. "Is there anything else you can think of that might be relevant? It's no accident that this was the memory the firebird chose to share with you. Before we jump to any conclusions, I want to make sure we know all the details."

"There was a forest," Echo said. "Trees. Stones. Grass." She scratched her head, fingers catching in the tangles of her hair, half expecting to feel brittle twigs in it. And then she remembered. "Oh. I'm guessing it was about four thousand years ago."

"How would you have known that?" The tone of Caius's inquiry was the tiniest bit insulting.

"The stars. Do you remember what you told me about the North Star shifting over time?" He nodded. "Well, when I was looking at the sky through Samira's eyes, it wasn't Polaris. It was Thuban, in Draco."

"I didn't think you were paying such close attention."

The Ala cleared her throat, louder than was absolutely necessary. Echo swiveled her head around to look at her, heat rising in her cheeks.

"The mention of the kuçedra concerns me, especially when linked to the firebird," said the Ala. She leaned back to rest on her heels and ran a hand over the raven-black feathers on her arm.

"Caius, what is it?" Echo asked again. Focusing on the facts made it easier to forget the sensation of steel ripping through skin. She looked back and forth between them. "You both seem a little on edge, and since we know at least one of the firebird's previous vessels died because of it, I think I'd like to know."

Caius's hand gravitated toward Echo's knee. When she made no move to stop him, he let it rest there. "After Rose died, my search for the firebird was elevated from curiosity to obsession. I wanted so desperately to end the war that had taken her life. My hunt was a sort of penance. I came across a great deal of information, most of it useless folklore and superstition, but there were some primary sources—most of them incredibly old—that mentioned a dark force meant to counter the light. It's like the Ala said: every action in this world has a reaction. Just as the firebird rose, so did this kuçedra. And if it happened at the same moment, then that might explain the otherwise inexplicable volcanic eruption that occurred on the opposite side of the world from where you were standing." Caius sighed. "You were right. It wasn't a coincidence. As to what we're meant to do about it"—he flung his hands up in a frustrated gesture—"I'm at a loss."

Echo looked at the Ala. "Any ideas?"

"I would like to consult my books," the Ala replied. She stood, straightening her skirts. "I'll telephone if I come across any pertinent information."

"And we'll do what we can on this end," Caius offered. "Though I'm not sure how much help we'll be."

The Ala accepted Caius's offer with grace, but she, too, seemed uncertain of what they would actually be able to accomplish from their hiding spot. After several hugs and promises of more food, the Ala departed. Her power electrified the air as she summoned the in-between, and Echo was left staring at the place where the Ala had been standing, the fading tendrils of the in-between the only sign she'd ever been there.

Echo flopped back on the mattress, throwing an arm across her forehead. There was a nascent migraine tingling at the space between her brows. The combination of past-life remembrance and contemplating the destruction of a dark force she was at least partially responsible for unleashing was almost too much to bear. "What now?" she asked.

"Well," Caius began, "to start, we need to get Jasper back on his feet." He smirked. "We can't have our best thief out of commission."

A stray lock of hair fell in front of Echo's face. She blew it upward with a strong puff of breath. "I resent that remark."

A soft smile ghosted across Caius's lips. "While you were asleep, the rest of us got to talking. Jasper said he knows a guy who might be willing and able to help." Hearing the former Dragon Prince spouting colloquialisms like *knows a guy* would never not be endearing. He was picking up their slang.

Echo snorted. "Of course he knows a guy. Who is this guy?"

"A warlock." The corners of Caius's lips turned down in a slight frown. "And one Jasper thinks might not be inclined to betray us. At least not immediately."

"So, do we just like . . . call him?" Echo hoped the answer was yes. Caius's attempts to navigate modern technology was her new favorite pastime. It had taken three days of suspicious staring before she'd convinced him to use the microwave. And they'd all agreed never to mention the time he'd put aluminum foil in it. Phones were a newfangled breed of sorcery he was just beginning to master.

"Apparently, this warlock responds only to requests made in person. And Jasper warned me that he could be exceedingly unpleasant."

"A warlock? Unpleasant? Surely you jest." Echo sat up, running a hand over her hair. It was still a mess from the night before, strands of it falling loose while the back felt like birds had nested in it. Under normal circumstances, she would have felt self-conscious, but sharing living quarters with four other people had corroded the integrity of her personal boundaries to the point where they hardly existed. "Leave it to Jasper's criminal acquaintances to be difficult."

"Present company excluded, I take it?" Caius chided.

She knocked her knee against his. "Of course. So when do we head out?"

"*We* aren't heading anywhere." Caius stood, holding out a hand to help Echo up. She did not take it. "I'm going alone. You're too valuable. Jasper's injured. Ivy needs to stick around to take care of Jasper. And Dorian is going to babysit you all, to make sure nothing exciting happens and no one sneaks out."

And by no one, he meant Echo.

"Absolutely not," she said. "Nobody goes anywhere alone. That's what you said the first day we holed up in this dive, remember?"

"You're staying here," Caius said, "and I will entertain absolutely no argument on the matter." There he went with his princely voice and his royal edicts. Echo was loath to admit it, but his points were maybe, slightly, potentially, infuriatingly valid. "And as you are so fond of reminding me," he added with a fleeting smile and a deep breath, "some rules are simply meant to be broken."

CHAPTER EIGHT

The streets of Seoul pressed in on Caius from all sides, the balmy July air suffocating. Neon-lit glass and metal canyons stretched in all directions, thrusting into the night sky with their garishly bright signage. His breath came in quick, uneven pants. Sweat beaded on his skin, and he worried that his scales were in danger of showing through the concealer Echo had smeared on his cheekbones. He balled his hands into fists, short nails digging into the flesh of his palms, and closed his eyes, shutting out the assault on his senses. It was easier to adjust if he didn't have to look at everything all at once. Echo had continued to protest his departure, right up until the moment he'd conjured a way through to the in-between in one of the warehouse's wide archways, in a large room on the ground floor that he assumed must have once been used for packing and shipping goods. She hadn't wanted him to go alone. Right now, he almost wished that he'd listened to her.

Dealing with modernity was easier with Echo by his side. It gave him the option of focusing on her instead of on the visual chaos of the world around him. At home, in his library at Wyvern's Keep, he had books from every era of human history, but there was nothing in a book that could encapsulate the reality of experiencing it all. He'd never considered himself claustrophobic before, but there was something about the crush of people around him, filling the nighttime streets of Seoul with energy and noise, that made his chest feel as though it were being compressed.

He reached into his pocket to touch the iron ball bearings he'd brought with him. Iron was the only thing that could neutralize a warlock's magic. The ball bearings were small enough to go unnoticed. Though they wouldn't deflect a spell entirely, they would lessen the effects of one.

Someone bumped into Caius from behind, uttering something in rapid Korean that sounded vaguely exasperated. Mumbling a quick apology, Caius set off down the street, scanning the array of signs for one bearing the same equal-armed cross that had helped them find the warlock in London. So far, Caius had passed well over a dozen small storefronts, each lined with blinking lights. Some sold inexpensive plastic trinkets geared toward tourists; others had placards out front that boasted a myriad of different foods, some local, some imported. A medley of scents wafted through open doors and windows. Caius was tempted by a stall selling soft rice cakes submerged in a sauce that promised to be as hot as it was red—*dukbokki,* the vendor called it—but he had a job to do and a warlock to find.

He nearly walked past the sign. If it hadn't been for the slight shimmer of air around an otherwise nondescript entrance, he would have missed the cross carved into the door's warped wood, overwhelmed as it was by the surrounding lights.

"Don't bother knocking," Jasper had told him. "Only newbs knock."

Newbs. The evolution of language was a strange and marvelous thing.

Caius pushed the door open. As soon as he crossed the threshold, he felt a faint buzz of energy, like he was walking through a wall of static electricity. He paused, one hand still on the rusted doorknob. It must have been the warlock's equivalent of a doorbell, announcing his presence. When no one rushed from the shadows, he let himself relax. A small, dying fern sat in a clay pot in a corner, while dust motes danced in the rectangle of light let in by the open door. Two metal folding chairs rested against a wall, right next to a brass accordion gate. A single lightbulb dangled from a chain in the center of the room, its faint glow barely enough to illuminate the space. Caius closed the door behind him. The sounds of the city outside immediately died, letting fall a silence too complete to be natural. An effect of a cloaking spell perhaps. Away from the city's chaos, Caius breathed a little easier, the pressure in his chest dissipating with each exhalation.

It took his eyes a moment to adjust to the semidarkness. After a few seconds, a loud rattle erupted from the elevator shaft behind the accordion gate. Inch by inch, an old-fashioned elevator slid into view, ascending from below. It was empty, save for a single dried rose in a vase in a small alcove in the far wall. Caius pulled back the gate and stepped inside, inwardly cringing when his weight made the elevator dip just enough to be terrifying. He had a complicated relationship with elevators. As with most modern contraptions, they hated him, and he hated them right back. Upon reflection, perhaps it wasn't that complicated a relationship after all.

He turned, looking for a panel of buttons. There was none.

Caius let out an exasperated sigh. *Damn warlocks.*

He turned to the small vase tucked into the alcove at the back of the elevator. It was cut crystal, decorated with a ring of human figures, delicate and detailed, writhing in either pleasure or agony, limbs intertwined, mouths agape with silent screams. The rose's sanguine petals were as soft as satin beneath Caius's fingertips. He followed the curve of the bloom down to the stem, trailing a light touch over the rose's leaves and thorns.

Nothing in this world came without a price, least of all favors from warlocks.

One of the thorns was slightly larger than the rest, beckoning Caius to dig the pad of his finger into it. He did just that. Pain radiated along the length of his arm, as if the thorn and the wound it caused were ten times their actual size. Blood welled up on the surface of his skin, and he held his finger where it was, pressed against the thorn's sharp point. The stem was stained crimson for only a moment before it absorbed the blood offered to it. With a jolt and a clang, the elevator began to rise.

After what felt like an eternity, the stuttering ascent ended. Caius pulled back another accordion gate and entered a corridor warmly lit by a series of small gilded chandeliers dangling from the ceiling. At the other end of the hallway, a burgundy velvet curtain covered the only doorway. A woman pushed it aside as he stepped into the corridor. She was tall, and as she moved, a slit on one side of her black silk gown revealed glimpses of a knife in a bejeweled sheath strapped to her thigh. A cascade of ebony hair fell freely around her shoulders, and her lips were the deep scarlet of freshly spilled blood. She held the curtains closed behind her as she let her gaze trail up Caius's body from his boots to his hair. Her eyes were devoid of pupils and white as cream.

She smiled, like a wolf baring its fangs. "Are you lost, little lamb?"

Little lamb, Caius thought. *How precious.*

"Hardly," he said. "I'm here to see the master of the house."

"And who might I say is calling?" asked the woman.

Jasper had warned him against providing a fake name, so he answered truthfully. "Caius. We have a mutual friend."

The woman simply arched one flawlessly sculpted eyebrow.

"His name is Jasper. He told me I could find assistance here."

The scarlet smile wilted at the sound of Jasper's name. "Is that so? Well, in that case, come along." She swept the curtain aside, gesturing Caius through. Before he could cross the threshold, a hand on his elbow stilled him.

The woman leaned into him, lips brushing his ear, the fall of her hair hiding her face from view. "Is he well?" she asked. "Jasper?"

Caius offered a shallow nod in response. Her behavior puzzled him. She had gone from well-mannered hostility to concerned curiosity just a touch too fast. It made him wonder how well she knew Jasper and why she didn't want her question overheard.

"Now, now, Taeyeon, it's rude to hog our guest's attention."

Taeyeon stepped aside, her soot-black gown blending with the shadows. Caius couldn't see the speaker right away, but what he did see was breathtaking. The exterior of the building had been as nondescript as those on either side of it, with a restaurant that appeared to specialize in a thousand kinds of dumplings on the ground floor, but Caius realized now that it was a front, fueled by magic. The far wall was dominated by an enormous clockface that doubled as a window, its wrought-iron gears and hands casting oddly shaped shadows on the hardwood floor as the city's rainbow of lights filtered through the glass. Large pillows were scattered about the space, interspersed with couches bearing sinfully plush cushions and artfully draped fur throws. Candles mounted in sconces along the walls illuminated the room. Bodies, so like the ones carved into the crystal vase in the elevator, were gathered in groups on both the furniture and the floor. Some were practically nude, though most were dressed like Taeyeon: fully clothed, but with strategic areas of bare flesh, just enough to capture the imagination. A woman with hair the color of amethyst held a champagne flute to the lips of a bare-chested young man, her free hand trailing along the raw, raised skin of a newly inked tattoo—a stylized *Q*—low on his stomach, right above the jut of his hip bone. The woman threw back her head as she laughed, keeping the champagne just out of the young man's reach. Caius could see part of the same tattoo on the woman's neck, right under her ear. These were Quinn's people, and he had gone as far as to brand them. The level of narcissism on display was so stunning it made Caius's head hurt.

A sofa shaped like an open circle dominated the place of honor in front of the clock. A group of men and women sat around a figure at the center, leaning into him like flowers craning for the sun. All of them were beautiful, but in very different ways, like a carefully curated collection of loveliness. Caius wondered if they had been chosen the way some people selected artwork with which to decorate their walls. The man at the center of it all, positioned like a modern-day Bacchus doted upon by faithful admirers, was bookended by two aggressively beautiful people, one male, one female. One of his hands rested on the woman's thigh, fingers splayed on her leather-clad leg, while the other tangled with the man's wavy platinum hair as they kissed. Everyone in the group, save for the man in the center, bore the same tattoo that marked the others.

"You must be Quinn." Caius was careful to keep his voice free of the distaste he felt. Two minutes in, and he already didn't like the warlock. Jasper needed better friends. "If that's your real name."

A lazy grin pulled at Quinn's lips as he drew back from the platinum-haired man. "It is. For the time being, at least."

Quinn patted the woman's thigh the way one would pet an obedient dog, and without a single spoken command, the group around Quinn dispersed, gravitating toward their brethren in other parts of the room. Quinn turned to Caius. Unlike nearly every warlock Caius had ever seen, Quinn's eyes weren't a sickly shade of white; his pupils were as dark as the night sky, sprinkled with pinpricks of light that looked like stars. With each blink, the stars swirled, orbiting each other like roving galaxies. Quinn's eyes must have been white beneath the glamour, but the magic was so deftly done that it was impossible to tell it was fake.

"And to whom do I owe the pleasure?" Quinn asked.

"Most never make it past the elevator." He ran his thumb along his lower lip, mouth shiny with what Caius assumed was saliva. Charming. Quinn's black hair was cropped close to his head, and he was shirtless, golden skin gleaming in the candlelight. Dark jeans sat low on his hips, and his feet were bare. An intricate pattern of scars crawled up his arms and chest, reminding Caius of the way ivy crawled up the sides of buildings. The scars were deliberate, perhaps even self-inflicted. Magic came with a price, and Caius wondered if Quinn had carved his out in blood and pain.

"My name is Caius. Jasper told me I could find you here."

Quinn tilted his head, mouth tightening into a thin line. "That's true," he said. "But you're hiding something, aren't you?"

He snapped his fingers, and Caius felt the concealer pull away from his skin like a film, leaving a not entirely unpleasant tingling sensation in its wake. A few of the people sitting on the cushions closest to Caius twisted to get a better look at him. They were all human, and fascinated by his scales.

"That's better," said Quinn. "Never try to trick a trickster." He leaned forward to pick up a glass on the low table in front of him. With languid grace, he settled back against the cushions. "Now, how is Jasper? It's been so long since I saw him last." Quinn patted the seat next to him. "Come, sit."

The way Quinn's dark eyes studied Caius made his skin crawl. He went to the sofa, taking a seat one cushion down from the one Quinn had indicated. Quinn snapped his fingers at the nearest of his acolytes, and within seconds, a glass full of something that smelled like brandy was presented to Caius.

"He's been better," Caius said, taking the glass from the

petite girl who offered it. She couldn't have been a day over sixteen, and she was covered in ink from her shoulders to her ankles. "Otherwise, he would have come himself."

Quinn smirked into his glass. "Oh, I highly doubt that. We didn't exactly part on good terms."

Caius had assumed as much, judging from the tight set of Jasper's jaw as he told Caius exactly where to go. There was history between them, but Jasper had been convinced that Quinn would respond to a summons if it came from him, even if indirectly. "He'll help you," Jasper had told Caius. "Trust me."

Caius set his glass down on the table. Accepting food or drink from warlocks was flirting with trouble; one could never be quite sure what type of edible magic one was ingesting. "Jasper is the reason I'm here. He's been hurt. Badly."

"Is that so?" Quinn's fingers marched along the length of Caius's thigh. "And how might I be of assistance?"

"There's a curse I need undone," Caius said. He removed Quinn's hand. "It was cast by a warlock and it can only be undone by a warlock."

"Why come to me? Any warlock worth his salt could do that, and for far less than my asking price."

"Jasper seems to think you're the best person for the job. I'm inclined to trust his judgment."

"You must not know him very well, then." The warlock's eyes narrowed. "Who hurt him?" Quinn raised his drink, and Caius noticed that his grip on the glass was so tight his knuckles were turning white.

"Firedrakes," Caius said. "Sent by the Dragon Prince herself."

Quinn paused, glass halfway to his lips. "Firedrakes?"

he asked, voice oozing incredulity. "What the hell is Jasper doing messing around with Firedrakes? He has more sense than that. Though judging from the company he's keeping"—Quinn gave Caius a pointed look over the rim of his glass—"maybe I overestimated him."

"The past three months have been chock-full of adventure. Jasper acquired his wound in defense of a friend."

"Huh," Quinn huffed. "Jasper engaging in heroics. Now, *that* I would pay to see." He knocked back his drink in a single swallow and then leaned in, encroaching on Caius's personal space. Though he appeared to be young, in his early twenties perhaps, magic clung to him like cologne. For power to stick like that, it took years—decades—of immersion. If a warlock kept his reserves of magical energy well fed, he could defy the natural progression of time, shedding his humanity over the years. There were any number of ways to do that. Most warlocks opted for blood and violence, buying their youth and power with someone else's pain after growing immune to their own, but now Caius understood why Quinn surrounded himself with a bevy of sensual sycophants. There was a certain magic to the element of attraction, found in the way one's heart beat faster when closing in for a kiss or the pounding of a pulse when love—or something that felt like love—was in the air. Quinn fed on their energy, or at least the promise of it, the way a vampire fed on blood.

"So you and our mutual friend Jasper need me to undo a spell only a warlock can break," Quinn said. "But before I agree to anything, I need to know one thing: how Jasper landed himself in the middle of a skirmish with Firedrakes." He canted his head to the side, his uncanny gaze raking across Caius's face as if seeking out the seeds of a lie. "And don't try to deceive me. We've already established that I'll see right through a fib."

"We were looking for the firebird." If Quinn wanted the truth, he could have it. Though Caius was under no obligation to provide him with the full truth.

The warlock's hand gravitated toward Caius's knee, slowly, as if expecting Caius to flinch. As if Caius would ever give him the satisfaction. He knew his grin was a little mad, but perhaps a little madness was what they needed. The encroaching hand froze, stalled by whatever Quinn saw in Caius's face.

"You're serious, aren't you?"

"Quite." Caius picked up his glass and swirled its amber liquid around.

After a beat, a smirk cracked Quinn's face. "You're insane," he said. "I like that. Adds a little spice to life." He stood and offered Caius a hand, which was pointedly ignored. "Let's go. Jasper is a dear friend, and I would so love to see him again."

CHAPTER NINE

Jasper watched as Dorian struck a match against the side of the box, the scent of sulfur and smoke rising in the air. The candles beside Jasper's bed had melted down to short, fat stubs, and Dorian had taken it upon himself to fetch a few more tea lights from the bag in the old-fashioned chest that held most of their survival necessities. The warehouse had always been a hideout of last resort; it was never intended for anything more than a quick ducking in and out as one ran from the law—human, Avicen, or otherwise. If Jasper had known that their ragtag group of runaways was going to wind up camping out for months, he would have spruced the place up a bit. Maybe even brought in a sofa. An honest-to-goodness place to sit. But no, such opulence was but a pipe dream for the time being.

He picked at the peeling paint on the baseboard beside his mattress and heaved a sigh, the tea in his other hand going cold. Ivy had brewed it for him. It had some kind of medicinal property to it that was supposed to stave off infection, but it tasted earthy and rotting. It did keep the wound in his abdomen from killing him, at the very least.

"Who's Rowan?"

Dorian's question drew Jasper's attention. He'd arranged the tea lights in a little semicircle on the floor, nestled in a pool of wax from the larger candles. It hadn't escaped Jasper's notice that Dorian had been rather stingy when it came to monitoring everyone else's gratuitous use of the candles, but Jasper had been allotted three tea lights each night instead of two. The favoritism wasn't subtle, but Jasper wasn't about to complain. Thawing Dorian's outer shell was a long and arduous process, but it wasn't like he had anything better to do. Humble progress was still progress.

Jasper swirled the pungent contents of the teacup. Bits of something herbaceous stuck to the sides. Delightful. "He's Echo's boyfriend. Or was, I suppose. Not quite sure what's going on there."

Dorian's silvery brows drew together. His eye patch shifted slightly, and he reached up to adjust it. Jasper had never seen him without it, not even when the Drakharin was sleeping. He wondered if it was fused to his head. Surely whatever scarring it hid couldn't be that bad. "Boyfriend?"

"Suitor. Gentleman caller. Romantic interest of the male gender."

"I know what a boyfriend is." Dorian rolled his one perfectly blue eye. Today, it was the color of the sky on a winter's day, bright and speckled with white, like snowflakes. Jasper had been trying to suss out a pattern in its ever-changing shades, to see if he could decode it like a mood ring.

"I just didn't realize Echo had one," Dorian said. "I wonder if Caius knows."

"Whether or not he does is Echo's business. Let's not meddle."

The corners of Dorian's lips twitched into a smile. "I'm surprised. You seem like the meddling type, especially when you're bored."

"Yes, but I'm also the self-serving type, and I don't know if I could survive another day in this hellhole if we stirred up a fight between forty percent of its inhabitants. I would kill everyone." Jasper studied the curve of Dorian's lower lip, the way the tips of his hair brushed the navy blue of his eye patch, the faint scarring on his cheek that spread from beneath it like a spider's web. "Well . . . maybe not everyone."

It was hard to tell by the paltry light of the candles, but Jasper was pretty sure that Dorian was blushing. As with his eye color, Jasper had developed an extensive catalog of Dorian's many blushes. The one that started at the base of his throat, peeking up from the collar of his shirt, was often found when Dorian was frustrated. The scarlet tinge at the tips of his ears belied anger. And the vaguely coral hint of blood rising in his cheeks was often a sign of embarrassment. Gods, Jasper could write a book about Dorian blushing. An encyclopedia. A multivolume encyclopedia.

Jasper set the teacup and saucer down by the mattress, chipped china clattering. "We need to get out of here," he said. "Or I'm gonna lose my frickin' mind."

Dorian reached behind Jasper to fluff his pillow. The move was so domestic that Jasper half wanted to giggle like a schoolgirl. "If you can stand up and walk out that door under your own power, I won't stop you."

Now, that was just mean.

"This is payback, isn't it?" said Jasper. "For the first time we met. When you were the one with the life-threatening wound and I was the one doing the harassing."

"Would I stoop so low?" Dorian said with another smile. He was freer with smiles lately, less self-conscious about the way they distorted the scarred flesh of his cheek.

"Oh, absolutely." Jasper rested back against the freshly fluffed pillows. "Hard to believe that was only a few months ago."

Dorian rubbed at his eye patch absently. It moved a centimeter, the band catching some of Dorian's light gray hair and rucking it up in the back. "Hard to believe we're the same people we were then."

"I don't think we are." Jasper smoothed down the disobedient tufts of hair on Dorian's head. Dorian stiffened, but he didn't move away immediately. Humble progress indeed.

Only when Jasper's hand lingered, fingers gently carding through the silky softness of Dorian's hair, did the Drakharin pull back. Jasper's chest tightened. This dance was getting old. "Why do you do that?"

Dorian retrieved a worn paperback from the small stack of books near Jasper's bedside. Since arriving at the warehouse, he'd read them all, but he started on this one again, curling up with it when he begrudgingly let Caius take the first night watch. Jasper angled his head to read the cover. *Wuthering Heights.* Forbidden love without the happy ending. Utter dreck.

"I'm not doing anything," Dorian said.

Jasper sighed. "I just thought we were moving past that."

"Past what?"

"Your emotional constipation."

"I am not constipated." Dorian looked down at the book in his hands. "I don't know what you want from me."

Jasper had learned to wield charm like a weapon from an early age. When he wanted something, he knew how to get it. He could sweet-talk a nun out of her habit if he wanted to. But that wasn't his goal with Dorian. No, that would have been a gross oversimplification of the yearning that had dominated his every waking moment the past several weeks. Jasper had never felt *want* like this before. Lust, he understood, but this wasn't the kind of desire that could be satisfied so easily. He wanted to crawl inside Dorian and count his bones. He wanted to know him, inside and out. He wanted to make him blush in a million different ways. He wanted to make Dorian smile, bright and true, without the faintest hint of a shadow lurking behind it. He wanted Dorian to stop hiding behind an eye patch and a century's worth of angst. But he didn't know how to say that. What he could say was "I want you to be honest with yourself."

"I am being honest with myself," Dorian protested. "I'm here, aren't I?"

"Where else would you be? It's not like we've got a lot of options."

Dorian shook his head. "Not here, in the warehouse." He placed his hand on the blanket, inches from Jasper's own. "Here." He paused, letting that one word sink in. "I don't have to be. I swore a long time ago that I would go wherever Caius went, but I don't have to sit here. I don't have to talk to you. I don't have to make you tea or fluff your pillows or listen to you complain about everything from the way your wound itches to the fact that we ran out of Pop-Tarts. I don't think you appreciate the enormity of that. And I don't think you should be eating Pop-Tarts. I don't trust food that comes out of boxes."

It was more than Jasper had ever heard him say in a single breath. He slipped the book from Dorian's unresisting hands and placed it atop the pile. Even though it hurt to push himself completely upright, he did so, sucking in a pained breath. This was not a conversation to be had lying down.

"I do appreciate it," Jasper said. "I understand."

Picking at a bit of dry wax on the floor, Dorian shook his head again. "No, you don't." He met Jasper's gaze. The color of his eye was a darker blue now, like the sea at dusk. "You're Avicen."

Jasper gasped, clutching at imaginary pearls. "Calumny and lies."

Dorian huffed out a tiny laugh. It was a lovely sound. "Those are the same thing." He glanced around the room, at the water-stained high ceilings, at the blackened windows, at the random spatters of paint on the hardwood floor. At everything but Jasper. "I hate your kind." He paused, rubbing the eye patch again. "I used to. Sometimes, I think I still do."

Something in Jasper's chest twisted. "Do you hate me?" He detested how small and insecure his voice sounded.

"Of course not," Dorian replied hastily. "It's just . . . when you carry something with you for so long, it's almost impossible to let it go. You forget what it feels like to not be held down by its weight." Finally, he looked back at Jasper, letting his gaze settle. Jasper knew his feathers lacked their usual jewel-toned shine and that his skin was a bit pallid, and he was struck by a malady the likes of which he rarely ever suffered:

self-consciousness. It was a ridiculous feeling, but he couldn't help it.

"I've hated the Avicen in a way you can't possibly comprehend," Dorian continued. "It runs so deep, it's like it's carved into my bones. It's been a part of me for so long that I don't know who I am without it. And then there's Caius. . . ." He let the words trail off, a rare acknowledgment of the ever-present elephant in the room that was his poorly hidden unrequited love.

"That's okay," Jasper said. "Because I know who you are."

"You've known me for the space of a few months, Jasper."

"And it's been long enough for me to figure a few things out." Jasper took Dorian's hand in both of his, fingers tracing the ridges of Dorian's knuckles. When Dorian didn't fight the contact, Jasper held on a little tighter. "I know that you're fiercely loyal. I know that you're capable of loving so intensely that you would ignore your own broken heart just to stay by your best friend's side. I know that you would put your own life in danger to protect the people you care about. And I know that you're brave enough to face down your own demons even when it feels impossible." Dorian squeezed Jasper's hand back so gently that Jasper was half convinced he'd imagined it. He dropped his voice to a conspiratorial whisper. "And to your last point, I'm not worried about Caius."

"Why's that?" Dorian asked, failing to fight the grin that found its way to his face.

Jasper smirked. "Because I'm prettier."

Dorian threw back his head and laughed, baring the fair skin of his throat. For the first time, Jasper noticed that Dorian had a dimple on his unscarred cheek. It seemed fitting. Two dimples would have been monumentally unfair to the rest of the world. No one was allowed to be that handsome.

Jasper was about to say something witty to see if he could summon forth that dimple once more when the door opened. He had only a few precious seconds to register that Caius had not returned alone before a low voice drawled, "Well, isn't this a touching moment."

Over Dorian's shoulder, Jasper spotted the last person he wanted to see, especially now. Dread coiled in his stomach, curdling like sour milk. His hand balled into a fist, rucking up the blankets. Dorian's gaze flickered down, then up to Jasper, then to the warlock who swooped into the room beside Caius. Dorian shot Jasper a questioning glance as his hand inched toward the sword that was never more than two feet from his person. It was a protective gesture that made Jasper's heart warm a little to see it.

"Quinn." Jasper tried to keep his voice as level as he could. He wasn't the person he'd been the last time he saw Quinn. He was better. Stronger. He could handle this asshole. "You always did have terrible timing."

CHAPTER TEN

Dorian had his hand on his sword before he'd even stopped to think about it; it was a reflexive action, driven purely by instinct. Echo sprang to her feet, pushing away from the table so quickly that a box of microwave popcorn plummeted to the floor, stopped only by Ivy's hand darting out to catch it. After the initial shock of seeing another person in the warehouse—besides the Ala, no one else knew they were there—they all froze, save for the man who stood in the center of the room beside Caius, staring down at Jasper like a cat appreciating the sight of a succulent mouse. The man's eyes were dark and peculiar, black speckled with glittering shards of white that reminded Dorian of starlight. An air of magic hung around him like a noxious cloud. A warlock. *The* warlock. Dorian hated him immediately.

Echo, being Echo, broke the silence. "Who's this clown?"

The warlock's strange night-sky eyes narrowed. "My name is Quinn." He kept his gaze on Jasper, who shifted uncomfortably and then winced in pain. "I'm a friend of Jasper's."

Jasper snorted. "We're stretching the definition of 'friend' a bit thin here, don't you think?"

Mouth pulling into a practiced smile, Quinn said, "Touché, my jaybird."

"Don't call me that."

Dorian lowered his sword but kept his hold on it. He liked the weight of it in his hand; it was solid, familiar. Unlike *this clown.*

Clearing his throat, Caius stepped forward, placing himself between Dorian's blade and Quinn. He shot Dorian a look that said, rather loudly, *Please put the sword away.* Dorian shot one back that simply said, *No.*

"Quinn is here to help us," Caius said. "To help *Jasper.*"

Dorian stood his ground.

"Oh, for God's sake." Quinn brushed past them, unconcerned with Dorian's blade. "You people came to me and now you're acting like I'm the intruder. Rude." He knelt down beside Jasper and extended a hand toward the fresh bandage on the Avicen's torso. Jasper sank back, deeper into the pillow. Dorian wasn't sure if he was seeing things or if genuine fear had actually flashed across Jasper's face.

"I'm not going to hurt you, Jasper. I just want to help." Quinn's voice was soft, but it had the same rehearsed quality as his smile. His hand hovered over Jasper's wound, as if waiting for permission. "You know I can."

The feathers on Jasper's forearms ruffled. The candlelight skittered off them, refracting their purple and gold highlights. "Yeah, yeah, I know," he said through clenched teeth. "Just make it fast."

"Jaybird, don't be like that. You're hurting. I can make it better." Quinn placed his hand over the wound, fingers lightly grazing the sides of the bandage. Jasper tried to flinch away from the touch, but he was too injured to go anywhere. There was a tightness to his eyes that Dorian had never seen before. Triumph flashed across Quinn's face, fierce and fleeting. This was a game to him.

Dorian edged the tip of his blade beneath Quinn's chin, applying enough pressure that Quinn had to either look up or risk being cut.

"He asked you not to call him that," Dorian said. "Don't make him ask again."

Quinn smiled, eyes shining like an oil slick. "And they say chivalry is dead." He looked back to Jasper. "You've been a busy boy, I see."

"That's enough," Caius said. He placed a hand on Dorian's elbow, forcing his arm back, and the sword away from Quinn.

For a moment, Dorian was tempted to disobey. There was a very short list of people for whom Dorian would battle a warlock as powerful as Quinn against his prince's direct order. Somehow, beyond all reason, Jasper had found a place for himself on that list. But even so, Dorian lowered the blade, giving in to the firm, persistent pressure Caius was applying to his arm. There was something about Quinn that made Dorian's skin crawl, as if ants were marching across the back of his neck.

It's because you're jealous, whispered a voice hidden in the deepest recesses of his mind.

No I'm not, Dorian hissed back, even though he knew he was being irrational. But he didn't want to stop being irrational. Not while a warlock was undressing Jasper with his weird starry eyes.

Quinn dragged his hand down Jasper's torso, fingers lightly touching Jasper's bare chest. Jasper sucked in a breath and held it, lower lip caught between his teeth. When Quinn's hand was positioned over the wound, he slowly lowered his palm so that his skin was flush with Jasper's. Quinn's eyes drifted shut.

Dorian tried to step around Caius, who held out his hand in another warning gesture. "What are you—"

Before Dorian could finish the sentence, Jasper sagged against the pillows with a relieved groan while Quinn sucked in a pained breath. The warlock opened his eyes and the starlit glamour was gone. They were white, pupils completely subsumed.

Echo stepped forward, but kept a healthy distance between herself and Quinn. "What happened to your eyes?"

Quinn removed his hand from Jasper's wound and rolled his neck. "Multitasking's a bitch. Hard to leech the power from a hex *and* look good doing it." His gaze drifted to the ground, and when he looked up, the blue-black star-speckled eyes were back. "That's more like it." Turning to Jasper, he asked, "How are you feeling?"

Jasper pushed himself up, and Dorian noticed that the movement didn't appear to cause him as much pain as it would have earlier. "Better," Jasper replied, arching his back with a groan. "A lot better."

"What did you do to him?" Dorian asked. He couldn't fight the bite in his tone even if he wanted to. And he didn't particularly want to.

"Magic comes with a price, and I paid it. I absorbed the

magic from the cursed wound and took his pain." Quinn's satisfied grin slipped back into place. "I healed him."

Quinn reached down, as if to touch Jasper's abdomen right next to the bandage. Jasper smacked his hand away. Even scowling, he was criminally beautiful. "Quinn, I swore you would never lay a hand on me again, and I meant it. That was an exception, not an invitation."

Again? Dorian's imagination concocted a series of situations in which Quinn would have laid hands on Jasper, each one more distasteful than the last.

Quinn retracted his hand. "I know it may be hard for you to swallow, Jasper, but I'm here as a friend."

Jasper snorted. "You don't have friends."

"I had you once." Quinn's voice was so serious, so quiet. If Dorian had to listen to it for a second longer, he would go mad.

"Warlocks aren't known for their selflessness," Dorian said. He rubbed a thumb along the leather on the hilt of his sword. It had been worn smooth from years of use, contoured to his grip perfectly. "What do you want in exchange for this?"

Quinn shrugged a single shoulder. His gaze slid from Dorian to Jasper and then back to Dorian. "Same thing as you, I suspect." He pushed himself to stand, wiping his hands on his dark jeans, eyes never straying from Dorian's. A chill started at the base of Dorian's spine, creeping upward. He was grateful for the familiar weight of the sword in his hand. Quinn's smile was a little too keen, as if he could read Dorian's thoughts.

Echo inched forward. "Dorian's right, though."

"I am?" He'd grown so used to fighting her on everything—especially when it came to leaving their self-imposed prison—that he'd nearly forgotten what it felt like to be in agreement.

She rolled her eyes. "Yes." To Quinn, she said, "What exactly is your price for healing him? You're a warlock. Your kind doesn't do anything without expecting something in return."

Quinn looked at Echo as if he were dissecting her, peeling back her layers to find out what made her tick. "I'm getting the sense that you're the clever one."

If Dorian had been anyone but himself, he might have missed the mild offense that flitted across Caius's face. His prince had always been the clever one. Until, perhaps, now.

Quinn carried on, voice resonating through the space as if he was performing for an audience. "As shocking as it might be for your pedestrian minds to consider, I've come out of the kindness of my own heart." He grinned. "I'm just helping an old friend in need. There's nothing untoward in that." Quinn peered down at Jasper. "No need to thank me."

"Wasn't planning on it," Jasper said, but his voice lacked the sharpness Dorian knew he could inject into it. The urge to pepper Jasper with questions about his history with Quinn was overwhelming, but Dorian did his best to quell it. He didn't have the right. He hadn't earned it.

Quinn didn't seem the least bit bothered by Jasper's attitude. "Always a pleasure, Jay." With a final flare of amused cruelty coloring his words, he added, "Oh, and happy birthday."

CHAPTER ELEVEN

"Whoa, whoa, whoa," Echo said. "I thought your birthday was six months ago. I stole a Rolex for you."

It had been a blustery day in January, the New York sky gray and cold, dotted with wispy white clouds and the occasional dark shadows of passing pigeons. The 6 train had been beyond warm, heated by the press of bodies crammed into the car during the morning rush. Echo had learned that if you wanted to pick a pocket, the best place to do it was on public transport at its busiest. Her mark had been a Wall Street type, with slicked-back hair and wing tips so shiny he could have seen his reflection in them, like Narcissus staring into a lake. A gleaming gold watch, probably worth more than his secretary's salary, was strapped to his wrist. Even the affluent opted for the train at rush hour—one stood a better chance of being struck by lightning than successfully hailing a taxi at 8:15 in the morning. A lurch of the train here, an "accidental" bump there, *et voilà*. After a mumbled apology for her invasion of the man's personal space, Echo had alighted from the 6 train one Rolex richer.

Jasper shrugged. "I just said that because I was in the mood for presents."

A wry grin graced Echo's lips. "Never change, Jasper."

"I don't intend to." Jasper pushed away the blankets and rose to his feet, slowly, as if he was expecting it to hurt. Echo could hear the sound of his joints popping from across the room. Quinn reached out to help steady him, but Jasper recoiled from the offered hand. Sliding his sword back into its sheath, Dorian brushed past the warlock and gripped Jasper's elbow, helping him take a few wobbly steps. Quinn and Dorian engaged in an argument that seemed to be conducted entirely with silent stares: Quinn's bordering on blasé amusement, Dorian's simmering with suspicion. Jasper refused to look at either of them, golden eyes focused on his unsteady feet.

Echo glanced at Ivy, who raised her eyebrows in response. That was just what their little group needed—a love triangle between an Avicen, a Drakharin, and a warlock. Because that emotional Chernobyl wasn't likely to blow up in anyone's face. Nope. Not at all.

Caius leaned in close, breath disturbing the hair near Echo's ear. A small shiver went down her spine. "I want no part in this," he murmured.

"Yeah, me neither." Echo turned to him. Their noses were a scant few inches apart. She took a tiny step back and turned to face the rest of the room, clapping her hands together. "I have a great idea. Let's go to the rave."

"The rave?" Caius asked.

"Yes, the rave. The party. In that warehouse on the other side of the tracks. Keep up, Caius."

"You want to go to the party?"

"Yes, I want to go to the party. That's what people usually do to commemorate the anniversary of a friend's birth. They party. Hard."

Caius blinked, as if he couldn't quite believe the words he'd just heard. "Are you mad?"

"Probably." Echo smiled. "Though we'd need a battery of tests to confirm a diagnosis."

He shook his head. "I'm serious, Echo. Parties are out of the question. It isn't safe."

"Nowhere is safe," she countered. "We can pretend that our little hideout is impregnable, but you and I both know that it's not. I can't go on living like this. I can't stomach another day staring at the same four walls and the same four people and eating the same four kinds of Pop-Tarts. I will go mad. I'll burn this place down."

Caius glanced over at the too-familiar faces staring at them. "I see your point," he said. "We don't even have four kinds of Pop-Tarts left. Jasper ate the last raspberry one this morning."

One couldn't easily find Pop-Tarts in England. The Pop-Tarts were irreplaceable. Jasper was not. "I'm gonna kill him," said Echo, "with my bare hands."

"Just let me know in advance so I have time to fiddle with the box that pops corn with its modern magic. Entertainment is always better with popcorn. You said so yourself."

Oh gods, he was adorable. And he knew it. Cabin fever was making him cheeky. "It has a popcorn setting, Caius. You literally just press one button."

"You both know I can hear you, right?" Jasper said as he pulled on a clean black T-shirt.

Echo ignored him. If there was ever a chance to discover any latent powers of persuasion at her disposal, now was the time. "C'mon. We'll only go for a little while—an hour. Just one hour. We'll peek in, see what all the fuss is about, and get it out of our system. It's Jasper's birthday. Did I mention that it's Jasper's birthday? Because it's Jasper's birthday."

Caius's lips quirked into the faintest ghost of a smile. He was beginning to cave. He just needed a little push.

"Oh, come on, what could possibly go wrong in a single hour?" Echo paused. Caius's eyes narrowed in contemplation. With a grimace, she added, "Inscribe that on my tombstone if it comes back to bite me in the ass." Echo darted in to press a chaste kiss to his cheek. He smiled fully, and for a split second, she felt the curve of his mouth against her skin.

"Fine," Caius mumbled, more than a little begrudgingly. "But we're not going out. It's too much of a risk. We'll have our own party. Here." Echo opened her mouth to protest, but Caius held up a hand. *"Here,"* he repeated, in a tone that invited no argument. "I'll even let Jasper pick the music."

"Oh, thank the gods," Jasper said. He kicked the blankets clean off his mattress, full of more energy than he'd had in months. "But whether or not His Royal Highness likes it, I am getting the hell out of here." He raised his arms in a luxurious stretch, and Echo noticed the way Quinn devoured the sight of Jasper like a shark circling its prey. Jasper tugged his shirt over his stomach; it had ridden up while he stretched and he only just now seemed aware of Quinn's attention. "If we're going to have a party here, then we need snacks."

Caius began to object, but Jasper plowed right over him. "You said it yourself, we're out of Pop-Tarts." He headed for the door, light on his feet. "Can't have a party without Pop-Tarts. And booze. And chips. Or as the locals call them . . . crisps."

"You're not going out alone," Ivy said. She elbowed Dorian in the side, pushing him forward. "That's the rule, right, Dorian?"

Ivy. Matchmaking. *Bless your heart,* Echo thought.

Dorian nodded. "Yes, that is the rule."

"I'll come too," said Quinn.

Jasper looked from one man to the other, his expression as guarded as Echo had ever seen it. When his gaze landed on Quinn, the brightness of his yellow eyes dimmed. But he covered up his reaction with a flippant shrug. "Whatever floats your boat." He pointed to Echo and Caius. "Any requests?"

"Food that occurs in nature," Caius suggested.

"Something salty," Echo said. "And also chocolate. And cake. And—"

Jasper cut her off. "I should have known better than to ask. Later, losers." He snagged the pouch of shadow dust they kept in a small bowl by the door—in case of an emergency—and left, the door banging into the wall in his wake. A flabbergasted Dorian and a bemused Quinn followed.

"Come back quickly," Caius said. "And be careful." Dorian nodded. And then they were gone. The loft was strangely quiet without Jasper's complaining. Hell, even when he was quiet, he filled the room with an undeniable energy.

Ivy plopped into one of the chairs in the kitchenette. "Do you think letting them go was a good idea?" She turned to Caius, her expression clouded with worry. "You said people might not just be looking for Echo, but for any of her 'known associates,'" she said, curling her fingers into air quotes around the last two words.

Caius sighed and raked a hand through his hair. "Aside from brute force, I don't think we could have stopped Jasper from leaving."

"You are not wrong, my friend." Echo picked up the television remote and hit the power button. She'd heard enough about volcanic eruptions and destroyed villages. Tonight, they would party. They would create a bubble of space and time in which nothing bad existed, where there were no enemies skulking in the shadows, no crushing world-saving responsibilities resting on anyone's shoulders. "Now, what do you say we fix the place up a bit? Make it look a little less like a bunch of bums decided to squat here."

Echo put Caius and Ivy to work. They folded clothes and arranged them in inconspicuous piles near the wall. The mattresses were piled one on top of the other, high enough to form a makeshift couch. Once Ivy draped the colorful afghan throws unearthed from the bottom of one of Jasper's trunks on top of the mattresses, they didn't even look that bad. The three of them talked, not about the kuçedra or the firebird or war brewing in far-off lands, but about frivolous things. Music. Food. Caius's hilarious aversion to modern technology. The disastrous love triangle forming among the absent members of their party. Despite the events of the past day, Echo felt a lightness in her chest. Here she was, prepping for a birthday party with her friends. If she ignored the world outside the warehouse and all the trouble it held, it almost felt like a normal night.

Then the cell phone rang. Echo and Ivy locked eyes. The

Ala was the only person who had the number, and she always let it ring once before hanging up and calling again so they knew who it was. The phone rang again. And again.

"Don't answer it," Ivy whispered, as if whoever was calling would be able to hear her.

The phone danced on the kitchen table, vibrations pushing it closer to the edge. Echo caught it before it fell. It buzzed in her hand once more before it went silent. No one spoke. The phone began to ring again. A tingle started at the base of Echo's spine. Fear. Anticipation.

Caius shook his head. Ivy mouthed, *Do not.*

Echo tapped the screen to accept the call. The ringing ceased. She held it up to one ear, but said nothing, waiting for the caller to break the silence first.

"Hello?" asked a voice on the other end of the line. "Is anyone there?"

The connection was bad, and the words were distant and broken, but Echo knew that voice. She cradled the phone in both hands and met Ivy's curious gaze from across the room. "Rowan?"

CHAPTER TWELVE

"Echo? Thank the gods it's you. I wasn't sure anyone was going to answer, but the Ala gave me this number in case of emergencies and this is definitely an emergency and—"

"Rowan," Echo said. Ivy and Caius drew closer. "Slow down. What happened? Is the Ala okay?"

The connection crackled and weakened. Rowan must be somewhere without reliable service. The Nest, perhaps. It was almost impossible to get reception down there. "She's okay. For now."

"What do you mean 'for now'?" Echo said. Fear clutched at her stomach, twisting it cruelly. "I do not like the sound of 'for now.'"

"Hold on." Rowan's voice faded, as if he'd put a hand over the receiver. She heard muffled sounds of talking, then some indiscernible noises, then the whoosh-whoosh of denim against denim. Rowan must have slipped the phone in his pocket. After nearly a full minute, his voice returned, quiet, his breathing slightly labored. "I'm at the Nest and I don't want anyone to know who I'm talking to. Altair had the Ala arrested."

"What?" The word came out as a squeak. Ivy pulled up a chair beside Echo, leaning against her knees to listen in on the conversation. Caius stood beside her, tensed, as if prepping himself for a fight. "Why?"

Rowan spoke fast and low. "Altair confronted her when she got back about where she'd been. He knew she'd gone to see you, but she wouldn't tell him where you were, so he's convinced the council that she's colluding with the enemy."

"Colluding? With the enemy? I'm the enemy now?" Of all the accusations Altair could have leveled at the Ala, that seemed to Echo to be the most unbelievable. The Ala was one of the oldest Avicen alive and she was almost universally loved. For Altair to have swayed the council meant that the Avicen were even more afraid than Echo had realized.

"The Warhawks saw what you did in the Black Forest," Rowan continued. "You attacked Altair. No one trusts you."

"In my defense, he was going to kill people I didn't want him to kill."

"Yeah." Rowan's voice was practically a growl. "Like that dragon bastard." Echo shot Caius a glance. *That dragon bastard.* "Don't think that escaped anyone's notice. He's going to put the Ala on trial, and if she's found guilty, they could kill her."

Echo's head spun. She gripped the side of the table. The Ala couldn't be killed. She couldn't. Physically, it was possible, though difficult, but a world without the Ala was a world Echo could not envision. And to die at the hands of her own people, stirred into a frenzy of fear and malice by Altair?

Unthinkable. "I'll come back," Echo said. "I'll tell them everything, I'll do whatever they want."

"Echo, no," Rowan said in a rush. "Altair is only trying to—"

His words were lost to a crash so loud Echo had to pull the phone away from her ear. "Rowan?"

He didn't respond. The call was still connected, and she could hear the sounds of chaos on the other end. Screams. The shriek of bending metal, the roar of something heavy collapsing.

The ghosts inside Echo's mind seemed to bang against the walls of her skull. Rose's voice cut through Echo's dawning horror. *You have to go home. You have to help them. They're dying. They're dying, they're dying, they're dying.*

Echo stood, her white-knuckled grip on the phone anchoring her. "Rowan?" Her voice was strangled. Desperation, Rose's and her own, choked her.

The call dropped.

She stared at the phone dumbly, as if it had betrayed her.

"Echo?" Ivy asked in a soft voice. "What happened?"

Echo's voice came, distant even to her own ears. "We have to go to the Nest." She was only vaguely aware of Caius's hand on her shoulder, the sound of his voice asking her if she was all right.

She was not all right.

Rowan had called her from the Nest.

The Nest was under attack.

The thought spurred her to action. She thrust the phone into Ivy's hands and dashed across the room for her backpack. From it, she retrieved everything she might need. An extra pouch of shadow dust went into her back pocket. The dagger slid into her boot. "We have to get back to the Nest," she repeated. Her words were quick, efficient. "There are no gateways here, Caius. I can't call the in-between by myself. I need you to get us there."

"Echo," Caius said. "Echo, what happened?"

She halted her preparations. A tremor ran through her hands that she could not stop. "They were attacked."

"At the Nest?" Ivy asked, her hands flitting to her mouth. "But how? The wards . . ."

Echo pulled the zipper of her backpack closed with so much force she almost broke it. "I don't know what happened, but I heard it." She locked gazes with Caius. "And Rose felt it. Something is happening. Something bad. Take me there."

The mention of Rose's name was enough to make Caius freeze. If he asked Echo how Rose knew or what it was that Rose had felt in whatever dimension of the universe she occupied when she wasn't busy interfering in Echo's life, she hadn't the faintest clue what she would say. But he didn't ask. He didn't demand a logical explanation. He simply reached for the pouch of shadow dust squirreled away in one of the kitchenette's cabinets and nodded. He would take her there.

"Echo," Ivy said, her voice breaking on the second syllable. Her fear, her uncertainty, practically vibrated off her in waves. "I don't understand."

"You remember the protocol, right?" Echo asked, taking Ivy's hands in her own. "The drills Altair made the Avicen run over and over and over?"

"In the event of an attack," Ivy recited, her hands holding fast to Echo's, "rendezvous at Avalon."

Echo nodded and pulled her hands from Ivy's surprisingly strong grip. Echo felt her reserves of calm dwindling. She needed to get through this. Rowan and the Ala needed her. Everyone back home did. "Jasper didn't bring a phone. When they return, you tell them what happened. Tell them Caius and I went to the Nest. Make sure they all go to Avalon, okay?"

Ivy nodded, but her brave expression looked like it was on the verge of crumbling.

"Ivy." Echo pulled her close and pressed her forehead against Ivy's. "You got all that?"

"Yes," Ivy said. She repeated the words with more strength. "Tell them what happened. Bring them to Avalon."

"Good." Echo turned to Caius and extended her hand. "Let's go."

In an instant, they were plunged into darkness as the in-between opened up around them. Ivy, the warehouse, and London all disappeared from view. Echo realized, a split second later, that Caius couldn't lead them to the Nest. He had never been inside it. He had no idea what to look for, and even if he did, he was Drakharin, and the wards around the main gateway would block his entry if he tried to access it directly. Echo needed to take the wheel.

She tightened her hold on Caius's arm and imagined the Nest's gateway: the graceful swoop of the swans' necks, their upraised beaks forming a perfect arch, the iron braziers burning on their backs. It was a marvel of Avicen architecture.

But what materialized around them as the in-between faded was anything but marvelous.

Pained moans drifted to Echo's ears as solid ground appeared beneath her feet. She didn't see the bodies, not at first. It was like trying to make sense of the scattered pieces of a jigsaw puzzle without the picture on the box. But then, slowly, details emerged. There were people trapped under slabs of stone, some attempting to move, others frightfully still. Both braziers had been lit when they fell, and smoke filled the cavern housing the gateway. Or what remained of it. A tangle of iron formed a loose circle around a field of debris, enough to still function as a gateway to the in-between. The detached metal head of a swan sat at Echo's feet, its sightless eyes staring at the chaos around them.

The gateway was decimated. Something had torn through the space with the ferocity of a cyclone. Wires dangled like macabre streamers, their exposed ends sparking with electricity. A shattered clockface lay atop a pile of rubble, and singed pieces of paper floated down like burnt leaves. Echo picked one up, and bile rose in her throat. It was a Metro-North schedule. The information booth at the center of Grand Central had rows of them available for passengers to take. Broken slabs of concrete littered the space, and she recognized the marble. It was the floor of the main concourse. A high-heeled shoe had fallen next to a scuffed briefcase. A man in a business suit—a human man—groaned in agony not five feet from where Echo stood. Her vision swam, and only Caius's grip on her arm held her upright.

The broken clock read 5:45. Evening rush hour. Something had struck the Nest—and Grand Central directly above it—at the busiest time of day, and it hadn't cared who it hurt.

CHAPTER THIRTEEN

Echo operated on autopilot. She smeared dirt across Caius's cheekbones—the area around the shattered gateway was filled with it. He needed to hide his scales or he would be blamed for all the senseless destruction.

She didn't realize that her ears were ringing until she saw Caius's mouth moving, forming the shapes of words, and heard nothing but a high-pitched buzz. It must have been shock. He lifted his hand to point at something. Echo followed the line of his arm and willed herself not to scream in despair.

One of the hallways leading farther into the Nest was blasted wide open, its arch cracked where shards of stone fell away. Echo walked to the nearest wall; it was black as if burned or covered in soot, but when she touched it, she felt nothing but a deep dread. Her fingers came away clean, though the dread lingered, sticking to her soul like a stain. The other hallways branching off the main room were untouched—whoever did this had picked a very specific direction. This was no aimless attack.

The bodies of the dead and dying lay on the ground, some still, some writhing in agony. Black lines crossed their exposed skin; their veins protruded slightly, as if swollen. Echo crouched down next to an Avicen woman. The woman's chest rose and fell in stilted, short breaths; her eyes gazed at the ceiling, not seeming to see anything. One of the woman's hands groped blindly beside her. Echo caught her hand and squeezed. It was the only comfort she could offer. The woman's throat worked as if she was trying to say something, but only a hoarse croak escaped her chapped lips.

Echo shook her head, helpless. "What did this?" she asked, not expecting an answer.

The woman swallowed, once, twice, then formed a single word: "Shadows." Her face went slack as the light fled from her eyes. Echo didn't know if she was dead or not. She let go of the woman's cold hand. Caius gently touched her shoulder, as if to encourage her to rise. To keep moving.

Shadows? Memory tickled at the edges of Echo's mind. The shadows in Samira's dream—could they be related to *this*? How? *Why?*

Echo rose to her feet; her body felt weighted down with a slew of emotions. Fear. Grief. The beginnings of rage. She forced herself to pass by the Avicen that had fallen in the corridors. None of them were moving. Black veins spread across their bodies, as if they'd been infected with some kind of toxin that had seeped into their bloodstreams. There was nothing she could do for them. She was too late. Too goddamn late.

Behind her, Caius's feet were eerily silent.

Echo followed the path of destruction. Doors hung

precariously from their hinges, and the gas lamps that lined the corridor lay shattered on the ground, creating a network of small fires that would only grow. Echo picked up her pace. As much as she wanted to scan the faces of passing Avicen for people she knew, for assurance that they were all right, she couldn't bring herself to look too closely at the ones who lay still. Some were unconscious, but some had to be corpses. She swallowed past the bile in her throat and kept moving, deeper into the Nest, following the blackened trail.

Echo felt Caius nudge at her knuckles. She gripped his hand so tightly it had to hurt but she didn't care.

"Echo!"

Caius dropped her hand, reaching for weapons he didn't have. Echo looked around frantically for the source of the shout. When she saw who it was, a strangled sob escaped her. Two little Avicelings, members of the group that had liked to follow her around like she was the Pied Piper, picked their way through the rubble, holding each other up. Flint's cardinal-red feathers made the bloody gash above his eye look almost black by comparison, while Daisy limped along, her downy blue feathers matted with sweat and dust. But they were in one piece. Echo jumped over a fallen support beam and swept them up in her arms, apologizing when Daisy winced in pain. Caius hung back, watchful gaze trained on the tunnel ahead.

"You're alive," Echo murmured, pressing her lips against their feathery heads. "Oh, thank god." She pulled back. "What about the others?" Her army of sticky brats. The orphans she helped the Ala care for. She was their Artful Dodger. That was what Ivy liked to call her. Tears blurred Echo's vision, and Daisy brushed them from her cheeks with a dirty hand.

"They're okay," Flint said with a sniffle. He tightened his

hold on Daisy. "They're trapped in the Ala's room, but we heard them through the door, and they're all okay."

Relief washed over Echo, but it didn't last long. "The Ala," she said. "Was she still in the cells?"

Daisy nodded. "Altair and Rowan were there, too." Fear made the Aviceling's eyes go wide. "Do you think they're hurt?"

The Nest's jail had been designed to nullify magic. Not even the Ala with all her power could transport in and out. If they'd been in the cells, they would have been helpless. Daisy's lower lip trembled, so Echo said, "I'm sure they're fine. I'm gonna go after them. You two find someone who can get the door open and free the other Avicelings. Do you remember the evacuation drills Altair made you all run?"

"The ones you said were a waste of time?" asked Flint. Blood trickled into his eye, and Echo wiped it away.

"Yup," she said, "those. Do it just like we practiced. Get help and then get out of here. It's not safe."

"When will we be able to come home?" Daisy asked, voice small and scared.

Echo shook her head, the urge to sob or scream rising in her chest. The answer was never, now that the Nest had been exposed, but Daisy didn't need to hear that. Not now. Not yet. "I don't know, sweetie."

A crash sounded from the far end of the hallway. Flint started trembling, while Daisy cried softly. Echo kissed them both on the forehead before ushering them away from the direction of danger. "Go. Get help."

She watched them go and tried to convince herself that it wasn't the last time she would ever see them. Caius took her hand in his and pulled her along. The sound of metal squealing and breaking made Echo quicken her cautious steps. The stench of gas hung heavy in the air, and she prayed it wouldn't lead to an explosion. Avicen streamed past them, away from whatever was causing those unbearable noises. Echo and Caius fought against the tide of moving bodies. Nobody gave the Drakharin in their midst a second glance. The closer Echo and Caius got to the noise, the greater Echo's sense of dread grew, almost as if the stain on her soul were spreading. Like an infection.

They were almost at the Nest's jail. Echo broke into a run, ignoring Caius's plea for caution. There were fewer Avicen here; the only ones who lingered had white cloaks soiled by dust and grime. Warhawks. Echo heard Caius's sharp indrawn breath behind her. If they realized who he was, he was dead. She spared him a glance; the dirt still hid the scales on his cheekbones well enough. She hoped it stayed that way.

The heavy metal door leading to the cells had been blown clean off its hinges. It lay, broken in two, in the middle of the corridor between the rows of cells. Melted iron bars twisted together, sticking out like a row of metal thorns. At the far end of the long room, Altair was on his knees, digging through the rubble with bloodied bare hands. He looked up as Echo entered, meeting her gaze. His orange eyes were hard and haunted, his mouth a taut, grim line.

"He ran down here when it attacked. He wanted to protect her" was all he said. He returned to his task, heedless of the sharp stones and scraps of metal that tore at his skin.

The air whooshed out of Echo's lungs, and if not for Caius's steadying grip on her shoulders, she would have fallen.

No. No, no, no, no. Her wobbly legs moved of their own

volition, bringing her closer to the person Altair was trying to dig out.

She fell to her knees beside the general and joined him, moving slabs of rock to the side, not caring about her own pain. A muffled groan sounded from beneath the rubble. It was wordless, but Echo recognized it anyway.

He was alive. Rowan was alive.

But it was not just his tawny feathers that Echo saw as Altair cleared away the debris.

A raven-black arm was draped across Rowan's torso, its dark feathers slick with blood. It looked as though the Ala had thrown herself atop Rowan to shield him from falling debris.

Altair let loose a string of curses in Avicet, too quickly for Echo to understand. Every sound blurred into white noise, and the ringing in her ears returned.

Altair lifted the Ala's limp body off Rowan with a tenderness Echo wouldn't have known he possessed. He cradled her in his arms, and Echo knew immediately that he never would have executed her. Not in a million years. Despair—true, deep despair—clouded his eyes. Echo knew he and the Ala had a history, but it wasn't until that moment that she understood how deep their history ran. She had thought they hated each other, but only something that had once been love could turn to a hate as petty as theirs. "This isn't what I wanted," Altair said, more to himself than to Echo. He looked up at her, expression stricken. "I only wanted to get your attention, to talk to you, to make you see reason."

The Ala shifted. Altair brushed dirt from her forehead, his fingers gentle against her skin. She coughed and tried to raise her head.

"Be still," said Altair.

The Ala reached for Echo, who seized the hand offered to her. "There was a woman in the hallway," Echo said, words tumbling forth in a rush. "She said shadows did this. How is that possible?"

"Ku . . ." The Ala choked on the word, as if speaking required more effort than she could spare. "Kuçedra."

The Ala's hand went slack in Echo's. Kuçedra? Echo's stomach dropped. She didn't know much about the kuçedra, but she knew enough to be sure that she didn't want to have to face it without the Ala. Which it looked like she was going to have to do. For now.

Rowan groaned again and blinked slowly, his eyes glassy, probably from a concussion. Aside from that, he didn't appear to be gravely wounded. The Ala had shielded him from the worst of the attack with her own body.

Caius reached down to help him stand and Echo turned back to the Ala. *Please don't die,* she thought.

As if answering a prayer, the Ala's chest rose and fell with a shallow breath.

Echo exhaled a relieved sob and placed a hand on the Ala's forehead, the only part of her that seemed safe to touch. She looked so frail in Altair's arms. The second Echo's skin made contact with the Ala's, her sense of dread spiked. The feeling she'd had near the gateway doubled.

At the edges of her sight, the shadows seemed to move, as if coming alive.

Echo rose, brushing her dirty hands against her jeans. She stepped away from Altair and the Ala, searching the dark corners of the room. "It's still here," she said.

Fire flickered to life in Echo's open palms. Her emotions were running hot. She didn't even need to think about summoning it. It simply sprang to existence against her skin. "Show yourself, you piece of shit."

And it did.

CHAPTER FOURTEEN

Darkness pooled in the center of the room. Echo realized with increasing horror that it wasn't a singular shadow, swollen to a massive size, but a collection of them, an amorphous, writhing mass. They were the same shadows Echo had seen curling around the trunks of trees in Samira's memory, and this time a primal part of Echo knew, with certainty, what it was. It was the darkness that had come before all things, that would outlast all things, that would consume the entire world whole if it was not stopped first. It was the thing the Drakharin in Samira's memory had feared.

It was the kuçedra. The Ala had said the name, but seeing it made it real.

The shadows ceased their undulations, as if recognizing Echo's presence.

As the darkness grew closer, the shadows began to coil around each other to form a single shape. Its neck was long and sinuous, its wings wide and thin, like a bat's. Clawed feet gripped the air as the beast was borne aloft by the powerful beat of its wings, tail flicking from side to side. With every flap of its wings, Echo thought she could hear a symphony of smothered screams, as quiet as a distant sigh. And that was when she knew.

They weren't shadows.

They were souls.

Trapped in that monstrous form was every life lost to the conflict between the Avicen and the Drakharin. Theirs had been a self-fulfilling prophecy. They had feared the darkness, and in that fear, they had created it. Their hate and violence had nursed the kuçedra as it grew, waiting for its destined foe.

Waiting for the firebird.

Waiting for Echo.

The souls trapped within it screamed, piercing Echo's eardrums until they felt like they were bleeding. The shadow grew louder and larger as she watched. Fresh souls, gleaned from the attack on the Nest and Grand Central, added to its mass. Its shape solidified: the wings scraped against the walls, the wickedly long tail swished through the air, beating at debris, and its fanged mouth howled in a grotesque mimicry of the wailing souls it held inside itself.

It looked like a dragon. It must have taken the form the Avicen feared the most, Echo realized. Even now, she could feel it leeching her fear, feeding on it. The Avicen's fear during the attack had molded it like putty.

Caius bent to draw the blade of a fallen Warhawk. Altair put himself between the Ala and the kuçedra, sword in hand. They were both skilled fighters, with centuries of experience between them, but they wouldn't so much as scratch this monster. How could steel pierce flesh made of darkness and despair?

"Get them out of here," Echo told Caius, never taking her eyes off the beastly form dominating the room.

"I'm not leaving you."

Of course not.

"Fine," Echo said through gritted teeth. "But do me a favor and stay out of my way."

With a bloodcurdling screech, the kuçedra attacked, lunging forward, its shadows expanding. From the corner of her eye, Echo saw Rowan lifted off his feet. He crashed into the bars of a cell and collapsed onto the floor. Caius leaped out of the way, tucking into a roll as the kuçedra lashed out. Altair darted in, slashing at the belly of the beast, to no avail. Their attacks didn't seem to inflict any harm, but they were good for one thing: distraction. The kuçedra wheeled on the men, momentarily forgetting Echo.

Fire blazed in her hands, crawling up her forearms with sizzling tongues of black and white. Power swelled inside her, greater than she'd ever felt before. She gathered as much of it as she could, focusing on the flames in her hands. The jail was illuminated by her glow. She felt like a force of nature. Instead of fighting the firebird for control of her body, she let herself become it.

The firebird was the light in the darkness. They were natural enemies, the firebird and the kuçedra, and the latter had made the grievous error of hurting people Echo loved.

The kuçedra's head swiveled. For a brief moment, staring into its black eyes felt like falling into nothing. The abyss called to Echo, beckoning her closer.

She lifted her hands and let the blaze surge forward. The

flames weren't merely black and white; this fire was a prism of light, containing every color of the spectrum, shining so brightly that it made even Echo's eyes burn.

Good, Rose intoned inside her skull. Echo felt Rose add her own strength to the flames. And she wasn't the only one. The too-tight feeling returned to Echo's skin, as if she would burst from holding all that power inside her. She felt them all—all the vessels of years past—pushing outward, lending whatever they had to give to the fire. Echo could not defeat the kuçedra on her own, but she was not alone; every soul the firebird touched blazed through her. The power was not hers; she was merely its conductor, directing it straight at the heart of the beast.

Soon, the room was so bright that Echo couldn't see a thing. With a final, heart-stopping scream, the kuçedra vanished, its shadows dissipating like smoke.

Echo collapsed to her knees and the fire died, plunging the space into darkness. She heaved, but there was nothing in her stomach to vomit. She had only minutes before she blacked out, depleted of power, and that was an optimistic guess.

She struggled to raise her head. Altair was staring at her, his gaze hard and calculating. What he was thinking, she didn't know, and in that moment, she didn't care. Caius rushed to her side while Rowan limped toward her, but all Echo could think of was the Ala. She crawled to the Ala's still form, taking one of her cold, clammy hands in her own as her vision blurred at the edges and her head swam.

Echo held her other hand up to Caius, and it took everything she had to say, "Get us out of here."

"No," Altair cut in. "I will not allow a Drakharin into our refuge."

They didn't have time for this. The Ala didn't have time. "He comes with me or you can forget about having the firebird on your side."

That did the trick. Though it was clear the idea filled him with no small amount of disgust, Altair nodded. "Wait on the shore, a mile north from the rendezvous point. I will meet you there." He turned to Rowan. "Go with them. Make sure you aren't seen."

"Yes, sir." Rowan's voice was quiet and pained, but there was strength beneath it. Resilience. His eyes met Echo's, and there was something in them Echo hadn't seen before. He looked as though he'd aged a decade in the past ten minutes. This was war, Echo thought. This was what it did. It took the innocent and remade them in its image. Rowan was no longer the boy who'd tried to teach her how to draw, laughing at her wobbly charcoal lines, or the young man who'd tried to sneak shy kisses when no one was looking. He was a soldier, not a child. None of them were children any longer. Rowan broke the hold of Echo's gaze and turned away. She wondered if he saw himself reflected in her eyes. If he hated what he saw. She felt Caius's presence beside her, humming like static electricity. "Get us out of here," she said again. "Please."

Transporting four people without the aid of a threshold must have been a herculean effort, but Caius did it. Echo had seconds to feel grateful as the in-between rushed around them and the rubble-strewn ruins of the Nest disappeared.

CHAPTER FIFTEEN

One of the first books Echo had ever stolen was a children's retelling of the story of King Arthur and the Knights of the Round Table. Delicate watercolor illustrations decorated its pages, giving form to a simplified version of the legend. In the supply closet she slept in at the library—long before the Ala had helped her set up a more spacious room on its uppermost floor—a seven-year-old Echo had lost herself in those tales of daring feats and valiant heroes and powerful wizards. She'd imagined that, even with her unwashed tangled hair and sneakers with worn-down soles, she was as brave as Lancelot and as beautiful as Guinevere and as mysterious as Morgan le Fay.

This Avalon was not the land of Arthurian legend. It was a small island in the Hudson River surrounded by strong wards that kept any activity on it hidden from human eyes. At the center of the island sat Avalon Castle, a relic of the excesses of late-nineteenth-century wealth. Once a summer home for the Carringtons, a family of eccentric billionaires made rich off steel, Avalon had been requisitioned by the Avicen after the last Carrington descendent died in the mid-1950s, leaving no children to mourn his passing or lay claim to an inheritance. Just as Jasper's East London warehouse had been tied up in a nightmare of red tape and false names to protect it from bureaucratic snooping, Avalon was currently listed as the property of one Fulton J. Hawthorne, a man wealthy enough to purchase an entire island with a remarkable view of the Hudson River, whom no one had ever seen before. Mainly because he didn't exist. The Ala had created him for the sake of the purchase. Even she needed a human face to hide behind on occasion.

Travel through the in-between could only get them so far. The island's wards made accessing the in-between within the castle an impossibility, so with Echo's guidance, Caius transported them to a small beach about a mile upriver from the island. She pictured the reeds along the shore, the water lapping at her feet. The Avicen performed evacuation drills once a year. Ivy and Rowan had grumbled about them, and even though the Nest was not Echo's permanent residence, the Ala had forced Echo to participate as well. Just in case, she'd said. None of the younger Avicen felt the drills were necessary. The Nest had never been attacked. To do so would have been a colossal error in strategy on the part of the Drakharin. After all, neither race had any desire to involve humans in their business, no matter how messy it got. But now, on the shore of the Hudson River, with the Ala lying prone on the riverbank, Echo had never been more grateful for the Ala's insistence that Echo do as she was told.

"Please wake up," Echo whispered into the Ala's ear. "I promise I'll never complain about anything ever again."

The gods only knew if the Ala heard Echo's plea.

Rowan and Echo tended to the Ala as best they could while Caius scouted the area. They were alone, but Echo thought that perhaps Caius felt as though the presence of a Drakharin at such a fragile time would be too much to demand of Rowan. Echo was silently grateful for Caius's discretion. She fashioned a sling for Rowan's injured arm. It wasn't broken, but he needed a healer. He flinched every time her hand brushed his arm, though she didn't think it was entirely because of the pain.

Two hours passed before a modest motorboat appeared in the distance, Altair's brown-and-white feathers recognizable even from afar. Echo watched him warily as he stepped off the boat upon reaching shore. Accompanying him was a Warhawk with charcoal-gray feathers encrusted with plaster dust and pale green eyes that flicked to Caius whenever he made even the smallest of movements. Altair and the Warhawk placed the Ala in the boat with as much gentleness as they could muster. As the others clambered into the boat, Echo held the Ala's unresponsive hand, as if, by sheer force of will, she could lend the Ala her strength. With only the soft whir of the boat's engine to cut the silence, they set out for Avalon.

The castle's battlements peeked through the mist that shrouded the island before the rest of its imposing mass came into view. Altair directed the Warhawk—Fern, he called her—to steer the boat toward the rear of the castle. The walls and wild overgrowth hid them from view. If Caius was spotted, his presence would cause a panic and the mud had flaked off his scales from the boat. The Avicen had been through enough; they didn't need the shock of thinking their safe haven had been breached by the enemy. With Altair giving quiet commands, they docked the boat in a small inlet shielded by the castle's high walls. Through it all, Echo kept her hold on the Ala's hand. Even Altair seemed to sense that she needed this contact, and when he pried the Ala's hand free of Echo's fingers to lift the Avicen woman out of the boat, he did so with surprising gentleness. They entered through a narrow passage by the garden, barely wide enough for Altair to fit through with the Ala cradled in his arms.

As Echo walked through the passages of Avalon Castle, it became clear that its glory days were long gone. Threadbare tapestries adorned the walls, their once bright colors faded to murky browns and grays. The stained-glass windows were missing several panes, so the sunlight fell on the floor in uneven patches of color. The air was thick with dust. Echo sneezed.

"Bless you," Rowan murmured. On instinct, she presumed. He blinked, as if surprised the words had escaped him.

"Thanks," she said, just as softly.

Altair led them to a richly appointed room high in the castle. He laid the Ala on the bed after Fern turned down the sheets. There was a tenderness to the way he pulled the bedclothes up around her. Echo couldn't stand to watch them shift the Ala's limp arms and rolling head. Unlit candles rested on the mantel and on the bedside table and on the trunk against the wall. Heavy drapes had been pulled aside to let in the morning light and meager breeze. Echo stood by the window, her fingers resting on its stone sill. A garden wrapped around the rear of the castle, wild and overgrown.

The Ala would have loved the room. Maybe that was why Altair had chosen it. Echo had always thought their enmity eternal, as old as the Elders themselves, but the morning's events had revealed some deep, secret history to which Echo had never been privy.

A healer entered, arms laden with herbs and tonics, accompanied by two more Warhawks. As the healer fretted over the Ala, Rowan gave voice to what they were all thinking: "What do we do now?"

One of the new Warhawks assisted the healer, but the other had eyes only for Caius. His scales were visible in the dim light.

"What is *he* doing here?" The Warhawk's words were slung like barbs, each one tipped with poison. The former Dragon Prince stood by the Ala's bed, hands at his sides, looking as harmless as he possibly could. But even to Echo, who knew that he was far from the nightmare the Avicen told their children about, Caius could never truly seem harmless. Nothing could hide his strength or his confidence. He'd been a fighter and a leader for too long; no amount of silence or projected softness would be able to cloak the truth of him.

"He was uninvolved in the attack *and* he is here at my invitation," Altair said. "If you have a problem with that, Sage, you are more than welcome to forfeit your sword and your cloak and join the children downstairs." He waited. The Warhawk bristled, but remained silent. To Rowan, Altair said, "You and Violet will accompany our *guest*"—Altair jerked his head toward Caius—"to his chamber. Speak of this to no one."

The Warhawk assisting the healer nodded as she handed over pouches of herbs that Echo knew would be useless. She must be Violet. The name was fitting: She had a cascade of pink and purple feathers that blended so well that when she moved, it was as if a candied sea moved with her. The edges of her white cloak were trimmed with gold, a sign that she was not only a soldier trained with sword and shield but also a mage. Perhaps sensing that her partner was about to say something rash, Violet moved to the bedside table, where she deposited the remaining herbs and then stood next to Sage, their shoulders touching. Sage's auburn feathers seemed to settle with the contact.

"Should we take him now, sir?" asked Violet.

Altair shook his head. "Not yet. We have matters to discuss."

"I am your captive audience," said Caius, with a pointed glance at his newly assigned guards. "Emphasis on *captive*."

"Can you blame us for treating you like a threat?" It was clear to Echo that Altair's patience was wearing thin. She wanted to tell Caius to keep his mouth shut, but she was too tired to insert herself into their argument. Altair plowed on. "How many of my people have you killed?"

Caius hesitated. Echo knew that he remembered the number of Drakharin that had fallen during his time as Dragon Prince. He had told her that he sent personal letters of condolence to their families, if they had any. It wasn't standard procedure, but he had done it anyway. If soldiers were going to die under his crest, he had said, they deserved to be recognized. But Avicen?

"I didn't exactly keep count," said Caius.

"How can you listen to this?" Sage said. She shrugged off the hand Violet laid on her arm. "We were just attacked. The Drakharin could be—"

Altair interrupted her. "It wasn't Drakharin. At least, not exactly."

Sage paused, deflated. "Then who?" Uncertainty flickered in her orange eyes, so like Altair's. Echo wondered if they were related, however distantly.

"The kuçedra," Echo said. Heads swiveled toward her place by the window, as if they had forgotten she was there.

"And why is *she* here?" Sage was spoiling for a fight. Echo understood. Sometimes anger was easier to deal with than grief. Echo let herself become Sage's target. "We all saw which side you took in the Black Forest. You attacked our commander in defense of Drakharin." An accusatory finger was pointed at Caius. "This Drakharin." She turned to Rowan. "This is the one who killed Ruby, isn't it?"

What? Echo's mind skipped like a scratched record. *She* had killed Ruby. Not Caius. And yet, Rowan's gaze skittered to Echo and then away. He nodded.

Altair watched them keenly, as if he was waiting for the holes in Rowan's story to show themselves.

Echo cleared her throat. "I—"

"It's true," Caius said. "We fought. It was my blade that felled her."

No.

Rowan had lied for her. And now Caius was helping him.

"And I am sorry for that." Caius looked at Echo, but his expression revealed nothing. "Sorrier than I can possibly say. I cannot bring back the dead, but I can help safeguard the living. We don't have to live as we always have."

Sage was ready to spit fire. "I won't fight alongside Drakharin," she said. "I can't. He can take his apologies and—"

Altair's voice rose above hers. "You will, or—"

Echo closed her eyes. The din in the room escalated as Violet tried to talk Sage down, and Altair shouted above them both. At some point, Rowan slipped out, claiming to anyone who could hear him that he needed some air, departing before Altair could give him leave. Caius did himself no favors by trying to counter Sage's vociferous assertions that the Drakharin were behind the attack. It was loud enough to wake the dead.

"Stop," Echo said. The discord was so great it made her feel as if she were suffocating. No one heard her. She raised her voice. *"Stop."*

It made no difference. They were caught up in centuries of patterned behavior. The Avicen and the Drakharin fought. They always had and they always would. It was the way of things. One confrontation led to another, and the cycle began anew. Conflict fed upon conflict, growing fat on their hate and their rage and their bile.

"Stop!" Echo's shout was accompanied by sparks falling from her hands, wholly unbidden. She curled her fingers into tight fists and fought for control. Of herself. Of the rising tide of enmity in the room.

All fell silent. Even Altair seemed taken aback.

"This is what it wants," Echo said softly. The fire that had been building in her chest died to embers. "This is what the kuçedra wants us to do. Fighting, war, hatred. Fear. It feeds off it. It gorges itself on our suffering." She pressed the heels of her palms to her eyes. "We can't do this. It has to stop somewhere."

"What do you suggest?" Violet's soft voice pierced the silence. She looked at Echo expectantly.

Echo wanted to hide from that look. How was she to

know? She was no strategist like Altair, or Seer like the Ala. She had never led armies, like Caius, or trained to be in one, like Sage and Violet. "I don't know."

"We work together," Altair provided. He fixed Sage with a hard stare. "As much as it pains us to do so, we must use all the tools at our disposal."

Was that what Echo and Caius were? Tools? Weapons in an arsenal?

"Let me talk to my sister," Caius said. "The new Dragon Prince. I don't think she was behind this attack, but I'll be able to tell if she's lying to me." He rubbed the base of his neck. "I'm not as blind to her treachery as I used to be."

Altair mulled the idea over. They all watched him in silence. His countenance gave away nothing of his thoughts.

"I can ask her for a truce," Caius added. *A little desperately,* Echo thought.

Skepticism colored Altair's response. "A truce? Do you honestly believe she would agree to such a thing?"

"No," Caius admitted. "But it might buy us some time."

They continued their conversation. Ever the politician, Caius had already positioned himself as some kind of Drakharin emissary among the Avicen.

"Can I have a minute alone with her?" Echo asked, her gaze falling to the Ala. Politics were not her strong suit. She didn't feel like negotiating terms or discussing strategy. She felt like a lost little girl, desperate to hold her mother's hand.

"We have no time to waste—" Altair began.

"Please." Echo hated how her voice fractured on that one word, but she could feel herself cracking, like a dam about to break.

Perhaps Altair's sympathy was a by-product of whatever

emotion stirred within his heart at the sight of the Ala prone upon the bed. Perhaps he sensed that Echo was about to shatter into a million pieces and he wanted no part in her unseemly crumbling. Either way, he nodded and ushered the Warhawks and the healer out of the room. Caius was the last to leave. He looked over his shoulder as he closed the door behind him, but Echo did not—could not—meet his gaze.

A vanity sat in the far corner of the room, its surface coated with dust. Echo pulled the matching stool up to the bed and slumped down on it. An acute heaviness settled in her bones. Had it really been only a matter of hours from the last time she had seen the Ala? The warehouse in London felt as though it belonged in another life. Echo took the Ala's hand in hers. The Ala was as still as a corpse, but her hand was warm. Black veins, darker even than the black of her skin, stood out on her arms, swollen, but this part of her was unblemished.

"One for sorrow," Echo sang quietly. "Two for mirth. Three for a funeral . . ."

The lullaby the Ala had taught her caught in her throat. Whenever Echo fell ill, the Ala had sung it to her. Echo remembered the way the Ala would brush the hair from her fevered forehead. The calming scent of the incense in the Ala's chamber, the warm glow of the candles. Echo had never known such safety, such love. Tears caught on her eyelashes, overflowed, ran down her cheeks. She held tightly to the Ala's hand and laid her head on the bedsheets.

"I'm sorry," she whispered. "I'm so sorry."

The Ala had shown Echo kindness. Had sheltered her after years of abuse and neglect left Echo small and starved and broken. And this was what the Ala had earned for her troubles. Suspension in a state between life and death. Echo's tears soaked into the cotton of the bedsheets. She allowed herself this one indulgence. The time had come, she knew, to put away childish things. But for now, she wept like a child lost, alone in the dark.

CHAPTER SIXTEEN

Ivy could count on one hand the number of times she'd been to Avalon. Most of the time, the Avicen evacuation drills ended at the shore, where boats driven by Altair's Warhawks would be waiting to ferry them to the castle. The first time she'd entered the sanctuary, she'd marveled at its vaulted ceilings and the aged stone walls that seemed to whisper secrets gathered over the years. Now all she could focus on was putting one foot in front of the other. She was dimly aware of the group behind her, following hot on her heels as she made her way through the castle's quiet corridors looking for Echo or Altair or anyone who could convince her not to let the panic rising in her gut overwhelm her.

Sneaking Dorian and Quinn in wasn't as hard as she thought it would be. Echo must have told Altair to expect them, because upon arriving at the shore of the Hudson River—a safe distance from where any Avicen might see them—she found a sullen Warhawk waiting near a boat, none too pleased to be tasked with the duty of bringing a Drakharin and a warlock into the Avicen sanctuary. So far, the only information Ivy had been able to glean from the Warhawk was:

"My name is Fern." Delivered with all the grace of a series of grunts.

"The Ala is alive, but unconscious. Don't know what happened to her."

"Your friend, Echo, is with her."

And lastly, with a sharp look at Dorian, "The other one is there, too."

The other Drakharin. Caius. Ivy caught the way Dorian's shoulders sagged with relief and his hand loosened on the pommel of his sword.

The Warhawk led Ivy to the wing where the Ala had been taken, Dorian, Quinn, and Jasper silent shadows behind her. Even the warlock seemed to understand the enormity of what had happened. Their home had been attacked. The Nest had been abandoned. Nothing was as it should be.

The castle had an air of the forgotten about it, as if it were only just now waking up from a long slumber. After what felt like an eternity, Fern motioned for them to proceed into a long hallway. Ivy took the lead. Better for the Avicen to see her face first rather than that of a Drakharin or a warlock or an Avicen whom they barely trusted. At the far end of the hall stood a cluster of people. Altair had his back to a closed door. Beside him stood Caius, who seemed remarkably short next to the Avicen general despite his six feet of height; two Warhawks; and Rowan, whose arm was held in a sloppy sling, clearly fashioned by someone who possessed only the most rudimentary of first-aid skills.

Dorian drew to an abrupt halt beside Ivy. She glanced at him just in time to see a pall pass across his features.

"Dorian?" she asked. "What's wrong?"

He stared straight ahead, as still as a statue, and as silent as one too. Ivy followed his gaze, and in an instant, she knew what troubled him: Altair.

How did you lose it? she had asked him in her cell in the belly of Wyvern's Keep.

Altair.

Good. I hope he kept it. I hear he loves a good trophy.

Decades of anger and resentment and, though Ivy knew he would never admit it, fear had hardened Dorian into the person she had first met in a dark dungeon cell. But months of tenderness, of kindness, of stories told in the dead of night and laughter shared in the light of day had softened years of calcified hatred. It was such a fragile progress, and Ivy could see it all beginning to unravel as Dorian laid his one lovely eye on the imposing figure of Altair at the other end of the hall, the ruin of his other eye hidden by the navy blue eye patch.

They had been so different then, she and Dorian. It had been only three months since she was held prisoner in the Drakharin stronghold, not a terribly long time in the grand scheme of things, but Ivy felt as though she had metamorphosed into a completely different person. She had once taunted Dorian's loss, had spat at his feet. And in return, he'd struck her while she was in shackles, leaving a bruise to blossom on her face in stages: red, purple, blue green, yellow. Forgiveness had not been easy to come by, but through some miracle—and by saving each other's lives—they had found it. Their uneasy alliance had become a friendship, and if there was one thing Ivy knew about friendship, it was that sometimes you had to carry your friends through their most difficult moments.

Altair showed no sign of recognition. His gaze flickered to Dorian and then away, registering him as the Drakharin he was told to expect by either Caius or Echo, and nothing more. Ivy wondered if he even remembered, or if Dorian had receded into the mass of nameless, faceless casualties that had fallen beneath Altair's blade.

Yet Ivy knew that for Dorian to come face to face with the man who had taken his eye, who had left him with scars that ran far deeper than the surface of his skin, was a challenge of extraordinary difficulty. She placed a hand on his forearm, not to prevent him from doing anything foolish but to show him that she was here. He was not alone. His body tensed beneath her touch.

She was standing on his bad side, the one without an eye, and he had to angle his upper body to look at her. In his face, she saw the old Dorian. Without breaking eye contact, she slid her hand down his arm and held his hand. It was a brief gesture. A quick squeeze and then a release. But it was enough. The old Dorian slipped away and the new one, the one he'd fought so hard to build on the shaky foundation of his former self, offered her an equally short-lived smile. It was barely more than an uptick of the corners of his lips, but that, too, was enough. Dorian had to face his demons—no way around that—but he knew he did not face them alone.

"There you are," Altair said as they approached. "Fern will show you to the rooms you've been allocated—"

"Where's Echo?" Ivy asked. There was no time to waste on pleasantries. Altair glared at her, no doubt filing away her impertinence. But she was no soldier and she couldn't care less if he viewed her as insubordinate. She'd followed instructions and brought the rest of their party to Avalon. She'd done her part for Dorian. And although the piece of her that had driven her to pursue the healing arts yearned to help the survivors of the attack, she knew that there was one person who needed her more.

Ivy entered the room quietly. When the door closed with a click, Echo's head shot up. Her face was tearstained and her eyes puffy, and when she saw Ivy, a fresh sob racked her body. Through the closed door, Ivy could hear Altair's deep voice relay instructions, but for the moment, nothing existed but the sight of the Ala lying still, the veins on one side of her body oddly swollen, and the sound of Echo's broken weeping. Ivy rounded the bed as fast as she could and gathered Echo in her arms. Tears soaked through her T-shirt as she brushed Echo's hair back. It was dirty, sprinkled with the same dust Ivy had seen on some of the Avicen, and tangled, but still soft compared with feathers. As a child, she'd been jealous of Echo's hair. It was like silk beneath her hands, and a rich dark brown that reminded Ivy of fresh soil. She'd envied Echo her ability to walk on the surface without having to hide. She used to think Echo's life was so easy compared to hers.

"It's okay," Ivy said. Echo made a noise halfway between a laugh and a sob. "All right, it's not at all okay, but it will be." She pressed her cheek against Echo's hair, barely noticing the dirt and the sweat. "I know it will be."

Ivy couldn't bring herself to look over Echo's shoulder at the Ala. If she did, she might start crying too. The Ala was the closest thing either of them had to a mother. Echo's mother might still be alive, but Ivy's had died in childbirth and she hardly remembered her father. When she was three, he'd gone off on a scouting expedition to the Philippines with a handful of Warhawks and had never returned. Even the sight of the Ala's hand, so dark against the white sheets, was almost enough to crack Ivy's heart in two.

"I can't lose her." Echo's voice was low and broken. "I can't."

"You won't," Ivy said. She would give her life to make sure that didn't happen.

Though they were separated by birth and biology, Echo was a sister to Ivy and she was hurting. Ivy held herself together, willed her tears to remain in place. There would be time for her to fall apart later. But now her best friend, who had been so strong for so many, needed someone to be strong for her. And while Ivy couldn't fight a monster or restore their ruined home, she could at least do that.

CHAPTER SEVENTEEN

Echo gave Ivy a minute alone with the Ala. She stepped out of the Ala's room and into the hallway just as Altair was mid-sentence.

"Sage, Violet, bring him to the east wing—"

At the sound of the door opening, all eyes turned to her. Echo knew her face was still splotchy from crying and her cheeks felt puffy and swollen, but with their various bruises and cuts, none of the others would be winning any beauty contests anytime soon. They hadn't seen her cry, so she could pretend it hadn't happened. The two Warhawks—Sage and Violet—flanked Caius. Sage's hand rested on her sword, fingers drumming against the pommel as if she anticipated resistance from Caius. Or hoped for it. To his credit, Caius was the picture of obedient compliance. He caught Echo's gaze, took in her disheveled state, and offered her the half smile she'd come to know so well. Rowan, on the other hand, refused to even look at her.

"Echo," Altair said, "Rowan will show you to your room."

"Um," she said. While she appreciated that Altair was either too emotionally detached to remark upon her tears or simply didn't care, she wasn't sure alone time with Rowan was the best idea he'd ever had. They weren't ready for that yet. *She* wasn't ready for that yet.

Caius seemed to catch on. "I'll go with her," he said.

Echo let out a relieved breath, not quite a sigh.

Rowan clenched his jaw so tightly that Echo could have sworn she heard his molars grinding together. "If you don't mind, I'd like to talk to my girlfriend alone."

Girlfriend.

He had called her his girlfriend.

Like he still thought she was. Like he still felt she was deserving of that title. Like the past three months hadn't happened.

Echo caught the way Caius's expression turned to stone. After a beat, he inclined his head in a gesture of chivalrous concession. "Of course," he said. His eyes cut to her briefly, but Echo couldn't read what she saw there.

She hadn't told him about Rowan. Not in so many words. Not as explicitly as he deserved. Caius knew that Rowan was important to her, but she'd neglected to mention the particular nature of his importance. Altair's curious expression made Echo want to curl into a tiny ball and evaporate into nothingness.

Without another word, Caius turned on his heel and marched toward the east wing, forcing his guards to scramble to catch up. Even though his current station was barely above that of prisoner, he maintained his imperious composure.

Echo watched his retreating form as Rowan and Altair

watched her. She couldn't bear the thought of looking at either one of them. Especially Rowan. But then Altair cleared his throat, and Echo couldn't ignore them any longer.

"Rowan will see to it that you have everything you need," Altair said. His burnt-orange eyes were heavy, either with exhaustion or with the horrible weight of the day. Echo was beginning to realize just how little she knew about the man who was now in charge of them. "Once you're rested, I can show you the others."

"Others?"

"The other victims," Altair explained. "The Ala wasn't the only Avicen struck down by the kuçedra."

It made sense, though Echo hadn't let herself entertain the idea of more victims, held in a state between life and death, with darkness crawling through their veins. She wanted to retreat to the Ala's room, to curl up at her side. But instead, she followed Rowan as he led her down a dimly lit passage. He didn't look at her as he walked, his stride slightly too fast, and for that, she was secretly, shamefully glad.

The walk from the foyer to Echo's room felt longer than it probably was. Despite what he'd told Caius, Rowan walked beside her in silence, letting the air around them fill with all the things they should have been saying and weren't. Echo busied herself by trying to memorize the path they were taking, but there were so many hallways with identical maroon carpeting and dark, dilapidated walls that she knew she'd get lost anyway. Most of the doors were closed, but through the open ones, Echo caught brief glimpses of rooms that spoke to the house's former beauty. A grand piano sat in a darkened parlor, partially covered by a sheet of old canvas. A library with shelves empty save for dust made Echo's heart scratch at the walls of her chest. She missed her library—her home. She wondered if it would look the same when she returned—*if* she returned—or if the fundamental fabric of her being was too altered by the events of the past several months for her to ever look upon her cramped little room, with its fairy lights and old-book smell, with the same eyes.

Rowan came to a stop in front of a door at the end of a long corridor. "This is you," he said, fiddling with an old skeleton key, gaze darting from the small window to his left to the faded carpet beneath his feet. "Altair had some of the Warhawks sort out rooms when you were with the Ala."

The key's tarnished brass highlighted the soft golden glow of his skin. Fading sunlight danced over the texture of his tawny feathers. Before any of this happened—before the firebird had ruined just about everything—Echo would have sunk her fingers into those feathers and pulled him in for a kiss, smiling against his mouth at his surprised laugh. The urge to do just that tugged at her with a persistence difficult to ignore.

When Echo didn't move to enter the room, Rowan finally looked her straight in the eye. "I'm right down the hall," he said. "Third door on the left. You know . . . in case you need anything."

He turned from her and began to walk away. Echo knew that if she let him go without trying to salvage even the tiniest sliver of their friendship, she would lose him forever. She didn't want that. It had been easy to forget him when she was with Caius. Easier still when Rose made her presence and her desires known. She'd thought she was ready to let Rowan go, but seeing him again, being this close without Caius or Rose standing between them, it was suddenly obvious that she'd been lying to herself.

"Rowan," she said. The tapestries on the walls seemed to swallow the sound of her voice.

He stopped, but didn't turn around. A current of shame washed through Echo. He couldn't even bear to look at her.

"I'm sorry." It wasn't enough, but it was all she had, all she could offer him.

Rowan didn't say anything, but he didn't leave either. His shoulders sagged an inch.

Once the words were out, the rest of what Echo had felt simmering beneath the surface poured forth of its own accord. It wasn't just that Rowan needed to hear it. Echo needed to say it. Ruby might not have been her friend, but she had been alive, and because of Echo, she wasn't anymore. The spirits of the dead deserved better than silence.

"I know I don't deserve to be forgiven for what I did, but I'm sorry. I didn't mean to kill her. I just wanted to make it stop. I wanted to keep everyone safe. I didn't think—I didn't—" Her voice cracked and hot tears pricked her eyes. Rowan's head angled toward her, giving her a view of his profile. "I'm sorry," she said again. "I'm so sorry."

Rowan kept his silence for so long that Echo gave up hope of getting a response. Dust motes drifted in the sunlight cutting across the floor. She turned to the door of her room. She had her hand on the brass knob when he spoke at last.

"I brought her back home."

The metal was cold against her skin. Now it was her turn to keep her eyes averted. A faded pattern was embroidered on the edge of the rug, picked out in thread she assumed had once been gold.

"I couldn't just leave her there," Rowan continued. "So I carried her back."

The fate of Ruby's corpse hadn't even occurred to Echo. She imagined Rowan struggling under the weight of Ruby's lifeless body. She thought about him trying to navigate his way through the in-between like that. She tried to picture the shock and horror on the faces of the Avicen waiting by the Nest's main gateway, a morbid tableau watched by the unseeing eyes of the arch's iron swans. Her knuckles whitened as she gripped the doorknob tighter.

Until a few months ago, the war had been an abstract concept to them. She, Rowan, and Ivy had sat in a café in London and laughed about the Warhawks and Altair and training that she'd been so certain Rowan would never need to use. A cease-fire had been declared long before any of them had been born; everything they knew of war had come from the pages of Avicen history books, stories too distant to seem real. But for all their imagined invincibility, the war had found them. And Echo had been the one to introduce Rowan to his first dead body. Unlike the Ala's band of orphans and runaways, Ruby had parents. Echo had met them only in passing, but she hadn't thought about them, either. Because of her, they had lost a daughter and Rowan had lost his innocence. The guilt was so massive, Echo felt like it was clogging her airway, preventing her from breathing.

"I know you didn't mean to do it," Rowan said. "I've had a lot of time to think about it. I've replayed it over and over in my mind. Sometimes, it feels like the only thing I can see."

He looked up at her, hazel eyes raw with emotion. "I just—I need some time, okay?"

Echo nodded. "Okay," she said, barely managing to croak out the word.

She watched his back as he left. He walked down the hallway and opened the third door on the left, just like he'd said. But he didn't enter the room. His hand rested on the knob, one finger tapping the brass. She couldn't see his face, but there was something to the set of his shoulders that she recognized. There was a way he breathed, slowly and with precision, when deep in thought. He was so quiet, so still, that she thought it might be best to go into her room and leave him to his contemplation. But then, he turned on his heel and said, "This is a terrible idea, but . . ."

He left the rest of the sentence unspoken and strode to where Echo still stood in front of her door. Before she could cobble her thoughts into a coherent shape, Rowan's mouth was on hers. His hands gripped her arms, firm but still gentle enough to allow her to slip away if she wished.

His lips were warm and chapped and heartbreakingly familiar. There was none of the studied grace of Caius's kiss, none of the artful elegance honed over two centuries of practice. Rowan's kiss was a little clumsy, but that artlessness was what made it perfect. Echo raised her hands to slide them along his cheeks, following the line of his jaw and then sinking her fingers into the soft feathers at the nape of his neck.

Echo had a second to think that he tasted like fruit punch before a memory that was not hers crashed through her consciousness.

The warped wood of the corridor's floor was replaced by grass, slick with rain, and muddy soil. The ceiling disappeared.

Thunderclouds darkened the sky. Rain—angry and persistent and flavored by the salty air of the sea—soaked her clothing. She would have been chilled to the bone if not for the body pressed against hers. The softness between her fingers was not feathers, but hair. Silky, dark brown hair. She opened her eyes.

No, not her eyes. Rose's. And it wasn't Rowan she was kissing. It was Caius.

Startled, Echo pulled away, and she was herself again.

She stepped back, feeling for the door behind her, needing its solidity to remind her of where she was. Of *who* she was. Her ragged breaths weren't pulling in enough oxygen. She was in Avalon Castle. Not on the island where Rose had died. She was inside, not out in the rain. And it was Rowan standing before her. Not Caius. Pain blossomed at the base of her skull, and she wasn't sure if it was because of the magic she'd used earlier or the mess of memories and identities crowding her brain.

Rowan dropped his hands. "I'm sorry," he said, voice soft. "I had to do that." He peered at her, brows drawn, sensing something was wrong, but not quite sure what. He was blaming himself for her reaction, Echo realized. *Crap.* He shook his head and added, "I shouldn't have done that."

Without giving Echo the chance to explain, he turned and went to his own room. The lock clicked behind him, and the quiet of the hallway swelled around her. She went into her room, half blind to its formerly lavish furnishings, her skull pounding with pain. She'd experienced slippage before, but not like that. The memories that came with the other vessels were rarely that forceful. She needed to lie down. If only she could talk to the Ala about it.

She touched a hand lightly to her lips. Her throat constricted and tears stung the corners of her eyes. The mattress was as hard as a rock; it barely sagged beneath her when she sat on it. She dug her fingers into the coverlet—the only thing about the room that seemed marginally new—and listened to the sound of her own beating heart. The castle was huge, but even here, she could hear the occasional creak of floorboards as Avicen milled about their rooms. And each and every one of them was depending on her to be some kind of savior. How could she save anyone when she couldn't even save the people who meant the most to her? How could she bear that kind of responsibility if all she brought her loved ones was pain? Echo was surrounded by people and yet she had never felt more alone.

CHAPTER EIGHTEEN

The next morning, breakfast was delivered to Echo's room by a sullen Warhawk. His resentment simmered hotter than the still-steaming porridge on the tray he carried.

"Thank you," Echo said, only half meaning it. "I know this is beneath you." The Warhawk offered her a curt nod in response and turned on his heel to leave, the sound of his boots muffled by the carpet, his white cloak billowing rather majestically behind him. Definitely too majestically for someone who had been relegated to breakfast duty. Echo wondered what he'd done to piss off Altair.

She sat on her bed and ate quickly. The porridge was in desperate need of sugar, and the coffee was bitter and badly burnt. Seconds after she scooped the last bit of porridge from the bowl, a knock sounded at her door. She left the dishes on the tray and sprang from the bed to answer it. Altair waited outside, his feathers immaculate, his white cloak as spotless as freshly fallen snow.

"There's something I'd like to show you," he said. And that was it. He turned and made his way down the hall, expecting Echo to follow. A brief rebellious urge seized her, but she ignored it in favor of grabbing her boots and pulling them on as she hopped down the corridor after him. Definitely not as majestic as a Warhawk.

Altair led her to what had once been the castle's ballroom. The high ceilings were decorated with a mural so faded Echo could barely make out the shapes. Fat little cherubs peeked through the peeling paint in one corner, while a beast that was either a narwhal or a disfigured unicorn pulled a carriage in another. The center of the mural was blackened with stains, most of which could be attributed to the chandelier hanging in the middle of the ceiling. The dawn of electric lighting had passed Avalon by, and smoke stains and ancient wax clung to the chandelier's brass frame. Crystal teardrops dangling from its many arms caught the midmorning light and cast it about the room in a kaleidoscope of rainbows.

Rows of cots lined the room. Two Avicen healers walked among them, checking on their occupants. They were so still. Like corpses. If not for the rise and fall of their chests, Echo would have thought they were dead. The skin she could see was covered in veins, black and swollen, just like the Ala's. Some were barely affected; others were so deeply lined with black veins that their features were obscured.

Altair walked between the rows, peering at each Avicen with an inscrutable look on his face. "The ones closest to the kuçedra suffered the worst, though even those with minor injuries have worsened despite our care." His voice was carefully modulated. It gave away nothing of his feelings. He could have been reading the nutritional information off the side of a cereal box. But when he turned to Echo, his orange eyes were full of something she'd never thought she'd see. Not in him.

Helplessness.

"We don't know what to do," Altair continued. "We don't know how to help them, or even if we can. The best we've been able to do is make sure they're comfortable. The human victims were taken to Lenox Hill Hospital. According to the reports we've picked up on the radio, the hospital has them in quarantine, but so far none of their treatments has proved effective in either curing the infection or slowing its progress. Not that they would. This . . . disease"—he spat out the word as if it were poison—"is magical in origin. They're as lost as we are. More so, I would wager. All we know is that those who came into direct contact with the kuçedra were affected."

Echo drew closer to the cot nearest the door. The Avicen lying on the crisp white sheets was a member of the Council of Elders. He was nearly as old as the Ala and had been in charge of food distribution in the Nest. Charon was his name, if memory served. Echo had seen him around the Nest and at the Agora. He had pale feathers, the color of cream. Not quite as white as Ivy's. One of his arms was covered in a network of dark veins; the other was untouched. The veins snaked up the length of his arm and across his collarbone: the contagion was spreading through his bloodstream. His body was putting up a fight, but the infection was winning. Beneath his closed lids, his eyes tracked with frantic movements, as though he was dreaming. Perhaps having a nightmare. Echo knew his eyes were the brilliant blue of sapphires.

Eyes like his were hard to forget. The kuçedra was a beast of shadow and suffering. The things Charon must have been seeing, trapped in a paralyzed body. . . .

"Do you think they'll get any worse?" Echo asked. She reached for Charon's hand, but one of the healers grabbed her wrist before she could touch him. The healer's hands were protected by latex gloves.

"I don't think that's a good idea," said the healer. Her pale yellow eyes, the same color as her hair-feathers, were bloodshot, as if she hadn't had a moment's rest since the attack. "We don't understand how or why the infection is spreading like it is, and we're taking every precaution to make sure it doesn't leave this room."

Echo drew her hand back. She could offer the wounded no comfort.

Altair stood beside her, looking down at Charon. "He was the only other council member who survived save the Ala and myself." A thin line formed between his furrowed brows as he laid a gentle hand on the sheets beside Charon. This was a side of the general Echo had never glimpsed before. It unnerved her. She felt as though she were seeing him without his armor. "To be honest," he continued, "we don't know what will happen to them or even if they're in pain." The hand on the cot balled into a fist, as if he needed to stop himself from trying to touch those horrible, blackened veins. "One cannot help but wonder if death would be a kindness."

Death. A dark thought occurred to Echo, darker still because it hadn't occurred earlier.

"What did you do with . . ." She couldn't finish the question.

"Our dead?" Altair offered. His voice was once again

dispassionate, as if he were discussing the price of a quart of milk. But then, he'd had far more practice desensitizing himself to the horrors of war than she. "Mage fire. The same way we used to clean up our dead after battles."

"Mage fire?" Echo had come across it in the Ala's books, but she'd never heard of anyone able to produce it. At least, not anyone she knew.

"The skill has gone out of fashion," Altair said. "But I've made sure there have always been those among us who know the old arts."

Arts. As if burning bodies so that nothing but unidentifiable ash remained was a thing of beauty. Echo suppressed a shudder.

"I can't do anything for them." She shook her head. "For the . . . survivors." If they could be called that. The medicinal scent of healing herbs and the stuffiness of the room overwhelmed her. She wrapped her arms around herself. She was cold, despite the warmth of the room. It was the kind of cold that settled into the bones, taking root deep in one's soul. "I don't know what you expect me to do."

Altair's gaze cut to her. The ferocity of it made her breath catch. This was the Altair she knew, the one who instilled the fear of god in his recruits, whose legendary bravery in battle had earned him the respect and the loyalty of his fellow soldiers. Was that what she was now? A soldier in a war that had begun thousands of years before her birth? Was she Altair's soldier? She had the sneaking suspicion he meant to mold her into something more than that.

"I expect you to do what we all must in times such as these," he said, deep baritone voice rumbling through the silent room. "I expect you to fight."

Echo looked away. She couldn't maintain contact with that steady, steely gaze. Her eyes roamed over the cots with their crisp white sheets and deathly still occupants. One of the healers looked up from where he was tending to an Avicen. In one hand, he held the washcloth he'd been using to wipe the unconscious Avicen's brow. From his other hand dangled a string of wooden beads, each one a different hue, almost all of them jewel tones. Back at the Nest, Echo had seen some Avicen wearing similar items, either as bracelets or necklaces. They weren't particularly popular, but she knew what they were: prayer beads. Each colorful bead was meant to represent a god from the Avicen pantheon, and the wearer often strung the beads himself, selecting the gods whose blessings he desired. On the healer's strand, there was a bead Echo had never seen before. The prayer beads were always a single color. One color, one deity. But this one was divided down the middle into two colors: black and white. Echo's gaze locked with the healer's, and he touched the two-toned bead with a gentle finger before returning to his ministrations.

Suspicion snaked through Echo's gut. She didn't want to ask, but she had to know. "What's that?" She kept her voice quiet, even though she knew sound wouldn't wake the afflicted. They were too deep in poisoned slumber for that.

The Avicen nurse seemed taken aback, as if he hadn't expected her to acknowledge his presence.

"It's for the firebird," he said, a slight quaver in his voice. He peered at her, his expression inscrutable. "It's for you."

Echo's stomach dropped. "Me?"

The Avicen nodded slowly. "Yes. You."

"Why?"

The nurse moved away from the Avicen he'd been tending

and took a few slow steps toward Echo. "We heard what you did. When the Drakharin attacked our forces in the Black Forest. You targeted their leader." His eyes skittered to Altair, no doubt remembering that Echo had also attacked the Avicen leader. But it seemed as though that detail was growing easier to ignore in the wake of the Nest attack. The Avicen needed a hero, and Echo could be molded into one so long as she cooperated with them in their darkest hour. How quickly the tide of public opinion changed.

Our forces. He made it sound like Echo was part of the *our.* All she'd ever wanted was to feel like she was one of the Avicen, but now that she did, it didn't feel the way she'd imagined. There was expectation in the nurse's voice. Hope. A desperate kind of hope that Echo feared she'd only disappoint. When Echo said nothing in return, the healer ducked his head and went back to his work, taking vital signs and making patients comfortable.

Oriflamme, she thought. *French. From the Latin, aurea flamma, "golden flame."* The word was originally meant to signify the battle standard of the kings of France, but it could also denote something more than that. A greater ideal. A symbol—or perhaps even a person—that armies would follow into battle. A point around which to rally. To fight. To die.

Echo felt Altair's presence as he approached behind her. "You're powerful, Echo." Altair almost never used her name. Usually, she was *the human girl* or simply *that one.* Depending on how rotten his mood was, *the wretch.* Occasionally just *you there.* "More than even you realize, I believe. I saw you in the Black Forest. I told them of your power." Echo turned to look at him. He raised a hand to his temple, where a scar disappeared beneath his brown-and-white hair-feathers.

The wound had healed, but the scar was still relatively recent. The skin was smooth, like a burn. "By the gods, I felt it."

The admission was the closest thing to a compliment she was likely to ever receive from him.

"You are capable of more than you know," said Altair. "And if you'll follow my instruction, I will help bring it out of you."

Within that plea—for that, despite his pride, was what it was, a reticent admission of her power—was everything Echo had ever wanted from him, from the Avicen in general. Acceptance. An invitation to become a part of the flock. A statement that she belonged, that she had a place among them. She just never imagined it would come from Altair. His had been the loudest voice on the Council of Elders when a vote had been called to determine if the lost, lonely human girl would be welcomed among them or left to her own devices. An orphan, for all intents and purposes. A wretch.

"You've never wanted me around, and now you're asking me to join you in this fight." A thought slid through her mind—something about gift horses and staring at their mouths—but she had to push. Pushing was what she did. "That must kill you."

He glared at her. But then one corner of his mouth lifted in a joyless smirk. "It does." He ran a hand through his hair-feathers. He looked tired. Not the kind of tired a good night's sleep would fix, but the kind that wore you down, slowly and steadily. "But you're a part of this"—he gestured at the makeshift infirmary, at the victims of the kuçedra's toxin, at the great wide world beyond Avalon's walls, which was changing with the shifting of cosmic forces too massive to be understood—"whether I like it or not. I saw you summon that fire. I know what power you possess. I know the magnitude of the weapon at your disposal. But I also know that a sword is only as good as the person who wields it. Even the best fighter needs to practice. I can offer you instruction, but you have to be willing to accept my help." He offered her another joyless half smile. "And I trust accepting my help is no easier for you than accepting yours is for me, but the world is changing, and we either change with it or we perish."

With that, he left her in the ballroom turned infirmary. The healers ignored her as she stood in the middle of the aisle between the cots, pondering Altair's words. She couldn't help but think that she was the sword and Altair wanted to be the person who wielded her. In the span of a few months, she had gone from unfortunate stray to a weapon of mass destruction. War was on the horizon, and the firebird had to play its part. Echo had a very strong feeling that, just as Excalibur had been created on an isle of magic and mystery, Avalon was where she would be forged into a weapon.

CHAPTER NINETEEN

Caius did not sleep. He dozed only when necessity demanded he rest. Relaxing enough to slip into a full slumber was an untenable notion, when he was sharing a roof with the raggedy remainder of the Avicen military. They, like the rest of their kind, had been decimated by the attack on the Nest, but their smaller numbers did not make them any less deadly. Caius lacked his own army to call upon. The forces of the Drakharin answered to the Dragon Prince, a title he could no longer rightfully claim. He was alone—Dorian was being held in another room to prevent them from *colluding,* as Altair had pointedly phrased it—and should the tides of fate turn against him, he was but one man against the dozens of Warhawks who had survived the attack or been away from the Nest when it occurred. He had every intention of assuring that did *not* happen.

His room had no window, but even through the thick walls of Avalon Castle, he could hear the trill of birdsong in the gardens surrounding the stone edifice. Compared with the silence the Drakharin maintained around Wyvern's Keep—it was a strict bird-free zone—it was almost a cacophony of sound. Without the benefit of the sun's arc through the sky, birdsong was the only way Caius had of telling time. When a nightingale heralded the end of the day, he knew the sun, hidden from him by stone and concrete, had set.

For hours, Caius paced the length of his modest room, his boots wearing tracks through the layer of dust caked into the ancient rug. He'd dozed with his boots on. He didn't trust the quiet peace of Avalon. Not with the kuçedra on the loose. Not when his sister was probably still plotting his capture (at best) and his death (at worst). He wouldn't be caught with bare feet in an emergency. He had slightly more dignity than that.

A knock at the door halted his circuit of the room.

Caius's hands twitched uselessly at his sides. What he wouldn't give to have his long knives back. He felt naked without them.

His visitor didn't bother waiting for Caius's response. The door swung open, and Altair filled the frame like he was in a doll's castle. The white feathers on the crown of his head nearly brushed the top of the doorframe, and his shoulders were practically as wide as the door itself.

"Good evening," Caius chirped. Echo's sarcasm was contagious. The greeting summoned a frown on the general's face, marring its stern, angular perfection. *Good,* Caius thought. He couldn't fight Altair—not when he was at the mercy of the Avicen's generosity—but he could annoy him. Centuries of animosity needed an outlet, even when he knew it was petty to antagonize Altair. This was the man who had sent Rose on her doomed mission to find the firebird with little regard for her life. Who had imprisoned Echo for daring to defy him. Who had cut Dorian's eye out of its socket for nothing but the sick thrill of it. Caius was rather proud of the fact that he stopped himself at an insincere greeting.

Altair wasted no time on pleasantries. "Before we proceed, I need to ask you one thing."

Caius arched a questioning eyebrow and let his silence speak for him.

"Why in the name of all the gods should I trust you?" asked Altair.

A broken half laugh escaped Caius. Altair's stern face only grew sterner. Trust? Between them? Honestly. *Honestly.*

Caius spread his arms wide. "How can I possibly answer that? I've killed more of your people than I can count and you've done the same to mine."

Altair crossed his arms. "Try. Or you don't leave this room. I will keep you alive because the firebird seems to care about your continued existence, but I am under no obligation to let you come and go as you please. You know the location of your sanctuary. I cannot let you leave unless I feel confident that you and I are not at odds." Something that was not quite a smile but not quite a smirk graced Altair's lips. "For now, at least."

The firebird. The way the general spoke of Echo as if she were a thing and not a person grated on Caius. But it also provided him with an opportunity. Altair had showed his hand, whether or not he had intended to.

"You might not trust that I mean you no harm," Caius said. Gods, *he* didn't even trust that he meant Altair no harm.

"But you can believe, beyond any doubt, that I would never do anything to hurt her."

The *her* required no specification. Echo's presence hung between them like a bartering chip, passed back and forth as they played this dangerous game.

And now, Caius knew, it was his turn to reveal his hand. A facsimile of trust would never be established without Caius giving Altair something meaty to sink his teeth into. "Echo is not merely my ally," said Caius. "She is my friend. And where she goes, I go."

The silence thickened. Altair seemed to mull Caius's proclamation over, as if testing it for holes or weaknesses. Revealing the depth of his feelings for Echo was a gamble, but it was one Caius was willing to take. If Altair thought he had something to hold over Caius's head when it suited him, then he was more likely to bring this conversation to an end.

"Very well," Altair said in slow, measured tones. He stepped aside, gesturing for Caius to walk through the door. "Then I believe you have an appointment with the Dragon Prince. The sooner we can confirm that she isn't responsible for the attack on the Nest and see about instituting a cease-fire, the sooner we can start hunting down the monster that is."

After a quick stop to retrieve Dorian from his room at the opposite end of the wing in which Caius was also housed, they departed the castle under the cover of darkness. Altair and two of his Warhawks—the angry one and the purply one, as Caius had taken to calling them in his head—shadowed their every move. For this to work, Caius needed privacy and a place from which to access the in-between, both of which they found a short distance from the castle, shielded from sight by a copse of trees. The island's wards prevented travel through the in-between, but what Caius had planned was more like cracking open a door without walking through it. The seam between land and river would have been the optimal place for their needs, but Altair wanted Caius to work the spell where no one would see the two Drakharin.

Now, Caius and Dorian stood in a circle of mushrooms—a fairy ring, the humans called it. Like entwined tree branches, the circle formed a natural doorway to the in-between. Circles, especially those formed through acts of nature, had their own energy about them, but only if one knew how to harness it.

Dorian drew a dagger from a sheath at his hip. It was a simple blade; the hilt was unadorned save for a plain bronze inlay on the pommel, and after years of use, the worn brown leather grip had contoured to the shape of Dorian's hand. Etched into the bronze was the winged dragon Caius had used as his crest during his reign as Dragon Prince. The dagger had been a gift from Caius on Dorian's one-hundred-fiftieth birthday. Dorian's blue eye had lit up, and he'd cradled it as if it was the finest thing he'd ever owned. "Your dominant hand, please."

Caius offered him his right hand. He could feel Altair's gaze on him, burning a hole in his back.

"It's been a while since we've done this," Dorian said, the tip of the dagger resting against the center of Caius's palm, indenting the skin without piercing it. "You remember how it works?"

"Like calls to like," Caius said. "Blood calls to blood. There is no blood bond greater than that between twins. My blood will call to her, and she'll sense its pull. She'll know how to find me through the darkness."

"If she feels like cooperating," Dorian muttered.

"I have faith in her," said Caius. He knew he shouldn't, but the part of him that still loved Tanith, no matter what atrocities she committed, couldn't shake the hope that he would be able to reach her.

"That's always been your blind spot." And with that, Dorian sliced Caius's palm, deeply enough for the onset of pain to be delayed by a few seconds. Blood welled up in his cupped hand. Dorian dipped his index finger into the growing pool of crimson and drew a line of angular symbols on Caius's arm from elbow to wrist. It was an ancient form of Drakhar, one that Caius hoped Tanith would remember when she felt the spell's tug. In order for the spell to work, she would need to replicate it on the other side. If she ignored his summons, then all this would be for naught.

Satisfied with the runes, Dorian rolled up one of his own sleeves and drew the same symbols, but reversed, on his skin. The mirror images would bind them, allowing Dorian to pull Caius back should he drift off, lost to the expanse of nothingness. The anchor could technically be anyone, even a stranger, but the spell was most effective when there was a bond. The relationship between the two men had evolved over the years, and it hadn't always been one between equals, but the bond was there and it was strong. No matter where Dorian's heart lay, he would always be Caius's friend. That incontrovertible truth was as undeniable and as unchanging as the sun's arc through the sky.

Dorian retreated to the outer edge of the circle, as far from Altair as the Avicen general would allow. The way Dorian's hand kept flitting to his eye patch had not escaped Caius's notice.

"When you're ready," Dorian said, "summon the in-between. The spell will be most effective if you conclude your business before the blood has fully dried."

Caius fought not to roll his eyes. "I know." He gave Dorian a small smile of feigned confidence. "Always such a worrier."

He jested, but Dorian was right. The blood would dry quickly and he wouldn't have much time. Just minutes. Some of his arguments with Tanith had lasted months. One exceptional dispute over who was to blame for an entire cabinet's worth of shattered glassware had lasted for years. Now he had a tiny window to somehow smooth over relations between the Avicen and the Drakharin, when the most stubborn person he'd ever known was sitting on the latter's throne.

Sometimes, one simply had to build Rome in a day.

Dorian caught his eye. "Ready?"

Caius braced himself.

No, he thought.

"Yes," he said.

He held out his bloodied hand and concentrated on that well of power within. Tendrils of ink-black darkness burst from his palm, as if the blood pouring from the wound had turned to smoke. It expanded, erasing from sight first Dorian and their Avicen companions, then the ring of mushrooms, and finally the crescent sliver of the moon.

The sensation was not unlike falling. The dirt and grass and pebbles beneath Caius's boots disintegrated into the ether. He was everywhere; he was nowhere. The in-between held him suspended, floating, a speck of life in a vast sea of darkness, weightless and aimless. There was no place on the planet that knew darkness this pure, this undisrupted by even the dimmest spark of light. It was as if he were adrift in the cosmos without the stars to guide him.

Now came the tricky part.

Tanith would be able to feel his blood calling to hers, but she would need to access the in-between as well. She would require her own anchor, someone to pull her back to solid ground. The last time Caius had done this spell, he had been his sister's anchor. They had trusted each other then, enough to place their lives in the other's hands. He had never known Tanith to let anyone besides him past her defenses. The armor she built around herself was even stronger than the gold-plated suit she wore into battle. Personal connections, she had once claimed, courted weakness. His sister was like castle-forged iron, made in the fire and shaped into something sharp and deadly.

Without an anchor, Tanith would be unable to meet him.

And so, when a faint flicker of light pierced the veil of blackness, Caius had to swallow his surprise.

The last time he'd seen his sister, she had been wreathed by fire, both her own and Echo's. Her gilded armor had been stained scarlet with the blood of the fallen, and her own blood had oozed from the wound at her shoulder. The wound that Caius had inflicted when his knife had found a gap in her armor. Tanith had always been fond of telling him he had good aim. He wondered if she admired it as much now.

The flicker of light grew, until suddenly, Tanith was there, standing before him in a diaphanous gown made of red silk. Specially modified armor plates covered her torso and a single shoulder. It was armor valued for its form, not its function; it was a statement. Do not mistake my beauty for softness, it said. Many had made that mistake with Tanith, but few ever repeated it.

Her long blond hair was in thin braids coiled around her head into a crown. The style was lovely and complex, and it, too, served a purpose. It kept the hair off Tanith's face and out of the way should she find the need to draw the longsword at her hip, held by a belt that matched her armor. Screaming dragons were carved into the metalwork. Another statement, this one vastly less subtle. Cross me and die, those dragons screamed.

Caius hadn't realized until that moment how much he missed her. Her absence from his life was like the phantom pain of an amputated limb. They may have stood on opposing sides of a conflict, but she was his sister, and nothing would ever change that.

"Hello, Brother," said Tanith. Both her arms were bare, and one of them bore the same runes as Caius's, also written in blood. The shapes were sloppy, as if she'd done them in a rush. He wasn't sure if he had imagined it or if there was a trace of wistfulness in her greeting. Her scarlet eyes weren't soft, but they weren't hard either, and for Tanith, that was something. Perhaps she had missed him, too.

"Tanith," he said. "I can't say I was expecting you to actually show."

"I almost didn't."

"Who's your anchor?"

Tanith's mouth stretched into a wry grin. "The royal treasurer."

"Oeric?" he asked.

That arrogant, vain, self-important buffoon? With hair the color of burnished gold and eyes his admirers liked to compare to gray winter skies, Oeric was handsome enough, but Caius couldn't imagine his sister falling for a pretty face and a fat purse. Unless access to a copious amount of gold was the source of Oeric's appeal. It would help to explain the sudden efficacy of Tanith's power grab. Those of the court who couldn't be bullied had likely been bought. Fear was a good motivator, but sometimes greed was better.

She rolled her eyes. "Yes, Oeric."

"I hadn't realized the two of you were so close," Caius said. "Though I suppose he does have his uses."

Tanith sighed, a familiar sound. It almost felt like they hadn't tried to mortally wound each other months earlier. "Spare me your judgment, Caius. There are a great many things you don't know about me. And I don't appreciate the insinuation that I would whore myself out for the throne."

"Well, did you?"

Her palm cracked against his cheek. The sting of her slap was nearly as bad as her fire. Caius worked his jaw, knowing he would probably have a hand-shaped bruise on his face later.

"Fair enough," he said. They didn't have time for the venomous banter of estranged siblings. It was time to discuss the only thing that mattered. "I assume you heard about the attack on the Avicen Nest."

A grin tugged at the corners of Tanith's mouth. "I did," she said. Caius was not surprised. The Drakharin had their spies, even among the Avicen. "I'll be sure to extend my condolences."

"Please tell me you didn't have anything to do with it."

The grin vanished. "Do you really think I'm that reckless? Attacking the Nest in broad daylight, surrounded by all those humans, would be insane. As much as the thought of Avicen casualties pleases me, I would never endanger my own people like that." She examined the blood on her arm, judgment radiating off her in waves. "I want to say I'm surprised you care so much, but you have a history of keeping the Avicen a touch too close."

Memories danced in Caius's mind, unwelcome and unwanted. Black and white feathers. A cabin by the sea. The smell of smoke. "I won't rise to your bait, Tanith. I'm here to ask for a truce on behalf of the Avicen. There is something far more dangerous out there, and it is much bigger than our old hatreds."

Tanith stared at him blankly. Then she burst into laughter. "Have you gone mad?" She sobered, her raucous laughter subsiding into faint chuckles. "I may not have had anything to do with the attack, but I can't say it wasn't . . . inspiring."

Caius frowned. "What do you mean?"

"I mean that two can play the game you started," she said. "You left quite the treasure trove of research behind in your haste to depart the keep. I know that the kuçedra is the firebird's counterpart. And I know that it can be bound to an earthly vessel, just like the firebird. You have your monster, and soon I will have my shadow beast. Right now it is a wild power, running loose like a feral dog. *I* will be its vessel."

Such a thing was madness. To even attempt to wrangle the power of an entity like the kuçedra would be certain suicide. It may have been the firebird's counterpart on this plane of existence, but Caius knew that some forces were beyond taming. "Tanith, you don't know what you're getting yourself into. The kuçedra cannot be held on a leash. I've *seen* it. You won't be able to control it. It will devour you. It won't be used as a weapon, targeted at your leisure. It will destroy anything it comes across."

She shook her head, sending a few strands of blond hair across her forehead. "You never had much faith in me, did you?"

Caius let out a bitter laugh. "Is that what you think? Tanith, I had more faith in you than anyone. If I'd had any less, I would have seen you sneaking up behind me to steal the crown before it was too late. I believed in you, and you used that to your advantage, whether or not you want to admit it."

Her lips were pressed together as if she were physically restraining words fighting to get free. Whether those words were apologies or rebuttals, he would never know. One of Tanith's hands rose to her bloodied arm, fingers curling as if to scratch, but she pulled back before she could ruin the marks. Caius could feel it, too, the blood slowly caking on his skin. It was their ticking clock.

"Don't do this," Caius said. "It's not like you, Tanith. You can be overzealous, but you're not reckless. Do you know what I think?"

"No, but I have the sneaking suspicion you plan on informing me." Her words were tough, but there was something about the tone of her voice that made Caius hope she could be reached. That some part of her, deeply buried though it might be, loved her twin brother enough to listen.

"I think you wanted me to reach out to you. I think you wanted me to try to talk you out of the insanity you're planning."

"Gods, you were always so condescending." It wasn't a denial. Her response was brusque, but Caius knew her. He knew her better than anyone else in the world, sometimes even better than herself. Hiding behind her words was a reluctant confession.

"Tanith, please, I am begging you—"

She barked out a laugh. "Begging? And to think, a scant few months ago, you were the Dragon Prince and now you're nothing more than a beggar. I suppose the higher you fly, the harder you fall."

"This isn't about my dignity. I am afraid for you. Maybe there's too much bad blood between us now to fix what's broken, but binding yourself to the kuçedra will solve nothing. If we fight, then we fight, but please, Tanith, please, don't go chasing the kuçedra. It is a creature of pain and death, and that is all it will bring, even to you. Especially to you."

Tanith's hand came to rest on the pommel of her sword, determination written in every inch of her posture. "You forget the point of war, Caius. It isn't pretty. It isn't noble. It is hard and cruel and unforgiving. There will be pain and death. There always is. That is the way of things." As she spoke, she seemed to deflate. She reached for him then, cupping his cheek in her hand. Her touch was soft, her palm cool and dry. Caius held his breath. "I never wanted you to be my enemy. Please believe that. I have caused you pain, I know. And I'm truly sorry. I did what I thought was right. What was necessary. But we must play the roles in which we've cast ourselves. You have chosen your side, and I have chosen mine."

The skin on Caius's arm itched. The blood was nearly dry. They had seconds, if that. He could feel Dorian on the other end of the tether, trying to pull him back. Caius resisted, but he wouldn't last long.

"Tanith—"

"Don't." She gave him a sad smile, a true smile. There was nothing biting or cruel in its shape. He wondered if she regretted the blood that she had spilled over the years, if the ghosts of the dead haunted her as they haunted him. "This war will end, as I promised it would. I will see to that. My only hope is that you will live to see that end, and one day, that you will forgive me for the things I have done and will do. But I am not seeking your permission, Caius. You do not rule me. You never have." She let her hand fall away. "Goodbye, Brother."

And just as abruptly as she had appeared, she was gone. In her place, there was only darkness. All the things Caius wanted to say were swallowed by the in-between. His skin tingled, and again, he felt Dorian's tug. This time, he let it take him. Sorrow made his heart grow heavy, and he wondered if he would ever see Tanith again. And if he did, whether she would still be his sister, or if dabbling with the forces of darkness would turn her into something unrecognizable.

He was still a little dazed when he breathed in the humid river air. His vision was blurry, and it wasn't until Dorian materialized before him, brows drawn together in concern, that he realized it was because tears had formed in his eyes. They didn't fall. They hovered on his lashes, waiting. He was already mourning his sister. She was strong—perhaps the strongest person he had ever known, but no one was that strong. The kuçedra was a monster beyond reason. It would not be controlled. Not by Tanith. Not by anyone.

Dorian cracked a weak smile and gripped Caius's shoulder. "I take it that went as well as expected." Behind him, Altair hovered, flanked by his Warhawks.

"We have to stop her," Caius said. His voice sounded thin, his words broken. "Tanith is going to doom us all."

CHAPTER TWENTY

Jasper, being Jasper, had claimed one of the nicest rooms in their part of the castle for himself. Echo didn't know how he did it. Bribery maybe. Or blackmail. Either scenario was just as likely. The bedroom was palatial, the mattress and chairs luxuriously plush, the view of the river astonishing. Trust Jasper to land on his feet wherever he fell, no matter how rocky the terrain.

Echo had rallied their little group to this meeting under the pretext of forming a plan—the feeling of being helpless grated on her nerves—but silence descended among them, each person lost to their own private troubles. The Warhawks Altair had ordered to guard them agreed to stand just outside the door more readily than Echo had thought they would. But as their gazes flitted to Caius and away, she thought maybe they'd spent enough time in the presence of Drakharin for one day. Rowan was nowhere to be found. Echo felt ashamed of how relieved she was to not have to see him.

"I have a contact that might be able to shed some light on the kuçedra," Caius offered after some time. "A professor in Edinburgh by the name of Aloysius Stirling. Well, technically a professor."

"What makes his professorship technical?" Echo asked.

"He has a reputation for being a bit of a crackpot," said Caius, his words laced with magnanimity. "He's still affiliated with the University of Edinburgh, but he doesn't teach anymore."

"Why didn't they just fire him?"

Caius shrugged. "He has tenure. Now he spends all his time researching the folklore and mythology of ancient civilizations, including ones that don't exist as far as humans are concerned. I found him when I was researching the firebird on my own. He had access to some excellent primary resources." An eager glint appeared in Caius's eyes that resonated with Echo. She knew that particular type of delight, the kind that accompanied extreme nerdiness.

"That might help us with figuring out how to deal with the kuçedra," Echo said. "But what about Tanith? We're sort of fighting a war on two fronts here."

From his perch at the window seat, Quinn said, "I have an idea."

It was Jasper who said what they were all thinking: "Really?"

The stars in Quinn's eyes danced as he rolled them. "Yes, really. It's no secret that there's a bounty on all your heads. The Dragon Prince has promised many pretty rewards for information concerning your whereabouts and even more for your capture." His smile was slow and lascivious. "One can't help but wonder what she would pay for the firebird herself."

Echo's back stiffened. Dorian reached for his sword, but his hand fumbled at the void where it normally hung on his hip. The Avicen had been wary about letting a Drakharin roam the halls armed, so a compromise had been reached: Dorian got to keep his sword, but he had to leave it in his room.

Jasper shot Quinn a withering look. "We are not delivering Echo to Tanith's doorstep."

"Yeah," Echo said. "Let's not."

Quinn bowed his head gracefully in Echo's direction. "I meant to suggest no such thing. I was merely pondering a hypothetical. Though it's not only the firebird the Dragon Prince wants." He looked at each of them in turn, his gaze lingering on Jasper, who fidgeted under the scrutiny.

"What are you suggesting?" Caius asked. He shifted his weight forward, the motion causing his knee to brush against Echo's. They both sat on the bed, their backs to the headboard. It would have felt more intimate had Ivy not been on Echo's other side, each of them providing a warm, comforting presence to sandwich her.

"It's simple really," Quinn said. "We're at a disadvantage because we don't know what your sister is planning or where she might attack. If she's telling the truth and she isn't behind the attack on Grand Central, then that means it was the kuçedra lashing out on its own." His gaze slid to Echo. "To find you, for whatever reason. But according to Caius's conversation with Tanith, she's going to make a move that involves the kuçedra one way or another. We need a man on the inside."

Caius and Dorian shared a look, as if they were transmitting information telepathically. After a long moment, Dorian offered Caius a brisk nod.

“Care to share with the rest of the class?” Echo asked.

“We have people within the walls of Wyvern’s Keep,” Caius said. “I may have been blindsided by my sister’s machinations, but I was not so foolish as to have ignored the possibility of treason within my court.”

“Is there a way to contact those people?”

“Well, during times of battle, the Drakharin use a form of blood magic to communicate across great distances.”

“Like what you just did with Tanith.”

Caius shook his head, paused, then nodded. “Yes and no. Tanith and I could communicate like that because we share a special bond—we’re twins. But there are other methods that don’t rely on an existing bond to tether two parties together. There are ways to use blood and metal to transmit information sort of like a radio.”

“I’ve read a ton of the Ala’s history texts—at least the ones that she translated—and I’ve never heard of that.”

Something a little like pride flashed across Caius’s face. “It was one of our best-kept secrets,” he said. His expression sobered. “But it requires two items previously bound by magic to create a line of communication.”

“We have my sword,” said Dorian, “but the twin blades to which it was bound were lost in the Black Forest.”

Twin blades? *Oh.* “Your knives,” Echo said to Caius.

A soft, sad sigh escaped him. “They were fine weapons. Now they’re probably rusting in the mud somewhere,” he said. “We have no way to communicate with anyone inside the keep. When I last left there, we were in a bit of a rush.”

Quinn paced the room, his strides long and leisurely. He stopped near the rolltop writing desk at which Jasper sat and leaned against it. “But what if we could place our own little spy within the keep? If he could smuggle an enchanted item inside, it would open up the lines of communication, would it not? Word on the street is that Tanith is offering a very generous reward for information regarding the whereabouts of a girl claiming to be the firebird or her known associates." The phrase *known associates* was accompanied by a pointed glance at each member of their motley crew. It sounded so official. *Known associates.* Like they were a gang. An old-fashioned gang. A ring of bootleggers in Prohibition-era America. Like maybe they should have old-timey names like Bugsy, or Lucky, or Machine Gun Pete.

Caius nodded slowly. Echo could see the idea dawning in his expression. "She wants you, Echo. But if she can't find you, she'll take anyone who knows you, especially if it's someone important to you. All the better to draw you out of hiding. She knows you'll do anything to protect your people, and she'll be looking to exploit that."

Echo fidgeted. *Her* people. She supposed they were, after all. They were her friends, as unlikely as some of them seemed. Caius met her eyes and offered her one of his rare smiles, the ghostly kind that was so fleeting you'd miss it if you blinked. Her stomach did something stupid. It always did something stupid when he looked at her like that. Her mind did something stupid, too, especially when she entertained the doubts that fluttered at the back of her head like restless moths. Doubts about whom he was smiling at. Whether that smile was meant for her or for another girl, one long dead.

"Okay, so she's fishing for info," said Echo. "How does that help us?"

"The plan," Caius said, "which I reiterate is insane, is to use Tanith's desire for information, or rather a source of information, to get inside the keep. Dorian and I set up a network of people within the ranks of the Drakharin military who are loyal to me." Caius paused. He frowned. "In case of coups, like the one I didn't see coming until it was too late."

"Hindsight's a bitch," Echo said.

Dorian snorted. Caius cleared his throat. "As I was saying, if we can place someone inside the keep, then we can communicate with them. Right now Tanith's defenses are raised. She'll see me coming from a mile away, but she'll be less likely to suspect a prisoner."

"How do you figure?"

"She's arrogant. That's always been her Achilles' heel. If she thinks she has the upper hand, if she thinks she has the power in a situation, she won't be as cautious. She's my sister. I know her. She used my blind spot to her advantage. Now we're going to use hers."

"What was your blind spot?" Ivy asked.

"Her." The word was clipped, like it cost Caius something to admit. "I loved her, and she used that to ascend to the throne. She's flying high on power right now, and that's going to go to her head. If she thinks she's winning this chess game, she'll get cocky."

"How do you plan on getting this person into the keep?" Echo asked. "Other than by being really, really sneaky?"

Quinn pushed away from the desk and swaggered to the center of the room. He never walked. He swaggered. He strode. Occasionally, he slunk. His lips cracked into a sideways smile and he gestured to himself. "That's where your not-so-trusty warlock comes in."

Echo frowned. Quinn's smile didn't waver. "I already don't like this plan," she said.

"Warlocks are a selfish breed. There are few things we prize over power, magic, and wealth. It's kind of our hallmark," said Quinn. "I'm going to deliver"—he spun around the room, his hand waving at each of them in turn—"one of you to her door, all wrapped up in a pretty bow."

"Okay," Echo said. "So we get someone inside, then what?"

"One of our agents inside the keep will make contact. There's a standard call-and-response known only to the people within Caius's circle. We can tell them to be on the lookout for people coming and going from the keep. There's a message we can leave, subtly, in the forest on the patrol route that wouldn't mean anything to anyone who didn't know what to look for. Then that person will guide and protect whoever we plant inside to acquire information that might assist us in our fight against the kuçedra and help our plant escape with the information we need."

"And what information is that?"

"A book," Caius said.

"What kind of book?" Echo asked. "And why can't you just remember what it said? I mean, you read it, right? You're an even bigger nerd than I am."

Caius looked mildly affronted. "My mind is not a steel trap, Echo. I discovered it when I was looking for the firebird. It's part of a collection of texts that contained information about the nature of the firebird and its related mythology. The kuçedra falls under that umbrella. I didn't pay that much attention to it at the time, as it seemed peripheral to my primary focus, but I remember it distinctly. The lore was . . . discomforting."

A pall fell across the room. There was no need for him to specify what was so disturbing. They had seen it in Grand

Central, and the ones who hadn't seen it firsthand had witnessed its effects: the black veins that even now were spreading across the skin of those it had touched.

"But why do we even need to get into the keep?" Echo asked. "Surely we can find that information somewhere else?"

Caius's gaze drifted down. His fingers drummed on his thighs. Echo was beginning to recognize his tells. Some she had cataloged herself; others she remembered in that distant way that meant the memories weren't really hers. Rose knew Caius and all his tics. And now Echo knew them too. This one meant there was something he had to say, but he didn't want to say it.

"There is only one copy of the text," Caius said, his voice soft, like he was telling her, and only her, a secret. Like he was confessing something. "I destroyed the others. I didn't want anyone else to access the information, lest they find the object of my quest before I did."

"Beat you to the punch by just a hair," Echo said with a small laugh. The air in the room felt heavy. The others didn't seem to notice. It was as though the two of them were having a private conversation in public.

Caius's lips smiled, but his eyes did not. "Indeed you did."

"And no one else knows what's in that book?" Echo asked.

"No," Caius said. "I made sure of that."

She had to ask. She didn't want to. She had to. "How?"

"By killing the people who owned the book before I did."

She knew he had killed. He'd been fighting a war long before meeting her. Before she'd even been born. And, she knew, one did not become the Dragon Prince by being nice and kissing babies like a politician currying favor from a fickle constituency. The Avicen spoke of the Drakharin's bloodlust as if it was a biological truth—an innate desire to hurt and kill. The truth wasn't as neat as all that, but there was a reason that perception existed. Among the Drakharin, strength and ruthlessness were considered virtues. In their leaders, they were necessities. Caius, at one point, had been seen as the embodiment of those virtues.

"Does that disappoint you?" he asked, again with that soft, private voice. His confessional voice. The question sounded like a challenge. Her answer, Echo realized, mattered to him. It mattered a great deal.

She labored over the right words. He was not the person Rose remembered—that phantom who existed in her mind. The softer Caius of Rose's memories had been hardened by loss and rage, and Echo could not hide from that truth. But then, neither could he. The sin wasn't hers to forgive, but she sensed that was what he needed from her.

"Well, it would have made our job a whole lot easier if you hadn't," she said, striving to keep her voice light. It was strained, but only slightly.

"Yes, well," Caius said, "hindsight's a bitch."

"That's all well and good," said Dorian. "But who would we send into the keep? It can't be you. Or Echo. It would need to be someone Tanith wouldn't see coming."

"It would." Caius's tone was laced with reluctance. There was no guaranteeing what Tanith might do to whoever was deposited on her doorstep. Echo couldn't bear the thought of any of them willingly putting themselves in that kind of danger.

"I'll do it," Ivy said quietly.

Echo sputtered, objections bottlenecking in her mouth. "What? No. No, that's freaking insane. No."

Ivy worried her bottom lip between her teeth. "Think about it, Echo. I'm the only person who *can* do it." She pointed at Caius. "You're obviously out of the question. Tanith wouldn't want to risk you forming an insurrection right under her nose, especially if there are still people loyal to you in the keep. And you, Dorian, she'd just kill outright. As a professional thief, Jasper has a reputation for being untrustworthy—"

"I resent that," Jasper interjected.

"You earned that," Ivy said. "And, Echo, you're way too valuable. I'm the only one who makes sense. Tanith knows we're friends. I'm valuable to you, and because of that, I'm valuable to her."

Caius tilted his head in consideration. "It could work."

Echo could scarcely believe what she was hearing. "Have you all lost your minds? This is *Ivy* we're talking about."

Ivy shot Echo an aggrieved glare. "What's that supposed to mean? You don't think I can do this?"

Un-freaking-believable. To think this had anything to do with Ivy's injured pride. "I'm not worried about whether or not you're capable, Ivy. I know you are. But you could die. For good. There's no firebird to resurrect you. No do-overs."

"We could all die," Ivy countered. "And if we don't do something to try to stop Tanith and the kuçedra and whatever else the universe feels like throwing at us, we will." She drew herself up, a feat complicated by her seated position. "It's my life, Echo. You've risked yours for us so many times. I can't do any less."

"I don't like it," Echo said, but the mood in the room was tilting toward Ivy's suggestion.

"You don't have to like it. You just have to not fight it." Ivy offered Echo a forced smile and added, "It's a plan. And it's the best chance we've got to get one step ahead of Tanith." She shook out her long white feathers, a nervous tic of hers that made something seize in Echo's chest. "Just another day hanging out behind enemy lines. What's the worst that could happen?"

"Oh, I don't know," Quinn said. "Death. Maiming. Excruciating torture."

Echo felt Ivy shiver. She knew the memories of Ivy's time in the dungeon of Wyvern's Keep simmered as closely to the surface as her own nightmares did. But Ivy gave no voice to her fears. She curled her hands into fists, as if readying to beat them back by force if necessary. Echo rested a hand on Ivy's shoulder and gave it a gentle squeeze. Ivy relaxed her tense muscles slightly.

Jasper delivered a solid kick to the warlock's shin. "Shut up, Quinn."

Echo pulled Ivy into a hug, burying her nose in the soft white hair-feathers at the nape of her friend's neck. "You have to promise me you'll come back," she whispered. "I can't lose both the Ala and you."

She felt Ivy nod against her shoulder, though the movement was a little too rapid, a little too jerky.

"I'll come back," Ivy mumbled into Echo's shoulder. "I promise."

CHAPTER TWENTY-ONE

Quinn lingered in Jasper's bedroom after the others had left. Jasper began the process of sorting through the limited wardrobe he'd thrust into a backpack before they left the warehouse. While he hadn't had time to consider his choices as carefully as he would have liked, the relative monochrome simplicity he preferred in articles of clothing meant that everything pretty much matched. With hair and eyes as vibrant as his, anything more visually arresting than a white T-shirt and jeans was often too much of a distraction. There was little point to unfolding and refolding the clothes, but it gave his hands and mind something to focus on that wasn't the heavy weight of Quinn's presence.

Soon, the silence became too much to bear. He had to break it. There was something about the warlock—there always had been—that wreaked havoc on Jasper's otherwise indestructible nerves. "What do you want?" he asked, as uninvitingly as possible.

"Oh, come now," Quinn said. "I can't catch up with an old friend? We've hardly had any time to chat since our reunion." There was a shift in his tone that made Jasper suspect Quinn had winced, but since Jasper refused to turn around to face him, he couldn't be sure. "Admittedly, said reunion was somewhat less than stellar." Quinn pushed away from the door, a movement detectable by the sound of the wooden floor creaking beneath his feet. He was standing behind Jasper now, the faint trace of magic that clung to him like cologne pressing against Jasper's back. The air shifted, as if Quinn had reached out a hand to touch Jasper—maybe his shoulder or his back, but really any body part was as unacceptable as any other—yet the touch never came. Perhaps Quinn had dropped his hand. Perhaps he'd grown as a person. Perhaps hell had frozen over.

"Is it too much to ask for us to start over?" Quinn asked. If Jasper hadn't known any better, the hint of sincerity in the warlock's voice would have sounded believable. Fortunately for him—and unfortunately for past-Jasper—he had learned that Quinn was not to be trusted. Not now, not three years ago, not ever.

Jasper shook out a soft black sweater he'd already folded, taking pains to refold it carefully so as to minimize wrinkling. "You and I both know the answer to that question, and it is a resounding, emphatic, indisputable yes. That is far too much to ask, especially after everything you've done."

"Does that long list of sins including healing you?" Quinn asked. "Because, if I may remind you, I did that out of the kindness of my own heart." He said it as though this were the most selfless thing he'd ever done. For all Jasper knew, it was. "*And* at the expense of my own comfort, I might add."

Now, *that* was classic Quinn. Hoarding good deeds for the sole purpose of shoving them in someone's face later. Their entire relationship—six months of Jasper's life that were unforgettable in the worst possible way—had been like that. It had taken Jasper an embarrassingly long time to wise up to the various methods of emotional manipulation in Quinn's arsenal. Being a bad boy had been part of Quinn's appeal, but the extent of his badness was something that Jasper had been woefully unprepared for at the tender age of sixteen. Now he knew better.

"Go away," he said, his refusal to turn around, to give Quinn the satisfaction of seeing the unease Jasper knew showed on his face, as staunch as ever. "I'm busy."

"Ah, yes, busy folding the same shirt over and over again?"

Jasper dropped the shirt, because that was exactly what he'd been doing.

"Look." Quinn stepped around Jasper and shoved a pile of clothes out of his way. He plopped down on the bed, and not even sinking into the uncomfortable softness of the mattress could make him look any less elegant or composed. That, too, had been part of his appeal. "You're right."

He was?

"I am?" The surprise wasn't that Jasper was right. That much was undeniable. The surprise was that Quinn would ever deign to admit it.

"I fucked up."

This was new. Jasper said nothing. He wanted to see how far Quinn would take this.

"And I'm sorry."

This was not just new. This was unheard of.

Quinn reached out to take Jasper's hand, and he was

stunned enough to let it happen. The remembrance of other times Quinn's skin had come into contact with his bubbled to the surface of Jasper's memory with the touch: the slide of arms around his waist, the feel of a palm cupping his cheek, the sting of nails scraping along his spine. The memories were a heady rush, as powerful as the shifting of tides, but Jasper would be damned if he let them pull him out to sea. He attempted to extricate his hand from Quinn's grasp, but the warlock simply held on tighter. It was the history of their relationship in a small, pitiful nutshell. "Unhand me," Jasper said. After a moment of deadlocked staring, he added, "Now."

Quinn dropped Jasper's hand.

That was easier than it should have been. It was definitely the fastest Quinn had ever acquiesced to a request. It had to be some kind of record.

"Look, Jay, I know I messed up, but—"

"First of all, stop calling me that. I've always hated it. Secondly, 'messed up' doesn't quite begin to cover what you did to me. You toyed with my life, Quinn. You put me in so many awful situations that I can hardly count them all. Do you remember that time you used me as bait to draw out those French warlocks you wanted to steal some enchanted trinket from? Because I do."

"That's just it." Quinn reached up to run a finger along Jasper's jawline. "You were bait. I never would have let anything bad happen to you."

Jasper slapped the offending hand away. Even Quinn's touch was toxic. It was a sweet poison that you didn't realize was sucking the life from you until it was too late. "And that's where you're wrong. *You* are the bad thing that happened to me. You lied. You cheated. You. Hurt. Me. I sent Caius to you because we were desperate, but don't you dare confuse that desperation with whatever fantasy you have of me running back to you. We are so far beyond that—*I* am so far beyond that."

It was astonishing to Jasper that the words in his head had actually left his mouth. When he fled Quinn the first time, he'd slipped away in the dead of night, knowing that if he were forced into a face-to-face confrontation, he would melt under that starlit gaze, just as he'd done a thousand times before, when Quinn had pleaded, with honeyed words and false promises, for him to stay.

"Fine," Quinn said, with an air of finality. He drew in a deep breath. "You're right. And I'm wrong, as usual. I know that I don't deserve your forgiveness." The stars in his eyes seemed to dim, as if hidden behind the cover of clouds. "But you have my apology all the same. And whether or not you choose to believe me, I mean it. Every word."

Jasper knew what lies sounded like. He trafficked in them. He had learned to wield falsehoods like weaponry, but he could hear none in Quinn's tone. That unsettled him. Badly. His voice had scuttled off to hide somewhere he couldn't find it, not even to throw the apology back in the warlock's unfairly symmetrical face.

The corners of Quinn's lips curved upward. "You're beautiful when you're befuddled."

It wasn't even that charming a compliment, and yet, something in Jasper's chest twinged at the words. But he had been down this path before. He knew where it led: nowhere good. At last, he found his voice; he dragged it, kicking and screaming, into his throat. "I don't care. I don't care if you're sorry. I don't even care if you mean it this time. I don't want to have this conversation with you right now. Or ever." His voice pitched half an octave lower, completely of its own volition. "Please," he said. "Just go."

With a sigh, Quinn stood, brushing lint that wasn't there off his black jeans. He squared his shoulders and planted his feet, as if he could force Jasper to accept his apology, to accept this new and improved Quinn through sheer determination. "Look, I'm a warlock, okay? This isn't news. And you know how a human becomes a warlock . . . through sacrifice and willful corruption, most of which is inspired by greed and lust. I am not a good person. I never have been. And I was fine with that . . . until I met you."

"Are you seriously giving me the 'you make me want to be a better man' speech? Is that what's happening here?"

"Maybe," said Quinn, a wry grin pulling at his lips. "But don't tell the other warlocks. They'd never let me hear the end of it."

A startled laugh escaped Jasper. Quinn took it as a sign of encouragement and stepped into Jasper's space. Slowly, he took Jasper's hand and pulled him closer. Their chests were nearly touching. Alarm bells rang in Jasper's head, but they were silenced easily enough. Maybe Quinn meant what he said. Maybe he had changed. It was a slim hope, but Jasper clung to it. Not because he wanted to pick up the tattered remnants of a failed relationship, but because the possibility Quinn was capable of positive change meant that maybe Jasper hadn't been such a complete and utter fool after all.

"We were good together," Quinn whispered, leaning close. He was taller than Jasper by only about two inches, but he'd always seemed giant. His breath rustled the fine feathers near Jasper's ear. "You know we were. We can be again. I'll be better, I promise."

And there it was. That pithy, two-word phrase that Jasper had relied on so many times before. A promise was never a promise with Quinn. It was more of an unlikely potentiality. Jasper stepped away, keeping his eyes focused on his feet. He needed space. He was a tactile person, and proximity was dangerous. It made saying no that much harder.

"He'll never love you."

Jasper jerked his head up. "Excuse me?"

"The Drakharin," Quinn said. When Jasper maintained his silence, he continued, "Oh, come now. I'm not blind. I see the way you look at him. And the way he looks at you. But you have to realize that soulful glances are all you're ever going to get from that one. Whatever baggage he's carrying around is entirely too heavy. It's dragging him down, and I don't want to see you get dragged down with him."

That was rich. That was so rich, Jasper hoped Quinn choked on it. "Since when do you care so much?"

Quinn reached out, hand nearing Jasper's face, but he curled his fingers into a loose fist before making contact. After a second, he dropped it. "I've always cared. I was just never very good at showing it." He closed the gap between them, leaving a few inches of air separating their chests. A deep enough breath would erase that small distance. Jasper kept his breathing shallow. "Let me show you now," said Quinn. "Please."

A knock on the door saved Jasper from having to respond, which was for the best, as he could feel his resolve beginning to crumble. He stepped away from Quinn, and it felt like a comet falling out of a planet's orbit—the warlock's pull was broken.

"Come in," Jasper called out before Quinn could tell the interloper to call again another time. The door swung open and a head of silvery hair poked in. Relief stole through Jasper. The pleasure he normally felt whenever he laid eyes upon Dorian's lovely, one-eyed visage was multiplied tenfold.

"Jasper," Dorian said as he entered, all brisk formality and military bearing. It was not lost on Jasper that Dorian deemed Quinn unworthy of a direct hello.

"Dorian, darling," Jasper said. "What brings you to my humble abode?" *Also, please stay, forever and ever, thank you.*

The tips of Dorian's ears went pink at the word "darling," but he didn't roll his eyes and tell Jasper to put a lid on it like he usually did. Maybe it was Quinn's presence. Or maybe he was coming around and seeing the light. The light being Jasper's raw animal magnetism.

Dorian cleared his throat before speaking. "I thought I left something in here."

"Your dignity, perhaps?" Quinn's voice dripped with sarcasm.

"I've had just about enough of your attitude," said Dorian. "Keep it up and there's no magic in this world powerful enough to protect you. Are we clear?"

Jasper had never been more attracted to another person in his life.

Quinn clenched his jaw so hard, he looked to be in danger of cracking his teeth. The sky in his eyes burned with the ferocity of a thousand supernovas. "Crystal." He approached the door, and Jasper braced for a confrontation. Dorian, however, stepped aside to let Quinn pass, as if, now that he'd made his point, he didn't have a single care in the world. Before stepping over the threshold, Quinn shot Jasper a heated look over his shoulder. "Just remember what I told you." With a final poisonous glance at Dorian, he left.

They both waited, perfectly still, until the sound of Quinn's footsteps faded. Dorian stood there, arms at his sides, every bit as awkward as a fish on dry land. Now that the grand gesture was complete, he didn't appear to have any idea what to do next. Hell, Jasper wasn't certain what to do.

After the silence stretched from awkward to unbearable, Dorian said stiffly, "My apologies."

"For what?" asked Jasper.

"For disturbing you."

Oh, for gods' sake.

It was hard for Jasper to believe that Dorian had been on this earth for more than two centuries and was still so woefully oblivious.

"You weren't," he said. "You couldn't even if you tried." He shoved a few belongings—a pocketknife with a serrated blade, an extra sweater, some healing herbs in the event of misfortune—into the backpack he'd had the foresight to grab before leaving the warehouse in London. He didn't want to have to rely on Quinn and his magic to patch him up again. "Not that I'm complaining, but why did you come? We both know you didn't leave anything here."

Dorian shrugged, but his shoulders were tense, as if he couldn't quite pull off nonchalance. "It seemed like the right thing to do."

"That's it?"

When Dorian spoke, he refused to meet Jasper's eyes. "I

noticed that Quinn hadn't left, so I decided to make sure you were all right. I don't like the way he looks at you."

It was, perhaps, cruel to prod, but Jasper had never been one to hold back. "And how does he look at me?"

Finally meeting Jasper's gaze, Dorian replied, "Like you're a conquest to be made."

"I'm afraid you're a bit late on that front," Jasper admitted. "Quinn and I met when I was sixteen. He came, he saw, he conquered."

Silvery-gray brows drew together. "You aren't some prize to be won."

To that, Jasper had nothing to say. Instead, he shoved the final few supplies in his backpack and zipped it shut. It was sweet that Dorian thought Jasper was better than that. Sweet and silly and terribly misguided.

CHAPTER TWENTY-TWO

Echo's room at Avalon was far more opulent than any place she'd ever called her own. A massive four-poster bed stood atop a platform raised off the floor by two steps, thick velvet drapes hiding the mattress from view. A tall bay window looked out on the garden below, an untamed riot of vibrant wildflowers and tangled weeds that had grown unchecked for decades. She'd left the window open to air out the room, which was in desperate need of a good dusting. A fireplace was set into the wall opposite the window, its embers long gone cold and lifeless. She closed the door behind her and let herself fall against it, her head thudding on the thick wood.

The fresh air in the garden that wrapped around the back of Avalon Castle was nice, but nice was not home. Home was the sugar-sweet smell of the vendor selling roasted nuts on the corner of Forty-First Street and Fifth Avenue; it was the broken-glass glitter of the sidewalk after it rained; it was the rumble of trains coming and going from Grand Central at all hours. This castle, with its battlements and drafty stone walls, would never be home. This lovely room was fit for a princess. Echo was anything but. She was a street urchin, rescued from a life of hunger and petty thievery by the Ala, who now lay in a room elsewhere in the castle, lost to the darkness that had seeped through her skin like poison. And the worst part of it all was that it was Echo's fault. *You are their destruction.*

She slid down the door, the stone floor hard and cold beneath her, and wrapped her arms around her legs, tucking her chin against her knees. She hadn't voiced the thought to Caius or Rowan. While Altair, she strongly suspected, would be only too eager to agree with her, but the others—they would perform whatever mental acrobatics they felt they must to absolve her of guilt. They cared about her, and that was what you did for people you cared about. You tried to make them feel better. You helped them lift the burdens that threatened to bury them alive. But Echo had to bear this burden by herself. The kuçedra had not randomly chosen to strike the Nest. No. It had been *looking* for her. Its darkness had sought out her light and it had begun by searching for her where her presence was strongest. She had only just arrived at Avalon, and so her presence had not yet seeped into its old stones, flaring up like a beacon for the kuçedra to follow. Or so she hoped. She had to leave before she turned this place into a target.

None of them were safe. Not the Ala, not Ivy, not Rowan, or Caius, or Jasper, or Dorian. So long as she and the firebird were one, so long as the kuçedra continued to hunt the firebird, the people for whom Echo cared would be brought down, one by one, until all that was left to her was solitude and despair. The weaker she became, the stronger the darkness; the blackness of her soul would feed it. She knew this as surely as she knew the sky was blue and fire was hot.

She breathed in and out, slowly, heavily, letting the weight of what she felt she had to do settle over her, letting herself grow accustomed to this new and terrible burden.

She had to save them. And she had to do it alone.

Packing was easy. She had so little to her name. She dumped the contents of her backpack on the bed—with the drapes pulled back, the bedspread was revealed to be a rich purple satin, so completely not Echo's style—and surveyed the items laid out before her, some more useful than others.

There were crinkled candy bar wrappers, some lint, a few coins in British and American currency, a crumpled list of toiletries they'd needed at the warehouse hideout, a half-crushed granola bar. Echo's chest tightened when her gaze landed on a pen with a ridiculous ball of pink fluff at the top. Ivy had found it in the library and given it to Echo for her birthday. It had been lurking in the bottom of her backpack for months. But since she doubted a creature made of darkness and pure evil would feel threatened if she waved the pen in its face, she left it in the pile of detritus that summed up her recent past.

She separated two items from the rest: the magpie dagger, removed from its sheath in her boot, and the locket Caius had given to Rose a century ago, the token of his affection that had led Echo to the Oracle, to her fate, and now, potentially to their doom. She lifted the locket and cradled it in her palm. Its surface was smooth, worn to a dull finish after decades of being hidden. The dragon on its face had a tail that curled around the bottom half of the locket and wings that arched over the top so that it looked as though the creature hoarded a priceless treasure. The chain—not the original one, for that had been lost to time—slithered through Echo's fingers like a snake, the metallic whisper of the links loud in the silence of the room. She slipped the necklace on, the chain catching on the loose strands of her hair, and tucked the locket into the neck of her shirt. The pendant fell at just the right spot against her sternum for her shirt to lie flat, the presence of the necklace neatly hidden from view. No one would know that she wore the former Dragon Prince's crest unless she wanted them to.

The dagger went back into her boot. She'd cleaned the blade as Dorian had taught her during the long and boring weeks they'd spent holed away in the London warehouse. It was sharp enough to slice through skin with ease and bright enough to reflect even the faintest scrap of light. There were times when, if Echo looked at it from the corner of one eye, she could see the crimson stain of her blood on the steel, but that was an illusion. She remembered the feel of it biting into her flesh as if the wound were still raw. Only a slight scar, the skin just a touch smoother and darker than that around it, remained to tell the tale. When she held the dagger in her hands, she could feel the weight of its years—it had belonged to Rose and now it belonged to Echo. How it would serve her against the kuçedra, she hadn't the faintest clue, but it felt comforting to have a weapon on her, one that she had tended to herself.

* * *

Before she left, Echo scribbled two notes on torn halves of a scrap of paper scrounged up from the dusty recesses of the desk in her bedroom. She thought about leaving a note for Caius, but she didn't know what to say. A connection had grown between them, that was undeniable, but she still did not trust it. How was she to know which emotions belonged to her and which originated with Rose? It was easier to push Caius out of her mind. Easier and cowardly. But she had only so much left in her to give, and she decided to give it to the people who had been with her from the beginning. Caius was not one of those people. Sorrow settled deep in her heart, and she wondered if it was hers or Rose's or a combination of the two.

The first note was addressed to Rowan. All it said was: *I'm sorry.* She didn't know what else to write. She owed him so much more than that. He deserved more. After a moment's hesitation, she added, *I love you.* He deserved to hear it at least once. And despite all that had happened, it was true. He was still her friend, her first love, her family. Nothing would change that, even if both their hearts were broken.

My dearest Ivy, the second note began, her penmanship a sloppy, hurried scrawl, *I'm off to fight bad guys. Sorry about the secrecy, but if I don't return, I bequeath to you all my earthly possessions, including that replica Romanov tiara you loved even after I told you it was fake. Also, find the laptop I stole from that guy in the library and delete my browser history. And please . . . take care of the Ala. Love, Echo.*

It was a lighthearted note, jovial both in its promise and its warning, but she couldn't bring herself to bid Ivy a proper farewell. The finality of goodbye was too much to bear.

Echo yanked the linens off the bed and the drapery from

the four-poster frame. She tied the ends together, fashioning the bedclothes into a rope she hoped was long enough to reach the ground. It would be the height of humiliation if someone found her in the garden the next morning, lying amid the unkempt shrubbery with a broken leg. Her plan was simple: crawl out the window, navigate her way through the garden and over the castle's outer wall with the aid of a maple tree that had conveniently grown right next to it, and abscond with the boat to a shore distant enough to let her access the in-between but not so far away that the Avicen on the island wouldn't be able to find the boat. That was one theft in which she'd take no pleasure.

Before Echo knew it, it was time to leave. Backpack on, hair pulled back into a sleek ponytail, she secured one end of her makeshift rope around a leg of the bed and tossed the other end out the window. She crawled down as silently as possible. She kept her mind on the physical tasks at hand. Finding footholds with the toes of her boots. Balancing her weight and praying the bed was sturdy enough to support it. When she reached the bottom, she jumped into the bushes and, quiet as a cat, crept through the garden and up the maple tree.

She couldn't look back. If she did, she wouldn't be able to do what she had to. It was, Echo thought grimly, like something from a story she'd encountered years ago. She'd gone through a phase of researching religions. The Ala had reared her on tales from Avicen myth, the result of which was that Echo was more familiar with their pantheon of gods and goddesses than she was with that of any human religion. Capitalizing on the library's vast collection, she'd gorged herself on tales from the Bible, the Torah, the Quran. She'd drawn comparisons between the Avicen gods and the human ones. The Avicen gods had names, the Ala had explained, but no mortal who walked upon the Earth knew them.

There's power in names, the Ala had reminded a curious ten-year-old Echo.

But even so, there was the goddess of love, a scarlet-feathered figure with two heads, one smiling with the euphoria of newfound romance, the other sobbing with the ache of heartbreak. The deities of the harvest—both male and female, for life could not exist without both—cropped up in every faith around the world, including the Avicen's. Their god of war had reminded Echo strongly of Ares, with his reputation for ruthlessness. And as someone who had shuffled off this mortal coil only to resurrect shortly after, Echo was uncomfortable considering the Avicen parallels with Christ-like figures. The thought of it made her sick to her stomach.

As she walked away from the castle, mostly dark now save for a few windows that flickered with weak candlelight, she remembered the tale of a city besieged by angels and a woman who looked back as she tried to escape, despite strict orders not to. The woman had turned into a pillar of salt. Echo had read the story one of the nights spent at the Nest, with Ivy holding a flashlight under the covers while Echo turned the pages. When she had asked Ivy why the woman had been punished for looking back, Ivy had simply shrugged and clicked off the flashlight. The darkness of the room had enveloped their words, granting them greater substance than they probably deserved.

"Maybe she couldn't help it," Ivy had said, snuggling into the mound of pillows on which they'd made their bed. Echo had lost count of the number of slumber parties they'd had in that room. "Maybe she was just scared. Maybe she wanted to go back, but she knew she couldn't or she would die too."

Echo hadn't understood the story then, but she understood it now. Looking back was easy. Even if everything you left behind was in flames, it was easier to watch it burn than it was to keep going, to march headlong into an uncertain future. But Echo did not have the luxury of stalling. She was no longer a girl, swept up in an adventure too grand for her. She was a part of it, a cog in the machine, a player on the stage. She was the firebird. Not a pillar of salt, but a means to an end. She was a weapon, a sword. She kept going, ignoring the way her heart pounded in her chest, thumping out two words in a steady rhythm.

Look back. Look back. Look back.

CHAPTER TWENTY-THREE

New York City had become a war zone. Tanks rolled through the streets, flanked by young men in pale green fatigues, high-powered rifles slung over their shoulders, caps pulled low over watchful eyes that darted here and there, into every corner, looking for enemies Echo knew they wouldn't find. The streets were empty of civilians. The ubiquitous hot dog vendors, who slung frankfurters through hail and sleet and snow, had abandoned their street corners. Coffee shops and delis were dark. Some had their metal grates pulled closed; others had been locked in a hurry as their owners fled in a rush to get as far from Grand Central as possible. The area between Fourteenth and Fifty-Ninth Streets was impassable on foot. Yellow police tape and parked police cars cordoned off Fifth Avenue.

It took the last of Echo's shadow dust for her to travel from the shore of the Hudson River to a utility closet on the platform of the Forty-Second Street/Bryant Park subway stop. She exited the tiny room to find the station deserted, save for a few scattered National Guardsmen patrolling the area. There was no crowd to hide her. The subway system had been shut down immediately after the attack, and Echo was the only soul foolish enough to try to use it. She evaded detection by ducking around columns and hopping the turnstile as silently as a rabbit. It was easier than she had expected. The guards were afraid. Of another attack. Of terrorists lurking in the shadows. Of bombs waiting to go off that might or might not be hidden throughout the transit system. It wasn't the first time the city had been caught in a stranglehold of fear, but it never got any easier. People forgot what it was like to be scared, to be uncertain. But their fear was useful to Echo now. Danger made the guards alert, but their fear made them sloppy. They didn't see a wraith of a girl flit up the steps and out of the station. They didn't spy her hopping from darkened corner to darkened corner through Bryant Park, the sandwich kiosks and umbrella-shaded tables providing her with just enough cover to sneak by. Slowly and methodically, Echo made her way to the library's side entrance, to the nondescript metal door that deposited maintenance workers and staff into their preferred smoking space, a small, open-air alcove littered with flecks of ash and occupied by a green municipal trash can cum ashtray. Echo waited a beat before trying the handle. The door was usually left open for convenience's sake. Her best chance of entering the library unseen was the possibility that no one had remembered to lock the door on their way out as the area was evacuated.

All eyes were focused on Grand Central. Clusters of guards ambled warily up and down Fifth Avenue, but no one was looking at the library, a pale gray mass against the darkness of night. Echo allowed the guardsmen to pass. Twenty paces. Thirty. When she was confident their backs were to her, their ears comfortably out of range, she twisted the door handle and pushed. The door glided open without a sound. She said a silent prayer of thanks to whichever member of the custodial staff had seen fit to oil its hinges so recently. When the door closed behind her—locked this time—Echo was submerged in complete darkness. With her hands on the walls on either side of her, she felt her way through the narrow maintenance corridor, around a tight corner, then down a wider hallway. Even without the benefit of light, her steps were sure. These darkened corridors had been her playground her entire life; she knew exactly where she needed to go.

A few more turns, two more hallways, and she was in the library's foyer. The spotlights that illuminated Grand Central for rescue workers and the National Guard bathed the nearby streets so brightly that enough light angled through the glass panes of the revolving doors at the entrance to shine feebly on the polished white marble of the library's floor. The busts of wealthy patrons peered down at Echo from their lofty alcoves, their stone eyes silently welcoming her home.

Like every other building in Midtown, the library had been evacuated in a rush. The front desk, where a blue-suited guard normally inspected bags to make sure no patrons left with books, still held traces of his presence. A coffee mug sat on an open newspaper, the ink smudged and the paper wrinkled by a few stray droplets and a ring of moisture near the mug's base, a milky white film settled atop the now cold liquid. Loose papers had fallen to the floor as students had dropped their research like trees shedding their leaves in autumn. Dirty footprints marred some of the pages, the work trampled in the haste to flee. A small stuffed bear with threadbare stitching stared at Echo from the middle of the staircase leading to the second floor. Its forlorn button eyes were dark with loss. Or maybe Echo was just projecting.

On quiet feet, she made her way up the marble stairs, through the stacks, down the pitch-black hallways whose lights she dared not switch on. Echo had known returning home would be painful. She hadn't predicted just how heavy her heart would feel as she walked across the familiar white marble, how her eyes would sting with tears that didn't quite fall as she gazed up at the painted sky on the ceiling of the Rose Reading Room, a false daylight compared to the night outside. Never before had she been able to walk through the library so freely, secure in the knowledge that there was no one to stumble across her. No employees burning the midnight oil. No night guards roaming the reading rooms. It was just her and the silence of the library.

The ward on the staircase leading to her room pushed back at Echo, the resistance lasting only as long as it took for the spell to recognize its caster. With a prick of her finger and a whispering of words that had taken on a new meaning since the last time she'd uttered them, her hands wrapped around the hilt of the dagger stuck in her chest—"By my blood"—she opened the door.

She clicked on the fairy lights. The homesickness that struck her was so sudden, so overwhelming, that she thought she would choke on it. Things were mostly where she had left them. Mostly. Her living space was a prime example of orderly chaos, the kind that would look like a mess to an outsider but always made sense to Echo. And while the treasures on the shelves and the books littering her desk and nightstand and random bits of the floor were all in their proper place, they were neater than she'd left them. The stacks of books by her bedside weren't quite as precarious as they had been. The crumpled candy wrappers had been moved from the surface of her desk to the wastebin beneath it. Her collection of matryoshka dolls was now arranged in order of height on one of her shelves, from the largest on the left to the smallest on the right, their painted eyes staring straight ahead, all facing the same direction.

Someone had tidied up her room in her absence. And the only person who could have made it past the protective ward without permission was the one who had helped her set it up. The Ala. She'd been taking care of Echo, even when Echo hadn't been around to yell at her for moving her things or appreciate the silent act of maternal love that it was.

Echo pressed the heels of her palms to her eyes. *You will not cry. You will not cry. You will not* freaking *cry.*

There was work to do. There were things to steal. Monsters to fight. Mystery illnesses to cure. Tears were not on the agenda. Tears got in the way; they were an obstacle—and a sloppy one at that—and obstacles were exactly the type of nonsense Echo did not have time for.

But tears were stubborn, even more stubborn than Echo was, and when she pulled her hands away, they fell freely down her cheeks, obscuring her vision. What she wouldn't give to go back in time, to the days when things made sense and her primary concern in life had been picking out the right birthday present for the Ala. A presence fluttered at the back of her mind; it was like the ghostly equivalent of someone rubbing her back with a soothing hand. The sensation wasn't quite as comforting as Echo assumed the vessel—whichever one it was—intended it to be, but it had the effect of forcing her to overcome the swell of emotion that had gotten the best of her. She pieced her focus back together, steadfastly ignoring the ache in her chest.

Work to do. Monsters to fight.

Echo swung her backpack off and set about stuffing it full of everything she might need for the task ahead. Her second-best lock-picking kit—the best one had been confiscated by a Drakharin guard during her brief stint in a cell deep in the belly of Wyvern's Keep—a small flashlight, her compact book of spells, a pair of slim leather gloves, a handful of granola bars, and a map of London marked with tube stations and other spots from which the in-between could be accessed in case of emergency. In the mesh side pocket went a bottle of water, and in the front pocket she stuffed two pairs of socks. One never knew when one might need a clean pair of socks. Almost finished. She dropped to her knees and began rummaging around beneath her bed. Behind the army of footwear—boots and sneakers and ballet flats collecting dust—was a small metal banker's box, its contents protected by a rusted brass combination lock. Echo slid the box out from underneath the bed, dust tickling her nose. She thumbed in the combination: 0621. June 21. The date the Ala had found her in the library and brought her into a world of magic. The date she'd been given a new home, a new family, and, unbeknownst to either her or the Ala, a new purpose. Within the box was a small pouch, left untouched for years and reserved for only the direst of circumstances. A note written in Echo's own hand was stapled to the pouch:

IN CASE OF EMERGENCY, BREAK (METAPHORICAL) GLASS. If her current circumstances didn't qualify as a dire emergency, she didn't know what would. She replaced the box and rose to her feet, weighing the pouch in her hand. It was full of shadow dust, but she would still need to use it wisely. Gods knew when she'd be able to stock up on more.

Echo let her gaze roam around the room. The aim was to travel light, but she wasn't sure when—or if—she'd ever see her home again. She wondered what would become of this place if she never returned. Maybe the spell would wear off after a few years and some unsuspecting library worker would stumble upon a strange room full of strange things. Maybe they'd make up stories about the girl who lived in the library, unseen, passing through the stacks like a ghost. Maybe she'd become an urban legend, a tale passed down through generations of library employees to kill time during their breaks. But then, maybe she'd defeat the evil threatening to destroy everything she held dear and return triumphant to take up residence in a room that felt far too small to contain her. Wishful thinking, she knew. Things never quite worked out the way she wanted, and she had little reason to believe this time would be any different.

Looking again at her unzipped backpack, Echo was struck with a sense of longing. This couldn't be it. She couldn't leave here with a bag full of strictly utilitarian goods. If she was headed off to her doom, she didn't want to go alone. Not completely. She refused to further endanger the lives of the people important to her by staying with the pack, but she could not—would not—allow herself to forget that she was loved. She *mattered.* And she would carry the thought of those who cared for her with her no matter where she went or what she did.

Behind the orderly matryoshka dolls was a framed photograph—the only one on the shelves. The picture had been taken on Echo's sixteenth birthday, and it had been a point of contention between her and the Ala for months afterward. The Avicen had a strict policy against photography, but Echo had snuck a camera into the Nest that day, an old Polaroid she had salvaged from the library's lost and found after eyeing it covetously for the span of a full week, the maximum amount of time she waited before pilfering in case someone returned to retrieve their belongings. Ivy had once asked her why she bothered waiting. Echo was, after all, a thief. Echo had said that even thieves had codes of honor and Ivy had accepted the explanation with a roll of her eyes and a demand that Echo pass her a slice of pizza. But that birthday had been special. It hadn't been a "sweet sixteen" in the truest sense of the term—the Avicen, being a race whose people could live for centuries, didn't attach any particular significance to the sixteenth year of life. But Echo was human enough to want the milestone marked in some way. The Ala had arranged a dinner picnic in her chamber of all Echo's favorite foods and invited Ivy and Rowan and a few of the Avicelings who clung to Echo whenever she stopped by the Nest. They'd sat on cushions on the floor, eating macarons from Paris and mochi from Tokyo and sopaipillas from New Mexico. Echo had taken the photo on the sly. In it, Ivy and Rowan were arguing over the last macaron while the Ala rested her hands on the heads of two Avicelings who had fallen asleep on her lap, their bellies full to bursting, victims of a vicious sugar crash.

The Ala had seen the photograph on Echo's bookshelf the following week and told Echo to get rid of it. If someone were to find it, the Avicen risked the kind of exposure they'd avoided for centuries living beneath the streets of New York. Echo had refused. It wasn't until weeks later, when a frame had miraculously appeared to house the photograph, that Echo realized the Ala had forgiven her for taking it.

Echo removed the photo from its frame, careful not to smudge it. She opened a drawer in her desk, hoping she had some plastic sandwich bags left. The frame was too heavy to bring, but she didn't want the photo getting wet or otherwise damaged. At the back of the drawer was a box of ziplock bags she'd shoved in there, and she let out a sigh of relief when she found a single one left. She sealed the picture inside the bag. As she ran her fingers along the faces of the people she loved so dearly, a word came to mind, surfacing from the depths of her lexicon.

"Setsunai," Echo thought. *Japanese. "Bittersweet." "Painful." Used to describe a particular and untranslatable cruelty inflicted upon the heart.*

She might never see them again. The Ala might never wake up. Ivy might never get to yell at Echo for running off on her own. Rowan might never know how much he meant to her. A tear dropped onto the plastic bag, and Echo wiped it away. No time for that. None at all. She put the photograph into the front pocket of her backpack, but after a moment's hesitation, she removed it and zipped it into the inside pocket of her leather jacket. That was better. She would keep them close. Her backpack might be lost, but the only way she'd ever lose possession of her leather jacket was if she were dead.

She drew in a deep breath to steady herself. Swinging

her backpack over one shoulder, she bid farewell, not just to the hidden room that had been her home for ten years, but also to the girl who had lived in it. She was a different person now, and she would be even more different still if she ever returned. And if she didn't . . . Well, that hardly merited thinking about.

Echo cast a final glance around the room and, to no one in particular, said, "Goodbye."

CHAPTER TWENTY-FOUR

The two guards deposited Caius in his room and locked the door when they left. He had no doubt that they were standing on the other side of that door, probably flanking it like good sentries.

He took in his surroundings and remembered there was no window, which was hardly surprising. The Avicen would have been beyond foolish to allow him any opportunity to escape. He knew where the refugees from the Nest were hiding, and while he didn't know their exact numbers, he could easily estimate how many people the castle could hold.

The walls were covered in old tapestries. Dirty white unicorns pranced around fenced enclosures surrounded by laughing children who held ribbons aloft. A fine coating of dust clung to the textiles. When he touched them, his fingers came away covered in gray silt. Years of neglect had woven the dirt deeply into the threads. He doubted even the most diligent restoration work would be able to uncover the tapestries' lost beauty.

On either side of the room's cold fireplace were two neat circles in the dust on the floor. Caius assumed that two vases, removed prior to his arrival, had once occupied those spots. The metal ring on the wall beside the fireplace was similarly empty, the pokers and tongs confiscated by his hosts. There was a writing desk crammed into a tight corner, its surface bare. Other than the door, there was no escape from this small, oppressive room.

Rowan's words played in his head like a masochistic mantra. *If you don't mind, I'd like to talk to my girlfriend alone.*

"Girlfriend."

It wasn't a term the Drakharin used, but Caius knew its meaning.

With a sigh, Caius fell onto the bed, splaying his arms wide as he sank into the mattress. He lay there, cursing the gods in silence. He cursed the god of love for making him feel. How much easier life would be if his heart were stone, impervious to beauty and cleverness and bravery. He cursed the god of tragedy for raining it upon him while he soaked up misfortune like a thirsty field. If there had been a god of cruel irony, he would have cursed that one, too. Eventually, he slept, plagued by dreams of laughing gods and girls too clever for their own good.

Without the benefit of natural light, Caius couldn't tell what time it was when he heard the lock tumble open. He couldn't be bothered to get up, dignity be damned. The disks in his spine groaned as he turned his head to see who had come through the door, though the angle flipped the world upside down. Rowan stood before him, arms across his chest, studying Caius with a stony look as the guards closed the door.

"Comfortable?" Rowan asked, voice simmering with the coals of resentment he'd no doubt spent the night stoking. Caius couldn't really blame him.

"Quite." He made no move to rise. It was petty, and he recognized its pettiness, but he wanted to see how long Rowan would tolerate this stubbornness before he dropped the facade of hospitality.

As it turned out, not very long.

"Get up. We're leaving."

They took the servants' stairs so they wouldn't be seen. Most of the Avicen believed the Drakharin were behind the attack on Grand Central, and Altair did not seem eager to dissuade them of that notion. For the time being, Caius was to remain hidden, out of sight. The servants' corridors were dark, the air dank and cold. Their path was illuminated by an old-fashioned gas lantern that Rowan held aloft. There were sconces on the walls, Caius noticed, but without tapers to fill them. Altair was most likely conserving supplies. No sense in wasting perfectly good candles on a path trod only by a Drakharin, his guide, and the occasional pink-tailed rat. Avalon hadn't been occupied in decades, and the passageway was in worse repair than the residential sections of the castle. Somewhere nearby water dripped from a broken pipe. Moss had taken up residence on the walls, and Caius's boots splashed through shallow puddles that had collected on the floor.

Rowan remained taciturn as they walked. Tension sang through the line of his back, as taut as a bowstring. It would be wise, Caius thought, to let Rowan stew in his own hate. But lately, wisdom had a habit of failing him.

"She fought well," said Caius. He did not specify of whom he spoke. There was no need. They both knew.

Bowstrings could only be held taut for so long before they snapped. Rowan came to an abrupt stop, the lantern swinging in his grasp as he turned. "Don't."

"I am trying," Caius said, ignoring the voice inside screaming at him to hold his tongue, "to be nice."

The Avicen's eyes narrowed, eyes nearly black in the lantern's feeble light, and for a second, Caius saw the makings of the fighter Rowan could become. "I don't want you to be nice," Rowan said through gritted teeth. "I don't want you to talk. I don't want you to even look at me. My commander ordered me to collect you and Echo, and so that's what I'm doing, but we are not friends. We will never be friends." Rowan stepped forward, the toes of his boots nearly touching Caius's. The Avicen was a few inches shorter, but there was nothing small about him in that moment. Caius met his level gaze. The boy would make a worthy adversary for those who crossed him. Caius hoped he was as good an ally. But rivers could not be crossed without first building a bridge.

"It is not your friendship I require," Caius said. "Nor even your respect. But I want you to know that you have mine. You and your partner fought well the night we met. She died with honor."

Silence stretched between them. Even the persistent drip-drop of water from the broken pipe went quiet, as if it, too, could sense that the moment was a powder keg waiting to go off. A wrinkle formed between the Avicen's brows as an inscrutable emotion flitted across his face. He turned, offering his back to Caius, but he did not resume walking. They stood there, in tense silence, until finally Rowan said, "Ruby was three weeks shy of her eighteenth birthday. Echo has blood on her hands because she was trying to protect *you*." The final word was like a punch to the gut. Rowan half turned to Caius and said, "Tell me, what honor is there in children killing children?"

Rowan didn't wait for a response. Even if he had, there was none that Caius could give. He had been bred for war, fed a steady diet of tales of courage and heroism from the time he was a babe in arms. His destiny, he had been assured, was to find glory on the battlefield, to christen his blade with Avicen blood. And so it had been for his father before him, and his father's father. But these young Avicen were different. They lived in a world far less insular than the one that had reared Caius. They saw their lives as full of options beyond a brutal end in a war that did not have one. The injustice, in their eyes, was that they had inherited a conflict that had little meaning for them. To die at the hands of their enemies, Caius understood, was to die for nothing at all. They fought over territories that were never truly theirs and wouldn't be so long as they had to build wards to survive and hide like rats in a cellar.

Caius said nothing more as they emerged from the cramped darkness of the servants' stairs, through a doorway disguised to integrate seamlessly with the hallway's plain wood paneling. Rowan extinguished the lantern and hung it from a hook on the servants' side of the entrance for the next person lucky enough to spend time with the mold and the puddles and the rats. The hallway was empty, save for the Warhawk leaning against the wall by the door at the far end.

Her arms were crossed over her chest, and her head bobbed up and down with the inconsistent rhythm of a person struggling to remain awake.

"Fern," Rowan called. The Warhawk snapped to attention, her hand flying to the pommel of her sword when she saw Caius approaching. The movement was driven by pure instinct. She stopped herself before she drew her blade, but her eyes remained wary and alert, her hawklike gaze focused on the scales at Caius's cheekbones. He did not bother greeting her. His good intentions had antagonized enough Avicen for the day.

"Echo give you any trouble?" Rowan asked.

Fern shook her head, her eyes never straying from Caius. How strange it must be for them, to harbor a Drakharin in their safe haven. "She's been as quiet as a mouse."

That didn't sound like the Echo Caius knew. Rowan frowned as if he shared that thought and brushed past Fern to open the door. Caius followed him into the bedroom, Fern hot on their heels, peppering their backs with questions to which neither of them paid any attention.

The window was open. Gauzy white curtains fluttered in the morning breeze.

The room was empty.

Echo was gone.

"Shit," Rowan said.

"Shit," Caius agreed.

CHAPTER TWENTY-FIVE

Breakfast, Dorian thought, breathing in the bitter scent of his coffee—black, no sugar—really was the most magical time of day. Or rather, it would have been if a dark cloud hadn't been cast over the spread the Avicen had so generously provided by a warlock who insisted on picking at the food on everyone else's plate. Everyone but Dorian's, that was. Even Quinn's sense of self-preservation was too strong to risk such a thing.

Ivy nibbled on a piece of bacon. Her toast had long since gone cold, and Dorian sensed she didn't want to eat the bacon so much as she wanted something to do with her hands. She was nervous. Brave, but nervous.

"Kummerspeck," Ivy said, apropos of seemingly nothing.

"What?" Dorian asked.

"It's a word Echo taught me. It's German, I think. It means grief bacon." Ivy looked at the strip of bacon in her hands and then gingerly put it back on her plate. "Has something to do with eating when you're stressed."

Jasper spread a liberal amount of orange marmalade on his own toast, the scrape of the knife loud in the early-morning silence. He sat on the opposite side of the table from Quinn, who had flitted from chair to chair trying to sit next to Jasper before eventually giving up when the act became too farcical even for him.

"Vocabulary lesson aside, is there a reason why I was pulled out of bed at such an ungodly hour?" Quinn stretched his arms high above his head, arching his back with a drawn-out yawn.

Jasper swallowed his toast. "Everything about you is ungodly."

"No flirting at the breakfast table," Quinn said with a wink and a leer. "It's unseemly."

A slow flush crawled up the back of Dorian's neck. He pulled at his collar. It was the coffee. All that heat. Nothing to do with the self-righteous indignation brought to a simmer whenever Quinn was around. Nothing to do with that at all. He pushed away from the window and set his mug down on the edge of the table. Ivy knotted her fingers together in her lap. He laid an encouraging hand on her shoulder. It wasn't his style to be physically comforting, but Ivy had stopped flinching at his proximity months ago, and through close observation—gods, everything in that warehouse was close—he'd gathered that she benefited from minor acts of physical affection from her friends. Some people were huggers. Dorian wasn't, but he would lend her his strength any way he could. The Avicen guard in the corner narrowed his eyes, as if Dorian were committing some heinous act by laying his filthy Drakharin hands on a perfectly nice Avicen girl. Three measly months ago, Dorian would have agreed. Personal growth, Caius had called it.

"Mission briefing," Dorian said. "Once the others join us, we'll go over every final detail together, but for the time being, I wanted to go over the basics. Quinn will deliver you to Wyvern's Keep, then he'll rendezvous with Jasper and me in the woods nearby." He nodded at Ivy. "Once you make contact with one of Caius's loyalists in the keep and retrieve the information that we pray to all the gods will help us battle the kuçedra, we'll help you escape."

Dorian reached into his pocket to retrieve the item he'd spent the better part of the night preparing. It was a fragment of a mirror he'd shattered, rounded into an even circle with the tools Altair's men had scrounged up. He'd chipped off the colorful enamel finish from an old jewelry box scavenged from the castle's storage rooms and glued the pieces to the opaque side of the mirror. Viewed from the front, it looked like a simple pendant. The reflective back, however, was far from simple jewelry. He held it by its chain, dangling it in front of Ivy. "This is what you'll use to communicate with me once you're inside the keep."

Ivy accepted the pendant from him gingerly. "And how exactly will a necklace accomplish that?"

Quinn wiggled his fingers. "Magic."

Dorian counted to ten and bit back a stinging retort. The warlock wasn't wrong; Dorian just wished he'd be quiet. Preferably forever.

"Open the clasp," Dorian told Ivy. "Carefully."

A small needle, just large enough to prick the skin, was

hidden inside the clasp. Dorian drew his own blade and held it up to the light. Ivy watched him curiously.

"Prick your finger," he told her. "And press the blood to the mirror."

She grimaced but did it. A bead of her blood sat on the shiny surface for a second or two before the mirror absorbed it. The pendant was clean, as if it had never been touched. A drop of blood appeared on Dorian's blade.

Ivy froze, one hand wrapped around her thumb. "Whoa."

"The mirror is small," Dorian said as he wiped his blade clean. "So we'll have to use a limited means of contact. One drop for abort mission, two for proceed as planned. That'll be my sign to meet you at the rendezvous point to make our escape."

Ivy swallowed thickly. "What happens if I abort the mission? Will I just be stuck there?"

Dorian sheathed his sword. He liked the weight of it against his hip. It was comforting, like a child's blanket. "If I receive the mission-abort signal from you, I will storm the keep and slay every Firedrake that gets in my way."

Jasper muttered something unintelligible and began fanning himself with a paper plate.

Ivy's eyes widened. "That's insane, Dorian."

He shrugged, as if embarking on a suicide mission weren't at all out of the ordinary, even for him. "No one gets left behind. I'm taking point on this mission, and you are my responsibility."

With a roll of her eyes, Ivy said, "Thanks, Dad."

Dorian frowned. "I'm too young to be your father."

"Yeah, you're really not, though."

Quinn cleared his throat and made a nuisance of himself

as he bustled around the table, pouring coffee and stealing more bacon than was fair. "It's a cute idea," he said, "but count me out of the harebrained heroics." He graced Ivy with an insincere smile. "No offense, love. I'm not much for rescues."

Dorian inhaled a slow and steady breath. And exhaled. And inhaled. "If you have nothing else to add, Quinn, may I suggest you take your heaping plate of bacon and leave?"

Quinn popped a strip of bacon in his mouth and chewed thoughtfully. "Just curious, as I've been nothing less than helpful since the moment I joined this band of ragamuffin misfits . . . what exactly have I done to offend you?"

Dorian waited for Ivy to pull her hair-feathers to one side so he could clasp the chain around her neck. "Your existence offends me."

Quinn pouted. "That seems a bit harsh." He reached out to trail a finger along one of Ivy's feathers. She flinched from the contact, pulling the chain through Dorian's fingers.

"I don't like you," Dorian explained. "I like her." Quinn's starlit eyes twinkled with amusement. He wouldn't look so amused with Dorian's sword protruding from his gut. Considering the slime that practically oozed from the warlock's every pore, Dorian thought it was not beyond the realm of possibility that such a fantasy might become a reality. "If you do anything—and I mean anything—to put her life in any more danger than it will already be in, I will kill you."

Quinn smirked. "You could try."

Jasper stiffened, his golden eyes bouncing between the two of them like a spectator at a sporting match. The words brought a smile to Dorian's lips. They were an echo of the very taunt he'd used on Jasper the night they met, when he'd been half mad from blood loss. He was a different person now, he could admit that, but he was no less deadly. He leaned into the warlock's space, close enough to kiss. "Oh, I won't just try. I will hunt you down. No matter how fast you run or how far, I will find you. And I will make you rue the day your wretched mother brought you into this world."

Jasper let out a low, impressed whistle. "Da-a-amn."

Suddenly, the door flew open, its knob slamming into the stone wall. Rowan doubled over, breathing heavily as if he'd been running. Half a second later, Caius appeared next to him in the doorway, nary a hair out of place. Rowan sucked in a deep breath, his forehead beaded with sweat. "It's Echo," he rasped. "She's gone."

"Oh, for fuck's sake," Ivy said.

"Language," Quinn remarked, idly inspecting his nails.

No fewer than three people replied, "Shut up, Quinn."

"Somebody has to go find her," Ivy said. "What do we do?"

"Exactly what we're meant to," Caius said. "You four have your mission." He looked at Rowan, who returned his gaze with a steady one of his own. "And now we have ours. As you said, somebody has to find her, and I'm fairly certain I know where she's going."

CHAPTER TWENTY-SIX

Early-morning fog shrouded the winding streets of Edinburgh's Old Town. The castle rose on its hill high above, the tops of its battlements hidden from view. Echo slipped the cardboard sleeve off her latte and wrapped her hands around the cup, more for comfort than warmth. Compared with the muggy heat of New York in July, the less oppressive Scottish morning was a welcome reprieve. It was still a bit too hot for the leather jacket she wore, but a soldier never went without her armor. She leaned against the blackened stone wall of one of the tall, slender buildings lining the close that shot off the Royal Mile like a tributary off a great river—the one in which Professor Aloysius Stirling's office could be found. Her patience was running thinner than the weak gray sunlight that fought its way through the clouds, but she waited. Still and silent.

Echo glanced at her watch. Just a little after seven o'clock, the time that, according to Caius, the professor arrived at his office every day, without fail. She'd made sure to arrive early enough to scope out the street and caffeinate herself. In New York, it would be two in the morning, when all good Avicen—and a couple of Drakharin and a warlock—would be tucked in their beds. She had hours before anyone noticed she was missing. In theory.

"Come on," she whispered, wishing that her limited range of magic had the power to conjure the professor from the dense fog. "Come on, come on, come on." Her watch—a dainty relic that had languished at the bottom of her backpack for months—ticked away the seconds. Every one in which the professor did not stroll down the narrow street was one second closer to the discovery of her absence. Time was a resource she could not afford to waste.

Just as her hope began to dwindle—maybe the professor was sick, maybe he'd been hit by a car or struck by lightning or decided to change his routine for the first time in years—she spotted a figure turn the corner at the other end of the close, tweed hat ducked against the fog turning into drizzle, arms wrapped protectively around a stack of books. He was a short man, getting on in years, with white hair poking out from beneath his hat. Everything about him seemed professorial, from the glasses he pushed up his nose to the worn patches on the elbows of his jacket. He had to be Aloysius Stirling. Only an Aloysius could pull off elbow patches without the slightest hint of irony.

Echo pushed away from the wall, dumped her half-finished latte into a nearby wastebin, and made her way down the street. The professor—or the person whom she really, really, really hoped was the professor—turned the knob and entered the building. Echo quickened her pace, half jogging to catch the door before it closed. She made it just in time, sticking the toe of her boot into the doorway. The man jumped, startled by her sudden appearance, the pile of books almost tumbling out of his arms. He cleared his throat, seeming to collect himself. His jowls were flushed slightly pink, either in annoyance or anger.

"Excuse me, young lady," he said in clipped Scottish tones. "Are you lost?"

That was definitely annoyance. He looked at her the way one would look at dog droppings on one's shoe. She tried not to bristle at his appraisal. Echo might have forgotten to put on a clean, unwrinkled shirt before leaving Avalon, bigger things on her mind and all. She probably looked like a ragamuffin. A sleep-deprived ragamuffin.

"Are you Aloysius Stirling?" Echo asked.

The man's eyes narrowed in suspicion. "That all depends," he said, "on who's asking."

"My name's Rose." Echo had decided using a fake name was the safest option. The flutter at the back of her mind might have been a hint of ghostly laughter. Or it might have been her imagination. These days, it was hard to tell what was what.

The man who was most certainly Dr. Aloysius Stirling, professor of mythology and folklore, slid the stack of books from the crook of one arm to the other. He made as if to close the door in Echo's face. She didn't let him.

Caius had warned her that the professor was notoriously guarded about his research. It had taken Caius months to earn Stirling's trust, but Echo didn't have months. She barely even had hours. She needed a shortcut into his confidence.

"I'm a friend of Caius's," she said, pulling the necklace out of her shirt to display the dragon crest on the locket's face. The professor's eyes widened in recognition. Her gamble had worked. "And I need your help."

The professor's office looked like it was inhabited by a man who wore tweed jackets and matching tweed hats. It also reminded Echo, in a way that twisted at something inside her chest, of home. Teetering piles of books were scattered around the room, though from a cursory glance, she could tell there was some sort of order to the scholarly chaos. The professor's desk was so littered with stacks of paper its surface was lost to view. The tomes appeared to be arranged by theme, but not by any genres one would find in a traditional library. The shelf on the wall opposite the entrance was filled with volumes that covered every imaginable facet of bird-related mythology. Separated from that shelf by a window overlooking the narrow close was a bookcase crammed with texts on dragon folklore found throughout the world.

Stirling's demeanor had changed the second he recognized Caius's crest. He'd ushered Echo up a claustrophobic staircase, making profuse apologies for everything from the way the ancient wooden steps creaked to the absence of a functioning lightbulb in the corridor leading to his office to the fact that the kettle wasn't warming the water fast enough. She'd declined his offer of tea, but he was having none of it. She would have his tea and his hospitality, whether she wanted them or not. After all, a friend of the Dragon Prince's was a friend of his.

"I still can't believe you know about Caius," Echo said as she took the chipped mug of steaming tea the professor offered her. Earl Grey. A man after her own heart. With her free hand, she waved at the bookcases. "About them."

Stirling chuckled, a sound as warm and as round as he was. "Oh, dear, did you really think you were the only human who knew of their existence?"

"Yeah, kinda." Echo shifted uncomfortably. It was much too warm for the leather jacket. "Caius seemed to think you'd be able to help us with our kuçedra problem."

Stirling's gaze transformed from jovial to assessing. He gestured for her to take a seat and lowered himself into his desk chair. Echo sat on one of the chairs situated on the other side of his desk; the chair was old, and its cushion hid a deep divot in the middle into which she sank. Stirling twined his fingers together over his generous midsection. "You'll forgive me, my dear, but I'm going to need more than a locket with the prince's crest on it before I start divulging sensitive information."

So that was how he wanted to play it. Echo wasn't surprised. You had to give something to get something. Unless, of course, you stole it, but this was not a situation in which petty thievery would solve her problem. "What if I told you that you were right? The firebird is real. Caius found it."

A glint flashed in the professor's eyes that Echo knew well. She had felt it herself, once upon a time. When she'd found the dagger, and the locket, and the key. It was the sense of a truth clicking into place, the satisfaction of having a belief become a fact. But Stirling's excitement was short-lived. He schooled his expression into one of calm curiosity with a healthy dose of suspicion sprinkled on top. "As much as I would love to believe such a thing, once more I'm left with just your word to back it up."

Echo's grin came unbidden. She shouldn't do the thing. She *really* shouldn't do it. Doing the thing was a terrible idea. This man was a stranger, and Echo had only Caius's faith in him as evidence that he was trustworthy, but the winged beast curled up inside her longed to be free. Who was she to deny it? "I have proof."

Stirling harrumphed. "Now, this I'll have to see."

"O ye of little faith," Echo said. If only she were as confident as she seemed. She projected every ounce of desperation she felt into her hands, as if it were a tangible substance she could marshal to her will. *Please work, please work, please work.*

She placed the mug on the professor's desk, adding a new mark to the mess of watery, ringlike stains on its ancient wooden surface. Stirling was apparently not the sort of man who wasted time with coasters. Echo cupped her hands and focused. Pain blossomed at the base of her skull. It was minimal at first, like an unopened bud straining for the sun at the start of spring, but the closer her power rose to the surface, the greater it became, like that very same flower unfurling its petals.

Fire sprang to life in her palms. Stirling jumped, his knees banging loudly against the underside of his desk. Tongues of flame, as black as night, as bright as day, licked at Echo's skin. The fire warmed her hands, but they didn't burn as they had in the Black Forest. She'd only managed to use her power before when experiencing a violently strong emotion;

this level of control was entirely new. The ache in her skull spread, sparking behind her eyes like a migraine. She pushed through it, focused on the magic churning in her palms.

"Sweet mother of god," Stirling whispered. One hand clutched at his waistcoat, above his heart, while the other fumbled a pair of spectacles from his breast pocket. It took him two tries to get the glasses on his face. "It's real," he breathed. His eyes reluctantly strayed from the black and white flames in Echo's hands to her face. He stared, agog. "You're real."

Echo sighed, letting the magic slip from her grasp. The fire died and her headache abated. She rubbed the back of her neck, where a dull throbbing lingered. "As real as they come." She picked up her mug and took a dainty sip of tea. "I think it goes without saying that if you speak of this to anyone—and I mean anyone—I will burn down everything you love. *Capisce?"*

Stirling was still staring at her hands, as though he could conjure forth more flames if he only wished hard enough. "Yes, yes," he said. "Of course."

"Now," Echo said, kicking her feet up onto Stirling's desk and crossing them at the ankles, "I believe you had some supersecret information to share."

"Remarkable," the professor muttered. He took his spectacles off and began wiping them with a monogrammed handkerchief that had seen better days. "Just the physics of it . . ."

Echo waved her hand in front of his face. His head snapped up, startled. "Professor?"

He shook himself as if coming out of a particularly vivid dream. "Right, right. The, uh, sensitive information." He cleared his throat and straightened his waistcoat. "Well, I'm afraid it's a long story and it doesn't necessarily cast me in the best light." His smile was a little shy, but also a little self-aware. "You see, I'm afraid I'm a bit of a misfit."

Echo offered her own smile in return. Caius was right about this one, she thought. He was okay. "Then you're in luck. Misfits are my kind of people."

CHAPTER TWENTY-SEVEN

Twenty years ago, before Echo was even a twinkle in her parents' eyes, Dr. Aloysius Stirling had been one of the most esteemed professors in the department of archaeology and anthropology at the University of Cambridge. Admission to his seminars was highly sought after, and his colleagues had nothing but kind words to say about the man who knew how each of them took their tea and could discuss the collected fairy tales of Charles Perrault with the same alacrity he possessed when lecturing on the early anthropology of Claude Lévi-Strauss.

All his colleagues save one.

Every hero needed a villain, and in Stirling's case, his antagonist was Dr. Walter Forsythe, chair of the department and known skeptic. While the rest of academia seemed content to take Stirling's eccentricities in stride—it was one thing to discuss fairy tales and another thing entirely to believe they were real—Forsythe would have none it. There was also, Stirling admitted, the small matter of the dalliance he'd had with Forsythe's wife, but, as he insisted with a flippant wave of his hand, that was neither here nor there. The real difference between the two men was competition of another sort.

"You see," Stirling said, lowering his voice and leaning over his desk, as if there were anyone around to overhear their conversation, "Forsythe had his eyes on my research. We both specialized in the cultural development of ancient societies, but I was always one step ahead of him." Another harrumph. "The only reason he became department chair was because he was better at rubbing elbows and playing politics."

Echo nodded sagely, as if she knew the first thing about elbow rubbing or politics playing. "Is that so?"

The professor straightened as though his spine were offended on his behalf. "Oh, I assure you, Walt had it in for me from day one."

"Or maybe he was just mad you boinked his wife," Echo mumbled into her mug. Stirling, lost in the hypnotic rhythm of his own narrative, didn't appear to hear her.

"Forsythe wanted me out, but thanks to the peculiar magic of tenure, he couldn't very well sack me and call it a day. No, he was a tricky beast. He used his not insignificant influence to make me look like a crackpot. That wily old toad cast aspersions on my good name."

"Aspersions?" Echo gasped. "He didn't."

"He did. Walt wanted me to look bad. He discredited me, smeared my reputation every chance he got, at every conference, every retreat, to every publication that would listen to his self-important blithering. He made it so no one wanted to publish me. He suspended my classes at the university, put me on indefinite leave—involuntary, I might add. But worse than all that, that great bloody bastard stole my research."

Stirling took a breath, steeling himself for a continuation of his tirade. From the top drawer of his desk, he withdrew a red tin, removed the lid, and offered it to Echo. "Biscuit?"

Echo plucked a Scottish shortbread from the tin. It was a tad stale, but still buttery and delicious. She knew she ought to put something in her stomach that had a main ingredient other than caffeine or sugar, but shortbread had the word "bread" in it, which meant it was practically healthy. Stirling helped himself to a biscuit and they sat in companionable silence for a moment before the professor remembered his outrage. "Right," he said, brushing shortbread crumbs off his waistcoat. "Where was I?"

"That great bloody bastard had just stolen your research," Echo supplied.

The embers of old wounds ignited in Stirling's eyes, stoked by years of simmering resentment. "It happens more often than you might think in the brutal world of academic blood sports, stealing research. Forsythe has done a damn fine job of keeping it from me ever since. And these were primary sources, never duplicated."

Now, thievery was something Echo understood. "Why didn't you just steal it back?"

A look passed across Stirling's face that was at once seething hatred and begrudging respect. "That no-good, deceitful"—his accent thickened as he let loose a string of profanities unique to the Scottish-English dialect, which Echo desperately tried to hoard in her lexicon of insults—"hid those texts very well. In a place I couldn't hope to access."

"Where's that?"

"The British Museum."

Oh. It had been months since Echo had broken into an institution of such magnificence, but she was sure she'd slide right back into it once she shook the metaphorical dust off her skill set and the literal dust off her tool kit. Just like riding a bike.

"Forsythe," the professor continued, "was offered the position of director shortly after my fall from grace. He likes tormenting me." Stirling took an extremely resentful sip of his tea. "Our paths crossed several months ago at a conference in Glasgow, and he took great pains to make sure I knew exactly where he'd hidden my papers."

Echo leaned forward in her seat, tea forgotten. This was it. The starting line. She needed a direction to run in, and Stirling was about to provide her with one.

"He put them in the Enlightenment Gallery. Under glass. Surrounded by alarms and the watchful eyes of museum guards. But they're there."

"Are you sure Forsythe was telling the truth?" Echo asked. She needed Stirling to be absolutely sure. There was no room for error. Not with Caius and Rowan and Altair hot on her heels and a monster made of shadows hunting her down.

The professor gazed forlornly into his cup of tea. His missing research might as well have been a lost love. "Sometimes, the truth is the very best weapon in one's arsenal," he said, "for nothing cuts deeper than brutal honesty."

Echo wasn't entirely sure they were still talking about missing books, but a lead was a lead.

Stirling sniffed haughtily and took another shortbread from the tin. "Forsythe knew the worst thing he could do to me was wave the jewel of my literary collection right in front of my face. And since he'd done such a thorough job of assassinating my character, no one would believe accusations of misconduct leveled at him by a nutty old crackpot like yours truly."

"What exactly *was* the jewel of your collection?"

"The only surviving copy of the 1838 folio edition of Phineas Ogilvy's *A Compendium of Fairy Tale Creatures,* complete with all two hundred thirty-five pages of copperplate etchings and watercolor illustrations." Wistful longing stole across Stirling's expression. "Oh, they were the finest illustrations you've ever seen. Such delicate watercolors. Finer than anything done by Audubon himself."

It sounded like precisely the kind of book Echo would have loved to hoard in her library room. "But what's so special about it? Does it have any info that'll help me?"

Stirling's smile brimmed with mischief. "No, as beautiful as the illustrations are, they're largely the work of the imagination. Though the page dedicated to the firebird might be relevant to your interests," he added with a wink. "The treasure you seek won't be found in the folio's pages, but in its spine."

"The spine?" Echo asked. "You hid something inside it?"

Stirling clapped a hand to his heart. "You have no idea how it pained me to do so, but the nature of my research into Avicen and Drakharin mythology was of such a secretive nature that I had to become creative with my hiding spots. Forsythe had cracked the safe I kept in my office—the rotten little slug—but I knew that no one would ever suspect me, the greatest fan of Phineas Ogilvy's work, to deface the most valuable text in his impressive oeuvre by removing and subsequently replacing its bindings."

Clever. Echo was fast warming to Stirling's particular brand of insanity. "What did you hide?"

"A map I had never been able to decode. It's written in a language so ancient, I was unable to decipher it."

A map. Echo never wanted to see another one of those as long as she lived.

The professor rummaged through the chaos of his desk, pushing aside piles of paper scrawled with illegible notes, notebooks so battered it was a miracle that their pages weren't spilling out of them, and glossy photographs of what appeared to be ancient texts, full of scribblings that pulled at Echo's memory. Though she couldn't read Avicet, much less antiquated forms of it, she recognized the swirls and slashes. All those years spent riffling the Ala's bookshelves had instilled at least that much knowledge in her.

"Ah, here we go." Stirling held a photograph with both hands, reverently, as if it were as fragile as the torn papyrus it depicted. "This," he said, pointing at a line of text near the bottom of the papyrus, "is a reference to a sacred place in both Avicen and Drakharin mythology. I discussed my findings with the prince—nice young man, that one—and as far as we were able to surmise based on context clues from the rest of the text, it's some kind of burial ground that dates to a time before the schism. The map in the spine of Ogilvy's folio shows its location."

"The schism?"

"The schism, or as some translations would have it, the partition. Or the rendering. All those sentiments are captured in the original language. It was the definitive division between the Avicen and the Drakharin. The birth, some say, of the firebird and the kuçedra. The starting point of the war."

"But I was told no one could remember exactly when or why the war started."

"No one alive, perhaps." Stirling set the photograph down gently between them on the desk. He got up and stretched, the buttons of his waistcoat hanging on for dear life. After putting the kettle on to boil again, he started pacing the room, hands in his pockets. Echo was ready to scream at him, to demand that he get on with it, when he finally spoke. "Everything I've come across in my research tells me there's something significant about that mystery location. It's tied to the events of the schism somehow. There are precious few archaeological sites that can shed light on the history of the Avicen and the Drakharin. They're both very good at leaving behind few traces of their presence."

"Mage fire," Echo whispered. It was how the Avicen and Drakharin cleaned their messes up. The Ala had explained as much when Echo asked how magical races had existed undetected by humanity for so long. The graphic descriptions of its usage had haunted little Echo for weeks.

"Come again?"

Echo shook the memory loose. "Nothing." She stood and brushed shortbread crumbs from her jeans.

Always such a sloppy eater, came a voice at the back of her head.

Shut up, Rose.

"If you don't mind my asking," Stirling said, "what do you plan to do with this information?"

"Isn't it obvious?" Echo said as she collected her belongings.

Her time in the professor's office had been a much-needed reprieve, but she had work to do. "I'm going to break in to the museum and steal the folio. Or at least what's inside it."

Stirling's hands fluttered as he crossed the room to pick up a green pitcher with a long spout on the windowsill. Echo got the feeling that he needed something to do with his hands to still their nervous movement. It must have been one hell of a folio. "Oh, do be careful with it," Stirling said.

"I will be," Echo said. "Scout's honor." She slung her backpack over her shoulder. "One more thing?"

The professor looked up from his watering of a half-dead fern. "Anything for a friend of Caius's."

"Don't tell him I was here."

Stirling froze, the water sloshing over the sides of the fern's earthenware pot. "Well, he is a dear friend of mine. . . ."

"It's for his safety," Echo said in a rush. "I might be heading into some dangerous situations, and I don't want him to follow me."

Clutching the pitcher to his chest, Stirling hesitated. "Oh, I don't know. . . ."

He was so close to agreeing. She could taste it.

"Please," she said. "I don't want him getting hurt."

Sometimes, the truth is the very best weapon in one's arsenal.

"Oh, all right, then." He mimed zipping his lips closed. "Mum's the word."

Echo smiled, surprised by how genuinely it came. "Thank you."

"And for the record," Stirling added, returning to his plants, "Walt's wife never loved him anyway."

CHAPTER TWENTY-EIGHT

Ivy had never been to Scotland as anything but a captive. She'd never felt the need to visit, not just because it had a reputation for being cold and damp, but also because all Avicen knew it was off-limits. There were parts of the British Isles that were relatively safe; London was too massive a city for the Drakharin to patrol—they were far more insular a people than the Avicen, and as far as they were concerned, the fewer dealings with humans, the better. But Scotland? That was their seat of power, and had been for hundreds of years. Few Avicen set foot on Scottish soil and lived to tell the tale. Ivy had defied the odds once. She wasn't entirely sure she'd be able to do it a second time. She shivered, though the grayish afternoon sunlight in the Highlands was warmer than she had thought it would be.

Quinn's hand on Ivy's arm was firm but oddly gentle. Perhaps, she thought, he'd taken Dorian's warning to heart, but when she felt his warm breath stir her hair-feathers as he leaned down to whisper in her ear, she knew that threats were not something that struck fear into his cold, dead heart.

"Frightened?" he asked, the smile she couldn't see evident in his voice. The question was rhetorical. She was shaking, and it had nothing to do with the weather; it was a full-body tremble, from her feet to her shoulders, and she knew the bastard could feel it.

"Of this place?" she said, jerking her head at the portcullis before them. The gaping maws of two stone dragons were situated on either side of the gate, reminding Ivy of gargoyles. Their fangs were sharp and their eyes seemed to follow her as she walked over the wooden drawbridge, which had conveniently been left down. The people inside Wyvern's Keep knew she and Quinn were coming, and had probably known for some time. The plan was, after all, to simply walk up to the front door, subtlety be damned. She fought to still her trembling. "Please. Been there, done that, got the T-shirt."

The words were such slim bravado, a page torn from Echo's book. How could she not be frightened? For herself. For Echo—wherever she was. For her Avicen brothers and sisters, dead, dying, banished from their home. In the span of a few months, the world had become a very frightening place.

Quinn snorted, disturbing Ivy's hair-feathers once more. She jerked her head away from him, and he laughed, tightening his grip on her arm. "None of that, now," he said. "You're supposed to be my prisoner, remember?" His fingers dug into her muscle painfully, and she winced. "Act like it." He released the pressure, but the warning was clear. It wasn't just her life at stake. If the Drakharin knew they were being deceived, Quinn's head would roll, just as surely as hers would.

They reached the gate. The bridge might have been left

down, but the gate was still shut, its points nearly scraping the arched entryway. The courtyard on the other side was empty, but Ivy spied movement in the shadows. They were not alone. And they were being watched. One of the slim windows above the portcullis darkened. It was a thin, rectangular hole cut into the stone, just wide enough for an archer to fire an arrow through it. Drakharin archers were the stuff of legend. Bedtime stories designed to frighten little Avicen children were full of them. Supposedly, they never missed. Ivy hoped she wouldn't have the opportunity to find out if the reality measured up to the myth.

The keep's battlements soared high into the cloudy sky, impossibly tall from where Ivy was standing. She gulped, feeling the contents of her stomach roil with her rising anxiety. "So," she said, "do we just ring the bell?"

There wasn't a bell, but if Ivy had learned anything from ten years as Echo's best friend, it was that sometimes the best way to handle a crisis was to quip one's way through it.

As soon as she'd finished her sentence, the gate started to descend, more silently than she would have expected. Behind her, she could feel Quinn straighten. It was showtime, and Quinn, she had deduced in their brief time together, was nothing if not an expert showman. "I don't think that'll be necessary," he said. "Our welcome party has just arrived."

In the courtyard, figures materialized out of the shadows. They wore simple leather tunics bearing the insignia of the Dragon Prince on the chest. It took two of them to pull open the massive wooden doors at the far end of the courtyard. Ivy's blood chilled as she caught sight of a familiar form, silhouetted by the firelight inside. Tanith stepped through the open doors, her scarlet cloak draped over a gown of golden silk, flanked by half a dozen Firedrakes in full armor. Halfway across the courtyard, she stopped and waited, her blond hair moving slightly in the breeze. Her silence was terrifying.

Quinn pushed Ivy forward, and she stumbled, her stubborn feet refusing to comply. The warlock showed little mercy as he pulled her along, his grip on her arm as tight as a vise. "I've come bearing gifts," he called out, his voice echoing across the courtyard.

As they drew closer to Tanith and her guards, Ivy's heart fluttered in her throat. She was afraid she might vomit. And wouldn't that be a shame, to puke on Tanith's lovely golden gown. The thought made Ivy giggle, and even she could hear the hysteria that colored it. Tanith arched an elegant eyebrow, her crimson gaze inscrutable, and the laugh died in Ivy's throat like an open flame doused with water.

"I believe there was mention of a reward," Quinn said as they came to a halt two yards from Tanith. He was playing his role well. Too well, Ivy thought. Not for the first time, the incongruity of the situation hit her. She was entrusting her life to someone who was, by all accounts, not to be trusted. "An accomplice of the firebird," he continued, "in exchange for enough riches to make the pope blush."

Quinn released Ivy's arm and shoved her toward Tanith. Ivy hadn't realized until that moment how much the warlock's touch—abhorrent as it was—had anchored her. Now, presented before the most fearsome person she'd ever had the misfortune to encounter, she felt alone, small, weak. Like a frightened animal. If she had a tail, it would be tucked between her legs. The fact that she kept her feet under her was a minor miracle. Her body was quaking so hard it felt as if her skeleton would shatter. One of the Firedrakes to the rear of the group caught her eye. It could have been her fear-addled mind playing tricks on her, but Ivy could have sworn he nodded at her almost imperceptibly, as if to encourage her to stand her ground.

"And who are you?" asked Tanith, her eyes drifting from Ivy to Quinn. On anyone else, it would have been a lazy gesture, but the new Dragon Prince's gaze was sharp. She was calm, but she missed nothing, not a single detail.

Quinn stepped forward, placing himself even with Ivy. He bowed deeply, head dipped low in reverence. "They call me Quinn, Your Grace."

Tanith scoffed. "Save your bowing for someone else." She stepped closer to them, and Ivy bit her tongue. Better to focus on the pain rather than the terror. She needed to do something to prevent herself from falling victim to panic. Quinn straightened. Tanith's hand shot out and grasped his chin, turning his head from side to side, studying his features. Quinn bore her appraisal with uncharacteristic silence. "You're a warlock," she said.

Quinn winked. At Tanith, of all people. Ivy wondered if he had a death wish. "The eyes aren't meant to deceive, my lady. The effect is merely to enhance. I take no shame in what I am, so I see no need to hide it."

"Of course you don't. I would think shame would be one of the first of many traits sacrificed on your path to power." Tanith took a step back and dipped her head in Ivy's direction. Two Firedrakes seized Ivy's arms, bracketing her between their considerable bulk.

"To the dungeon?" one of them asked. Ivy was surprised at how young his voice sounded. It was the one who had maybe nodded at her. But then again, maybe he hadn't. It was entirely possible that fear was causing her to hallucinate. The mention of the dungeon, where she had spent several lonely, maddening days before being rescued by Caius and Echo, made her head feel strangely light.

Tanith met Ivy's gaze and held it for a brief, silent moment. Eventually, her lips curled into a small smile. "No," said Tanith. "Prepare the uppermost room in the tower." She stepped closer, her cloak brushing the toes of Ivy's shoes. Tanith stared down at her—she was taller than Ivy remembered—and continued, "Bring the warlock to the great hall. We'll discuss the terms of his reward there. And then I'll head up to the tower to join our guest. Perhaps the little bird will sing if she's comfortable. My preferred methods proved so disappointingly fruitless last time."

Ivy supposed that was a nicer way to say that being tortured hadn't worked so well. A swell of pride surged through her, but it was quelled when Tanith reached out to cup her chin.

Her next words pierced Ivy like shards of ice. With another cruel smile, Tanith added, "Welcome back, little dove."

CHAPTER TWENTY-NINE

London, to Echo's surprise, was beginning to feel a bit like home. She'd gone straight from Edinburgh Waverley station to King's Cross, emerging from the blackness of the in-between through a rarely used utility closet. Wisdom dictated that she should have hopped from station to station by way of a scattered path across the globe, muddling her tracks to make it that much harder for anyone to follow her through the in-between, but shadow dust was not an infinite resource. Conservation was key. A rare surge of gratefulness went through her for all the days she'd learned to live on little before the Ala—

No.

She couldn't let herself think about the Ala. Couldn't let her mind stray to places where she would find only pain. She had to focus on the task at hand, and the task at hand was navigating the rush-hour crowd in one of the world's most notoriously busy rail stations. Hopefully, it was busy enough that she would be nearly impossible to find. A needle in a stack of needles, as it were.

Hands in her pockets, Echo passed besuited men and women hurrying to catch their trains, gaggles of tourists taking pictures of the high glass ceilings above the National Rail tracks, and harried Underground employees barking into walkie-talkies held in one hand while pointing out directions for the lost with the other. In the station's main concourse, a small queue was forming, where both children and adults had stopped to photograph themselves pretending to push a half-submerged luggage trolley through a wall. The smell of Cornish pasties wafted from a nearby stand, reminding Echo of her empty stomach and her even emptier wallet.

As soon as she stepped outside the station, the familiar scent of London assaulted her. Every city had its own smell, some more noxious than others. New York in the summer was all sweat and asphalt, with the occasional whiff of hot garbage. London's atmosphere almost always held the promise of rain, even on clear days. It wasn't humid the way New York was, but then few places were. It was more like there was always a reprieve from the summer heat on the horizon and you knew you wouldn't have to wait too long to experience it.

Echo's path was a straight shot down Tottenham Court Road and a left at Great Russell Street; then she came upon the British Museum.

Standing on the sidewalk, facing the building's Greek Revival facade with its massive Ionic columns framing the front doors and its pediment depicting the progress of human civilization, Echo realized that breaking into this vaunted institution was going to be far trickier than strolling into the Met with Caius at her side.

It was an hour until opening, and the dark, imposing gates—spiked at the top to discourage plucky heroes and curious youths from scaling their heights—were still closed. Echo weighed her options with care. She could try to find an entrance that would allow her to access the in-between, but her knowledge of the museum layout was scant to say the least. The last time she'd visited, two years prior, Rowan had been at her side. The museum had been showing an exhibit of drawings on the grotesque. Rowan was dismayed to find the show had more of a scholarly bent than he desired. It was a little too much *Temptation of Saint Anthony* and not enough graphically envisioned viscera. The only thing to catch his eye had been the "mermaid" in the Enlightenment Gallery, which was actually just the upper half of a monkey sewn onto the bottom half of a fish. In the great scheme of things, Rowan wasn't terrifically difficult to please.

With her supply of shadow dust running low, Echo would have to be crafty about entering the museum after hours. The time she'd bought herself by leaving Avalon in the dead of night was rapidly dwindling. Echo shoved her hands in her pockets and huffed out a breath. Waiting might be the death of her. As if she hadn't already died once.

After sunset, Great Russell Street was relatively quiet. A few stragglers wandered past, on their way toward the much busier Tottenham Court Road. Soon enough, the street was empty and Echo was alone. Now all she had to do was climb the fence—which was going to be harder than it sounded—find a way in that didn't involve shadow dust, disable the guards, and locate the book Stirling was certain Forsythe had hidden in plain sight.

Echo took the gloves out of her backpack and pulled them on. The palms had a rubber grip that would make scaling the gate that much easier. She tied her leather jacket around her waist. She'd be needing it shortly.

It was not the most graceful of climbs. There weren't any convenient footholds halfway up, and more than once, she slid down the wrought-iron rails before figuring out how to leverage her weight between them. She shimmied up until she reached the top, her eyes level with the spiked golden finials. With one hand and both legs clinging to the rail for dear life, she unwound her jacket from around her waist, said a quick prayer to whatever deity cared about garments, and draped it over the top of the fence. It would pain her to tear holes in the jacket, but it would pain her more to tear holes in herself. With a mighty heave, she swung one leg over the top of the fence. Getting down, she thought, would be a million times easier.

Easier, that is, if it hadn't been for what she saw rounding the corner. Two people—men, judging by their height and considerable bulk—approached, their forms outlined in the streetlight near the corner. Atop their heads were the unmistakable hats that marked them as London police.

Echo's leg slipped, the denim of her jeans slick against the iron rail. She flung herself over the fence, snatching her jacket as she tumbled, and landed on the museum side, her bones rattling with the force of the fall.

Everything hurt. Echo forced herself to scramble into the bushes, hoping that, combined with the relative darkness of the evening, they would be enough to hide her. Her body would be one giant bruise in a few hours, but she'd gotten over the fence, albeit not quite the way she'd planned. The police officers' footfalls approached. She held her breath. The pouch of shadow dust was in her pocket. If they spotted her, she would have to run to the gate's entrance and hope that it had enough magic stored from all the people entering and leaving the museum to operate as a threshold to the in-between.

The sound of the officers' chatter grew louder. "—and then she said I wouldn't know real romance if it bit me on the arse!"

Manly chuckling, and then: "You reckon she'll take you back?"

More chuckles. "She always does."

They passed by Echo without so much as slowing down. She let out a shaky sigh, her rib cage aching from the movement of her chest. She poked her head out of the bushes. The coast was clear. With a final glance around the museum's plaza and the street beyond the fence, she jogged toward a side entrance. She'd seen employees using it during the day, mainly maintenance workers. If she was going to sneak in unnoticed, it was a far less conspicuous option than the front door.

A siren wailed as a fire truck sped down a nearby street. Echo stared at the locked door. Had it been a simple lock—even a dead bolt—getting through would be a breeze. She'd yet to meet a lock she couldn't pick. But the key-card reader beside the door presented an interesting dilemma, its illuminated red dot mocking her. The author of the book of spells she normally relied on for heists hadn't seen fit to include a chapter on disabling electronic card readers. Once inside, she knew how to disable the security cameras and induce temporary sleep in the guards, but she wasn't sure the same spell would work on the door. She drummed her fingers against the plastic, worrying her bottom lip between her teeth. If only she could cut the power to it . . .

Sparks burst from Echo's fingertips. She yanked her hand back instinctively, but it wasn't burnt. A smile tugged at her lips as she rubbed her fingers together. The little red light blinked off as curls of smoke rose from the card reader. Securing her backpack more tightly around her shoulders, she opened the now unlocked door and went through it. She pulled it shut behind her, submerging herself in darkness, and entered the museum.

CHAPTER THIRTY

Ivy had expected to be kept in the dungeon. Now, as she took in her accommodations, she was glad that the cage chosen for her was a luxurious one. Decorated with fine silks and plush carpeting, the only real indication that the room was a prison were the bars on the bay window, and even those could be hidden by a heavy velvet curtain. The window was open, and the smell of the sea reached her, a faint hint of salt and ocean spray flavoring the air.

"I hope the room is to your liking," the Dragon Prince said. Tanith's voice still held the rhythmic, rolling accent of the Drakhar language even though she spoke English for Ivy's sake. "I want this visit to be more pleasant than your last."

Visit. As though Ivy hadn't been kidnapped and carted off half unconscious like a sack of potatoes by warlocks sent to ransack Perrin's shop in the Agora. As if she hadn't been forced to listen to Perrin's torture and his final shuddering breaths. As if Tanith hadn't used pain to extract information from Ivy that she didn't have.

Ivy didn't acknowledge Tanith or turn to look at her. She couldn't face those bloodred eyes or the self-satisfied smirk on Tanith's face or the fire-bright gleam of her golden armor. Not yet. Instead, she continued to catalog her surroundings. The bedroom was decorated with the detached elegance of a guest room. The spacious bed was enveloped by a deep green damask canopy heavy enough to block out the brightest morning light. In front of the stone fireplace was a small sitting area with a divan upholstered in aubergine velvet and two high-backed chairs with curving arms and matching footrests. A mahogany table sat in the midst of it, a silver tea set atop it.

It was the highest room in the keep's tallest tower. Ivy felt a little like a princess in a fairy tale, one of the dark, twisted ones. Her room may have been outfitted for comfort, but it couldn't be more clear that she was a prisoner, not a guest.

She turned to face her captor. Tanith cocked her head to the side, blond hair falling in soft waves over armored epaulets. Ivy opened her mouth. And closed it again. She was too afraid to speak. Tanith cut a terrifying figure and knew it.

"I'm afraid we got off on the wrong foot," said Tanith. She clasped her hands behind her back, perhaps in an effort to look harmless. It didn't quite work.

The inanity of the comment was too much to stomach. Ivy found her voice at last. "You tortured me." The words came out stronger than she herself felt. She held tight to her anger. It was better than being afraid. " 'The wrong foot' doesn't even begin to cover that."

Tanith was silent for a moment, eyes narrowed as if

assessing Ivy's mettle, and Ivy fought not to wilt under that gaze. "I would apologize for that, too, but we both know that would be a lie," Tanith finally said. "I did what I believed I had to do. I will not ask for your forgiveness, nor do I expect it. I merely hope that you and I may come to an understanding."

"And what sort of understanding would that be?"

Tanith strode across the room, coming to a halt in front of the fireplace. She dragged a finger over the mantel, then inspected it as if looking for dust. Caius was a bit of a neat freak; maybe the character trait was genetic. "Contrary to what you believe," Tanith said, "I don't like to cause pain. If pain is the most efficient way to bring about a desired result, however, I will inflict it as I see fit."

"You don't have to threaten me," Ivy said. "I know what you're capable of." For a moment, she could almost feel the burn of Tanith's fire again, held so near to her feathers that they singed. The smell of that had lingered in Ivy's memories for weeks. "I remember."

Tanith turned her gaze to Ivy. "You have no idea what I'm capable of. What I did to you was nothing." The effort it took for Tanith to soften her voice was obvious. "But our situations have changed. It wouldn't be in my best interest to hurt you now. Or kill you."

"I didn't think my life mattered to you at all," said Ivy.

"In the greater scheme of things, it doesn't. I've slaughtered hundreds of your kind. Your death would be but a drop in an ocean. But there is someone who cares if you live or die: the firebird. Your demise would be devastating to your friends."

"If you're looking for information, I won't give you any. Unlike you, I don't betray the people I love."

Tanith's smile was tight-lipped. Ivy hoped her words had hit close to home. She couldn't hurt Tanith with weapons or fists or swords, but words . . . words she could use.

"You see," Tanith continued as if Ivy hadn't spoken, "killing the firebird wouldn't have accomplished anything other than removing a piece from the chessboard. But I don't want that piece removed, I want it in play. And I want it at my mercy. I cannot force Echo to cooperate by threatening her, but I can use you to persuade her. She is a brave girl, I'll give her that. She faced me in the Black Forest with the courage of a seasoned warrior."

Tanith turned toward the door, sweeping her cloak behind her. "But love makes us uniquely vulnerable." Something flitted across the Dragon Prince's face, too fast for Ivy to comprehend. "I'm relying on the firebird's love for you to trump that steel will of hers." The door opened as though the guard on the other side had some sort of sixth sense. Tanith glanced back at Ivy. "In three days' time, you will be escorted to the courtyard through which you entered the keep, secured to a stake with chains as thick as your wrist, and set alight by my own fire."

Ivy's stomach dropped as if she were standing aboard the deck of a ship in danger of capsizing. An execution. Tanith was planning her execution. Ivy had known she was walking into the viper's nest, but she hadn't expected a fatal bite to come so quickly. She swallowed past the thickness of her suddenly dry tongue before speaking. "Why three days?" she asked. "If you're just going to kill me, why wait?"

Tanith smiled, slow and satisfied, as if Ivy's fear were exactly the succulent snack she'd been craving. "It's not that I particularly *want* to kill you, little bird. But I want Echo to believe that I will. And I need to give the news time to reach her ears so she'll come running to your rescue. She doesn't fear death. Not her own. But yours? That she fears." With that, Tanith stepped through the door, one hand tapping a jaunty rhythm on the knob. "I'll have some food sent up. You've had a long day. You must be hungry."

Before Ivy could muster a reply, Tanith was gone. As the door closed, its lock turning with a decisive click, Ivy caught a glimpse of a single guard. She must not be seen as enough of a threat to merit more than one. And why *would* the Dragon Prince see her as anything but a means to an end? A wriggling worm on a hook designed to draw out bigger prey. To Tanith, Ivy was barely a pawn in this game, an inconsequential piece that could be sacrificed with few consequences. To Tanith, Ivy was nothing.

A trembling hand rose to clutch the pendant at her neck. Its thin edges dug into the flesh of her fingers. In three days' time, Ivy would be dead. Three days.

With a ragged exhalation, she released the pendant, her fingers aching but now steady.

Three days.

Three freakin' days.

It wasn't much, but it would have to be enough.

CHAPTER THIRTY-ONE

The maintenance entrance of the British Museum let Echo into a pitch-black hallway, where she promptly knocked over not a single broom but a small army of them. She groped wildly, hoping to catch at least one or two before they fell, but the handles danced out of her reach and clattered to the floor, the sound of wood hitting marble echoing through the corridor. She cringed.

Well, that was certainly one way to announce her presence.

Shlemiel, she thought. *Yiddish. "Someone likely to spill a steaming-hot bowl of soup at dinner."*

The beam of a flashlight slashed through the dark. Echo ducked behind several boxes of cleaning supplies, the smell of disinfectant tickling her nose.

The security guard holding the flashlight called out, "Who's there?"

With a silent curse, Echo began the spell she'd used a

hundred times before. She traced an Avicet rune on the floor, the lines and swirls summoned from sheer muscle memory. "By the shadows and by the light," she whispered furiously, "may I pass beyond all sight. From here to there, as quick as air, as I will it, so shall it be."

With each word uttered, she felt the power of the spell rising within her. She concentrated on the words, on the way they felt in her mouth, on the sounds they made in the shadowy stillness of her hiding spot. The symbol she had traced with her finger appeared on the marble floor, glowing with a faint white light.

Huh.

That had never happened before.

The symbol faded as quickly as it had appeared. Motes of light danced in the air before her and dispersed, like the delicate seeds of a dandelion in the wind. The flashlight cut out, and a second later, Echo heard the thump of the guard's body as he slumped to the ground, overcome. The green light on the security camera near the ceiling faded to black.

Echo's head began to ache from the spell's magic. It was a small price to pay, and if it was the worst thing she had to deal with in the museum, she'd count it as a blessing. Maybe things would be easy from here on out. Maybe she would find what she needed; figure out a nice, bloodless way to stop the kuçedra; heal the Ala and the others stricken by its dark poison; and be home in time for supper.

But then again, maybe her next trial was simply waiting to spring when she least expected it. Because that was just how her life tended to work.

Echo rose, dusting herself off, and headed down the corridor to the Great Court, at the museum's center.

Schlemazel, she thought, feeling along the wall to find her way in the darkness. *Also Yiddish. "The person likely to have the steaming-hot bowl of soup poured on her."*

Dr. Walter Forsythe, according to Professor Stirling, kept meticulous records of every book under his purview and guarded the collection of texts in the Enlightenment Gallery, formally the King's Library, with the tenacity of a mythical dragon protecting a trove of treasures.

Unfortunately for Dr. Forsythe, the safeguarding of the current King's Library had not been designed to withstand magic the kind of which Echo was ready and willing to wield. Nobody ever saw her coming. That felt like a superpower in itself.

The exit of the maintenance corridor opened into the museum's central hub, the Great Court. Echo stepped over the guard, mindful of the flashlight that had tumbled out of his hand as he fell into his sudden slumber.

Even at night, the Great Court was resplendent. The soaring glass roof let in just enough light to illuminate the triangular panes that created a curving, dome-like effect. Echo kept her footsteps quiet, though the chances of her being discovered were slim. Every guard and security camera in the vicinity would be out of commission.

She passed through the Great Court and entered the foyer near the main entrance. The Enlightenment Gallery was on her left, and if the memory of her first time in the British Museum after hours served, the door was locked at night. But this time, the door was partially ajar. Hushed voices came from the room, too quiet for Echo to pick out words. She tiptoed closer, pressed against the wall so she would be out of sight of whoever was speaking. Everyone should have been asleep by now. That was how the spell worked, and it had never failed her before.

There were at least two people, maybe more. She crouched to slip the dagger from her boot and then inched forward, straining to hear the conversation. The voices fell silent.

She could wait, but the spell she'd cast wouldn't last forever. And she'd come too far to turn back now. Whoever was in there must have known she was coming—she could only hope they didn't know exactly what she'd come for. Either way, she would have to fight them for it. Echo steeled herself and laid a gentle hand on the door.

Now or never.

She sprang forward, pushing the door open and staying low. People had a tendency to aim at chest level when caught unawares, and she had no clue what kind of weapon her adversaries were armed with. Hopefully, if they pulled a trigger—literally or metaphorically—any shots would go right over her head.

The door bounced off the wall. No shots came. No arrows were fired. The gallery interior was dark save for the light from the blue-tinted spotlights that illuminated the building's facade. Marble statues so white they seemed to glow cast eerie shadows on the bookcases lining the walls. Near the front of the room was a fireplace full of neatly arranged logs meant purely for show.

And leaning against either side of the mantel, not looking the least bit surprised to find her there, were Caius and Rowan.

Caius cocked his head to the side, his grin almost lost to shadow. "We really need to stop meeting like this."

With a groan, Echo rose. "Really? You had how many hours to come up with a good opening zinger and that's what you went with?"

Rowan rolled his eyes. "That's enough, both of you." He cast a look at the dagger in Echo's hand and frowned. She wondered if he recognized it. The last time he'd seen it, it had been protruding from between his Warhawk partner's shoulder blades. But if he did recognize it, he neglected to say anything other than "I don't think you'll be needing that."

Echo relaxed her grip on the hilt. "Guess not." She knelt to slide it back into its sheath, pulling her pant leg down to hide the tip of the pommel sticking up from her boot. "How were you unaffected by the spell?" she asked. "It should have knocked you both out."

They both reached into their pockets and produced two identical pouches with an Avicet rune scratched into the leather. Rowan shook the contents of his pouch into his hand, revealing a chunk of amber, a few seeds, and the head of a spoon that had been snapped off its stem.

"Protective charm bags," he explained. "Remember that time you brought me here and showed me how to do the spell?" Echo nodded. Rowan poured the ingredients back into the bag and said, "Well, I got curious and looked up counter-spells after that. Turns out all you need to repel an attack like that is some amber, a couple of quince seeds, and, for some reason, a spoon. Something about deflecting the spell from the wearer. We made these in a bit of a rush, but they did the trick."

Seeing Caius and Rowan together made Echo's head hurt almost as badly as performing magic had. It wasn't right. They belonged to two separate worlds—Rowan occupied one bubble in Echo's landscape of *known associates* and Caius another. It wasn't as bad when they had a buffer of other people between them, as they had at Avalon, but now it was just the three of them. Echo would have sold a kidney for another person—preferably Ivy, with her naturally soothing presence—to make the situation less awkward. You really only needed one kidney anyway. The sound of a throat being cleared cut through the darkness.

"So," Rowan asked, "what are we looking for exactly? The professor was either unwilling or unable to cough up that bit of information. He just told us where to find you and made us promise not to hurt you or steal anything else from the museum." In an atrocious Scottish accent, he added, "Knowledge is meant to be shared."

Echo sighed. There would be no outrunning them. They were far too stubborn for that. There was a lot of work to do and precious little time in which to do it. "I'm looking for"—at Caius's quirked eyebrow, she amended her statement—"*we're* looking for a book."

Rowan raked a dubious glance across the bookcases that spanned the not inconsiderable length of the room. "Well, that really narrows it down. There are hardly any books in here at all."

There were thousands of books, all safely nestled behind glass.

"It's a folio," Echo said. "*A Compendium of Fairy Tale Creatures,* written and illustrated by Phineas Ogilvy." She clapped her hands. "Better get to work." *And split the two of you up.* As it was, she was surprised they'd lasted as long as they had without killing each other.

The three of them searched the shelves, peering through glass at hard-to-read titles. Echo was beginning to despair of ever finding the book when a triumphant shout came from Caius's corner of the room.

"Found it," he said, pointing through the glass at a large leather-bound folio.

Echo made short work of the lock on the bookcase. She slipped the volume out, sliced through its binding with her dagger, and eased the spine away. A piece of paper, folded many times over to fit inside the spine, fluttered to the ground. Caius picked it up and carefully unfolded it.

"What does it say?" Echo asked, peering over his shoulder. The map wasn't like any she had ever seen before. There didn't appear to be any landmasses or passages marked on the parchment. Instead, all she saw was a jumble of pictographic symbols arranged in concentric circles. "What do those mean?"

"I'm not entirely sure. . . ." Caius held the paper up to the shaft of moonlight that fell through the high windows. As soon as the light hit the page, the shape of a continent appeared. Echo caught her breath. A rounded eastern shore and a collection of familiar curving islands off the coast—it was Asia. In the upper right corner a stone bridge suspended between two mountain peaks slowly came into view.

"Brilliant," Caius said softly. "Ink that appears only in moonlight. It's a beautiful bit of magic."

Faint lines glowed on the page, connecting segments of the intricate pictographic symbols.

"It's Chinese," Caius said.

"You can read Chinese?" Rowan asked.

"Yes."

"Of course you can," grumbled Rowan. Echo elbowed him in the ribs.

Caius ignored them both. A wrinkle formed between his eyebrows as he concentrated, mouthing words silently. Finally, he said, "It's a reference to the Tian Shan mountains in northwest China." He traced a line of text and read aloud: "'Where all things begin, so must all things end. The cradle of life is a pyre come death.'"

"Creepy," Echo said. "What does it mean?"

"Humans call the range the Tian Shan mountains. In Drakhar, they are called *Amrydalik ker Darask.* It means 'Beginning's End.' It's a sacred place in both Drakharin and Avicen mythology. I've heard of it, but in all my time hunting the firebird, I never came across anything that would make it seem relevant." Caius pointed to the drawing of the bridge. "And this is how we're going to get there."

Echo clapped him on the back, harder than she meant to, and he almost dropped the map. "Nice work." Her eyes fell to the folio on the table beside them. Space in her backpack was at a premium, but it didn't look that heavy. And one good deed deserved another.

"What are you doing?" Rowan asked as Echo slide the folio into her backpack. "Didn't you say you had a rule about not stealing books?"

"It's not really stealing if you're returning something to its rightful owner," Echo explained. She zipped up her backpack and put it on. The extra weight was hardly noticeable. She left the gallery, Rowan and Caius following her through the door and into the concourse. Thousands of people came through here every day. The veil to the in-between should be thin. "If we live long enough to make it back to Scotland, I'm going to return it to Stirling." She reached for both their hands. Caius saw the request in her eyes and nodded. "Buckle up, boys. We're going to China."

CHAPTER THIRTY-TWO

They emerged from the in-between on a short, narrow stone bridge, suspended hundreds, quite possibly thousands, of feet above the ground between two soaring peaks. Echo barely had time to appreciate the feeling of something solid beneath her before the wind knocked one of her feet off the bridge. She fought for balance, arms flailing. A hand shot out—with the wind whipping her hair into her face, she couldn't see whom it belonged to—grabbed her arm, and yanked her back onto the bridge. She collided with a broad, solid chest.

"Almost lost you there." Caius's voice rumbled against her ear. His tone was light; if it hadn't been for the rapid rise and fall of his chest, Echo wouldn't have known he was ruffled in the slightest.

She peered over her shoulder and immediately wished she hadn't. From where they stood, the ground wasn't even visible. All Echo could see were thick ribbons of fog pushed along by the wind that screamed between the mountains like a vengeful god. An arched entryway was cut into the mountainside on either end of the bridge. Chinese characters were carved above both arches. One of the entrances was sealed with heavy rocks. The other opened to the blackness within the mountain. It was as if someone had blocked the bridge off to ensure there was only one way to go.

"Can you read it?" Echo asked, gesturing to the inscriptions.

Caius tilted his head toward the eastern door. "Those are the characters for 'death' and 'rebirth.'" Turning toward the doorway on the western side of the bridge, he added, "And those are the words for 'light' and 'dark.' I think we're in the right place."

Behind Echo, a throat cleared. She turned to find Rowan standing there with a frown on his lips and a disapproving look on his face. "If the two of you are done canoodling, I believe we have an ancient temple to find."

"I do not canoodle," Caius shot back.

Echo stepped backward, careful to keep both feet on the bridge. It was about three feet across and maybe fifty feet long. Ancient ropes swung on either side, but the security they provided was flimsy at best, deceptive at worst. They wouldn't have held her weight if she had stumbled against them. Their presence would have mocked her as she pitched over the side and plummeted to her death. The wind continued to buffet her, an insistent reminder that the threat of an ignominious death by winding up as a splat on the earth in the middle of nowhere in China was still a very real possibility.

"Nice landing spot you picked, Caius," Echo said. "Remind me to never trust you with anything ever again."

Caius shrugged. "We're on a mountain. Our options were limited." He nodded to Rowan. "But you're right. No time to waste." Looking toward the western door, he added, "This way." He spun on his heel, heading into the mountain's cavern through the western arch. She watched him go, unwilling to face Rowan and his judgmental stare. As it was, she could still feel his irritation bristling at her back even if she couldn't see his expression.

"He just assumes people will follow him, doesn't he?"

Echo turned. Rowan, hair-feathers snapping in the wind, met her gaze with a glare that she realized was only partially intended for her. His anger, it seemed, was spread evenly between her and Caius. A silver lining, perhaps, if a rather slender one. At least she wouldn't have to bear the brunt of his bad mood all by herself.

"He was a prince for a hundred years, Rowan. I guess he got used to it." She took off down the bridge, toward the archway through which Caius had disappeared. A particularly strong gust of wind slammed into her, eager to hasten her demise. *Not today, Mother Nature.*

She stepped through the archway. Her ears roared with the sudden silence, as if they missed the wind's wild howling. She looked back. Rowan was still standing on the bridge, but he wasn't looking at her. His gaze was on something in the distance, or maybe on nothing at all. His brows were drawn tightly together. It was his thinking face. A death trap of a bridge wasn't the best place for contemplation.

"You coming?" Echo asked.

Rowan started as if lost in his own little world. "Yeah," he said, hastening down the bridge. Echo couldn't help but notice that he had a much easier time keeping his balance than she did. Added bulk. Had to be. He caught her eye and smiled. For a moment, it felt like old times, even if she could see telltale signs of how forced the smile was: the tightness of his jaw, the way the smile didn't quite reach his eyes. But he was trying, in his way. He gestured for Echo to head down the stairs first, in the direction Caius had gone, deeper into the mountain. "Lead the way, firebird."

A winding staircase led them down into the mountain in near darkness. Echo switched on her flashlight as the last of the light from outside disappeared. The beam flickered, then died. Caius cursed as his met with the same fate. They were still near the top of the stairs, the mountain's darkness punctured only by the light slipping through the opening that led to the bridge. Unease settled deep in Echo's gut. She'd never been afraid of the dark before, not the way children tended to be. But then, she'd never had reason to fear the shadows until she discovered the kind of monster that could hide in their depths.

Echo smacked the side of her flashlight with her palm. The batteries managed to emit a final, weak beam of light before dying. For good. Her feet were glued to the top step, Caius a few feet below her, Rowan at her back. "Why won't the flashlights work?" Her voice echoed in the cavernous space, bouncing off the walls and down the stairs. "The batteries were brand-new."

"It's the magic," Caius said, voice barely above a whisper, and reverent, as if he were standing on holy ground. "It's strong here. Can't you feel it?"

"Not really sure I want to feel it, to be perfectly honest," Rowan muttered.

Caius shushed him. "Close your eyes. Listen."

Fear spiked through Echo. An irrational, primitive sort of fear. The kind her Neolithic ancestors must have felt in the dead of night when they could hear predators lurking. The darkness was complete enough that she didn't think closing her eyes would make much of a difference, but there was a slim chance Caius knew what he was talking about. He was older, after all, though Echo wasn't sold on the wiser part of that equation. But she complied, squeezing her eyes shut.

"Listen," Caius whispered again.

Echo listened. At first, she heard nothing but the sound of her own breathing, the quiet susurration of Rowan's jeans as he shifted position behind her, the thumping of her heartbeat in her ears.

And then she heard it.

No. Not *it*.

Them.

It would have been easy to mistake the noise for wind rushing through the opening at the top of the stairs, but there was a strain of something else, something sentient, woven through it. The sound was like a thousand voices whispering in distant rooms in tongues too ancient to be understood. Echo recognized stray phonemes here and there. There was the guttural rumble of Drakhar consonants, the lilting melodies of Avicet, quickly spoken and heavy on the long vowels. But it was like trying to make sense of Old English. The words were familiar, but still foreign. She strained to listen, to catch as much of the whispers as she could, but their overlap combined to create a single buzzing sound, like wind through densely packed trees.

"What the hell is that?" Rowan asked. His voice interrupted the whispers like a rock thrown into still water.

"The dead," Caius said.

"Like ghosts?" Rowan's voice cracked on the second word. Echo sympathized. She had enough dead people in her head. She wasn't keen to add to her tally of unwelcome voices.

"Yes," Caius said. "Like ghosts."

"Well, shit." Rowan's boots made a scraping sound on the loose pebbles as he took a few steps toward the entrance. Was he leaving? He couldn't leave. Not now. Not because of some ghosts.

Echo turned to catch him and drag him back, but all she managed to do was pivot into the poke Rowan had aimed at her back. His finger dug into her ribs, right in her most ticklish spot. She jumped and nearly lost her footing.

"What the hell was that for?" she asked.

"Two things," Rowan said. "One, you're the firebird." He waved something in her face that looked, in the dim light, like a club. "Make fire." When Echo didn't immediately do so, he sighed. "It's a torch, dummy. There were two on either side of the door."

Oh.

"I'm not a dummy," Echo mumbled, reaching for the torch. "You're a dummy."

Caius sighed, very loudly and very pointedly.

Echo did not acknowledge his obvious disdain, but she did what Rowan asked. She made fire. Her fingers trailed up the length of the torch as she focused, imagining what the end result would be. A dull knot of pain formed at the base of her skull, but she ignored it. It was weaker than the ache she'd felt at the British Museum. This was a much smaller act of magic, but Echo preferred to think she was getting stronger. That she was in charge of the power and not vice versa. A tongue of flame burst from her hands, leaping to the head of the torch in black and white sparks. Upon contact with the old, fraying linen wrapped around the torch, they turned the bright amber color of a normal fire. The brightness of it was so sudden, Echo's eyes watered.

"There," Rowan said. "That's better. I knew I kept you around for a reason." His smile was tight, but he was trying to act like nothing had changed. Like they were the same people they'd been months ago. They weren't, but Echo didn't begrudge him the fantasy.

She did the same with the second torch and passed it to Caius.

"You said two things. What was the second thing?"

Rowan swallowed, as if unsure whether he should say the thing he was about to say. "The ghosts," he started. "The voices. Are they anything like your voices? You know, the ones in your head."

Echo had never told him about the voices. The Ala must have shared that bit of information. When the Ala awoke, they would be having words. "When you put it like that, you just make me sound like a crazy person," Echo said. "But no, not really. These voices are like listening to an old record. It's a little fuzzy, a little distant. It's almost like the white noise between radio stations. There are words hidden in the sound, but I can't make them out." She tapped the side of her head. "These voices are crystal clear when they want to be."

"Like Rose?" Caius asked. His tone was free of inflection, his expression carefully neutral. He'd be a great poker player. But Echo wasn't fooled.

"Yes," she said, not unkindly. "Like Rose."

He nodded briskly and turned away. Echo suspected he didn't want her to see the look on his face. She let him have his privacy. The light from his torch reached only a few feet below them, as if whatever awaited at the bottom was swallowing it.

"Onward and upward," Echo quoted, mostly to herself. "To Narnia and the north."

"We're walking down a staircase," Rowan said as they followed Caius down the spiraling steps. "If anything, that would be south."

Echo smiled, genuinely glad to have him around, even if the wounds between them had yet to heal. "Shut up, Rowan."

CHAPTER THIRTY-THREE

Ivy whiled away the hours reciting the names of herbs and their uses. Crushed mugwort was good for burns and minor skin irritations. Mixed with a bit of honey, it could fade bruises. Burdock root to treat toxins in the blood. Pokeweed extract to relieve inflammation of the joints. She sorted through her knowledge as if she were flipping through a catalog, watching the sun descend, its light diffused by fog.

True to her word, Tanith sent food. The same Firedrake who had nodded at Ivy in the courtyard delivered her evening meal. Twisting the hem of her sweater in a white-knuckled grip, she watched him enter, arms laden with a tray topped with silver domes. He set the tray on the low table in front of the fireplace, glancing at Ivy, who sat curled up on the window seat. Black hair fell across his forehead, brushing the tops of his eyebrows. His eyes were nearly the same color as his armor, pale yellow at the edges and darker gold near the pupil. He offered her a small smile. "You have to eat something," he said in halting Avicet.

That took her by surprise. She hadn't expected a simple soldier to know the Avicen tongue. Caius did, but he was a nerd. Ivy tightened her arms around her shins, watching him over her knees.

"The food is not—" He hesitated, tripping over the words. "There is no—" He gestured helplessly at the tray, muttering something in Drakhar.

"Poison," Ivy supplied in Avicet. It was her first tongue, but the Avicen at the Nest had taken to raising their young bilingual. It was hard to live in New York—even underground—and not speak English. Even now, the word felt strange in her mouth. It had been so long since she'd spoken Avicet to another person. The Ala had tried to force lessons on her, but as Ivy grew older, she discovered a growing list of reasons to slack off.

The Firedrake smiled at her, a little sheepishly. Like Caius, he had a smattering of scales on his cheekbones that angled up toward his temples. They were faint in the dim morning light, but the dying fire in the hearth caught their slight iridescence. His face lacked the aristocratic angles of Caius's; it was a soft face. A kind face. "Poison," he repeated. His accent was terrible.

"I see," Ivy said in English. Could this be her contact? The phrase Dorian had taught her settled on the tip of her tongue, but she couldn't bring herself to say it out loud. What if she was wrong? It was meant to be an innocuous phrase, one that would fly under the radar if need be, but if she came off as suspicious in the slightest, then she might not even have three whole days left before she got a little friendlier with a burning stake than she ever wanted to be.

"You speak English?" The Firedrake sagged with relief. He rubbed the back of his neck. "I was worried. My Avicet vocabulary is pathetic, to be honest."

Ivy didn't find his linguistic shortcoming the least bit surprising, but she said nothing. Outside, the fog slowly descended on the water, like a curtain falling after a show. Ivy's view was interrupted by the harsh black bars on the window. She caught her lower lip between her teeth and sent a silent prayer to the Avicen god of good fortune.

"You can trust me," the Firedrake said softly. His gaze held hers for a minute, as if he was trying to communicate something without words. He reached into his scarlet cloak and pulled out a white napkin folded into a bundle.

"I heard the Avicen have a taste for sweets," he said, settling the small bundle on the edge of the tray.

Ivy met his eyes once more, searching their sunshine-yellow depths for any hint of malice or deception. She found none. Earnestness seemed to ooze from his pores. Ivy pushed herself off the window seat, her knees creaking from having been in one position for too long. Shaky legs carried her across the room. She knelt beside the table, sinking to the floor with a dull thud, and unwrapped the napkin. Cradled in the white linen was a small cake in the shape of a flower, glazed with honey and topped with slivers of almond. She popped the cake in her mouth to buy herself time. Nerves tied her stomach in knots, threatening to reject the sugary sweetness. She could do this. It was this or the stake.

The Firedrake lingered. Ivy wiped the crumbs from her mouth, suddenly self-conscious. "Thank you," she said.

"Tanith's gone," he told her. "For a few hours, at least." Running a hand through his dark hair, he took in the room. He seemed a bit awkward. Shy, even. "I told the guard on the door I'd take his shift." His smile was a tiny bit crooked. "He's got a girl down in the kitchens he never gets to see. And I think maybe you and I have something to discuss."

Ivy stared and tangled her fingers together. This was it. The Firedrake was either Tanith's clever way of finding out if Ivy had ulterior motives or he was Ivy's man. Only one way to find out.

He smiled again, as if to encourage her, and she hated how she noticed the way his left cheek dimpled but his right didn't. When he spoke, he kept his voice low, even though there wasn't supposed to be anyone listening in on the other side of the door. "My name is Helios."

Helios. Like the Greek god. It suited him. His hair was black as the midnight sky, but his eyes were a bright yellow, like the crayon a child might use to color the sun. He was dressed in what Ivy now recognized as a less formal version of the Firedrake armor. Gone were the gilded metal and the fancy braided epaulets. Instead, he wore dark brown leather armor—it looked thick enough to provide protection from glancing blows while allowing for ease of movement that full armor would prohibit. A crimson cloak was fastened about his neck with a golden pin in the shape of a dragon coiled in on itself to form a circle, wings tucked close to its body.

Ivy closed her hand around the pendant and wished for a certainty she knew she would never feel. She settled on the small sofa, and Helios followed suit. He was silent, waiting for her to speak. She thought of the phrase Dorian had told her to say when she was confident that she had found someone trustworthy.

Despite the fact that the sky had been as cheerful as a slab of granite for the past three days, Ivy looked at Helios and said, "Lovely weather we're having."

She waited, hope and anxiety churning her stomach. Her nerves were so frazzled and her heartbeat so loud that she almost missed his response.

"I'm sure the gardeners will appreciate it," said Helios.

That was it. The response Dorian had told Ivy to expect. Standard call-and-response, he'd said. Relief washed over her, so powerful that it felt a bit like drowning.

"We have to move quickly. Caius"—Ivy paused, noting the way a crease of confusion formed between Helios's brows—"the former Dragon Prince," she amended, "hasn't abandoned you. He wants his people to know that their prince is with them, and that the firebird is on their side."

Her wording was deliberately vague. Saying the firebird was on their side wasn't necessarily the same as saying the firebird supported the Drakharin in the war, but Caius had stressed the need for a "flexible truth," as he called it. It wasn't entirely false, but it felt like a lie—yet even Ivy had to admit that swaying enough Drakharin to form an alliance with Echo and the Avicen to defeat Tanith would be easier if they got the full story from Caius directly, and not some Avicen prisoner.

Helios nodded. "I can do that."

"And we have to get me out of here before Tanith kills me."

"Yes, let's avoid that."

"Dorian is close and he'll come to help get me out, but we have to move fast." Ivy pictured the map Dorian had drawn for her, the one she had stared at for hours while the others were sleeping, a small tea light her only illumination as she committed each twist and turn in the labyrinthine tunnels beneath Wyvern's Keep to memory. There was the possibility that Helios would know the way to the tunnel opening at the back of the keep, but she didn't want to divulge that detail just yet. He could be a triple agent, for all she knew, pretending to work both sides. If she divulged her escape route and was wrong about him . . . then there would be little chance she'd live to see sunrise.

Ivy reached behind her neck to undo the clasp on the pendant's chain. On its mirrored side were two red dots: Dorian's message, written in his blood, asking if she was okay. She swiped her thumb over them and they disappeared, clearing the way for her response. She pricked her finger on the tiny needle hidden inside the clasp and dabbed two drops of blood on the mirrored side. They soaked into the glass and disappeared. Dorian would receive her message; she had made contact. Now all she had to do was risk life and limb to find and abscond with valuable information on Tanith's schemes and escape the keep. No big deal.

"Here," she said, offering the pendant to Helios. "Dorian told me to pass this along once I'd used it to contact him so we can get messages into the keep without anybody else having to be kidnapped."

"I'll see that it gets to who it has to get to," Helios said as he accepted the pendant. It disappeared into the folds of his cloak. Part of Ivy wanted to snatch it back—without it, she had no way to contact Dorian. Its absence left her even more vulnerable than before, but a plan was a plan, and she had sworn that she would stick to this one.

Helios seemed to pick up on her anxiety. He took her hand in his and gave it a quick squeeze. Ivy's pulse thudded in her throat. "It'll be okay," he said. "You're going to get out of here. I'll come back for you, I promise."

He stood up and made his way to the door.

But Ivy needed to know one thing before she let him go. "Why are you doing this?"

Helios turned to her. He was silent for a few moments before he said, "I was there. When Tanith called the vote."

Caius hadn't talked about that night much, and Ivy had been left to wonder about the turn of events that had led to him on the run and Tanith on the throne.

"Most of the nobles voted for her," Helios continued. "I think they were afraid. Some abstained and a few brave souls even voted against her."

"What did Tanith do to them?" Ivy asked. She almost didn't want to know.

"She lined them up in the throne room and asked them, one by one, if they were interested in changing their votes."

"And did they?"

"Some did. Some didn't. When she got to the end of the line, she set them on fire with a snap of her fingers. Every single one of them." Helios swallowed thickly before continuing. "I'll never forget the way it smelled."

"But if they changed their votes, why did she do it?"

"She said there was no room in her court for those of questionable loyalty." Helios twisted a bit of his cloak in his hands. "I watched them burn. And I did nothing."

Ivy hugged her knees to her chest, appetite forgotten. She couldn't wrap her head around how wretched it must have been to see people you knew burned alive for daring to stand up for what they believed in. The world was full of cruelties, both small and large, but Helios's story was a special kind of terrible.

"There was nothing you could have done," she said.

"Strange how that doesn't make the guilt go away." Helios met her gaze, his eyes shining like liquid sunshine. "That's why I'm doing this. Because I did nothing before, and I can do something now."

With that, he left. And all Ivy could do was wait.

CHAPTER THIRTY-FOUR

Dorian sucked in a deep breath, relishing the crisp night air. The woods near Wyvern's Keep smelled like home. After months of being cooped up in a London warehouse, the scent of the forest was a relief. He brushed his fingers against a tree, tracing the cracked veins in its bark. He and Caius had ridden through these woods so many times. They would skulk out of the keep alone, without the retinue of guards that normally accompanied the prince outside its walls. Dorian had objected the first time Caius had proposed they sneak out unguarded, but the prince was persuasive. It hadn't taken much to whittle down Dorian's defenses. A pleading look, a pout that Caius would never admit to, a promise that they would be gone for only an hour, and Dorian was putty in the prince's hands, just as he'd been since the moment they'd met.

He cast a backward glance at the Avicen and the warlock following him through the thicket near the lake. Quinn had rejoined Dorian and Jasper after delivering Ivy to the keep, which took longer than Dorian had expected. Quinn claimed Tanith had taken her sweet time negotiating the terms of his reward, and Dorian grudgingly admitted that it was precisely the kind of pettiness he'd expect from Tanith. Jasper was less than pleased at the prospect of a night spent in the woods, but they had little choice but to approach the keep on foot. Should they try to reach the keep through the in-between, alarms attuned to the wards around its outer walls would announce their presence and a contingent of Firedrakes would be on them in minutes. Dorian had overseen the establishment of the wards himself. He knew their strengths. They were sound, but no fortress, not even Wyvern's Keep, an imposing stone edifice that had stood unbreached for centuries, was impenetrable so long as one knew where to look.

"Dorian," Jasper whined as he slumped against a tree, "are we there yet?"

Quinn sidled up beside Jasper, exasperation written in his every weary move. The warlock hadn't broken a sweat despite their daylong trek through the woods, but his patience appeared to be running thin. "Jasper, I swear to every god in every pantheon, if you ask that one more time, I will hex you."

Jasper stuck out his tongue. Quinn responded with a lecherous wink.

"Keep your wand in your pants, warlock," Dorian said. "We'll make camp here for the night and proceed in the morning. Patrols don't run through this part of the forest." Or at least they didn't as far as he knew. His information was admittedly a touch outdated. He hoped he was still right. "We should be safe so long as we stay to the trees."

Setting up camp was a simple affair. Since the smoke from a real fire would broadcast their location to anyone with eyes, Quinn built one from dry wood and magic that emitted nothing but a cold, odorless glow like embers of coal. Dorian might not trust him, but the warlock did have his uses. Jasper busied himself with picking burrs out of his feathers while grumbling under his breath about the indignity of nature. Quinn offered to help, but Jasper brushed him off. Dorian pretended that watching Quinn be rebuffed—again—didn't bring him an inappropriate amount of joy.

After carving a circle of protection runes in the dirt around the camp, Dorian pushed a log toward the fire and took a seat, unstrapping the sword at his back and resting it against the tree beside him.

"That's a mighty big sword there," Quinn said as he waved a hand over the fire. Warmth began to emanate from it. "One might suspect you're compensating for something."

"And I bet you'd know all about compensating," Dorian said.

"Ooh, burn," Jasper said with a soft chuckle. He met Dorian's gaze and some of the tightness fled from his smile.

Dorian didn't return the smile, but he wanted to. Instead, he rolled up his sleeves and unsheathed the knife in his belt. He pressed the blade into his forearm, fighting back a wince when it pierced his skin. He angled the blade so the metal caught the blood welling up from the wound. It wasn't a deep cut. The message he planned to send wasn't long. He drew two dots on the blade with his own blood, then wiped it clean and waited for a response. Two dots from him meant "All good?" Two dots from Ivy would mean "All good, proceed." He prayed he'd see two dots soon.

Quinn's lip curled in disgust. "How barbaric."

Dorian ignored him. Once their mission was completed

and Ivy had been retrieved, safe and sound, he would be glad to see the back of Quinn.

"You know," Jasper said, "since I met you, I've done more camping in the woods than I have in my nineteen years of existence."

"Should I apologize for that?" Dorian asked.

Jasper smiled. "Probably, but you're cute, so I'll let it slide."

Quinn retched. "I'm gonna throw up." He stood, wiping his hands on his trousers. "I'm going to find us something to eat. Try not to do anything stupid while I'm gone." He sauntered off. The fire crackled merrily, but as Quinn had promised, not a single wisp of smoke rose from it.

Jasper settled on the log beside Dorian. He crossed his arms and hunched over as if he were cold. While July evenings in the Scottish Highlands rarely ever approached what one would call warm, it wasn't nearly cold enough to justify Jasper's huddling.

"What's wrong?" Dorian asked. He couldn't look away from the blade, not for any extended period of time, but his gaze flicked to Jasper, just for a second.

Jasper shrugged and kept his eyes on the fire. The light made them shine like topaz. "Nothing."

Dorian arched a brow. Jasper ignored him, but the source of his trouble was obvious, and it had been since Quinn arrived, bringing with him a shared past full of hurt and regret. "You let him have too much power over you," Dorian said, attention back on the dagger.

"I know," Jasper said quietly.

One dot appeared on the bloodied steel of the blade. Dorian waited, his heart in his throat. If that girl had been sent into the Dragon's den only for the plan to go awry, it would be on his conscience. But then a second, fainter dot materialized next to the first. The mission was on. Dorian was more relieved than he could say, since their plan relied on a great deal of luck. A contingency plan had been in place from the first day of Caius's reign; Tanith was not the first Drakharin to make a grab for power, simply the only one who'd been successful. The network of loyal Drakharin Caius had spent decades building operated on anonymity. Not even Dorian knew whom Ivy would encounter within the keep's walls. At seemingly random intervals on the hike toward the keep, Dorian had left groups of three stones arranged in small pyramids at the base of blackthorn trees he knew were on the standard patrol route. They wouldn't mean anything to someone who didn't know what they were looking at, but for those in Caius's network, the rocks were a signal. Watch for me, they said. Any unusual activity in the keep would be noticed. Any arrivals would be questioned—in secret, of course—to determine if they came bearing messages from their erstwhile prince. Ivy's arrival—or her abduction, rather—was the tacit signal that Caius was trying to contact his supporters. One of them would make contact with Ivy, and judging from her message, someone had. Dorian only hoped that whichever loyal subject came to her aid would help her carry through the next—and most dangerous—part of her mission.

So far, their plan had gone off without a hitch. Dorian hoped, with a desperation he would never vocalize, that the rest of it went as smoothly. If Quinn did his part and Ivy succeeded, they would be home free in a matter of days, though every time he saw the way Jasper reacted to Quinn, Dorian's misgivings grew. The warlock was not one to be relied on, and yet, here they were, relying on him.

"Why Quinn?" Dorian asked, no longer able to keep to himself the question that had been plaguing him for days. "I don't get it. He's not exactly brimming with good qualities."

Jasper shrugged. "I guess it's just nice to feel wanted sometimes."

Ridiculous. People like Jasper were chronically wanted. They were beautiful and charming and irresistible. They were flames to which mere mortals were drawn like flies. For the first time, Dorian considered that maybe Jasper's confidence was an illusion, a mask. He rubbed at his eye patch. He knew a thing or two about masks, having hid behind one for the past century.

Jasper picked up a stick and stoked the fire even though its magical nature meant it hardly needed stoking.

"I just don't understand why you would give him the time of day to begin with," said Dorian. "You could have anyone you want."

Jasper shot Dorian a look he couldn't quite read. He hadn't meant to say that last bit out loud, but now that the words were in the open, hovering in the air like traitorous little hummingbirds, there was no rescinding them.

After a moment, Jasper looked back to the fire. "Apparently not *anyone*."

Dorian had nothing smart to say to that. Jasper had been patient with him, but a century of rage and hate and unrequited love wasn't something that could be conquered in a matter of months. Lately, however, he'd found himself wishing he could brush it all aside. He hadn't understood at first why Caius had gravitated so quickly to Echo, but he was beginning to appreciate the desire to seize an opportunity for happiness. How nice it would be to forget everything that had made him the way he was: cantankerous, introverted, and generally unpleasant. But he couldn't be what Jasper wanted or needed or deserved. He just couldn't.

Jasper's sigh was audible in the silence of the evening. "There was something about Quinn that made me feel safe."

Safe? Dorian thought. "Are we talking about the same Quinn?"

"I know it sounds ridiculous, but it's true. I was sixteen when I met him. Can you imagine that?" Jasper glanced at Dorian, his expression a pale version of his reliably mischievous grin. "And Quinn was . . . well, he was Quinn. He kept me so close the first few months. It was like nothing existed but the two of us. He became my entire world. He was the sun and the moon and the stars, and when I was in his orbit, nothing else mattered. He liked it that way, and for a while, I thought I did, too."

"Jasper, that isn't healthy."

"Yeah, I know that now. I left eventually, but I still remember what it felt like to have him be the only thing that mattered."

Dorian shook his head. "Infatuation is a poor substitute for love."

Jasper shrugged. "But something's better than nothing. Or at least, that was how it felt at the time. Especially when the real thing seemed so far out of reach."

Again, Dorian lacked a response. He hated thinking of Jasper ever feeling desperate for affection or a place to feel safe, but he couldn't give him that. Not now. Maybe not ever.

The sound of twigs cracking underfoot signaled Quinn's return. Dorian wasn't exactly glad to see him, but he was somewhat relieved that he didn't have to continue the conversation. He'd started it, but he knew he couldn't finish it. Not adequately.

In one hand, Quinn dangled a fat rabbit by its back legs. Its white fur was spotless. It had been killed without any visible wounds. Magic, Dorian presumed.

"Jasper, dear," Quinn said, swinging the rabbit. "Come help me with dinner."

"Still not your dear," Jasper grumbled, but he stood and went to Quinn.

Dorian watched as Quinn jostled Jasper's shoulder playfully, leaning in to whisper something in Jasper's ear that elicited a grudging laugh. When Quinn smiled, wide and brilliant, Dorian could almost see his appeal. The smile appeared to be genuine; it made perfectly shaped dimples form in his cheeks and made the stars in his eyes shine even brighter. There was a magnetism to Quinn, but that was the way the best predators worked. They drew you in, and you didn't even realize you'd walked right into their trap until it was too late.

CHAPTER THIRTY-FIVE

Time took on an elastic quality as Echo, Caius, and Rowan descended the spiraling stairs, deeper and deeper into the mountain. Below, there was darkness and more darkness. Their torches created an island of light in a sea of black. Echo tried to count the steps, but the hushed whispers of the dead distracted her. She settled for praying that they'd reach the bottom soon. Her knees were beginning to hurt.

All three of them kept silent. It was as if the strange sanctity of the mountain absorbed their will to make noise, to disrupt the voices of those who'd lived and died among the stones. Each step had been smoothed by time, a slight curve worn in the middle. People had been passing through this mountain for centuries. Millennia, maybe. Echo wondered how many of them had survived the trip. The thought that her voice might join in the ghostly chorus occurred to her—not for the first time since they'd begun their descent—but she pushed it away. She just hoped there wasn't a pit of skeletons at the bottom of the winding staircase. She really, really, really wasn't in the mood for corpses. Especially not on a mostly empty stomach.

As if on cue, her stomach emitted an embarrassingly loud grumble. Behind her, Rowan choked back a snicker. Echo shot him a caustic look over her shoulder, her cheeks flushed. "What?" she snapped. "I skipped lunch."

Rowan's lips pulled into a sideways grin. "The truest sacrifice I've ever known you to make."

Echo scoffed. She marched down the stairs, head held high, eyes on the steps, which were illuminated by warm, amber torchlight. "Let me tell you something about sacrifice—"

Caius held up a hand, halting a few steps below. "Shut up, both of you."

Under his breath, Rowan muttered, "Rude."

With his free hand, Caius beckoned Echo forward. "Look at this." He lifted the torch high, its light crawling up the wall as if fighting the shadows for coveted territory. There were paintings on the wall, primitive ones that reminded Echo of the caves of Lascaux, a place she hadn't gotten around to visiting yet. Another item to add to the list of things to do if she lived long enough. The figures were outlined in brownish-red paint, still vivid despite their antiquity. They had faded only a little with age; sunlight had never penetrated this place, so the darkness had preserved them.

"What is it?" Rowan asked, crowding Echo on the steps.

"A bird," said Echo. "And a dragon."

She reached out to trace the swooping line of wings. The bird's talons were locked in combat with the claws of a great dragon. Swirls of smoke and tongues of flame curled from the dragon's mouth and nostrils. The bird's beak was open in a silent, frozen screech. The creatures formed a loose circle, their wings meeting beneath their feet and at the apex above their heads. Echo's fingers hovered near the wall. The ghostly whispers had faded to background static during the long descent, but they grew louder the closer her hand moved to the painting. The voices built and built, becoming a roar in her ears. The moment her fingers brushed the red paint, the roar became a scream, echoing through the mountain with the force of a thousand cries. Her knees buckled. If not for Caius's quick reflexes and steadying grip, she would have tumbled down the stairs to her doom. The drawing burned beneath her touch, the red glowing as if lit from within. The voices coalesced into a single shout, one phrase slicing through Echo's mind like a warm knife through butter.

She snatched her hand away, expecting to find blisters on the pads of her fingers, but her skin was unmarred.

"Echo?" Rowan knelt beside her, worry and panic clouding his hazel eyes. "What was it? What just happened?"

Her voice was thin and reedy, but she found it. "It's not paint," she gasped. "It's blood."

Neither Rowan nor Caius appeared as disturbed as Echo felt. "Didn't you hear that?" she asked. "The screaming?"

Rowan shook his head. "No." His eyes were a little too wide as he and Caius helped pull her to her feet.

Welcome to my new life, Echo thought. *It is super weird.*

"As a matter of fact," Caius said, turning to study the image on the wall, "the whispers stopped." He cocked his head, his eyes going unfocused. "They're back now, but when you touched the wall, it was as though the air was sucked out."

Rowan nodded. "Like a vacuum."

Caius extended a tentative hand toward the painting. After a moment's hesitation, he laid a single finger on the dried blood. They waited, breath held. Nothing happened. "It appears the magic in these walls wants to react to you and only you." He rubbed his finger against his jeans to wipe off the dusty red residue. "What did it sound like? The screaming."

Echo closed her eyes. The hushed whispering washed over her. The cadence of it had changed. There was an urgency to it now, as if the voices were excited about something. The sound caressed her as it resounded through the mountain, prickling her skin into goose bumps and making the space between her shoulder blades tingle. She couldn't shake the feeling that she was being watched by a thousand eager eyes. One phrase stood out among the many phantom voices, repeated at uneven intervals like an inconsistent chant.

"Enu busana." Echo opened her eyes. Rowan was frowning in puzzlement, but Caius was mouthing the words to himself, silently. "Does that mean anything to you?"

Caius glanced at her, then back at the painting. "It's from a language that died many years ago, long before the development of modern Drakhar and Avicet. One of my old tutors knew it well and taught it to me when I was researching the origin of the firebird. If memory serves—though my grasp of the language's finer complexities is admittedly somewhat rusty—then I think I know what it means."

"Well?" Echo prompted. "Spill. The suspense is killing me."

"Us," Rowan said, his animosity buried for the moment beneath his curiosity. "The suspense is killing *us*."

Caius ran a hand through his hair, mussing it up on one side. "I'd like to consult a more knowledgeable scholar than myself on the nuances of the linguistics. . . ."

"Look around." Echo waved at the black expanse above and below their position on the stairs. "Unless you've got a more knowledgeable scholar hidden in your pocket, it's just us. What does *enu busana* mean?"

"'It has returned,'" said Caius. "Or, 'she or he has returned.' I'm a tad rusty on the pronouns of primitive Drakhar-Avicet."

"It has returned," Rowan said softly. His eyes locked with Caius's and, as one, their gazes slid to Echo. Rowan gave voice to the thought she did not want to speak. "Maybe 'she' and 'it' are one and the same."

"It's the firebird," Echo said. She cradled her head in her hands, cupping her palms over her ears. It did nothing to silence the ghostly whispering that filled the mountain with a frenzy of agreement. "It's me. They—it—whatever is in this mountain recognizes me. Or whatever's inside of me."

Her mouth went dry. *It has returned.* She *has returned.* It was too much. It was all too much. She could ignore the enormity of her present situation when she had something to do, somewhere to be, a task to occupy her mind, a theft to occupy her hands. But it came crashing down around her now, like a wave breaking against the shore. She snatched Caius's torch from him. He didn't try to stop her. Perhaps he sensed her need to do something, anything, besides consider the implications of what it all meant. Flickering torchlight spilled onto the steps below, illuminating the stone with a caramel glow. More petroglyphs lined the walls, all drawn with the same reddish-brown paint. Blood, Echo reminded herself. She wondered whose it was. Who had hewn these stairs, who had opened a vein so that centuries later, she would find a mountain full of paintings depicting a story so old that no one alive could recount it. By the unsteady light of the torch, the paintings appeared to be moving. Echo held still, fighting the tremor in her hands. The blood-drawn figures were stationary. A trick of the eye, then. That was the more comforting option, so she chose to believe it.

She took one step forward. Then another. And another. Caius and Rowan followed her.

Caius leaned forward to ask, "Are you all right?"

His breath was warm against her neck. That, too, was comforting. She huddled around that small comfort. "Not really." It felt good to admit it. She didn't have to put up a front here. The ghosts of the mountain knew her, and so did the two men at her back. All in different ways, from different angles, but they knew her. She had nothing left to hide. "But it doesn't matter." Her stubborn feet didn't want to continue descending the steps, but she forced them, one foot, then the other. "There's something down there," she said. "And it's been waiting for me for a very long time."

CHAPTER THIRTY-SIX

"If I have to walk down any more stairs," Echo grumbled, "I'm going to give up. I will live on these stairs. I will grow old on these stairs. I will die on these stairs."

Caius threw her a smirk over his shoulder. He'd wrested the torch back from her and taken the lead. If there was anything at the bottom, he'd told her, he wanted to encounter it first. "That seems a touch melodramatic," he said, fumbling slightly as his foot reached for the next step. "Cheer up, Echo. We're at the bottom."

The landing was a small, conical space, its ceiling swirling up with the staircase, its dirt floor pockmarked by stray stones and the odd root poking up from the ground. They faced a narrow, arched opening opposite the stairs. Where it led was hard to tell. The light from the torches seemed reluctant to penetrate the darkness beyond the arch. Behind Caius, Echo popped up onto her toes. Her chin barely made it past his shoulder. He stepped aside so she could see.

"Ooh, a door," said Echo. "I wonder where it leads."

The promise of a new and exciting mystery had rejuvenated her spirits. A sane person would have been frightened by the prospect of what they might find, but not her. Her curiosity overwhelmed all sane emotion. Caius's curiosity seemed tempered by the need to keep Echo safe. And Rowan too, she supposed. Though it was clear the scars of their first meeting in the Metropolitan Museum of Art had not scabbed over well enough for Rowan to appreciate Caius's presence.

"I'd rather not barge in without a plan," Caius said. "If we could just—"

Echo plucked the torch from Caius's hand with alarming speed. He grabbed for it, but she danced out of his reach. She was slippery. Like an eel. "Luckily for you, barging in without a plan is my specialty." She tipped an imaginary hat to them. "Gentlemen."

A series of problems arose the second Echo ducked through the doorway and emerged on the other side.

The first problem: She was no longer standing in a dark cave. The room in which Echo found herself was not unusual per se. There was a faded leather couch, the cushion on its right side, the one closest to the end table, sagging in the middle from wear. A television was set against the wall opposite the couch, static on its screen as if someone had turned off the cable and forgot to turn off the set itself. An old wooden coffee table sat between the two, its surface covered with dog-eared copies of *Cosmopolitan* and *National Geographic,* empty glasses with lipstick on the rims, a neat pile of used textbooks, and an ashtray that was near to overflowing. The carpeting was a forest green that had been cheerful once but was now the color of regurgitated spinach. A smell hung in the air, like stale smoke and even staler beer.

The room itself was not unusual in anything other than its location, which Echo knew, without the slightest shred of doubt, to be on the other side of the world, in a completely different hemisphere from the one she had been in not two minutes prior. And also for the minor fact that it was a room she had sworn she would never set foot in ever again. She knew this room. She knew it despite the fact that she had longed to forget it and the house it was in and the people who lived under its roof.

Echo stood in the living room of the house in which she'd grown up, before running away, before meeting the Ala, before embarking on her new life. And somehow, she'd gotten there from a cave hidden within a mountain in China.

The second problem was when she looked back at the door behind her, the one through which she'd entered, it was nowhere to be found. All she saw in its place was peeling wallpaper and a framed still life of a bowl of peaches.

She would have called out to see if Caius or Rowan could still hear her on the other side of the wall, but her voice had escaped her and was determined not to be found. The familiarity of the room was too much. She had left. She had sworn never to return. Never, not ever. She willed her feet to move, but they were rooted to the ground. She could handle a great many things—killer shadow monsters, homicidal monarchs, terrorist attacks on Grand Central—but not this. Everyone had their limits. This was hers.

"Looking for this?" The question came from behind her, spoken in a voice gone raspy with smoke and slightly slurred with alcohol, accompanied by the squeaky swinging of the saloon doors leading to the kitchen. That voice. Echo's blood turned to ice in her veins and her vision prickled at the edges as if she might faint. It was a voice she hadn't heard in ten years, a voice she'd never wanted to hear again, not as long as she lived. It was her mother's voice.

Echo turned slowly, the way people did in horror movies. Her mother stood on the other side of the room, her parched, processed blond hair pulled into a messy bun atop her head, her eyes bloodshot as if she'd been up all night drinking. It was a look Echo knew well. There was a small stain on the sleeve of her mother's pink tracksuit. It was red. Not bloodred. Wine red. A black-and-white composition notebook dangled from her mother's manicured fingers; in her other hand, she held a mostly empty glass of wine.

This isn't real, Echo told herself. *None of this is real.* It couldn't be. She'd been in China, thousands and thousands of miles from the home she'd left behind. And she hadn't entered the in-between. She would have felt that familiar drop as she'd entered its void. No, this had to be some kind of test. Another instance for her to prove herself worthy of whatever was on the other side of . . . whatever this was.

But, by the gods, it felt real. Her mother took another step forward, wine sloshing in her glass, and Echo instinctively retreated. She took half a step back before her shoulder blades hit the wall. There was nowhere to go. Her mother was in the center of the room now. The stone archway was gone and the only way out was through her. Whatever nightmare the mountain had deposited Echo into, she would have to live out, whether she wanted to or not. And she really, really didn't want to.

"Found your diary." Her mother's words tripped over

themselves like drunks stumbling out of a bar after last call. "Is this the kind of shit you've been wasting your time on when I'm at work?"

Something else was wrong, Echo could feel it. Everything was as she'd remembered it, as if the mountain had mined her memories to reconstruct her old house as faithfully as it could. Each and every detail was painstakingly rendered, from the ash burns on the carpet near the end of the couch her mother always sat on to the way her mother's breath smelled like a distillery, even from halfway across the room. But something was off. Something wasn't right. Echo's eyes darted around the room, never quite letting her mother out of sight, an old habit that felt like hopping on a bicycle after not riding for years. Violent drunks were unpredictable. One should never let them out of one's sight.

"I'm talking to you," her mother said, her voice rising with anger. Every fiber of Echo's being screamed at her to run, to hide, to ward off the beating she knew was to come, but her feet were planted so firmly that she might as well have grown roots deep down into the earth, like a tree. "Look at me when I'm talking to you."

Her mother stumbled toward her, knee knocking into the coffee table. The pile of textbooks swayed, one falling to the ground. *An Introduction to Calculus.* Calculus? But Echo had left home when she was seven. She hadn't been taking calculus at age seven. She was smart, but not that smart. That was a high school class, and Echo had never gone to high school. She might have, in an alternate universe in which she'd never run away.

Her mother bent, awkwardly, like her joints hadn't been greased, and set her wineglass on the table. "You always did have an active imagination," she slurred, opening the book. Only a few feet separated her from Echo, and Echo could see the name scrawled on the book's cover. It was a name she'd walked away from a decade ago, a name she'd shed like snakeskin when the Ala told her she could choose her own. And it was written, unmistakably, in Echo's handwriting. But it couldn't be hers. She couldn't have written that. This wasn't her life. This wasn't real. She had left home. She had escaped. None of this was real.

Her mother skimmed through the pages, one painted red nail scratching across the lines of text as if she could draw blood from paper. "And you've got little drawings, too."

She flipped the book around so Echo could see it. The page was covered in Echo's handwriting, small and neat and cramped. Bursting from the margins were illustrations. A girl with long, flowing feathers for hair and eyes as black and wide as a dove's. A boy with feathers as sleek as a falcon's, and another with scales gracing the angular cut of his cheekbones. On the next page two figures held hands, one wearing an eye patch that had been filled in with the blue ink of a ballpoint pen, the other with a shock of feathers atop his head in all the vivid shades of peacock feathers. A woman with skin so black she looked like she'd been formed from the night itself took up almost an entire page. Lines of white had been left blank to signify feathers.

"Nice little family you made," her mother said, turning the book back around. Echo almost reached out to snatch it from her grasp, but her palms had gone cool and clammy, her fingers refusing to obey the signals her mind was sending them. "Nice way to spend your time while I'm out there busting my ass to put food on the table." Loose papers fell from the back of the book where they'd been tucked in as if hidden. Echo knelt down to retrieve them before her mother could.

They were college applications, half filled out. There was even a handwritten draft of an essay. The first sentence read: "Growing up with an abusive alcoholic is a character-building experience, to say the least." Before Echo could read any more, her mother yanked the papers from her hands, leaving nothing but a torn corner of the essay in her loose fist. Her mother read the opening of the essay in silence, her face slowly reddening.

Echo remained where she knelt, like a woodland creature cowering before a predator. If she didn't move, maybe the monster wouldn't see her. But the monster always saw her, always found her, no matter what Echo did.

Her mother's voice pitched low and dangerous. "Is this how you see me?" She threw the paper to the floor. In comical slow motion, it flitted down, down, down.

Scuffed tennis shoes approached. "You think you're better than me?" Her mother's foot struck out and caught Echo directly in the stomach. The wind whistled out of her lungs and she clutched an arm protectively over her gut. It had been years since someone had kicked her like that, but her body remembered the pain, the bone-deep humiliation. Footsteps retreated to the kitchen. Bottles were rummaged through in the refrigerator. A cap was popped open. "I read your diary," her mother said. "You think your prince is gonna come and save you? Your imaginary friends with the feathers?" Her voice, already thickening, grew closer. Echo cowered just as she always had. "You are nothing. D'you hear me? Nothing. And you'll never be anything more than—"

Echo heard the first syllable of a name on her mother's tongue. The old name. The one she'd left behind.

I am not that girl.

Another voice, the same one that had haunted her dreams asked: *Then who are you?*

She didn't look into her mother's eyes as she pushed herself to stand. She didn't respond to the name she no longer called her own. This life of fear and hurt and isolation was not hers. This house was not hers. This monster had been slain already, not by a knight brandishing a weapon like in her stories but by the decision to leave. And Echo had. None of this was real; it was an illusion crafted by magic from the raw material the mountain found in her memories. But she was certain about one thing.

I am a sword.

She stood, and the life that was not hers crumbled like paper burned to ash.

CHAPTER THIRTY-SEVEN

Her mother was gone. As were the coffee table and the peeling wallpaper and the stack of college applications and the room in its entirety.

Slowly, Echo sank to her knees, exhausted. Breaking free of the hallucination's shackles had been harder than she would have anticipated. She was kneeling in the middle of Fifth Avenue, between Forty-Second and Forty-First Streets, right in front of the library. Her instincts screamed for her to run, to get out of the way before an overzealous cabdriver mowed her down. But no cars drove down the avenue. Puddles of slick black fluid pooled beneath the husks of rusted vehicles that crowded the street. Smoke flavored with the scent of oil clogged the air. The windows of the buildings on either side of her were dark, all the lights out despite it being twilight. The clouds were gray, but not the gray of rain clouds; it was as if someone had scorched the sky. The white stone lions that flanked the stairway leading to the library's entrance were gray with filth. One of them was missing a head. It was deathly quiet. Not a soul in sight. When Echo rose, her left boot caught on something. She looked down. It was a license plate, but not one of the newer ones with the yellow background. This one was old and had once been white, though the layer of grime that covered it made it hard to read the numbers. Through the muck, a red outline of the Statue of Liberty stared up at her, its torch held aloft, blue capital letters boasting NEW YORK above it.

Her surroundings were as real as the house she'd left behind, and also just as fake. The minor details gave it away. The incorrect license plate. The black-and-white checkered stripes on the yellow taxis that had been abandoned at haphazard angles all over the avenue, as if their drivers and occupants had fled on foot in a hurry, away from whatever it was that had wreaked such havoc on the city. Cabs hadn't been checkered in New York City for ages. For as long as Echo could remember.

None of it was real. But the smell . . . By god, that smell was real enough. Echo held one hand over her nose, but that only made it worse. Something both slick and sticky transferred from her hand to her face. She looked down and bile rose in her throat, tangy and acidic. Blood coated her hands. Some of it was old and drying, darkening as it oxidized in the rank air, but some of it was fresh and bright. She stumbled backward, her hands held in front of her as if they belonged to a stranger, but she couldn't run from herself.

"You have some nerve coming back here."

Echo spun around, eyes darting left and right as she looked for the speaker. From behind the hulk of an overturned city bus emerged a figure with a rifle slung over its shoulder. A hood masked the speaker's face, but the voice—a woman's—sounded familiar. Familiar, but slightly off, like the rest of the hallucination. That was what it had to be. It was the mountain, playing more tricks.

The speaker approached cautiously, as if expecting Echo to attack at any moment. Echo raised her bloodstained hands, palms open to show she meant no harm. "Who are you?" she asked. "What happened here?"

The speaker stopped. The hooded head tilted to the side. One gloved hand reached for the rifle and unslung it to hold it at the ready, but not aimed at Echo. Not yet, anyway.

"Please," said Echo. She lowered her hands slowly. On second thought, displaying the blood that drenched them was perhaps not a terrific idea. She didn't know to whom the blood belonged or how it had gotten all over her hands, but if it had come from a friend of this person's, then maybe it was best not to brazenly show it off. Again, she asked, "What happened here?"

A tendril of smoke rose from a tangle of metal beside the bus. It might have been a motorcycle once, but it was so badly mangled it was hard to tell. The speaker let the silence hang between them for a few tense moments before moving. She raised a hand to her hood and pushed it back. The white feathers were matted with sweat and dirt, but they still shone brilliantly in the ruins of Midtown, catching the feeble light around them like flowers desperate for the sun. Ivy glared at Echo with one black eye. The other was gone, replaced by a mass of scar tissue. Burn scars dominated the right half of Ivy's face, the feathers near her temple blackened with soot. "You happened here."

"Ivy?" Before Echo could take one full step forward,

the rifle was pointed squarely at her chest. She froze. "Your eye . . . I don't understand."

Ivy's lips twisted into a grimace. "Is this a joke to you?" She cradled the butt of the rifle against her shoulder. "Haven't you hurt us enough?"

"I didn't . . ." Echo shook her head. She had to get out of here, but she could spot nothing in the immediate vicinity that seemed to be a viable exit from the dream or hallucination or vision or whatever it was. The mountain was trying to teach her something. There was a method to this madness, but Echo had no desire to puzzle it out. All she wanted was a way to leave this horror show behind. This was not her Ivy. Ivy carried herbs and poultices, not high-powered weapons. Ivy was a healer. Not . . . whatever it was this Ivy had become. "Where is everyone? Where's Rowan?"

"You killed him." The rifle's barrel dropped a few inches, as if it had become too heavy for Ivy to hold. "And Caius. And Jasper. And Dorian. You tore down every single person who tried to stop you. I was the last person left who believed you could be saved." She snapped the gun up, her vigor renewed. "I won't make that mistake again."

Before Echo could beg or plead or try to explain, Ivy pulled the trigger. The bullet tore through the flesh and muscle of Echo's abdomen, the shock of it knocking her off her feet. She clutched her stomach. Her own blood mingled with the blood on her hands, but what poured out of her body wasn't red. It was black. As black as oil. As black as shadows. Boots crunched over gravel and stray scraps of metal. Echo struggled to keep her eyes open. Ivy came into view and towered over her, the barrel of the rifle pointed at Echo's face. Echo opened her mouth, but her words were drowned in a gurgle of blood. She felt her power pulse in time with her heart—she could summon it. It was there, simmering beneath her flesh. But she would not hurt Ivy. She would *never* hurt Ivy, no matter what this nightmare version of her best friend said. Echo wasn't a monster who would harm the ones she loved.

She wasn't.

She wasn't.

Was she?

"And they said you couldn't be killed." Ivy's tone was devoid of emotion, her one good eye as dead as her voice. "Let's see if this does the trick."

Again, Ivy pulled the trigger. An eternity was compressed into the space of a single second. The boom of the shot. The smell of gunpowder igniting. This time, Echo felt no pain as darkness engulfed her.

CHAPTER THIRTY-EIGHT

Light, bright and vengeful, seared Echo's eyes as she fell out of the void, her knees landing on packed dirt and dry grass with a painful thud. Her fingers dug into the earth, capturing fistfuls of pebbles and dead leaves, as she heaved in deep, shaking breaths. The world spun and her eyes burned.

Power surged within her, fueled by anxiety. She couldn't hold it back. It was like trying to close floodgates after a wave had already rushed through. Fire flowed from her hands, scorching the earth and rushing around her, forming a circle. Her eyes watered and struggled to focus as she looked around. She was in a cavernous room with two arched doorways. The one behind her must have been the one she'd fallen through after leaving that nightmare hallucination. The expansive space glittered with the light of her fire. Veins of silver ore wove through the rough-hewn stone walls like a vast circulatory system. A faint glow emanated from the silver, as if it were lit from within by some strange magic. The sound of her breathing reverberated through the space, adding to the low drone of whispers that Echo had all but ceased hearing after the first few hours walking down those stairs.

In the center of the room stood a massive fountain, its basin filled with rich, dark dirt and stringy red weeds that grew despite the lack of sun. Droplets of water trickled from the eyes of a stone beast perched astride the basin, its head angled downward as if in mourning. It was neither purely a bird nor a dragon; it possessed the traits of both creatures. Its outspread wings were coated in feathers so expertly carved they appeared to be fluttering in the wind. Great taloned claws gripped the edge of the basin. Scales covered the creature's legs and torso, blending seamlessly with a ruff of feathers on its chest. Though its fangs were as long and deadly as those of a saber-toothed tiger, there was something unbearably melancholic about its countenance.

Who are you?

The whisper came from all around her, spoken not by one voice but by hundreds. Thousands.

"I don't know," she said in a soft, broken voice.

What are you?

"I don't know," she repeated.

But she did know. She wasn't a girl. Not the one who had lived in that awful house or the one who'd taken up residence in the library or the one who had fallen in with a race of magical beings beneath the streets of New York. She was more than that, and less. She was the firebird. She was a creature. She was a monster. It didn't matter if she outran her childhood. She had left a home designed to turn her into something dark, and darkness would not be denied. Her past had primed her for corruption, and the cosmic force coursing through her veins had found a seed inside her that could be watered. The firebird was neither good nor bad, the Ala had told Echo all those months ago when she had first learned of its existence, before her journey had led her here. Its nature was ambiguous, determined by the nature of its vessel. And Echo knew the truth now. Even if she won a battle against her demons, she was still losing the war.

The fire continued to burn all around her, and she was powerless to stop it.

CHAPTER THIRTY-NINE

When Caius emerged from the darkness, the sight that greeted him made his heart ache even more than it already did. The residue of what he had witnessed—of what the mountain had shown him—clung to him like the stench of smoke after a fire. He brushed the memories away as he focused on the girl in front of him.

Flames of light and shadow danced around Echo's huddled form. Her face was buried in her knees, and even with the crackling of the fire, he could hear her shuddery breaths, punctuated by the occasional soft hiccup. The blaze undulated with the rhythm of her uneven breathing.

"Echo?" he called out quietly.

She didn't look up when she said, "Leave me alone."

He paused, remembering the horrors he had just endured. "What did you see?"

Echo sniffed and shook her head. "I don't want to talk about it." The fire continued to burn. "I can't control it." She tightened her grip on her knees. "I can't make it go away, no matter how hard I try."

She squeezed her eyes shut in concentration. The fire around her began to abate, but small flames continued to burn, leaving sooty marks on the ground in the shape of a circle.

Caius took a tentative step forward, and when Echo didn't protest, he walked to the edge of her flames. He could not advance any farther unless she allowed it. Provided she *could* allow it.

"You're stronger than this," he said. "You control your power. It doesn't control you."

She shook her head again and a ragged sound tore from her chest. It took Caius a moment to recognize it as laughter, though it was mirthless and hollow. "I'm not strong," she said. "I'm a coward. All I do is run away." She looked down at her hands. "And now I'm a monster. I can't run from that no matter how hard I try." As she spoke, her voice rose, and the fire rose with it.

Caius was forced to step back or be burned. "No," he said. "You're not. I don't know what you saw, but you are no monster."

She glanced at the fire around her. Tears gleamed on her cheeks in its glow. "I am," she said. "I will be. I saw it."

Gods, what Caius wouldn't have given to cross the threshold of flame and embrace her. Her voice was strained, as if she was curling in on herself, trying to force the wild parts of her being into a cage too small to contain them. "You're not," he said. "You are so good, Echo. Better than anyone I've ever met."

He locked gazes with her, and for the barest sliver of a

second, it was as though Rose was looking at him through Echo's soft brown eyes. Damn the fire. He approached the circle, and Echo tried to warn him off, her voice rough with desperation.

"Please, Caius, I can't stop it. I don't want to hurt you."

"You won't." He stepped forward, free of doubt, and the moment his foot crossed the barrier that divided them, the flames extinguished. He was unburned. "See? You're not a monster. You care about people. Deeply. That means you would do anything in your power to keep the people you care about safe."

He sat next to her, their knees just barely touching, and held out his right arm. After a moment's hesitation, she shuffled closer, pressing herself against him and tucking her head beneath his chin. There were no tears, no racking sobs. Only the slight hitch in her breathing and the tense set of her shoulders indicated her unease.

"I'm so sorry," he said into her hair. "You shouldn't have to carry this weight alone. I can't carry it for you, but I can carry it with you." Echo shuddered in his arms with another repressed sob. "I'm here," he whispered, praying his voice could pull her from her torment. "I'm here."

A hundred lost years sat on his lips, but he let them lie there, unspoken. A century ago, he had failed Rose. He would not do the same with Echo.

With a sudden jerk, she stiffened in his arms. Her head shot up, almost colliding with his chin. "Rowan," she said. "Where's Rowan?"

Caius placed a hand on the nape of her neck as though trying to calm a frightened horse. "He has to fight his own demons, just as we did." Echo's expression darkened, remembering whatever it was she'd seen. With a confidence Caius wasn't quite sure he believed, he added, "He'll come through. I don't know him well, but I know that boy is as stubborn as an ox."

Echo sighed, her whole body shuddering. "I hope he's okay. He never should have come. It's too dangerous." She rubbed her nose against her sleeve. "How the hell am I supposed to be what everyone wants—no, *needs* me to be if I can't even protect the people I love?"

Caius hugged her tight. "You can and you will." He gestured at the ring of soot, where the fire had been. "You protected me just now."

Echo sat up and turned to face him fully, her head canted to the side as if measuring him. He realized, then, what he'd just said. She had referred to the people she loved, and he had counted himself among their number. He could have tried to cover his carelessly chosen words, but he didn't. A part of him—an undeniably large part—wanted them to be true.

Silently, Echo reached out and traced the planes of his face. Her fingers slowed as she caressed the smattering of scales on his cheekbones. Her hand wandered over his brow, his cheeks, the line of his jaw. It was a quiet touch, as light as a feather. She touched him like he was something precious, as if he were made of all the stars she never got to see through the haze of polluted urban skies. Caius's eyes drooped closed, and he leaned into her hand. It was delicate, but there was strength there. She was small, but she was steel.

"Caius?" Her voice was as soft as her caress.

He hummed in response. When she didn't continue, he cracked his eyes open. She was studying him, expression guarded.

"Do you love me?"

He blinked. Since the moment he'd met her, his emotions had been a jumbled mess, scattered about him like a child's toys, but he couldn't deny what was in his heart. He couldn't deny the way his pulse raced at her touch, or the way his breath caught in his throat when she said his name, especially when she said it so softly, so sweetly. The loss of Rose had been hard, and he had resigned himself to a lifetime of emptiness in the wake of it, but Echo had slotted herself into the vacant hole in his chest and nested there, filling Caius with hope for a future that was far less bleak than the one he'd imagined.

His answer was simple and honest: "Yes."

Echo sucked in a deep breath and held it, white and black flames materializing in the air, summoned by whatever she was feeling.

"I haven't loved many people in my life," she said. Her expression was still closed, still guarded, but her eyes were raw and open.

"Neither have I."

"It's not an easy thing for me to say."

Caius reached for her, touching her face the way she'd touched his. Softly, gently, with fingers unsure of their welcome. "You don't have to say anything."

Echo nodded, and he cupped her cheek in his hand and wrapped his other arm around her waist. He wanted to draw her in, to press his lips against hers until she forgot her own name, but he didn't. He waited until she came to him. She leaned in and brushed her nose against his. Still, he didn't close the distance between their mouths. They shared air for several agonizing seconds, her proximity tightening the coil of heat at the base of his spine. The plea hovered on his lips until he couldn't take it anymore.

"Please," he breathed.

The kiss was as sweet as honey. Her lips were chapped yet soft, and they moved against his with excruciating slowness. His eyes were closed, and he could feel the fire around them growing as its warmth spread.

Caius had meant what he said. Echo didn't need to tell him anything. He already knew.

CHAPTER FORTY

As if on cue, a figure fell through the opening from which Echo had emerged, landing on the ground with a sputtering cough and the sound of dry heaving, a sensation she knew all too well. The dim light glinted off the feathers on Rowan's head, making them glow as bright as gold. He held one hand over his stomach, and the other cradled his temple, as if the seams of his skull were threatening to split. He was mumbling something under his breath over and over like a mantra.

Echo pushed Caius's hands away and stood. The chill of the cave seeped into her skin. She hadn't realized how warm he was. She shivered once and forced herself to walk away from him and toward Rowan. When she reached the Avicen, she fell to her knees in the dirt beside him, her own hands settling on his arms. He rocked back and forth, his jeans stained with dirt, his mumbling reaching a fever pitch. Caius had brought her back to herself, and she would do the same for Rowan. She didn't let herself think about what Caius had just confessed. She had known, in some deep part of her, what he felt for her. But now was not the time to dwell on such things. At least, that was what she preferred to believe. It was a more comforting thought than admitting to herself that the depth of Caius's emotion frightened her, just a little. She was too much of a coward to confront it. Besides, Rowan needed her more at this moment.

"It's not real," Rowan whispered hoarsely. "It's not real. It's not real. It's not real."

Echo took his hands and pulled them away from where he was beginning to claw at himself. She clutched them tightly and rested her forehead against his. "That's right," she said, rocking with him. "It's not real. This is real. I'm real."

Rowan twitched, then reared back, his eyes wide and afraid. "Echo?" he asked. He sounded so young, so scared.

She held on to his hands, refusing to let him pull away from her completely. "Yeah," she said. "It's me." She brought one of his hands to her face and rested her cheek in his palm. "Same old me."

He cupped her face as if she were made of glass, fingers tracing her cheekbones with reverence. "You're alive." It felt more like a question than a statement.

Oh. *Oh.* That had been his nightmare. Her death. She knew how creative the mountain's magic could be with the visions it conjured. It had probably been gruesome. It must have been, to put that look on his face.

"I'm alive," she said. Twigs cracked and pebbles scattered as Caius stepped away from where Echo and Rowan huddled and walked off a short distance. Perhaps he was giving them a moment alone. Perhaps he simply couldn't bear to see them like this, wrapped around each other like the rest of the world didn't matter. As if *he* didn't matter. Especially not after what had just happened between him and Echo.

With great reluctance, Echo relinquished her hold on Rowan. He let her go with minimal resistance. She stood, brushing dirt off the knees of her jeans. Rowan gathered himself and stood as well. Their eyes met, then skittered away from each other. She thought of him kissing her back in Avalon, of the way his arms felt around her, of the tickle of his feathers against her face. From the rising color in his cheeks, he was thinking of those things too. She turned and walked toward Caius, who was staring up at the statue, his posture rigid and still as stone. She wanted to apologize for shoving him aside for Rowan, but she had a feeling that would only make things worse.

She looked at the statue so she wouldn't have to look at him when she asked, "What did you see?"

He was silent for a moment, then said, "I don't wish to talk about it."

He moved away from her, rounding the statue's base as if he couldn't bear to be near her. It had not escaped Echo's notice that he hadn't been able to look at her either.

CHAPTER FORTY-ONE

Caius felt Echo's eyes on him as he circled the basin, but she didn't push him to speak. She let him go, her objections, if she had any, kept to herself. He'd told her he loved her. That seemed more impossible than a magical fear cave hidden inside a long-forgotten mountain. He was stupid. Beyond stupid. It was a moment of weakness, he told himself, spurred on by the trauma of what he'd just witnessed. But not even he could believe that.

What he'd seen in that cave . . . a sea of flames, as endless as the universe itself, burning every inch of his flesh, the sound of Rose's screams piercing his ears. It was a nightmare he knew well, and that had been his only saving grace. He had pulled himself from that particular agony before, in his dreams. But he had saved himself from reliving the loss of one love only to anticipate the loss of someone else who had carved a place for herself in his heart, an organ that wasn't quite as dead as he had believed it to be.

In the months after the events of the Black Forest, cooped up in an enclosed space with Echo, Caius had let himself become acquainted with a notion he thought he'd left behind: optimism. About himself. About Echo. About their future. Not necessarily one that they shared but that of their respective peoples. And maybe, if he allowed himself a moment of brutal honesty, he wanted to consider a future for himself that involved her. But theirs had been a self-made bubble, bound to burst at some point.

Echo had Rowan now. Rowan was a good soul, of that Caius was certain, as much as he was loath to admit it. And the boy wasn't burdened with a century of heartache. Bearing that weight had made Caius brittle, as though his heart had gone stale in his chest from years of abuse and neglect. Echo deserved better. Gods knew she had enough ghosts of her own without adding Caius's to the mix.

He had to focus on the task at hand. Matters of the heart could wait. He inched closer to the statue, squinting up at the beast's downturned head. Bored into the inner corners of its eyes were two small holes from which the water flowed, moistening the dirt in the fountain's basin with the creature's tears. Even the whispering of the mountain's ghosts grew mournful in the statue's presence, as if they, too, had suffered a great loss. There was a sanctity about the space, as though they had wandered into the remnants of a temple.

"Caius, look." Echo pointed toward the rim of the basin. She had shucked off the moment they had shared before Rowan showed up with an ease that discomfited him. Nevertheless, he kept his mouth shut and looked at what she was pointing to. Curved around the basin's circumference were runic symbols in the same ancient language as the book in the Enlightenment Gallery at the British Museum. It was the written form of the language the ghosts had cried out in when Echo had touched the painting made of blood. She knelt down, holding the torch aloft. "What does it mean?"

Caius joined her in the dirt, his knees resting on the fountain's base. He brushed away the delicate red leaves that spilled over the side of the basin. With reverent fingers, he traced the lines of the first phrase. *"Enu sutagan,"* he read. "'It destroys.'" He moved on to the next phrase. "*Enu kamalan*. 'It saves.' Or, 'it protects.' Like I said, my grasp of the language is a little rusty. The verb conjugation is similar to Drakhar, but the vocabulary is something else. Older than Avicet. A distant relation, I think."

"What's the 'it'?" Echo asked. Her eyes drifted up to the stone beast, carved countless centuries ago and left there, weeping into its basin of soil. "Is it another reference to the firebird, or . . . ?"

Caius had only ever seen one being who possessed both feathers and scales, who was neither solely Avicen nor Drakharin but both: the Oracle, an ancient Seer who had survived wars and disasters and the passage of time, only to be struck down by Tanith's fire. His hands itched to grab his sister by the shoulders and give her a good shake. The Oracle had been their one source of information about a past so distant, most of its writings had been lost, and Tanith had brought her long life to an end in a fit of rage.

"I don't know," Caius said. How hateful were those three little words. "It could be a reference to the prophecy, but it's more than a little vague."

Echo sighed. "I am so done with prophecies."

Caius couldn't agree more.

"What are these?" Rowan plucked a leaf from the scarlet weeds growing in the basin. He rubbed the thin leaf between his fingers, pulverizing it into a cherry-red paste that stained his skin. After a few seconds, he dropped the remnants of the leaf as if scalded and frantically wiped his hand on his jeans. "Holy shit, it burns. Ouch. Shit. Ouch." He sniffed the red paste that lingered on his skin. "And it smells like Satan's toilet seat."

Caius leaned closer to the weeds, careful not to touch them. Whole, they were odorless. The delicate stems swayed with his breath.

"How do they grow down here without any sun?" Echo wondered aloud. "How can anything grow in this darkness?"

"I've seen this before," Caius said. "It's called bloodweed." From his back pocket, he retrieved a handkerchief requisitioned from Jasper's supply at the warehouse. A voice in his head that sounded remarkably like Echo reminded him that "requisitioning" was just a fancy word for stealing. With the cloth protecting his skin, he pulled up one of the weeds, roots and all, and folded the handkerchief around it. "I've never seen living specimens, though, only illustrations in old texts I came across while researching the firebird." His gaze strayed from the weed to Echo. Her cheeks flushed pink, and his chest tightened at the sight. She blushed easily, like Rose. Echo cocked her head to the side, no doubt wondering why he was staring at her so intently. He cleared his throat. *Focus, you lovestruck fool.* "I had assumed they were extinct as I've never come across them in the wild, at least nowhere with light. But perhaps they require darkness to thrive."

"I didn't know botany was one of your specialties," Echo said, trailing a finger along the lip of the basin. She walked around the fountain, each step bringing her closer to Caius. There was something beguiling about the way she looked in the dim light. Her hair—an otherwise nondescript brown—shone with chocolate shadows and caramel highlights. Her skin, pale from being cooped up in a warehouse, away from the sun's rays, glowed in the torchlight. The proximity of her was almost suffocating. Paired with the weight of the mountain bearing down on them, it made Caius feel suddenly claustrophobic.

He shrugged. *Focus.* "It's not. But there was a drawing in one of my old texts that bore a striking similarity to these plants. I dismissed them as insignificant at the time. Those old books are full of herbal remedies for common ailments, most of them stemming from old wives' tales. Colicky babies, rheumatic joints, irritable bowels."

Echo scrunched up her nose. "Gross."

"Indeed."

She drew up beside him and examined the weed he held in the handkerchief. Her presence buzzed along the side of his arm as if her body heat were a palpable force.

"Let's take a bunch," Echo said. She fished her gloves from the depths of her backpack and put them on. Caius held the handkerchief while she plucked more weeds and deposited them into his open hands. When they had filled the handkerchief to capacity, she tore sheets of paper from a notebook and wrapped up even more weeds in makeshift envelopes.

Rowan watched them, confused. "What are you doing?"

"It's a mysterious plant that grows in the dark." Echo packed her leafy plunder into her bag. "Maybe it can help fight the dark too."

Caius wished he had her faith. But, he thought, perhaps that was what set her apart. If she was part of a greater prophecy, destined to bring about an end to all that plagued them, then her faith, her ability to believe in a solution even in their darkest hours, was what made her a worthy vessel for a force such as the firebird. The statue loomed above them, watching with its tearful gaze.

"Why leave this here?" Caius asked.

Echo paused in her packing. "To remember?"

Her words reminded him of a conversation they'd had a lifetime ago, in the shadow of a headless sculpture, before Echo's hands had become stained with blood. It was the first time he'd let himself notice her—her strength, her beauty. He shook his head, both to clear the memory and to convey his objection. "I don't think so. Why would someone build a memorial here? Deep in the belly of a mountain where no one could see it?"

"Hope," Rowan said softly. The orange glow of the torch warmed his tawny feathers, granting him an unearthly halo. "*Enu busana.* It has returned. Someone left it here for you."

"But why?" said Echo. No one had an answer for her, not even the ghosts who continued their infernal whispering, their voices prickling the skin on the back of Caius's neck like a cold wind. "And why make us go through that nightmarish cave to get here?"

"We had to earn it," Caius said. He wandered the circumference of the cavern as Rowan and Echo filled her backpack with more of the bloodweed, looking for an exit. The cave seemed like a one-way trip. Caius trailed a hand over the silver ore threaded through the walls, brushing aside the network of dry vines that hung over it, when all of a sudden, his hand slipped through an opening in the wall, masked by those very same vines. It was a hole in the rock, the mouth of it showing nothing but darkness. The void seemed to have a gravitational pull of its own. It tugged at something deep in Caius's gut, a magnetism calling to him, beckoning that he give himself to its black depths.

"Echo," he called, resisting the pull and stepping away. "I found something."

Caius and Echo pulled loose the vines covering the hole while Rowan held the torches aloft. It was narrow, about half the width of a normal door, and short, coming up to Caius's collarbone.

"That's going to be a tight fit," he noted.

Echo was already stripping off her backpack and jacket.

"No," Caius said.

"Yes," Echo replied.

"No," he repeated, with more force to the word this time, as if that would make any difference. Echo's obstinance was both her greatest asset and the bane of his existence. A different tactic, perhaps. "Please," he said softly.

She paused, one sleeve of her jacket still on, the other trailing on the dirt floor.

"I'll go first," Caius said. "Then you and Rowan will follow. If there's something in there, I'd like to encounter it first."

"He's right," Rowan said. "If there's a monster in there, let it eat him first."

Not quite the solidarity Caius would have preferred, but it would do. Echo, for all her bravado, didn't protest further. She must have witnessed something truly terrible during her test to give in so easily. Beside her, Rowan watched Caius squeeze through the narrow gap with disinterested eyes. If a monster did await on the other side, Caius knew of at least one person who wouldn't mourn his passing. He took that cheerful thought with him into the dark, and in an instant, he was gone.

CHAPTER FORTY-TWO

I'll come back for you, Helios had promised.

The confidence in his voice was the confidence of boys. Ivy had heard it in Rowan's voice every time he did something stupid, which was often. He'd used that tone when he swore they wouldn't get lost in the abandoned tunnels beneath Grand Central the first time they'd snuck out of the Nest to visit Echo in the library. They had. He'd used it when he swore that starting a relationship with Echo—which Ivy had learned about when she found them kissing in the street like savages—wouldn't put a strain on their friendship. It had. And now here was Helios, another fresh-faced boy, making assurances that Ivy wasn't convinced he could keep.

Promises were such delicate things, easily broken, but sometimes a flimsy promise was better than none.

Sleep eluded her. Every time Ivy closed her eyes she saw all the ways in which their plan could go awry. They would both be imprisoned, certainly, and not in a luxurious guest room with a big, squishy bed. She wondered if Tanith would make her watch Helios's interrogation—his torture—the same way she'd forced Ivy to witness Perrin's suffering. If Tanith was to be believed, Ivy had some strategic value to the Drakharin, but she wasn't sure that value was enough to counterbalance Tanith's inevitable rage.

Hours passed and dawn broke, bathing her room in butter-yellow light. Ivy wrapped a blanket around her shoulders and watched as sunbeams skittered across the surface of the sea, breaking into shimmering fractals on the waves. The sight was beautiful but fragile. Ivy huddled deeper into the blanket and waited.

And waited.

And waited.

She tried to busy herself, but there were few options available to her in her finely furnished cell. She sat, and when she grew tired of that she paced. And when she grew tired of that, she sat down again, and watched night slowly fall.

"Ready to run?"

At the sound of Helios's hushed whisper, Ivy spun around. He stood in the doorway, one hand on the knob and a dark blue cloak in the other.

He'd kept his promise. He'd come back for her. Her escape was at hand.

"Here," he said, offering her the cloak. "It's cold outside."

Ivy wrapped the cloak around her shoulders. It was soft and woolen and smelled faintly of woodsmoke. She wondered if it was his.

"Is it safe?" she asked as if that weren't a ridiculous

question. Of course it wasn't safe, but the primitive part of her brain that feared violence and bodily harm needed some kind of reassurance.

"As safe as it's going to be," Helios replied. "Tanith left with a small retinue of Firedrakes about an hour ago. I don't know how long she'll be gone, but most of the guards are having dinner in the mess hall. Shift change is happening, so our window is small, but it's there." He pulled a flask from his back pocket and took a liberal swig. He wiped his mouth with his sleeve and offered the flask to her.

Ivy politely declined, but he quirked an eyebrow as if to ask again, and she relented. She didn't know what was in the flask, but it burned all the way down, scorching her esophagus with its potency. It was vile. Helios looked a tiny bit proud. She handed the flask back and steeled herself for whatever was to come.

"Let's roll," she said.

The keep was a testament to the Drakharin's fascination with their creation myth. One corridor had a mural that spanned its entire length—the mural must have been fifty feet across—and showed the evolution of their kind, from primitive, fire-breathing dragons to tall, elegant figures, with smatterings of scales their only connection to their past.

"Wait!" Ivy tugged on Helios's hand, pulling him into an alcove inhabited by a tall statue of a winged dragon. She didn't remember which of them had reached out first, but his hand was warm in hers as he led her through the keep's empty corridors. She suspected that he needed the comfort as badly as she did. So far, they hadn't had any encounters—she had finally told him about the tunnel—and as much as she wanted to keep it that way, she knew there was more work to be done before she could flee.

He gaped at her as if she had lost her mind. Maybe she had. They were in a carpeted hallway with reams of heavy velvet covering the cold stone walls, which seemed to swallow the sound of Ivy's whisper. Another small comfort in the nest of vipers they would soon escape. Hopefully.

"Are you mad?" Helios hissed. "Or just suicidal? Because I do not plan on dying tonight, and you are complicating that plan. Tanith could be back at any moment, and I am getting you out of here whether you like it or not."

"No," Ivy hissed. "I came here with a mission, and I am going to see it through whether you like it or not." She squared her shoulders and tried to make herself seem as imposing as possible, which was probably not very imposing at all.

"I do not like it," Helios argued. He peeked out of the alcove as if he'd heard something, but after a few seconds of silence, he turned his attention back to Ivy. "I truly do not like it." The corners of his mouth quirked up. "Not that that matters. What's the plan?"

"There's a book I have to find. One of Caius's." At Helios's confused expression, Ivy added, "A very important book that might contain information to help us fight the giant, scary monster that destroyed the Nest."

Helios nodded slowly, as if he were dealing with a lunatic. "Tanith has been using the Dragon Prince's study." After a beat, he clarified, "The old Dragon Prince. All his books are there."

"Take me." Ivy injected every ounce of confidence she could muster into her voice, but the consequences of failure loomed in her mind. At best, she would find information that would prove useful, something she could take back to Avalon and use to help people. At worst, she and Helios would be captured and killed. It was a dangerous choice, to stay when she should go, but some choices weren't really choices at all. She'd made hers before she even embarked on this adventure. The point of no return was miles behind her.

A series of emotions flickered across Helios's face: Deeper incredulity. Stubborn resistance. Then, finally, grudging respect. "Fine," he said, taking her hand. The contact made Ivy feel a little bit braver. "But if we die, my ghost is going to make your ghost miserable in the afterlife."

Ivy waded through stacks of books. Some were piled in teetering towers on the floor; others were scattered across leather seats and mahogany side tables, their spines cracked open to reveal where pages had been ripped out. The massive desk at the room's center was littered with papers, both faded with age and marked up with fresh ink. Ivy rifled through the mess, hunting for books that might contain a neat, foolproof plan to defeat a monster composed of shadows and suffering. Not that she had the foggiest idea what such a tome would look like.

"We don't have much time," Helios whispered. He had one foot in the study and the other in the hall as he kept watch. "You have to hurry."

"I know, I know," Ivy said, sifting through the clutter for something—anything—useful enough to justify her presence in the keep. Regret surged through her. This had been a terrible idea. Shame on the person who'd thought of it.

Almost as soon as her hope began to flag, she found it:

a book about the firebird. Its battered red leather cover bore a gold-embossed bird, its wings spread to show feathers tapering into flames. The book had been left open to a page furiously marked up with ink as red as blood. The page's illustration, however, was not of a firebird. Or any bird. The figure looked like a dragon made of smoke and shadow. Just like Echo's description of the kuçedra that had torn apart the Nest as if its walls were made of paper. Ivy flipped through the pages. There were smaller, more rudimentary illustrations of what looked like battles and piles of corpses, all of which featured the beast hovering like a malevolent god. She turned a page and sucked in her breath when her mind made sense of the crude drawings; there were figures lying prone, as if dead, their limbs marked with blackened veins. Like the Ala. Like all the others wounded by the kuçedra. On the next page, another crude figure bent over one of the prone forms, a cluster of red plants clutched in its hand. On the page after that, the previously stricken figures were rising from their deathbeds, bodies clear of the black veins. Ivy scanned the page, hope bubbling desperately to the surface. There was a cure. They might not yet know how to fight the kuçedra, but they could fight the disease it caused. Tiny problem: the text was entirely in Drakhar.

"Helios, come here," she whispered. He did. She held up the book, pointing to the passage beneath the illustration with the red plants. They needed to move on, but her curiosity got the better of her. "What does this say?"

Helios shook his head, squinting at the page as if trying to summon its secrets. "No idea. This type of written Drakhar is old. Much older than me. The Drakharin haven't used these runes in centuries."

A new voice interrupted them. "What in the name of the gods is going on in here?"

Ivy snapped the book closed and spun around. Two Firedrakes had entered the study, as silent as cats even in full armor. Suspicious glares bounced between her and Helios. This was bad. This was very, very bad.

"Relax," Helios said as he approached them slowly, hands raised to show that he was unarmed. Ivy wasn't sure that unarmed was their best option at the moment. She clutched the book tightly; she wouldn't let them take it from her, not unless they killed her first. But as per usual, she had already been written off as a threat, and neither of the Firedrakes seemed the slightest bit interested in a stolen book.

One of the Firedrakes jerked his head in her direction. "What's the little bird doing out of her cage?" He said it in English, not Drakhar. Probably just to taunt her.

Helios closed the distance between himself and the Firedrakes, ambling up to them as though he didn't have a care in the world. "Well, you see, here's the thing—" His fist lashed out, connecting with one Firedrake's jaw with the sickening sound of bone snapping. The other reacted, but he was slow. Helios knocked the sword from his hand, but the Firedrake recovered quickly and trapped Helios in a headlock. Helios's fingers scrabbled at the arm at his throat, his face turning an alarming shade of red.

There was a small dragon-shaped sculpture holding down a few papers on the desk. It looked heavy enough to do some serious damage if wielded properly. Ivy shifted the book to one hand and grabbed the statue with the other. She marshaled every ounce of strength she had and brought the statue down on the Firedrake's golden helmet. He groaned and his grasp weakened, allowing Helios to slip away. The Firedrake slumped to the ground beside his equally unconscious partner.

"Holy crap," Ivy said, setting the statue back down on the desk. There was an indent in the Firedrake's helmet where she'd struck it.

Helios rubbed his throat and grinned at her through ragged breaths. "I didn't know you had it in you."

Ivy looked at her hands, shocked. It felt as though they belonged to a stranger. "Neither did I."

Helios took a small knife from the belt of one of the fallen Firedrakes. For the first time, Ivy noticed how many blades were tucked away in their armor. She guessed that the element of surprise, no matter how flimsy, rendered even the sharpest weapons irrelevant. Helios offered her the knife hilt-first. "In case you need it," he said.

Ivy accepted the blade, but her fingers shook. She was a healer, not a fighter. Hitting someone over the head was one thing, but this? Stabbing another person? Feeling steel bite through their flesh while their blood spilled out of them? That was something else entirely. She didn't want to be the kind of person who could do that, but as Helios led her through the keep, she began to worry that listening to her conscience was a luxury she could no longer afford.

CHAPTER FORTY-THREE

The muddy terrain of the forest gave way to rocks and slushy sand closer to the shore. The imposing facade of Wyvern's Keep was visible now, looming in the distance like a darker spot of black against the night sky, a few of its windows illuminated by firelight and candles. There was a rocky outcrop that would shield them from view once they arrived at the tunnel opening that Dorian had instructed Ivy to find, but they had to get there first.

Dorian thanked the gods for their run of good fortune when they reached a small stream that marked the point where they would be within range of the archers posted along the keep's walls. Quinn and Jasper came to stand on either side of him. "From here on out, they'll be able to shoot us," Dorian said.

"So, this is the danger zone?" Jasper asked, eyeing the stream. He said it like he was quoting something, but the reference was lost on Dorian. Jasper had been uncharacteristically silent since they'd broken camp and departed that morning. The remainder of the trip had lasted the entire day, which was fine by Dorian since the cover of darkness was a requisite part of the plan to get in and out with minimal fuss and bloodshed. Less fine was the way Jasper clammed up in Quinn's presence. The longer he was around the warlock, the less he seemed like himself.

Quinn shot Jasper a look that was far too intimate. "As much as I adore your brilliant plumage, Jaybird, now's the time to cover up. Your feathers catch moonlight like they're desperate for the attention." With a dismissive wave at Dorian's silvery hair, Quinn added, "And you might wanna do something about that."

Jasper's feathers ruffled. He didn't return Quinn's subtle jab with one of his own, but instead focused on smearing mud on his feathers, while Dorian did the same to his hair. While Dorian would never dare utter the thought aloud, he was sad to see Jasper's feathers covered so. Quinn was right about one thing: they absorbed light in an unearthly fashion, the golds and indigos and fuchsias somehow brighter at night than they were during the day.

"You missed a spot," Quinn noted. His fingers grazed a clean patch of feathers, and Jasper flinched away from the touch. His face was arranged in a careful mask that betrayed nothing of his true feelings, but there was something a little too like panic in his eyes.

"I've got it," Dorian said. He elbowed Quinn out of the way, pointedly ignoring the warlock's starlit glare. Jasper seemed to relax into Dorian's touch. It was the perfect moment for a wisecrack designed to make Dorian blush; therefore it was worrying when Jasper didn't so much as attempt to flirt.

"You okay?" Dorian asked, keeping his voice soft. He didn't much care if Quinn eavesdropped, but he had the feeling that Jasper might.

Jasper offered him a shadow of a smile. "Not really," he whispered back, "but I will be." His eyes darted to where Quinn stood, gazing at the keep in the distance. "Soon enough."

Soon enough. As in, when they didn't need Quinn anymore. They were minutes from the keep. Their business would be concluded soon enough indeed. Then it would be back to New York, Ivy in tow, and they'd have no need for Quinn's services.

The mud was cool and cakey. It squished between Dorian's fingers as he combed it through Jasper's feathers. A contented sigh escaped the Avicen's lips, and Dorian was suddenly aware of the intimacy of the moment. It felt right, touching Jasper like this. As though he could keep doing it all day.

As soon as the thought occurred to him, he dropped his hands. There was enough mud on Jasper's feathers to hide them from sight. Dorian cleared his throat and stepped back, resolutely not reading into the Avicen's arched eyebrow and too-perceptive expression.

"How do I look?" Jasper asked.

"Muddy." Dorian's voice was half an octave deeper than normal. Because Jasper and Quinn were Jasper and Quinn, they both cast him knowing looks.

Not fair, Dorian thought as heat rose in his cheeks. Jasper's lip quirked up on one side. *Not fair at all.*

"Ugh." Quinn stalked off toward the keep, exaggerated disgust radiating off him.

"I take it that means the wards are safe to cross," said Jasper.

"So it would seem." Dorian glanced at Jasper's profile. It was aquiline and regal, even in the darkness. "You don't have to come, you know. You can stay here."

Jasper's affronted glare was answer enough.

"Right," Dorian said. "Onward."

The plan was not to deactivate the wards. Not completely. Dorian knew that simply turning them off would trigger all sorts of alarming results, none of which he had the time or the energy to entertain. The plan, as it stood, was to render a small section of the wards inert—small enough that it would evade notice, but large enough for an Ivy-sized person to get through. The ward would still be intact, but a section of it would cease to perform its designated function. They had only minutes before even that amount of tampering set off the alarms, but Dorian was hoping it would be enough. If everything went according to plan—a rarer occurrence than he would have liked—then they would be home by sunrise.

And the entire endeavor rested in Quinn's slimy warlock hands.

The trio stood upon a narrow, rocky bluff in front of the opening of a drainage tunnel, just out of view from the keep's rear turrets. The smell wasn't fantastic, but it wasn't as pungent as Dorian had feared a sewage runoff might be. If Ivy's escort did his job, she would soon emerge from within the depths of that tunnel, smelling the worse for wear but ideally in one piece. A few feet to either side and they would be visible. Jasper huddled closer to Dorian than was necessary, which he didn't particularly mind. Quinn's shoulder brushed Dorian's with every minor movement, and that he *did* mind.

"Give me your hand," Quinn said, looking at Dorian expectantly, a naked blade in one hand while he held out the other. "I just need a drop of your blood."

This was the part of the spell Dorian had been dreading most. His blood was necessary for the spell, as he had been the one to seal the wards when they were first established, but the thought of allowing Quinn near him with a sharp object was more than a little unsettling. The scar in his eye socket itched. But he was a seasoned warrior of the prince's guard, and he wouldn't let a warlock make him cower like a child.

He offered up his hand and bit the inside of his cheek to keep himself from wincing when Quinn sliced open his palm with gleeful ferocity. Blood poured from the cut in generous rivulets.

"Just a drop?" Dorian asked. He wanted to press something against the wound to slow the bleeding, but giving Quinn the satisfaction of knowing how much it hurt was nowhere close to being an option.

Quinn gave a one-shouldered shrug and knelt down to sink the knife into the dirt. "My hand slipped."

Dorian felt the barely there buzz of magic in the air. Beside him, Jasper shivered, as if cold. But the night air was warmer than usual for Scotland, even at the height of summer, and Dorian knew that Jasper had felt the electric hum of magic as well.

Quinn straightened and raised one hand. He mumbled words in a language Dorian did not recognize. An area about six feet tall wavered the way air seemed to quiver in the heat. "And now, we wait."

"Goody," Jasper said, tucking his hands into his armpits. The feathers on his forearms were still ruffled, sticking up from the drying mud. "This is exactly how I like spending my Friday nights."

"Jasper," Dorian said, "it's Tuesday."

"The point still stands."

The urge to count the seconds was strong. With every passing moment, their situation grew more precarious. The tunnel was pitch-black, and Dorian itched with the desire to storm the keep himself. He wanted to barge in, sling Ivy over his shoulder, and march out of there, but that would be counterproductive in that it would most likely result in the deaths of, oh, everyone.

Under his breath, Jasper whispered, "Come on, Ivy. Come on, come on, come on."

Dorian shared the sentiment. He was sure that it would be some time still before Ivy would deign to call him her friend, but she was one of those people who was so kind and genuine that it was difficult not to like her. Jasper, it seemed, had likewise been charmed by her. Dorian reached out and gave Jasper's shoulder a quick squeeze. For solidarity, of course. Nothing more.

"There," came Quinn's harsh whisper.

Dorian squinted. He could barely make out a spot of white approaching through the tunnel. The closer it got, the more it appeared that Ivy was glowing in the dark. Her feathers were whiter than snow; they were the white of starlight. It was going to take an obscene amount of mud to camouflage them.

Another person walked beside her, but other than making out a shock of black hair and a dark red cloak, Dorian was too far away to see who it was.

They were almost in the clear. Almost home.

But since things so rarely went according to plan, that was the precise moment when they were ambushed from above.

An arrow landed in the dirt at Dorian's feet, and he shoved Jasper to the side without pausing to think twice. Gold metal glinted in Dorian's peripheral vision. At least they charged him on his good side. He turned just in time to see two soldiers clad in gleaming armor leap across the rocks on the other end of the bluff.

Firedrakes.

Dorian crouched low and drew the dagger from his boot. A sword would have been pointless; it was likely he was about to find himself in close combat with more than one Firedrake, and there were archers firing down on them, though judging from the significant lag between volleys of arrows, there weren't very many. Two archers, he estimated; three at most. Ivy and whoever was accompanying her wisely chose to stay in the tunnel. He prayed they would stay there until the fighting was finished.

Quinn, snake that he was, was nowhere to be seen. But his voice carried through the still night air. "Nothing personal, Dorian, but I prefer to hitch my wagon to the winning side of this crazy train. You guys are all cute and noble, but you don't have half of Tanith's resources. And it doesn't hurt when the winning side is offering a prize for cooperating."

A prize? Dorian shot a look at the place where Jasper should have been. He was gone. *Of. Course.*

He almost wished that Quinn's betrayal were a surprise,

but he had called it from day one. Dorian might have been the youngest captain of the guard ever appointed, but he was no fool. When a situation failed to go according to plan, the best thing was to have a backup plan in place.

Quinn emerged from the darkness, one arm slung around Jasper's neck in a manner that managed to look both tender and threatening, while Jasper clutched his backpack with trembling hands. Dorian met Jasper's amber eyes, and something clenched in his chest. For Jasper, the contact must have felt like poison seeping into his skin. Dorian inched out of his hiding spot, dagger in hand. He held his breath and waited for the arrows to fall from the heavens. When no such thing happened, he breathed a sigh of relief.

A Firedrake popped up from behind a nearby boulder like the worst kind of jack-in-the-box, but before Dorian could engage him, a figure snuck up behind the Firedrake and slit his throat with nary a sound. The Firedrake's body sagged, and the Royal Guard that had taken him down nodded tersely at Dorian over a lifeless golden shoulder. The Royal Guards might have been beholden to the Dragon Prince, but Dorian knew his own men. They were on Caius's side, with or without the title.

Sometimes, Dorian loved how good he was at his job.

The sounds of struggle were muffled as Royal Guards emerged from the shadows, dispatching the half a dozen Firedrakes that had set upon Dorian. While in the woods, Quinn must have made contact with someone in the keep to strike some kind of deal. Had Tanith been in residence, Dorian doubted they would have been met with such a small party, but he was glad that his guess about her keeping to the schedule he'd set for visiting the garrison on the southern border had been correct. A single Firedrake stood against his brothers, fighting on the side of the Royal Guards. *Helios,* Dorian thought. He'd been the one to contact Ivy inside the keep. *Good.* He was a decent soldier and an even better man.

Quinn looked less sure of himself as he watched one gold-armor-clad body fall after another. But he still had Jasper by the neck, and that was high on Dorian's list of things that were utterly unacceptable.

"Let him go," he demanded.

The stars faded from Quinn's eyes, replaced by the sickly whiteness that was their true form. The blade he'd used to cut Dorian's palm was now at Jasper's throat. "No." It was impressive how much petulance he could inject into a single word. "Unless you want me to slit his pretty throat, you will let me leave, unharmed. Jasper here is my reward."

Reward. As if Quinn hadn't already lost.

Dorian twirled the dagger in his hand, careful not to cut his fingers. He'd shed enough of his own blood already. "Do you know what your problem is?"

"Enlighten me," Quinn said.

Dorian hoped his grin was as violent as he felt. "You always underestimated him."

Jasper twisted in Quinn's arms, heedless of the blade that nicked his throat, and an iron collar clamped around Quinn's neck before he had the chance to react. Anvil-forged iron. One of the few materials in the world that could stop a warlock from drawing on his magic, so long as the iron was pressed against their skin. Jasper had been carting the collar around in his pack for days, and Dorian had hoped they wouldn't need it. Not because he harbored any sympathy for the warlock but because needing it meant things had gotten messy. At least this mess had a satisfying conclusion. Quinn's hand flew to his throat, clawing at the collar as if it burned. Dorian hoped it did. Jasper's triumphant smile made that thing in Dorian's chest clench again.

Dorian climbed over the rocks to reach Jasper, nodding his thanks to the guards he passed.

Quinn's eyes were fully white now. He no longer had the magic to disguise their hideousness. He spat at Dorian's feet and looked up at Jasper, his expression twisted and cruel. "Can't say I saw that coming. Looks like our little lapdog has teeth after all."

Jasper's grin wilted. "You know what, Quinn? Fu—"

The insult Jasper was about to hurl at the warlock fizzled in his throat when Dorian punched Quinn with all his might. Quinn's ugly white eyes rolled back in his head and he slumped to the dirt, blissfully unconscious. Unconscious people were silent, and silence, Dorian thought, was such an underrated virtue.

Jasper looked at Dorian with a mixture of awe and adoration. "Was that really necessary?" he asked, genuine joy in his renewed smile.

"Yes," Dorian said. "We kept telling him to shut up." He waved at Ivy to signal that it was safe to emerge. "He really should have listened."

Just as he'd hoped, they would be home by sunrise. His fist wasn't happy, and he was fairly certain he had split the skin on his knuckles against Quinn's jaw, but it hardly mattered. Some small pains were worth the inconvenience.

CHAPTER FORTY-FOUR

Exiting the temple was far easier than entering it had been. The familiar feel of the in-between had greeted Caius the moment he walked through the door. Usually, when using the in-between to travel, one had to visualize an image of a destination and hold on to it. Intention was always an important part of magic, but it was especially critical when it came to the in-between. A wandering mind could leave a person floating in that strange and dark space for eternity.

But when Caius entered the doorway, he'd been whisked away before he'd had enough time to fathom what was happening. The gateway must have been enchanted to deposit anyone who used it in a specific place, because he didn't have to imagine a location to exit the darkness. In seconds, the all-consuming blackness of the in-between faded and he was standing on a patch of dry yellow grass. The mountain loomed behind him. He was in a large valley situated amid the range's towering peaks. The ground was dry, but he could smell water and damp leaves nearby. He took the time to examine his surroundings. The gateway had left him in a small circular clearing. About a hundred yards to the west was a small lake. Bare tree trunks protruded from the water, giving the lake the appearance of a drowned forest. To the east was a modest clearing, surrounded by trees tall enough to grant some cover from the elements.

A few minutes passed before Echo and Rowan appeared beside him, one right after the other. Caius didn't miss the way Echo's hand found Rowan's, almost instinctively, it seemed, as the black tendrils of the in-between faded. Her gaze darted around the clearing before she realized they weren't in any danger. She dropped Rowan's hand when she met Caius's eyes. She tried to communicate something with her gaze, but Caius looked away. His head was a mess around her. Messier than it had been when he'd known Rose. That affair had been rife with its own complexities, but at its heart, it had been two people, drawn together by curiosity first, attraction next, then, eventually, love. This . . . thing with Echo was anything but simple. Caius knew he was projecting his feelings for Rose onto her. He had to be. But there was something else lurking in his heart. Something meant for Echo alone. But he—*they*—didn't have time to untangle that mess. He needed to distance himself. Not just for his sake, but for Echo's.

"There's a clearing that way," Caius said, pointing in the appropriate direction. His voice was cold even to his own ears, his face a mask of perfect placidity. "We'll make camp there. There's a lake to the west."

Echo nodded, her expression questioning. Caius returned her looks with a blank stare. She didn't press him for an explanation of his behavior, and for that, he was grateful.

"I'll send word to Altair," said Caius. "I have no doubt he's keen to know what we've all been up to since your . . . departure."

With that, he left. He could feel Echo's eyes on his back as he walked toward the lake. A small part of him told him to go back, to try to explain why he was acting hot one minute and cool the next. But when he thought about the way she and Rowan seemed to gravitate toward one another, a larger part overwhelmed that urge. She had a history with the Avicen she didn't have with Caius. His history was with Rose. It was a shadow of the past, a memory of a life that would never be. Each step took him farther from Echo, in more ways than one. He had confessed to loving her. In that moment, he'd felt a clarity he hadn't in years, but her silence spoke louder than anything she might have said. Her own heart was divided at best. At worst, it belonged to another.

Dusk in the submerged forest was a marvel to behold. Branches worn bare by water and wind thrust up from the surface like bony fingers reaching toward the sky. Fading sunlight danced across the turquoise water, broken up by the canopy of leaves surrounding the lake. Caius stood on the shore's incline, his boots squelching in the mud. He closed his eyes and drew in a deep breath, savoring the fresh air. It was so different from the smog that suffocated London or the faint odor of pollution that hung about New York like a stubborn perfume. Reeds rustled in the breeze. Somewhere in the distance one bird called to another. Birdsong was still a novelty to Caius, who was accustomed to the silence of the woods around Wyvern's Keep. Birds had learned long ago not to roost there lest they be driven out by Drakharin hunting parties. He'd spent his share of summers riding through that forest, first with Tanith at his side, then, when their paths diverged, with Dorian. Once, they'd found a lone albino peacock strutting through a meadow, its white feathers dragging through the grass. It was a regal creature, but it had chosen the wrong place to rest. Caius had felled the bird with an arrow and it had been served at dinner that evening, trussed up to best display its plumage. How times had changed. How Caius had changed.

He hadn't gone far from their camp. It hadn't been a lie that he needed to report to Altair that they had located Echo and were in the process of investigating the kuçedra's origins. But he could have done all that from their camp using the communication spell he'd taught Altair and his Warhawks and the utilitarian switchblade he'd plucked from a supply closet at Avalon before chasing Echo to Scotland. He needed a moment to himself, away from the sight of Rowan and Echo. Together. Close in a way that made Caius's stomach hurt.

He drew the blade tucked into his belt. He'd contact Dorian first. Make sure they were still on track. Sending Ivy in alone had been a desperate move, but desperate moves were all they had left to them. He rolled up one sleeve. It would be safer to nick the flesh of his forearm. Wounding his hands would only compromise his ability to fight should he need to. The way things had progressed in recent months, he wasn't about to let himself be lulled into a false sense of security by the calm of the forest. One must be ready for battle at all times. It was one of the most important lessons he'd learned as a soldier. It was a shame he'd let himself forget it during his reign. If he'd been vigilant, he would have seen Tanith sneaking up behind him, one hand on her sword, the other ready to snatch his crown.

His skin prickled in the breeze. He cut himself, scrawled a message in the Drakhar shorthand he and Dorian had devised ages ago, and passed along his message: *Found E. All safe.* The blade absorbed the blood and a new message appeared on its surface: two parallel lines with a diagonal line cutting across them. Short for "mission accomplished."

Now to contact Altair. Caius set the sharpened edge of the blade against his skin and readied to draw it down, when heat seared through his arm. The knife fell from his fingers. Blood welled on his skin, some of it dripping down to his wrist to bead on his fingers. Symbols appeared in the blood, Drakharin words written by a shaky hand, the very same words he'd used to connect with his sister days earlier. Pain brought him to his knees, the mud soaking the leather of his breeches. Not all of the blood was his.

Caius.

The voice in his head was unmistakable despite the agony laced through it.

"Tanith?" he gasped into empty air. But he knew she heard him.

Help.

His sister never begged. Not when she'd taken an arrow to the chest during the first raid she led, on an Avicen settlement on the Continent, or when she'd broken her leg falling off a horse and had to drag herself to safety lest she be trampled underfoot during the last battle in which she and

Caius fought together. He had never seen anyone grit their teeth and bear their pain without a single complaint the way Tanith did.

But wherever she was now, she was hurt. Badly enough to call out for her brother, despite their rift, her cry defying the miles between them. There was no artifice in her voice. Only pain and fear.

Please.

Caius groped in the mud for his sword, his hand unsteady as he sheathed it, not even bothering to wipe the dirt from the steel. It was the kind of negligence that would have earned him a clout around the ears from his old swords master, but that didn't matter now. Nothing mattered but the feeling of Tanith's pain along the connection they shared.

Caius, please. What have I done? Oh gods, what have I done?

What *had* she done? He couldn't fathom what had left his sister in such a state. The kuçedra was involved somehow, he knew it. The thought of it attacking Tanith, after what he'd seen it do to the Avicen at Grand Central, was too much to consider. He had to tell Echo and Rowan. They'd find Tanith. Wherever she was, the kuçedra was bound to be.

Help me. Help me help me help me.

Her pleas devolved into a broadcast of wordless agony, almost enough to bring Caius to his knees once more, but he fought on.

"Hold on, Tanith," he choked out. He could taste blood in his mouth, but none of it was his. Tangled reeds and fallen logs conspired to trip him as he fought his way through the underbrush. "I'm coming."

CHAPTER FORTY-FIVE

Dorian scrunched his nose against the musty smell of the wine cellar deep within the belly of Avalon Castle. Weak candlelight fought to fill the space, though it was a losing battle. The vaulted stone ceiling was shrouded in darkness, and shadows lurked in every corner. Dust caked the rows of green glass bottles and gathered in the crevices of wine barrels.

He had come down to the cellar after receiving Caius's message shortly after their return to Avalon. He was glad they'd found Echo and gladder still that Caius was with her. She was good for him, impetuous as she was. Dorian was surprised by his lack of jealousy. Caius was happy, and that was enough. His prince had pretended to have a heart of stone for so long, but Dorian had seen through the facade. Caius had been hurting, and now he had found a way to cope with the tangled mess of his heart. Dorian hadn't realized how much his own happiness had been entwined with Caius's until he felt that burden lighten.

A phrase came to mind, a stray snippet of text from one of the books he'd found in Caius's study, written by some human named Bulgakov.

The one who loves must share the fate of the one he loves.

Dorian had shared his prince's pain, and now, like Caius, he had a chance to alleviate his own, free from the shackles of the past, if only he was brave enough to take it.

He turned the corner, heading for the room at the far end of the hall that served as Avalon's prison. The iron collar had neutralized Quinn's power, and the matching iron manacles that Altair had ordered him in upon their return were mostly insult added to injury. Without magic, the warlock was as dangerous as a rabbit. A lone figure stood at the end of the hall, dim light casting a long shadow on the floor behind him.

Dorian paused, watching Jasper stand before the door that separated him from a quiet Quinn. The warlock was either still unconscious or he'd been gagged. Win-win, as far as Dorian was concerned. Jasper's hand rose to lightly touch the iron padlock sealing the door shut. It had been joined by a series of additional locks that shone brightly even in the poor lighting. They must have been new. Dorian waited, silent, wondering.

"I know you're there." Jasper's voice carried in the cavernous space, reverberating off the walls so that even though the words were softly spoken, Dorian heard them just fine. "I can hear you breathing."

"I thought I might find you down here," said Dorian. With measured steps, he closed the distance between them, coming to a halt a few feet from Jasper, who was still facing the door. "You were noticeably absent."

"Let me guess—Echo and her Scooby Gang are planning further hijinks."

Dorian didn't know what a Scooby Gang was, but it sounded about right. "You're usually the type for hijinks."

Jasper snorted softly. "Not really in the mood." He let his hand fall to his side and turned around. "I just wanted to make sure . . ." He looked back at the padlock, then down at his feet.

"He's not going anywhere," Dorian assured him. "And even if he did manage to escape, I wouldn't let him get anywhere near you."

Jasper's gaze cut upward, sharp and yet somehow still vulnerable. Dorian hadn't planned to say that quite so bluntly, but he didn't regret the words and the promise they held. Not in the slightest. It was cool and damp in the cellar, but there was a warmth in his chest that expanded with the softening of Jasper's face.

"Thanks," said Jasper, voice quiet in the darkness. "I'm not used to being like this. I'm not usually the type that needs to be saved."

"We all need saving sometimes." It was probably the truest thing Dorian had ever said. Caius had saved him once, and Dorian had loved him for a century afterward. "There's no shame in that."

The hint of softness that snuck into Jasper's expression felt like a shared secret. The candlelight brought out the golden highlights in his feathers, and Dorian wondered what they would feel like sliding between his fingers without mud in the way.

"You're stronger than you know," he told Jasper.

"So are you."

With a self-deprecating laugh, Dorian said, "I'm not sure that's true."

"You're here, aren't you? Surrounded by Avicen. That

can't be easy for you." A cocksure little grin tugged at Jasper's mouth. "I know I'm a special exception."

He was. Gods, he was. But Dorian wasn't nearly as brave as Jasper gave him credit for. Admitting his desires to himself was one thing. Acting on them was another matter entirely. When in doubt, he mused, change the subject. "You should get some rest. If we're going to go toe-to-toe with the kuçedra, we should meet our foe bright-eyed and clearheaded."

Jasper wilted, just enough to make something deep in Dorian's chest tighten. "Yeah. Rest. Very important."

"You've been through a lot," Dorian added. "You deserve a good night's sleep."

Jasper nodded, gaze darting to the oak barrels piled into pyramids. "Maybe I'll go do that." He didn't so much as lean in the direction of the exit.

"Right," Dorian said. "I'll just—" He rocked back on his heels, unsure of himself in a way he hadn't been in years. He felt like an awkward adolescent. It was embarrassing. "I should go," he said while making absolutely no move to do so.

Jasper licked his lips. It was nothing more than a quick flash of his tongue, but the movement drew Dorian's eye. "You could," Jasper said. "Or . . ."

The conversation was rapidly spiraling out of control, and Dorian wasn't sure he could stop it. He wasn't even sure he wanted to.

Jasper reached for him, tracing the joints of Dorian's index finger with his own. The touch was featherlight but electric. It was as though the skin on his finger were connected to every nerve ending in his body. His heart pounded so hard he was sure Quinn would be able to hear it through the thick wooden door.

"Or you could stay with me," Jasper finished. "I'm not the only one who's earned a good night's sleep."

Dorian swallowed. He couldn't answer. They'd shared space before, slept within feet of each other. First in the warehouse in London, then again in the woods beyond Wyvern's Keep. But this was different. There was a promise in Jasper's words of something that Dorian wasn't sure he could handle. The silence filled the room, punctuated only by the harsh rasp of his own breathing.

Slowly, and with great gentleness, Jasper twined his fingers with Dorian's.

"Look," Jasper began, "I'm not great with this slow burn we have going. I tend to fall into things with people as violently as I fall out of them." He jerked his head toward the padlocked door. "Exhibit A is locked up in there. But for you . . . I could do slow. As slow as you like. Whatever you want. Nothing you don't."

When Dorian failed to respond, Jasper stepped into his space, their chests brushing with each inhalation. This close, Dorian could see the individual streaks of color in Jasper's eyebrows, a microcosm of the indigo and fuchsia feathers on his head.

Jasper's hands trailed up Dorian's arms and came to rest on his shoulders. Less than an inch separated them in height, but Jasper still had to stretch onto his toes to place the gentlest of kisses on Dorian's eye patch. His lips hovered there for a moment before he lowered himself back to the ground. He kissed the scar tissue on Dorian's cheek, then a spot on his jaw right beneath his ear that made the synapses in Dorian's brain misfire. Jasper's breath tickled the side of his neck.

"See?" Jasper mouthed the word against Dorian's throat. "I can do slow. Just tell me what you want."

And so Dorian did. The only way he knew how.

He cupped Jasper's chin with one hand while the other pressed into the Avicen's lower back, bringing them as close as was physically possible. He poured everything into that kiss, every ounce of frustration and fear and hope he'd felt since the day he entered Jasper's life, half-dead and covered in his own blood. Jasper's teeth caught on his lower lip, and Dorian barely registered the growl that started low in his chest. Jasper's hands clutched at his biceps, fingers digging deep into the muscle. Dorian brought his hands up to card through Jasper's feathers, and they were every bit as silky as he'd imagined. And oh, how he had imagined this, late at night, lying on a rocky forest floor, the stars the only witness to his silent yearning. Jasper matched Dorian's ferocity, but after a few moments, he seized control of the kiss, turning it into something slow and sweet.

When they pulled back for air, Jasper smiled, bright and true, a puff of laughter on his lips. "Took you long enough," he said.

The complexity of language was still too much to ask of Dorian's addled brain, so he answered with a chaste kiss at the corner of Jasper's lips, where another small smile was forming. Jasper sighed against his mouth.

"We should go," said Jasper. He took a step back, but Dorian followed, his body acting of its own accord, as if he were a moth drawn to the flame. "I think this'll be a lot better when my evil ex-boyfriend isn't on the other side of the door."

Clearing his throat, Dorian nodded. "Yes. Let's." The words came out thin and reedy, oxygen-starved.

He stepped away from Jasper, and the cool air of the cellar was the most wicked kind of torture against his feverish skin.

Jasper pulled a bottle of red wine off a nearby rack. He examined its label, but the text had long since worn off. Regardless, he slanted his eyes up at Dorian, a mischievous spark dancing in their amber depths. "A fine vintage, I'm sure."

"I have no need for liquid courage," Dorian said. And he didn't. Not now.

Jasper's lopsided smirk deepened. "We'll see," he said with a wink.

And in that moment, in that bubble of stolen time, Dorian found it hard to care that an ancient evil was looming on the horizon, or that the halls were full of Avicen, or that his prince and the firebird were probably off causing all kinds of trouble. All that mattered was this sliver of time and the warmth of Jasper's hand in his as they climbed the stairs, leaving the ghosts of their pasts behind.

CHAPTER FORTY-SIX

They made camp in the small clearing Caius had indicated, though he had made himself scarce. Echo watched Rowan build a fire; it would be cold once darkness fell, and they'd need the warmth. She nibbled on one end of a granola bar unearthed from the depths of her backpack. It tasted like ash. Wisps of smoke rose from the kindling Rowan had collected. Smoke became flames as the dry twigs and grass caught fire. Pleased with his handiwork, Rowan rose and brushed the dirt from the knees of his jeans. He spared a glance in the direction Caius had gone. When it became clear that Caius was not returning right that instant, Rowan made his way to where Echo sat.

"What did you see?" he asked. He lowered himself onto the log beside her. "You know, if you feel like sharing. No pressure."

Echo picked at the log's bark, flicking it off with her fingernails. For someone who hadn't gone camping a day in her life, who had no latent desire to ever go camping, she'd spent more time in the woods in the past three months than she cared to. The things she had seen clung to her still, like a film. She let out a deep breath. The air was comfortably cool compared with the sweltering humidity of summertime New York. There, it was all glass and concrete and metal, baking in the sunshine. In this land untouched by civilization—human or otherwise—the air was clean and fresh and carried the scent of wet bark and soggy leaves from the direction of the sunken forest.

It would be easy, Echo thought, to pretend the past few hours hadn't happened, to push them so far down into the well of her memory that she'd never be able to retrieve them. They would rot down there, lost like the fragments of her previous life, too painful to recover. But forgetting was a luxury she could not afford. The mountain and its ghosts had made sure of that. Her torments had been selected with care and for a reason. There was a lesson to be mined from her time in the cave's temple, and it didn't take Echo a great deal of digging to unearth it.

"I saw the things I fear the most," she said. Beside her, Rowan went still, either unsure of what to say or giving her the space to speak as much or as little as she pleased. Listening had always been a strength of his. He never pushed or cajoled. Never forced a truth the speaker wasn't ready to relinquish. He simply waited, patient. Kind. She didn't deserve him. No one did. He was pure in a way Echo had never been. The mountain had seen fit to remind her of that, too.

"I saw my mother," she said quietly.

Rowan plucked a dandelion sprouting from the dry earth.

A breeze caught its seeds and carried them away. He and Echo watched in silence as the puffy white down danced like wisps of cotton on the wind. After the dandelion fluff dispersed into the air, off to pollinate the next patch of soil, Rowan said, "You never talk about her."

Echo shrugged, her shoulders tight, the muscles in her neck tense. "There's not much to say, I guess. I ran away from that part of my life. Literally. I haven't really felt the need to look back. It's the past. It's over."

She could feel Rowan's eyes on her, studying her profile. Hers stayed locked on the horizon, watching the sun sink between the masses of two distant peaks, a triangle of pale gold against a backdrop of dusty pinks and purples.

"I don't think that's true," Rowan said. "The ghosts or the magic or whatever it was that lives in that mountain showed you what it did for a reason. Nothing's ever really over. Maybe we stop dealing with things, but they're still there. You wouldn't have seen your mom if your past wasn't still affecting you. What exactly happened in your vision? Or nightmare, or whatever we're gonna call it, because I really don't freaking know what the hell just happened to us."

"Don't call her that."

"Call her what?"

Echo didn't even speak the word. She didn't want it to sit on her tongue, cancerous. A poison.

"Mom?" Rowan asked.

Echo's nod was tight and shallow. "It's too . . . familiar," she said. "I need distance."

"Okay," Rowan said. "But don't think I didn't notice you avoiding the question."

A small part of Echo hated him in that moment. She cast him a sidelong glance. "You're annoying when you're perceptive. More so than usual."

He offered her a lazy half smile and flicked a bit of bark at her. "Sorry, not sorry." He nudged her with his shoulder, an amicable gesture. Friendly. Platonic. A quick thrill flashed through Echo at the contact. They'd been so careful not to touch each other since her return to New York that she'd almost forgotten how natural it felt. "You know you can tell me anything," he said. "Anything at all." He tapped the side of his head. "My brain is a vault. All your secrets are safe with me."

A soft huff of laughter escaped Echo. "A leaky vault, maybe." Maybe Rowan was right. She'd borne her secrets for so long that she'd grown accustomed to their weight, like a snail lugging around a shell. But—and just hours ago, this scenario had seemed so impossible it wasn't even worth considering—maybe she didn't have to carry them around with her anymore. Perhaps Pandora's box was better left opened.

"When we were in the temple," said Echo, "I saw her. Her face, her hair. Every detail was spot-on. I've done a pretty good job of not picturing her face all these years. Somewhere down the line, I convinced myself that if I forgot her face, I would forget her. That it would all seem less real if I just pretended it was nothing more than a bad dream."

"What did she do?" Rowan asked. "When you were little?"

"She hurt me."

He didn't ask how. And they both knew there was no point in asking why. There was no logic involved when parents harmed their children. It contradicted the bonds of biology, violated the rules of nature. The details, Echo thought, were less important than the damage inflicted. The events of her early childhood had shaped her, for better or worse. They had provided her with the lens through which she viewed the world. They had become the material with which she'd built the stone walls around her heart. Few had ever breached those walls, and each time someone did, it was nothing short of a minor miracle.

"I was just a kid," Echo said. The injustice of it was something she would never outgrow.

"You still are," Rowan said.

Echo shook her head. "In years, maybe, but you don't stay a kid for very long when you're shown just how awful and ugly people can be." She examined her fingernails. Brownish dust was caked around her cuticles. Her hands were in dire need of a good wash. "When I think about my childhood, I don't remember school or birthday parties or cartoons. Do you know what I remember? The only thing that comes to mind?"

"What?"

"Fear. That's it. It's like this yawning chasm in my memory has swallowed everything that's not fear. It's like a black hole. I remember what it felt like to be afraid to leave my room in the morning. To expect to be hurt if I dropped a plate or didn't put away the dishes just right. I remember fear and pain and humiliation and the unique sense of betrayal that comes from the realization that the one person in the world who should love you automatically, unconditionally, doesn't. There's nothing quite like that."

The sun continued to drop below the horizon. Soon, shadows would creep through the trees, blanketing the valley in the cover of night. There was an ache in her chest that felt like a knot. Talking to Rowan felt like pulling at that knot with clumsy hands in a vain attempt to unravel it. Airing her burden hadn't made Echo feel any lighter, but now that the words were tumbling forth, she felt powerless to prevent their escape.

"Sometimes, I wonder what went through her mind the first time she hit me. I don't remember if she was drunk or sober. Not that it really matters; she was awful either way. But I've always been curious. I was her child. She gave me life and it was like she didn't even care." And now the awful truth, the secret worry she'd kept hidden, even from herself. "Sometimes, I wonder if it's genetic. I don't know if she was always rotten, or if her soul went bad gradually, like sour milk. But if she could turn bad, then maybe I can too." Echo gnawed on her lower lip. The skin felt trapped and dry, yet the discomfort, however minor, was a welcome distraction. "But there's one thing that still confuses me. I saw the vision with my mother and you saw a nightmare with me dying, right? We both had to overcome those dreams or hallucinations or whatever you want to call them in order to escape and enter the temple, but . . ."

Her voice trailed off. The image of her city in ruins was as vivid as it had been when she'd been in it. Every detail stood out in excruciating detail: The smoke curling against an ashen sky. The bite of a bullet as it pierced her skin. The way the hatred in Ivy's eyes had been flecked with sorrow.

"I didn't see one vision," said Echo. "I saw two."

Rowan's brow furrowed. "Two? Why would the mountain make you go through that twice?"

Echo shook her head, equally perplexed. "I don't know. All I know is that I saw myself standing in the middle of Fifth Avenue, surrounded by chaos and destruction, and it was all my fault. It wasn't like the first vision. I didn't have to overcome anything to get out." She remembered Ivy's finger on the trigger, how her friend's hand hadn't shaken even the slightest bit before pulling it. "I died, I think. And then I woke up in the temple."

Rowan hummed in consideration. "Maybe it wasn't a test."

"What do you mean?"

"Well, we all had to face a fear to get to the temple. We had to face the thing that scared us the most and overcome it to, I don't know, prove that we were worthy or something. And we all did. But maybe your second vision wasn't a test."

"Then what would it be?" Echo asked.

Rowan's expression settled into grim lines. He looked older than he had when they'd entered the mountain. "I think it was a warning, meant only for you."

"Because I'm the firebird," Echo said. "And the prophecy never guaranteed I'd be good or evil, light or dark. It could go either way." A thought occurred to her, sudden and terrible. "Maybe that's why the kuçedra is drawn to me. It can sense the darkness inside me."

Rowan took her hand and held it tightly between both of his. "There might be darkness in you, but there's light, too. There always has been. And it's a lot stronger than you realize. I'm not talking about Echo the firebird. I'm talking about Echo the person. I *know* you. I've known you since you were a snot-nosed brat, stealing anything shiny or edible you could get your grubby little hands on. Your genetics don't determine the kind of person you are. Neither does your upbringing. Being good is a choice you make, and I've seen you make it every day for the past ten years, in the way you take care of the Ala and the Avicelings and Ivy and me. You are kind, and you are brave, and you care about people. Really, truly, selflessly care. Do you realize how rare that is? If kindness and bravery were easy to pull off, the world would be a much sunnier place. And if you can't believe in yourself yet, then know that I believe in you. I believe in your goodness and your light, especially when you can't see it." He shrugged, punctuating the movement with a weary sigh. "Maybe the mountain had a more tough-love approach to reminding you that it's your choices that define you, not fate."

Echo wanted to believe him. She wanted it more than anything else. "But . . . Ruby." The name was heavy between them, like a stone sinking to the bottom of the ocean. The memory of that night rose to the surface. A splash of blood on marble tile, warm and viscous and as bright as a gemstone. The scrape of steel against bone. The squelching sound the dagger made as she pulled it free. The way the soles of her boots slipped in the widening pool of Ruby's blood. "That's the kind of stain that doesn't wash away."

Rowan's shoulders stiffened, his lips pressed together in a tight line. His hold on her hand slackened, but he didn't let go. "I've thought about that day a lot. For a while it was the only thing I could think about. I kept wondering what I could have done differently. If I could have saved her. If I could have stopped you from doing what you did." He kept her hand in one of his and ran the other through his hair-feathers, smoothing down the unruly strays. They gleamed gold and bronze in the dying light. When he looked at her, Echo felt as if she were gazing into the eyes of a stranger. He'd changed so much in her absence. His youthful softness had hardened as he'd traveled the path from boy to man. There was experience in those hazel eyes. Wisdom. Compassion. And determination.

"I thought about every possibility, every potential scenario. And do you know what conclusion I came to?"

Echo arched an eyebrow in lieu of a question.

"I realized—Altair helped me realize that I had to forgive myself. I couldn't move on, I couldn't learn from any of it if I let my guilt consume me. And in forgiving myself, I found that I was able to forgive you."

"There is no way in hell Altair said that last part."

A rueful smile played at the corners of Rowan's mouth. "No, not in so many words." He chuckled softly, and the sound of it was a little sad, a little tragic. "Turns out forgiving you is a lot easier than forgiving myself. But I have to try." He gave her hand a gentle squeeze. "I think that's the best anyone can do. We never, ever let ourselves forget the things that have happened, good or bad, but that doesn't mean we're trapped by them. They inform us. They don't define us."

Echo leaned against his side. When he didn't protest, she rested her head on his shoulder. "You got a lot smarter in my absence."

"Yeah, well, someone had to pick up the slack with you gone." He raised his shoulder, jostling her playfully. "Although I think my supply of sappy self-awareness has been depleted. How about we—"

His words were cut off by the sound of someone crashing through the bushes, twigs snapping underfoot. Echo and Rowan scrambled to their feet. Caius burst into the circle of their camp, his eyes wild, the sleeve of one arm soaked with blood. "It's Tanith," Caius gasped. His forehead was covered in a sheen of sweat. "We have to find her. Now."

CHAPTER FORTY-SEVEN

They stood on a forgotten spit of land miles from civilization, the crisp salt scent of the North Sea filling Echo's lungs with a powerful longing. It reminded her of homesickness, but this home had never been hers.

Hiraeth, Echo thought. *Welsh. "Homesickness tinged with sorrow."* It was the only word she could think of to describe what she was feeling—what Rose was feeling.

Her skin felt too tight, like there wasn't enough room in her body for all the emotion it held. When the dark swirls of the in-between faded, Rose had surged forward, summoned by recognition. The island hadn't changed much since her death. The gently sloping hills were still covered with long, yellow-green grass that swayed lazily in the breeze. The shore was still composed of pebbles that gave way to wet sand. The sky was still full of streams of drab white clouds cutting across a field of gray, as if the heavens themselves hid their colors in mourning.

The most noticeable difference was the cabin. What had once been a modest single-room dwelling, with a chimney cheerfully puffing smoke and a cluster of stubborn flowers growing in the equally modest garden, was now nothing but barely visible ruins. Weeds poked up from between the rotted remnants of the floorboards, and moss coated the logs that had survived the blaze. The bricks from the fireplace had collapsed in a messy pile.

Caius stood in what had once been the center of the cabin, his hands at his sides, his face inscrutable. Not a single tear fell from his dry eyes. He didn't even frown. He simply kept his gaze, shadowed with grief, trained on the ground.

"What's he doing?" Rowan's voice was a hushed whisper, as if he, too, could feel the island's funereal pall, even if he didn't understand why sorrow clung to this place like a heavy perfume.

"Mourning," said Echo.

Rowan nodded, silent. Caius was not—would never be—his favorite person, but there was something about witnessing a soul shrouded in grief that had the power to soften even Rowan's belligerence.

Echo knew, without being told, that this was the first time Caius had returned to the island, to the cabin, this woeful monument to a love forged in secrecy and destroyed by fire. He had never visited the spot where Rose's ashes had been left, either absorbed by the dirt or carried off by the wind, never to be given a proper burial. Echo felt Rose retreat, as if she, too, were swallowed whole by memories of happiness lost and a future stolen.

When Caius spoke, his voice was rough, as if chiseled by sadness. "We should go. We have to find Tanith." His eyes were the darkest shade of green Echo had ever seen. "The battlefield isn't too far from here."

As they picked their way around rocks and the odd plank of wood marking the location of the village that had been leveled during the fighting, Echo slipped her hand into Caius's. His fingers tightened around hers in a silent gesture of gratitude. If Rowan felt even the slightest inkling of condemnation to her gesture, he kept such thoughts to himself. This wasn't about him. This wasn't even about Echo. This was about Caius and his pain and doing the least she could possibly do to alleviate it, to remind him that he wasn't alone.

They came to a meadow of knee-high grass dotted with little clusters of white and yellow flowers.

In the center of the meadow, a lone figure knelt, nearly hidden by the tall grass. Blond hair whipped around her head, and the edges of her scarlet cloak fluttered in the wind.

Caius relinquished his hold on Echo's hand. "Stay here," he said softly.

Echo took a step forward, ready to argue, but Rowan's hand on her arm stilled her.

"Echo. Please." The plaintive quality of Rowan's request was more effective than the hold he had on her forearm. She would stay put. For now.

She studied the sight before her, some primal alarm beginning to sound in the back of her mind. There was something about the downward tilt of Tanith's head and the defeated set of her shoulders that silenced Echo's protest. Tanith didn't look dangerous; she looked sad. Echo inched forward. Rowan barely even put up a fight. His curiosity, it would seem, was just as strong as hers.

Caius approached his sister, feet barely making a sound. "Tanith?"

She looked up, expression drawn and hesitant. "Caius?" Her voice was small and scared, as if she weren't certain whether her brother was real or imagined. Her hollow cheeks were tinged pink, dirtied by a combination of tears and dried blood, and her eyes were puffy and red-rimmed. Her golden gown was soiled, and her exposed arms were covered in gashes. This was not the fearsome warrior who had rained fire down on the Black Forest. Echo felt a tug of something she thought she would never feel toward the person who had snuffed out lives as easily as blowing out candles: pity.

But that pity dissolved the closer Echo came to the place where Tanith knelt. She hadn't come to this island alone. Wind rustled the grass, revealing hints of crimson fabric and gilded armor arrayed in a circle around Tanith: Firedrakes, nearly hidden by the tall grass, bodies frightfully still. They were all dead.

Tanith lowered her head again as Caius and Echo approached, her red eyes transfixed by the sight of blood on her hands. "I needed a sacrifice," she said softly, as if to herself. "It wouldn't come without a sacrifice."

A sacrifice, Echo thought. Like the one she'd made to unleash the firebird. But that had been a selfless act, powered by her desire to save not herself but her friends. This . . . this was a senseless act of violence, designed to court a darker power. A binding required a death. Echo had given the firebird hers. Tanith had given the kuçedra the lives of those who had followed her here.

"I had to come here," Tanith continued. "The ritual said . . ." Her voice fractured and the words scattered.

"What?" Caius prompted. "What did the ritual say?"

Tanith's voice was small and broken when she answered. "I had to find the place where my heart felt its darkest." Her eyes slid to meet Caius's. "This is where I hurt you the most. You loved a girl and I stole her from you." A black-veined hand hovered near Caius's chest, over his heart. "I'm sorry," she whispered.

Echo inched even closer. The gashes on Tanith's arms weren't random. Even with the crusted rivulets of blood running down her skin, Echo could see that the marks formed the shapes of runes. The veins in her forearms showed blue black through her pale skin.

They were too late, Echo realized. The kuçedra had already been bound to Tanith. The Dragon Prince had performed the ritual, and the darkness had found its anchor, its vessel. It lived in Tanith now just as the firebird lived within Echo. No longer was it a wild force weaving a path of indiscriminate destruction through the world—now it had a will to guide it.

Caius fell to his knees beside Tanith and pulled her into his arms. She rested her head on his shoulder, her body racked by a harsh, broken sob. "What have I done? Oh gods, what have I done?" Caius stroked her hair from her face while she mumbled the question over and over, begging for absolution that would never come, not now that she had called such a force to her side and bound herself to it. No longer was the kuçedra a free entity, wandering the earth like a lost and monstrous child. It belonged to Tanith, body and soul, the way the firebird belonged to Echo.

"I'm sorry," Tanith mumbled again and again. "I'm so sorry."

Caius cradled his sister's face in his hands. He was gentler than Echo had ever seen him. "It'll be all right," he promised. "We can fight this, Tanith. Together."

"Caius, we can't help her," Echo said. As she watched, something black and viscous began to spread through the veins in Tanith's arms, racing through her bloodstream. Dark tendrils wound around her neck, stretching toward her jaw, her cheeks. Inching closer and closer to Caius's hands.

"She's right," Tanith agreed, her voice distant and sad. She lifted a hand, reaching for Caius's cheek. "I'm sorry, Brother."

White-hot fear coursed through Echo. Somehow she knew that if Tanith's hand touched Caius, something terrible would happen. The veins in Tanith's hand grew even blacker, like shadows pumped through them instead of blood.

She was contaminated. And if she placed any infected part of her on Caius, the contagion would seep into him. The kuçedra had claimed Tanith, and now, like a parasite, it wanted to spread.

Echo shouted a warning and raised one hand, acting without thinking. Flames leaped from her palm, racing through the air to crash against Tanith's side. Shadows spooled around Tanith like a shield, but the force of the blow was enough to knock her away from Caius. She pushed herself to her hands and knees, looking down at her black-veined arms in a daze. Caius started toward her, as if to help her stand. Echo pulled him back.

"No," she said firmly. "There's nothing you can do for her."

His face was stricken. He looked helpless. "But I have to help her."

Echo shook her head, sadness swelling with her urgency. "She's beyond our help now." She bit the inside of her cheek hard enough to draw blood. "Caius. Please."

Tanith struggled to her feet, gown shredded from the knees down, red eyes darkened by shadows. Her lips curled back into a snarl, and Echo knew then that Tanith was lost. Orange fire crackled to life around Tanith's fists, and she lifted her hands, lining up her target.

Echo tugged on Caius's arm. Fire, wild and uncontrolled, burned a ring in the grass around Tanith. They had only two options: flee or die.

With a snarl, Tanith surged forward, grabbing Caius by the arm and pulling him toward her.

Echo lunged before she had time to consider that it was maybe a terrible idea. Rowan reached for her, but she was faster, slipping through his grasp as she threw herself forward. She collided with Tanith and Caius with enough force to send them all toppling to the ground in a tangle of limbs. She could not let Tanith infect Caius with whatever dark magic was pumping through her veins. Echo's hand shot out to smack Tanith's away. The moment their bare skin connected, the world around Echo fell away. Gone was the salt of the sea air, the tall yellow grass, the blood-soaked earth. It was almost like traveling through the in-between: she felt the same weightlessness, the same sense of being everywhere and nowhere as her molecules floated through the unseen spaces of the world. But when she opened her eyes, it was not the velvety blackness of the in-between that greeted her. She was standing in a quiet room bathed in the warm glow of firelight.

It was a library. A modest one, much smaller than Caius's study in Wyvern's Keep, though the architectural details were similar. Above the lintel, a dragon's head stared down at her, curling horns rising from the top of its head. A fireplace in the corner was burning merrily, logs crackling and popping as the bark peeled and turned to ash. The walls were lined from floor to ceiling with shelves, on which books were stacked two rows deep. The wooden shelves buckled under their weight. A desk stood before a bank of windows, its surface buried beneath sheaves of parchments and scrolls held down with pots of ink and rounded stones. Frost climbed the windowpanes. Echo took a step toward the desk and felt the swirl of heavy skirts against her legs. Skirts? The last time she'd worn a skirt was the Easter before she'd run away from home, when her mother had wrestled her into a pink velvet monstrosity and dragged her to church. Echo looked down and saw that she was wearing a crimson wool gown thick enough to ward off a winter chill. A golden silk cloak was fastened around her shoulders and spilled over her gown.

She raised a hand to her face, afraid of what she would find. Her fingers traced her features, but they were not hers. The cheekbones were higher, the jawline more defined. Her hair was piled on her head in elaborate braids far more intricate than anything Echo had ever worn. And, she noticed as she pulled loose a few strands, it was blond.

CHAPTER FORTY-EIGHT

Echo was in Tanith's memory. Echo *was* Tanith in this memory. Her legs were long, her arms well defined, her muscles honed from decades of training. Her body moved of its own accord, as though Echo were merely a passenger along for the ride. The door to the library opened, and a man entered, closing the door behind him only after he scanned the hall outside as if to make sure no one had followed him. His golden hair was slicked back and his pale skin shone like alabaster in contrast. Iridescent scales dusted his temples, and his eyes were the gray of storm clouds. They softened when he met Echo's—Tanith's—gaze. With two long strides, he closed the distance between them and took her in his arms. His kiss was fierce and bruising, his hands clutching fistfuls of her cloak.

She pulled away, her breath a deep sigh. "Is it done?" she asked. The words felt strange on her tongue, and it took Echo a moment to realize she was speaking Drakhar. This was a memory. Like the one she had endured as Samira during the Ala's hypnotic trance.

The man nodded, his eyes lingering on her lips. "Yes, my love."

She turned away, her cloak brushing against the man's leather boots. "Do not speak of love to me, Oeric. It is an indulgence I cannot afford. Not now, when the crown is just within my reach."

The man—Oeric—stiffened at the rebuke. "The votes are yours," he said. "And as far as those who could not be bought . . . I'm sure you'll be able to think of some way to win their compliance."

She nodded, turning to a large tome left open on the desk. It was a list of names, written alongside insignia that looked like coats of arms. Tanith's fingers—callused from years of handling a sword—dragged along the names, crossing invisible lines through some, tapping on others. "Everyone has a weakness," she said, a finger landing on the name at the top. *Caius, Prince of Dragons.* "Power is a game. To win, one must find those weaknesses and exploit them. It is simply a matter of exerting the right amount of pressure at the optimal time."

"And your brother?" Oeric asked. "How much pressure will you be exerting on him?"

Tanith's hand lingered over Caius's name. Slowly, she dragged her finger across the letters, slashing an invisible line through them. "He is not to be harmed," she said. "Detained, perhaps, after the vote. But not harmed."

"My love, surely you see the folly in allowing him to—"

She spun, striking out as quick as a snake. Her hand closed around Oeric's throat, her thumb pressing against his windpipe. "I said"—her voice was low and deadly, laced with the promise of pain—"that my brother is not to be harmed." She squeezed. Oeric's fingers scrabbled at her hand, but he might as well have been trying to pry off bands of solid iron. "Do you see now, what I mean about exerting pressure?" Her grip tightened again, and Oeric's eyes began to water. "You need only exert the right amount to get what you want."

She released him. He doubled over, hands on his knees, and drew in several shuddering breaths. With a gentle hand, she touched his shoulder and he peered up at her, expression wary, as if he expected to be hurt. She helped him stand and caressed the bruises already beginning to blossom on his neck. "I do not intend to hurt the people I care about unless absolutely necessary, Oeric. This isn't about punishing Caius. This is about doing what's right. And you want to do what's right, don't you, Oeric?"

He nodded, trembling under her touch. "Of course I do."

Sparks appeared at the corners of Echo's vision. The world shifted and re-formed around her. The room in Wyvern's Keep changed: the rug transformed into knee-high yellow grass; the stone floor softened into brown earth. The ceiling opened up to gray skies, the light of the fire burning in the hearth blazed with the sun's pale brightness. The memory was pulled from Echo gradually, peeled off in layers until she was left kneeling in the dirt, her hands inches from Tanith's arm. Echo gazed into crimson eyes blackened around the edges of the irises. She saw her own alarmed expression mirrored by Tanith's face, but the Drakharin recovered far quicker than Echo did. Bloodstained hands pushed against the ground as Tanith sprang to her feet, her movements quick and jerky, as if she wasn't quite in full command of her body. Maybe it was the kuçedra, pulling Tanith's strings like a puppeteer, forcing her to reach for Caius once more, her arms locking around him like a vise. Fire erupted from the earth, creating a barrier around Tanith and Caius.

Echo didn't make it past a kneeling position before a wave of vertigo overtook her. The island appeared to be spinning and Echo buried her hands in the long grass to steady herself. Magic electrified the air. It was too much for her. Firebird or not, her body was still human and she could only take so much magic. Rowan called to her, his voice drowned out by the crackling flames. The orange of Tanith's fire was consumed by black wisps of smoke. It took a handful of moments for Echo's brain to make sense of what she was seeing. The fire was giving way to the in-between. Somehow, Tanith had summoned a gateway to it. In the middle of the field. Far from any natural threshold to anchor it. Such a thing should have been impossible. Calling forth a door to the in-between without a proper threshold wasn't one of Tanith's strengths. It was Caius's. But this didn't appear to be his doing.

Echo had half a second to meet Caius's eyes, to see the genuine fear in them, before both he and Tanith were swallowed by a plume of black smoke. Tanith's fire merged fully with the darkness of the in-between and surged upward for several terrifying seconds. Then, the circle of black fire disappeared, unable to sustain itself without its mistress.

The smoke cleared. Tanith and Caius were gone.

"Caius?" The distant, rational part of Echo knew there was no point in calling his name, but she couldn't help it. She reached back, groping wildly for Rowan. His hand, strong and warm and rough from sword practice, found hers, and he pulled her close. It was just them and the bodies of the Firedrakes. A vulture circled overhead, waiting for them to leave so that it could fall upon its meal.

"Caius is gone," Rowan said. He began tugging Echo toward the shore, where they would be able to access the in-between and flee. "Echo, come on, we have to go."

She dug her heels in, refusing to follow. She couldn't tear her eyes from the spot where Caius had stood. Gone. He was gone. Just like that. Gone, gone, gone. "No."

"Echo!" That one word was packed with every bit of exasperation and fear she imagined Rowan must be feeling. He moved to stand directly in front of her and seized her hands, hazel eyes pleading. "We can't stay here. We have to go back. We have to tell Altair what happened. He has to know."

Echo tore her eyes from the empty patch of grass she could still see over Rowan's shoulder.

"We have to save him." Even as she said it, she knew that she was asking the impossible.

But because Rowan was Rowan, he didn't tell her so. He didn't bring logic into it. He merely nodded and said, "We will. But first, we need to go back to Avalon. I don't understand what just happened here, but I know it's not good. The others need to know. We need to prepare for"—he shot a look behind him, taking in the cooling corpses and the burnt grass and the blood seeping into the ground—"whatever the hell is coming our way."

Echo couldn't bring herself to answer. She simply let herself be led away, knowing she had lost.

CHAPTER FORTY-NINE

The relative tranquility of Avalon made Echo want to scream, to rip out her hair, to throw a tantrum of unholy proportions. But all she could do was meet Altair's furious gaze from across a mahogany table in the dining hall and repeat, for what felt like the millionth time, "I told you: I left. I followed Caius's lead to Edinburgh. Got info that took me to London. Found the map. Found them"—she tilted her head toward Rowan, whose thigh bounced as he fidgeted in his seat, the other member of their little group conspicuously absent—"then the three of us went to the Tian Shan mountains, where we found the temple with those red weeds. The bloodweed."

Said weeds had been confiscated as soon as Rowan and Echo had returned to Avalon. As they were marched to the dining hall on Altair's furious orders, Echo had overheard a passing group of healers discussing Ivy's return. The knowledge that Ivy had made it back safely, Dorian and Jasper towing an unconscious Quinn behind them, burned in Echo's chest, her relief as bright as the rising sun.

Her backpack had been searched and the weeds had been handed off to the healers in charge of the infirmary, where the survivors were worsening with alarming speed. A dozen had died in the night, including the only surviving council member besides Altair and the Ala. If the radio reports were to be believed, though, the Avicen were holding up much better than those in Manhattan. Every human victim of the attack on Grand Central who had been similarly infected had succumbed to the kuçedra's poison and died. The Centers for Disease Control and Prevention was at a loss for an explanation. They were running out of time. For the Avicen still living. For the Ala. Time was a luxury no one had. Every beat of Echo's heart felt like a ticking time bomb. Avalon wasn't safe as long as she was here. Her presence painted a target on the island. She would leave again, and soon. She'd acquired the bloodweed, and now the Avicen had it. They could figure out what to do with it. But before she ran away again, there were a few matters to be taken care of. Namely, Altair's displeasure.

The general steepled his fingers, his orange eyes drifting shut. Echo suspected he might be counting to ten in his head to rein in his anger, but she couldn't change the truth. She'd run off, against his orders and in violation of her promise to him. The general was a man of his word and therefore not a man who took broken promises lightly. "And then, according to the two of you"—Altair's pointed gaze made the fidgeting Rowan abruptly freeze, like a rabbit spotting a fox lurking in the grass—"you made camp, after which the Drakharin—"

"Caius," Echo interrupted.

Altair's gaze cut to her, but she refused to flinch. It took more willpower than she'd care to admit. Greater women than she had quailed under that gaze. "Then Caius," he continued, "felt a summons from his sister, the reigning Dragon Prince."

Echo nodded. "That's right. The story hasn't changed from the last eight times I told it."

A booted heel came down hard on her toes. In lieu of wincing, she dug her teeth into her lower lip, her eyes darting to Rowan, who was staring straight ahead, his own gaze locked on a point slightly to the left of Altair's head, as if he weren't busy trying to grind her toes into dust. *Message received,* Echo thought. *No talking back to the general.* And while he was at it, Rowan might as well ask water not to be wet.

Altair tapped his pen on the desk, looking down at the notes he'd been taking during their interrogation. His brow crinkled, and for the first time, Echo noticed a few lines near the corners of his mouth. They looked like frown lines, though Altair was, like the Ala, practically immortal. The operative word being "practically"—he could, like other powerful Avicen, live a long, uninterrupted life spanning centuries, barring a violent death. Echo hadn't thought he could get wrinkles, but then, she supposed, war had a way of taking its toll on everyone, even hardened soldiers like Altair.

"And then the Drakharin—*Caius*—transported you all to an island in the North Sea where you encountered the Dragon Prince."

"Yes," Echo replied. "The island where Rose lived a hundred years ago." *Before you sent her on a suicide mission. Before Tanith burned her to death within her own home.* "You remember Rose, don't you? The girl you sent off to die because you wanted to find the firebird before anyone else?"

Rowan's heel slammed into Echo's shin this time, but she kept her eyes on Altair's, her back straight and her shoulders square.

"Rowan?" Altair said, his gaze never leaving Echo's. He placed the pen on his notebook very, very slowly and laid his palms flat on the table very, very deliberately.

"Yes, sir?"

"Will you give us a moment? I'd like to have a word alone with Echo."

Rowan hesitated, torn between his loyalty to his commander and his . . . whatever with Echo. She still wasn't sure what they were to each other, if they were anything at all. But an order was an order, and Rowan was far more adept than she at following those. He left the room, casting a loaded glance over his shoulder as if to warn her to be on her best behavior in his absence. She returned his stare with a raised eyebrow and no promises.

"Follow me," Altair said, standing. "There's something I want to show you."

They left the room through a set of double doors opposite the one Rowan had used. Altair maintained his stony silence as they walked through the halls of the castle and up an interminable flight of stairs. Finally, they emerged onto the rampart overlooking the wing that had become the Warhawk barracks. There was little wind to interfere with the sounds rising from the courtyard in which the soldiers sparred. The ring of steel was punctuated by the occasional bark of a command or the grunt of someone doubling over in pain after failing to block an impending blow. A wrought iron fence divided the courtyard in two, and on the other side, a small circle of Avicelings sat watching the Warhawks practice. There were fewer children than Echo remembered. Fewer Warhawks as well. Two Avicelings stood out, a girl with hair-feathers the color of the summer sky and a boy with coloring as red as a cardinal. Daisy and Flint. Bored with the display, Daisy lolled her head back. She must have spotted Echo on the rampart, because she elbowed Flint in the side and they waved up at her. Echo waved back.

"It was never you I hated." The deep rumble of Altair's voice made Echo jump.

Such a statement was not quite what she had expected. It was almost . . . nice.

"It was the idea of you," he said.

Now, that was more like it. "Oh good, I was worried for a minute you were about to get all warm and fuzzy on me. Can't have that."

Altair turned to her with a glare that was just short of piercing. "Must you always be so"—he paused, groping for the right word—"insouciant?"

Echo shrugged and shoved her hands in her pockets. "Insouciant is my middle name." Altair heaved a frustrated sigh. "But please," she said, "do go on."

Altair inclined his head toward the courtyard, where Daisy was chasing Flint with a slug, the red-feathered little boy not the least bit slowed down by the sling that cradled his right arm. A few other Avicelings shrieked as someone started a mud fight. Mud, Echo knew, was a bitch to pick out of feathers. She'd had to do it for both Rowan and Ivy countless times during their childhood, and she didn't envy whoever was on child-wrangling duty later that afternoon.

"Everything I do," said Altair, "I do for them."

"That is disturbingly warm and fuzzy coming from you."

"You were a child when the Ala found you, and a lost one at that. She could never leave you to fend for yourself. It's not the kind of creature she is. A child alone isn't safe in the human world. The things they do to their own . . ." Altair's voice trailed off, as if he was haunted by memories to which Echo was not privy.

"Trust me, you don't need to tell me about human cruelty," she said. "I know it better than I'd care to."

Altair looked at Echo, as if taking stock of her. "Yes," he said. "I heard."

"The Ala told you about me?" she asked, stunned. She assumed the Ala had made a convincing case for keeping a human child among the Avicen, but Echo had never truly stopped to consider what that would have entailed. A sob story was bound to win hearts, and hers, chock-full of abusive parenting and too many days spent curled under a desk in the library, her stomach cramping with hunger pains, was a story worth a few sobs.

"Of course she did," Altair said. Something in his voice softened as he spoke of the Ala. "Bringing a human into our home was no small matter. It required a unanimous vote among the council, and I was the last to be swayed."

"Color me shocked," Echo mumbled.

"I am not without compassion, Echo." Altair rested his hands on the parapet. His knuckles were covered in a constellation of scars, his fingers calloused from handling weaponry. "But I was afraid."

Echo's shock was so severe that if a strong gust had barreled into her at the moment, she would have toppled right off the rampart. "Afraid?" she asked, incredulous. "Of what?"

"You."

"But . . . I was just a kid."

Again Altair peered down at the Avicelings, who were now making mud angels. "Ours is a dying world. Our magic is diminished, our numbers are shrinking, and our territories grow smaller with each passing day. Humanity's realm continues to expand, and I wonder if we'll soon lose even the small corner of the world we occupy. Every moment of every day, I ask myself how I'll protect them. How I can keep each and every one of my people safe."

"And I threatened that safety," Echo said. *Just like I am now.*

"Through no fault of your own." A soft breeze danced across the rampart and Altair raised his face to it. His brown-and-white feathers gleamed in the sunlight, his bronze features sharp and still. He was every inch the noble general, the brave leader. "You cannot help being human any more than I can help being Avicen." He turned his orange eyes to her. They burned with the ferocity of his emotion. "But I see now that the world is changing, whether or not I want it to. And though you are not one of us, not truly, our fates are intertwined."

"Why are you telling me this?" Echo asked. "Why did you bring me up here?"

"To give you perspective," replied Altair. "So you can see what it is that I see."

Echo looked over the parapet, past the crumbling stone walls of the overgrown garden, past the reddening leaves and silvery bark of the maple tree arching over the courtyard. Below, the Warhawks prepared for war and the Avicelings played, louder and more energetic than she'd ever seen them, as though they could forget the catastrophe that had brought them to this island if only they moved fast enough.

"I brought you up here so that you could appreciate the weight of what I'm going to ask you," said Altair. "You have magic of your own now, and a power that not even I fully comprehend. Use it well. Use it wisely." He nodded his head in a sort of bow toward the Avicen below. "Use it for them. Shelter them as they sheltered you."

The phrase that Echo had carried like a talisman when faced with the specter of her past in the temple came to her in that moment, stronger than ever.

I am a sword.

"I will," Echo said, her words carrying the weight of a promise. "Till my dying breath. But you know I can't stay. The kuçedra went to Grand Central looking for me, and I don't want to bring it here, too. It's bad enough I've been here at all."

Altair nodded. "Yes, the kuçedra was following your . . . scent . . . in a way." His lips tilted upward in a rueful smile that seemed at odds with his stern features. "Do you have such little regard for my abilities as a strategist that you assume such a thing hasn't occurred to me?"

Echo bit her tongue. To say yes would be an insult. To deny it would be a lie.

Altair gestured at the perimeter of the island. "The wards protecting this island are the most powerful our mages could design. The inhabitants of Avalon are undetectable by magical surveillance. That includes the kuçedra, as far as we understand its abilities."

"But that's the thing," Echo said. "We don't understand its abilities. Everything we know is pulled from myths, legends."

There was no way to keep the island safe, not with her on it. The power of the firebird flowed through her veins, making her shine like a beacon in the night. Her blood was potent.

Her blood. Her freaking *blood.* Echo knew a thing or two about wards designed to keep enemies out. And if the firebird was as powerful as the prophecies said, then how powerful would its blood be? *By my blood,* Echo thought, remembering the words she had spoken so many times to pass through the shield that had protected her own home. Her blood had opened the door for the firebird to enter this world; maybe she could use it to keep the kuçedra out of the Avicen sanctuary if it was incorporated into the island's existing shield.

Echo grabbed Altair's arm. He frowned, surprised by the touch. "I have an idea," she said. "It's nuts, but it just might work."

CHAPTER FIFTY

Now that her mission was complete, Ivy was left feeling suddenly useless. She gave the healers in the infirmary the text she'd stolen from Caius's study and spent the rest of the afternoon hiding from the watchful gazes of the other Avicen. She was a rarity: a pure-blooded Avicen who had broken bread with the enemy, who had brushed shoulders with creatures of legend and lived to tell the tale. The few times someone managed to corner her, she had been peppered with questions she had no desire to answer. Even Altair wanted to question her, and barring that, he wanted to put her to work, training other healers and putting their supplies in order. Right now Ivy wanted to be selfish with her time. Just for a little while.

She rounded a corner just in time to see Dorian and Jasper slip into one of the bedrooms in the east wing. She had heard of Quinn's treachery and of his past with Jasper. She guessed that combination of factors was the kick in the pants Dorian needed to get his act together.

About time, she thought.

Everyone was still having their own adventures. Ivy had had one of her own and it had left her feeling high, as if her blood had been transformed into pure adrenaline. The thrill of being useful in a way that was completely within her control was intoxicating, but it had faded quickly as people scattered, drawn away by their own tasks and worries, drifting out of Ivy's orbit. Her usefulness had been depleted.

And that was how she'd wound up here, holding a stale pastry in a folded napkin, standing in front of a closed door as one of Sage's former Warhawks gave her a curious but blessedly silent glance.

There was only one person who hadn't looked at her like he needed her for anything. His usefulness had also run out, and he had been shown to this room, put away like a toy soldier in a cupboard, waiting until someone needed him again, when he would be taken out and dusted off and wound up once more.

Ivy knocked. After a few seconds of fumbling and muffled curses, the door swung open, revealing a tousled Helios, his ink-black bangs falling artlessly across his forehead, his honey-colored eyes alight and alert. When he looked at her, he blinked several times, as if he hadn't been expecting her.

He didn't say anything right away, and Ivy wanted to slink into a dark corner and die. She felt suffocated by shame. She could make up an excuse. She could say she had only stopped by to check on him and had to attend to Very Important Business somewhere far, far away. But then he smiled, and it lit up his whole face, as if her presence had flipped a switch inside him. He looked down at the pastry in her hands and laughed, a low rumble that made warmth spread through Ivy's stomach.

"Returning the favor?" he asked, smile continuing to radiate sunshine.

Ivy shrugged. She could be cool. Totally cool. Cool as a cucumber. "I thought you could use a snack."

Helios laughed once more and threw open the door. With a courtly bow, he stepped aside, gesturing her into the room, and said, "M'lady."

The broad-shouldered Avicen guarding the door put a hand on Ivy's arm to prevent her from entering. "I don't think that's a good idea."

Ivy didn't know the guard. Not really, anyway. She had seen him in the square at the Nest when the Warhawks did their drills, but he was a stranger to her. More so than Helios. A few months ago, the fact that he was Avicen and Helios was not would have been enough to make her heed his warning, but if she had learned anything since the night she'd patched up a half-dead Dorian, it was that their old allegiances were not divinely ordained. They were arbitrary rules, designed to divide.

When Ivy tried to tug her arm from the guard's grasp, he said, "We don't know if we can trust him."

Her gaze cut to Helios. His expression held the beginnings of disappointment, and his hand tightened on the doorknob. He was expecting her to agree with the guard, to cast doubt on his character.

Ivy wrenched her arm free and slipped on her best scowl. "You may not trust him," she said, "but I do."

She was rewarded with another sunshine-bright smile from Helios.

As soon as she entered the room and the door closed behind her, her nerves returned. She felt shy, like a wallflower on her first date. Heat suffused her cheeks. "Is it okay if I stay?"

Helios took the pastry from her and set it on a small table by the bed. He broke the little cake in half and offered her the bigger piece. Against all odds, his smile widened. "I'd be honored if you would."

CHAPTER FIFTY-ONE

Caius had never known darkness like this.

One moment, it felt like he was falling through it, the blackness of the space around him so impenetrable, he half feared it would rush into his lungs were he to open his mouth. The next moment, it felt as though he were suspended in a sea of nothing, weightless and formless, his own body one with the dark. Tanith was nowhere to be seen, though the sensation of her steel grip digging into his arms persisted, a phantom pain that anchored him in that indescribable place.

Over the years, Caius had grown accustomed to all manner of darkness. There was the darkness of the in-between, something he learned to wield during early adolescence; both he and his sister had come into their own unique abilities at the same time. He remembered Tanith running through the halls of Wyvern's Keep, blond curls streaming behind her as her childish laughter ricocheted off the dark stone walls, fires bursting to life in previously cold sconces in her wake.

During those precarious first few months when their powers manifested themselves, their guardians—a collection of tutors and advisors after their parents' deaths—had ordered all flammable items removed from Tanith's bedroom. She had a habit of igniting her surroundings in her sleep. For months, she slept on the cold stone floor, surrounded by her one indulgence: a blanket, for even if that burned, her flames never hurt her.

Caius's early days of manipulating the in-between were equally fraught. As a child, he used to sleepwalk; once he came into his power, his sleepwalking turned into something far more dangerous. He'd fall asleep in his own bed only to awake elsewhere in the keep with no recollection of having gotten there. He'd tried everything: securing himself to his bed with steel chains, downing draughts brewed to inspire dreamless slumbers, wearing herb-infused charms concocted by the court's most senior mages to inhibit magical abilities. None of it worked. Caius's relationship to the in-between was too strong, they said. He, like Tanith, would simply have to master his newfound power through sheer force of will.

Centuries of bending the in-between to his will had made him confident. Arrogant, even. He thought he'd known darkness, but this . . . this was beyond his control. He was a prisoner to this darkness, ensnared in its inky blackness.

A slight pressure, like the caress of a ghostly hand, trailed over his forehead, brushing away the hair that had fallen across his brow.

It's time to wake up, Caius.

A voice was summoning him. It was familiar, and should have been comforting, but there was a strain sewn through it that was wrong, all wrong.

Brother. Wake up.

Tanith. It was Tanith's voice, but it was not. The words themselves were calm, but Caius could not help but feel that she, too, was ensnared by some wild power beyond her control.

And that was when he remembered.

The island.

The bodies of her Firedrakes, slain by her hand.

The kuçedra, its shadows coursing through her veins like blood, bleeding into the crimson of her irises.

The in-between rushing at him, called by his power but not by him.

His eyes flew open, and as suddenly as he had fallen into the darkness, he broke free of it. A surge of recognition flitted through him. He was in his own bed, in which he hadn't slept in months, in his own bedroom in Wyvern's Keep. Light seared his vision, and he squeezed his eyes shut once more.

"So sorry about that, dear brother," came Tanith's voice, thick and distant through the haze of pain in his skull. "You know how I forget myself sometimes."

But Tanith never forgot herself. She prided herself on meticulous control of her abilities. Caius wondered if she clung to the uncertainty and fear of those early months of learning to handle her power, if she used those memories as motivation to never let her control slip again. Again, he noted the undercurrent of something in her voice—something other, something not Tanith.

The reddish glow he could see even through closed lids dimmed. Cautiously, he cracked one eye open, then the other. Tanith perched on the side of his bed, her golden armor pristine, not a single blond hair out of place. The blood had been cleaned off her hands. But her eyes . . .

Some emotion must have flitted across his face—shock, betrayal, disgust, for he felt them all, simmering just beneath the surface—because Tanith raised a hand to her right eye, a sheepish grin tugging at her lips.

"Ghastly, isn't it?" she asked.

Caius wasn't sure "ghastly" quite covered it. The capillaries in her eyes had gone black. Darkness bled into her crimson irises, as if threatening to conquer them.

"Power," Tanith continued, "doesn't come without a price. But if the price I have to pay is my vanity, then I think I got the better end of the deal, don't you agree?"

Caius tried to sit up, but pain lanced through his body and he fell back against the pillows. There were more on the bed than he remembered. Tanith reached behind him to fluff one, and the sleeve of her tunic slipped back. Bile rose in Caius's throat at the sight before him. The protruding veins in her arm were as black as coal, a stark contrast to the paleness of her flesh.

He reached out to touch her, but as soon as his fingers grazed her skin, she recoiled as if his touch burned. She yanked her sleeve down in a show of self-consciousness the likes of which Caius hadn't seen from her in decades.

"Tanith?" His voice was a hoarse whisper, his throat parched and sore. He closed his eyes again and all he could see was the grotesque tableau that had greeted him on the island: the blood-drenched grass, the lifeless bodies of the Firedrakes Tanith had slain, the darkness crawling along her skin like a disease. He opened his eyes and met his sister's gaze, disturbing as it was. "What have you done?"

"What you drove me to."

Her words cut through him as surely as steel. "What I—Tanith, I don't—"

She held up a hand to silence him, and for once, he complied. Any other day, he would have gleefully argued with his sister, but now he wasn't certain that the person sitting beside him was his sister. Not entirely.

"We could have worked together," said Tanith, pushing a lock of hair behind one ear. The veins on the back of her left hand were beginning to blacken. "When you found the firebird, we could have mended what was broken between us. We could have used it for a greater good, but you took it for yourself." She shook her head in short, sharp twitches. It was as if she was talking to herself, not to him. "Perhaps you were punishing me. For my arrogance. For my lack of faith in you. For the sins I've committed against my own blood." Her hand snaked out to clasp his. When he tried to pull away, her fingers dug into the bones of his wrist with a strength he knew she hadn't possessed before. "But I found another way, you see, and it's all thanks to you. Your research led me here." She gestured with her free hand to her eyes, to the blackened veins trailing down her arms. "The firebird is not the only cosmic force in this world that can be harnessed."

Caius pushed himself up, ignoring the pain in his aching limbs, deaf to the screams of his tortured muscles—gods, what had his sister done to him? "Listen to me, Tanith, you don't understand what you're dealing with. The kuçedra cannot be controlled. Not by you, not by anyone."

Tanith's laugh cut through the air like shards of broken glass. It was like nothing Caius had ever heard before. If remnants of his sister were trapped somewhere inside this monstrosity, she was losing the fight. He could hear it in the jagged edge in her voice; he could see it in the darkness coursing its way through her blood, propelled by a force too chaotic to be contained.

"And that's where you're wrong, Caius." She held up a hand and blew into her cupped palm. It was a gesture he'd seen her make a thousand times before, but now, instead of flames bursting to life in the cradle of her palm, shadows, thick and viscous, writhed there as if they had a life of their own. At first he thought it was the same substance that gave form to the kuçedra, but then he felt it. A tugging, deep at the core of his being. His energy plummeted, shrinking as the mass of shadows in Tanith's hand grew. She was drawing on his power, his energy. The aches and pains in his body surged with a ferocity so stunning it stole his breath.

"This is what the kuçedra is. This is what it does," Tanith said, twirling her hand in the air. The shadows danced around it, chasing each other like a school of fish. Caius felt himself deflating as she continued to draw on his power. "It takes and takes and takes."

She flicked her fingers and the cloud of shadows vanished. It was a wasteful expenditure of magic, but Tanith showed no signs of having exerted herself. And why should she? None of the magic was hers. Air rushed back into Caius's lungs, but that sweet relief was short-lived, as pain settled deep into his bones, plaguing every muscle fiber, every beat of his heart with a fresh wave. Magic never came without a price, and it seemed that he was to be the one paying it for Tanith.

Speaking was an exercise in agony. "How?"

Tanith leaned over him, brushing the hair off his forehead. He would have shrunk from her touch had the muscles in his neck and shoulders felt like cooperating. "You are my blood, Caius. We are connected, you and I. We always have been and always will be. What is yours is mine," she said, summoning another small cloud of shadows in her free hand, draining more energy from Caius, "now that I have the power to take it."

She stood and turned away in a swirl of crimson. Her cloak dragged across the stone floor as she made her way to the door. The lock, Caius noticed, had been altered so that it could only be opened from the outside. While Tanith's back was to him, he cast a surreptitious glance at the windows. Through a crack between the heavy green drapes, he saw that they'd been bricked up. It had been hastily done, and pinpricks of light showed at the seams. But even a rush job would be difficult to overcome in his current state. Difficult, he knew, but not impossible.

He looked back at Tanith to find her standing in the now open doorway, her expression calculating. The look, at least, was all Tanith. He'd seen her stare down enemies with that cunning gaze before, and a small part of him felt a thrill of fear at being the target of it. He arched an eyebrow in question, feigning a nonchalance he did not feel.

"I'm not evil, Caius." Tanith broke eye contact first. If he hadn't known any better, he would have sworn he saw a hint of doubt flit across her expression.

"I never thought you were," he said, for lack of anything else. It was true, even if he wasn't entirely certain the force possessing her now wasn't evil. His sister, the one he knew, the one he loved, even after all the loss and bloodshed between them, was not evil. He knew her heart as well as he knew his own, or at least he thought he had, once upon a time.

"By the way," she continued, tone hardening as she spoke, "your friend, the little snow-white Avicen girl, stole one of your old books and one of my Firedrakes." Her scarlet gaze cut to Caius, the blackness seeming to grow with each passing second. "Not quite as helpless as she used to be, is she?"

She clenched her hands into fists. Dark energy crackled around her hands like electricity. Caius fell back on the bed as a surge of pain overwhelmed him. Tanith barked out a laugh and dropped her hands to her sides, releasing him. He sucked in a deep breath of air. His head swam and his vision grayed at the edges.

"Rest now, Caius," Tanith said, one hand on the door's new and improved lock. "You've reached an end, but I'm afraid it's not a happy one." She brushed dirt that wasn't there off her cloak. "Not yet, anyway. You may not believe in me now, but you will. You'll see. With this power I shall herald in a new era for us, for our people. They will no longer live in fear of the Avicen or in the shadow of humanity. I will bring us victory, and through victory, there shall be peace."

Peace. It had never been a concept that held much interest for Tanith. The way she'd phrased it—they'd always steered clear of humanity. Neither the Avicen nor the Drakharin had ever had any desire to dabble in the human world or to invite it into theirs. Humans were a young civilization, much younger than theirs, and like all young things, they were rarely careful with their toys. And that was what Caius knew his species would become under a mass human gaze: a toy, a curiosity, something to poke and prod and slice open just to see how its insides worked.

"Tanith." The name felt like poison on his tongue, but he forced himself to continue. "What are you going to do?"

Her answering smile was beatific. "The kuçedra and I want the same thing. Blood. Pain. Death. I'm going to break them," she said. "And I'm going to start with *her*."

CHAPTER FIFTY-TWO

For the rest of the day, Echo, Altair, and the surviving Warhawk mages—a cohort that included Violet of the purple-pink hair-feathers—brainstormed ways of tailoring Avalon's existing wards with a new spell. The blood of the firebird might save them all. But building spells was not in Echo's skill set. She could follow a list of instructions, but there was a vast world of magical knowledge that eluded her. Constructing a spell wasn't like whipping up a batch of cookies, or so Echo had been told by a scandalized Violet after asking why they couldn't just take some of Echo's blood and slap something together with it. Creating a new ritual was a complex task—not one to be rushed into without considering the metaphysical implications. Or whatever. Echo's eyelids had begun to droop around two in the morning. Altair had sent her to bed with orders to rest. The mages would plot and plan and argue and debate while she slept. By the time she woke, they would—hopefully—have a spell that would make

Avalon the safest place on earth. Echo fell asleep as soon as her head hit the pillow. Let the mages plan the magic. She would be more than happy to open up a vein once they figured it all out.

Screams pulled Echo from her slumber. Her blankets were on the ground and her legs were swinging out of the bed before she had time to think. The air was clogged with the smell of something burning. That was not good. That was very, very not good. Because where there was smoke, there was fire. Rose's presence fluttered through Echo's mind. *And where there is fire, there is Tanith.*

She pulled her boots on, lacing one up only high enough for her to fit the scabbard of her dagger inside. She was halfway to the door when the castle shook, as if someone were trying to blast their way through the thick stone walls with heavy cannon fire. Echo opened the door and hurtled down the hallway, toward the screams. They were louder now, more urgent. And some of them were high-pitched, like those of children.

The Avicelings. They were housed near the Warhawk barracks, which should have been the safest place in the castle. Adrenaline coursed through Echo's veins, propelling her down the winding corridors with as much speed as her muscles could muster. The castle shook again with the ferocity of an earthquake, nearly hard enough to knock Echo off her feet. She rounded the corner that should have left her near the top of the grand staircase, but all that greeted her was a dead end and a small wooden cabinet, the kind for holding linens or some such household nonsense. She let loose a string of curses that would make a sailor blush. There had been no time for her to properly familiarize herself with the layout of Avalon Castle. She'd been there for less than two full days before striking out on her own, and now her haste was coming back to bite her in the ass.

She retreated, trying desperately to retrace her steps. Altair had brought them into the castle using a circuitous route to avoid detection—mustn't let the Avicen know one of their worst enemies was in their midst—and after several wrong turns, she finally—finally—made it to the east wing. Fallen stone blocked off the rest of the castle. Echo's room had been set apart from the others: Ivy, Jasper, Dorian. She said a silent prayer that they would be safe, trapped as they were. She skidded to a stop, her feet reacting quicker to the carnage than her brain. The still form of a Warhawk, surrounded by chunks of stone and wooden shards from a broken bench, blocked her path. A tapestry lay about his legs, as if he'd tried to hold on to it as he fell. His skin was so thoroughly covered in blackened veins that it was hard to tell if he was still alive. Echo knelt down beside him, careful not to touch him. She couldn't risk being taken out of commission before she'd even made it to the source of this man's pain.

Slowly, painfully, the Warhawk's chest rose with a labored breath. The sound gurgled out of him, as if there was fluid in his lungs. "Help them," he croaked. He reached for her, but his hand fell limply to his side before he could complete the motion. "Save them." And just like that, the light faded from his eyes as life fled his body. His gaze rested, unseeing, on the ceiling, the capillaries in his eyes turning from pinkish red to deepest black as the contagion continued to spread through his body even after his heart stopped beating.

I will, Echo wanted to say. *I promise.* But dread constricted her throat, and it was all she could do to push herself to stand, to step around the Warhawk's dead body. She wanted to close his eyes, to do him that one small act of mercy, but she didn't dare touch him with her bare hands. She didn't even know his name.

The corridor was littered with debris. The wall on the other end had been blown out, leaving an almost perfect circle of an opening. Through the hole, Echo could see that the expansion off the east wing, the area in which the Warhawks had taken up residence, had imploded. Muffled screams reached her through the fallen rocks and beams of wood rising from the ground like stalagmites, their tips blackened with what Echo knew was not smoke damage. She had seen it before, on the news broadcast about the volcanic eruption, on the walls of the Nest after the attack, on the face of the clock from the information booth at Grand Central.

The kuçedra had come again. No, that wasn't right. *Tanith* had come looking for her, her body acting as the kuçedra's cage.

The wards, Echo thought. *The wards should have stopped it.* They should have hidden her presence, as Altair had said. But the kuçedra didn't need to sense her to find her. Echo had looked into Tanith's soul and Tanith had looked back. She had known about Avalon. She'd seen it in Echo's memories as clear as day. It didn't matter if the wards shielded Echo from detection. Tanith had been all but handed a road map on a silver platter. The Avicen sanctuary had been violated the moment Echo's mind touched Tanith's. And Echo had been too blinded by her grief over Caius to think such a thing would happen. *Stupid. Stupid, stupid, stupid.*

Tanith could have seen the view that had greeted Echo as the boat carried them toward the island, the battlements rising through a dense fog like something out of a fairy tale. She could have heard Altair explaining the layout of the castle, where different groups were housed, the location of the barracks. Their destruction had not been accidental. It was strategic. Take out the fighters, then pick off the weakest among them. Like ducks in a barrel.

A scrap of Nietzsche hovered at the edge of Echo's memory. *And when you gaze long into an abyss, the abyss also gazes into you.*

Echo pushed herself forward, over the rubble, through the razed section of the garden that separated the Warhawk annex from the main castle, around the fallen mass of the castle's outer wall. She could hear the cries of the people trapped beneath the wreckage. The Warhawks who hadn't been near the annex flowed in the direction of the worst of it, toward their dead and dying comrades, toward the monster that had caused it all.

The sky outside was dark, charcoal-gray clouds blocking the light of the moon and the stars. But even against the backdrop of night, the stain of the kuçedra was visible still, darker than the darkest night, as black as a hole in space, consuming everything it touched.

First the Nest. Now Avalon. There was nowhere left for the Avicen to run. If they lost this home, they would be forced to scatter in the wind, dispersed to cramped safe houses throughout the country, torn apart as a people in exile.

No, Echo thought. The light summer breeze was not cool on her skin as it should have been. It was too warm, too clogged with smoke and dust and despair. She didn't want the

Avicen to have to run. She didn't want them to have to hide. They had given her a home when she had none. She would protect theirs if it was the last thing she did. And, if she was brutally honest with herself, it just might be.

A voice boomed across the small island, amplified by the same magic that held its speaker aloft, floating above the mess she'd made. Tanith's power flashed around, cutting through the swirl of shadows that surrounded her like cracks of lightning. She was flying, which should have been impossible. And yet.

"Ah, the firebird," Tanith said. "So nice of you to join us." She spread her arms wide, her bloodstained cloak flapping open to reveal tarnished golden armor. Her blond hair was laced with streaks of black so dark they seemed to absorb the light around her. "Do you like what I've done with the place?" She lowered herself, her feet not quite touching the one stubborn wall of the annex that remained standing. "I did it just for you."

Echo took half a step forward, intent on wiping the smirk off Tanith's face any way she could, when her jeans caught on something sticking out from behind a slab of stone. She looked down, ready to kick away the offending piece of debris, when she saw a skinny arm, covered in downy red fluff. Flint. She would have knelt down to see if he was okay, but she didn't want to draw Tanith's attention to him. From the corner of her eye, she could see that he wasn't trapped beneath the broken wall's weight; he was hiding. "Go." She tried not to move her lips as she spoke. "Run."

A tiny voice replied, "I'm scared." Flint huddled deeper into his precarious shelter. Echo spared him a quick glance.

He wasn't alone. At least two other Avicelings were hiding with him. *Help them,* the Warhawk had said. *Save them.*

Echo didn't know how. She didn't know if she could. But she had to try.

"When I tell you to run," she whispered, "run."

She walked away from the stone shelter, her stride long and confident. Crimson eyes tracked her movement. Echo was glad Tanith had come alone. Most of the Warhawks had been in the barracks, and the ones who had rushed to the scene had already sustained injuries in the time it had taken for Echo to arrive. She spotted the orange hair-feathers of one Warhawk she recognized—Sage, one of Altair's lieutenants. The right half of her body was covered in a network of wounds, some old and scarred, some fresh and weeping with blood that was almost black in the night. She was standing by the body of a Warhawk whose candy-colored hair—a cheerful pink—was shocking against the blood that covered almost her entire face. Violet, Echo recalled. Sage's sword was held loosely in her left hand.

Sage followed Tanith's gaze to Echo. Their eyes met across the distance. The Avicen nodded once, shallowly. Maybe it was an acknowledgment of Echo joining the battle. Maybe it was a commiseration. A sort of "We're all going to die here tonight, might as well be polite" gesture. Echo tilted her head in the direction of the Avicelings' hiding place. *Help them,* Echo thought. Sage narrowed her eyes and then nodded once in understanding. Good. Echo focused on Tanith, floating above the ruined section of the castle.

Remember what Caius told you, Rose's voice whispered in Echo's mind.

What? Echo thought at the voice. *He told me a lot of things.*

But Rose had fallen silent, either unwilling or unable to share her wisdom.

"Useless," Echo spat.

And then it occurred to her. The first day Echo and Caius had spent alone together, when they'd broken into the Met to find the key that opened the door in the Oracle's chamber, he had held her hand beneath a bridge in Strasbourg and conjured an entrance to the in-between. When she'd asked him why he'd used such an obvious seam between their world and the in-between, he said that just because you had power didn't mean you had to use it. It was a lesson he wished his people would take to heart. But Echo hadn't known the truth then. That the new and terrible Dragon Prince was his sister. That it was her flexing of her muscles and her magic that he had so strongly disagreed with. And right now she was expending energy keeping herself afloat. Leave it to the Dragon Prince to act like she was too good to stand.

Power, Echo knew now, was not an infinite resource. Magic had its cost, even for the kuçedra. She wouldn't have been able to chase it off in Grand Central if its magic had been limitless. She needed Tanith to waste her power. But the only way to do that was to get her to use it. And there was no way that could happen without more destruction, more loss of life.

"Where is he?" Flames crackled in Echo's fists, dancing up her arms. Her hair stirred in the current of her own power. "What did you do with him?"

"My brother is lost to you, firebird," Tanith called out. "He was never yours and he never will be."

White-hot hate boiled inside Echo. If Caius was hurt, if he was dead, she would paint the broken stones of Avalon with Tanith's blood if it was the last thing she did. She climbed atop a pile of rubble. Tanith watched her, amusement dancing in her strange crimson eyes. Black veins, just like the ones that had snaked up her arms when they'd found her in the field, framed her face, leaving most of it strangely untouched. It was almost as if the kuçedra's poison wanted to spare at least some of her golden beauty.

"You want me?" Echo shouted. "Come and get me!"

The kuçedra peered at her through Tanith's crimson eyes, black bleeding into the irises. Echo saw the truth of the kuçedra's desire in those eyes. It wanted to bend Echo to its will, to swallow the light of the firebird until it was extinguished and all that was left in its stead was the darkness of its despair.

It wanted to break her.

Enu sutagan. It destroys.

Try, Echo willed the thought to reach the kuçedra. Tanith twitched her head to the side, as if listening to a far-off shout. *Try to destroy me.*

CHAPTER FIFTY-THREE

Tanith launched a volley of attacks in Echo's direction. Her aim was wild, erratic. Stone exploded on either side of Echo, pelting her with shrapnel that embedded itself in her skin. Everything Caius had ever told Echo about his sister had painted the picture of a battle-hardened tactician. There was nothing tactical in these strikes. They smashed through the remaining walls of the barracks with all the precision of a hastily lobbed grenade. This was sloppy. Echo could work with sloppy.

She darted away from the huddle of Avicelings behind the stone. "Run!" she shouted, not turning to see if they did. Drawing Tanith's fire was Echo's priority, and she could only pray that Sage got the children to safety. A shower of earth erupted as Tanith pounded the courtyard with a fresh barrage of flame. Echo ducked behind a tangled mass of stone and steel. Weapons, warped from the searing heat of Tanith's attack, had bent and broken as they were buried by collapsing stone walls. The stones themselves were as hot as coals.

Fire licked at the stones, reaching for Echo. She answered its call with her own, a black-and-white blaze that circled her like a shield. Tanith's power beat down on Echo, driving her to her knees. Every ounce of strength went into her barrier of flame. It absorbed the crackling shadows like a sponge.

"I grow tired of this game, Firebird." Tanith's voice grew closer and there wasn't a shred of sanity in it. Her fire died as abruptly as it had erupted. "Come out and play."

Echo dug her hands into the dirt, balling them into fists. Her own power quieted. The soil was dry, both from the warmth of summer and from the unrelenting heat of Tanith's fury. It was so hot, the air burned Echo's exposed skin, and every breath she drew scorched her lungs.

I can't do this. Tanith was strong, stronger than she'd been in the Black Forest, and even then, she had been too powerful for Echo's magic. Now she had the full force of the kuçedra chained to her. Echo could feel Tanith's approach on the other side of the mound of debris. Armored boots clanged over the weapons of dead Warhawks, every step bringing with it a fresh wave of despair that threatened to force its way down Echo's throat and suffocate her. She heard the sound of metal crumpling to the ground as the last Warhawks standing fell under the onslaught.

That was not one of Tanith's abilities. It was the kuçedra. It sought to leech the fight from Echo's body by wearing down her mind. Fear seized Echo, squeezing her until it felt as though she would burst. Where the hell was Altair?

The plan to let Tanith burn herself out suddenly seemed

like a childish fantasy. A fool's errand that Echo had undertaken, misguided by her own desperate hope.

Tanith's voice prickled along Echo's skin like a rain of needles. "This is hardly sporting of you. Hiding like a mouse."

Echo huddled deeper in the rubble, the despair projected from Tanith's body—too close now—and fueled by the kuçedra practically blinding her with its might. Movement caught her attention, a flash of white against the backdrop of night. White, she thought, like a Warhawk's cloak. She latched on to the sight, kept it in the center of her vision. The white streak moved along the edge of the ruined courtyard with speed and precision.

"You are nothing to me, Echo," said Tanith. "Nothing. Come out and meet your end with some dignity."

Nothing.

That one word was sharp in its ugliness, striking at the part of Echo that was the weakest. The part of her that was still a little girl, haunted by demons that feasted on her fear. Nothing, just like her mother said.

No. I am not *nothing.*

Echo pushed away from the rubble. Tanith's sickly red eyes widened in surprise, as if she hadn't been expecting Echo to actually heed her request to come out and play. On the other side of the courtyard, the white form revealed itself at the same moment Echo did. Altair stood on the fallen rampart, his sword arm gashed open and bleeding freely. The blade was steady in his hand despite the pain Echo knew he must be in. Their eyes met across the ruined expanse of the barracks. Grim determination burned in his expression. She had promised him that she would use her power wisely, and he was going to buy her the time to do just that.

"Dragon Prince!" Altair shouted.

Tanith spun around, her feet barely skimming the stone beneath her. Locks of her hair defied gravity, undulating around her head like Medusa's snakes. Strands of gold and black wove together, almost beautiful in their ethereal dance. Sparks rained down from Tanith's fists, turning the surfaces they touched as black as soot.

"General." Tanith rolled the word around on her tongue as if savoring its sweetness. "So nice of you to join us."

Altair's long stride brought him closer, never once faltering even as he navigated the uneven footing. Tanith vacillated between him and Echo, seemingly divided. One part of her kept angling toward Altair, but another appeared drawn to Echo's presence as if magnetized.

"Remember what I told you," Altair said. His eyes were trained on Tanith, but his words were meant for Echo.

Altair pounced, his sword arcing through the air. Tanith roared, her power surging forward, toward Altair, away from Echo. This must have been how he planned to buy Echo time. With his life. He was just a man. Strong and brave, but just a man. And a lone man could not stand against the dark.

Tanith's burst of power sent Altair careening into a half-fallen wall. He struggled to his feet, and with a snarl Echo heard from the other side of the courtyard, he lunged again.

Tanith watched him approach. She smirked, golden tresses whipping about her face with renewed fervor.

"He burns so brightly," Tanith drawled. "Such a shame to snuff him out."

The fire Echo expected didn't come. Tanith flew toward Altair—giving up all pretense of walking—and they collided in a tangle of limbs and armor. They wrestled, so fast that

Echo couldn't follow. Rocks and dirt lifted off the ground, carried aloft on the rising tide of Tanith's power. She was expending it without realizing it. It leeched from her, wild and uncontrolled.

Tanith's energy was not limitless. Expending the firebird's energy drained Echo of her own. If the kuçedra truly was the firebird's counterpart, then the physics of it should be the same, Echo thought. All she had to do was let Tanith tire herself out.

Echo was transfixed by the sight of Altair and Tanith fighting, the latter holding back from unleashing the full force of her power, for some reason. Maybe she was toying with him. Maybe she wanted to see how far she could push him before he broke. Something protruded from Echo's boot and dug into her calf hard enough to bruise.

Rose's dagger.

She groped for the hilt, feeling along the edge of the scabbard where it pressed against the inside of her boot. The blade slid free, its steel shining in the light of her flames.

Enu kamalan. It protects.

Echo sliced open the palm of her left hand. The bite of steel barely registered as her blood welled up in the wound. It smeared over the magpies on the dagger's hilt as she switched hands and cut open her right palm. The dagger fell from her hand, the white bellies of the magpies stained scarlet.

Shelter them. Altair's words rang as clear as a bell. *As they sheltered you.*

"By my blood," Echo whispered, pressing her hands into the dirt. She didn't know what she was doing, not really, but instinct and improvisation had gotten her this far. Maybe they would get her just a little bit further. She felt the island pulse beneath her as if it were a living thing. And it was, in its way. It breathed through the blades of grass and the leaves of trees. It fed on the sunlight that bathed the petals of its wildflowers and drank deep from the river that flowed around it. It welcomed her blood as it welcomed the rain. Nature had a power of its own. If Echo could join that power with hers, she would be unstoppable. She thought about the wards they'd discussed into the small hours of the night, the theories Violet had mentioned that Echo had only half understood. In her mind's eye, she built a dome around the island. There was one theory of magic she knew well, for it was the basis of all magic: at the heart of any spell was an intention. If the intention was strong, the spell would be too. Echo poured her intention into the soil and felt the island soak it up.

I am a sword, Echo thought. *I am a shield. Now get the hell away from my people.*

She bled into the dirt, focusing on that thought. There's always a choice, Caius had told her once. She could choose to be a weapon, or she could choose to be a shelter. She made her choice and poured herself into the soil, binding herself to the island with magic and blood.

Two harsh cries rose from the spot where Tanith and Altair were fighting. Echo looked up as Altair fell. A hole had been punched through his armor and crimson streaks decorated his breastplate. Beside him, Tanith held something in her hand. Viscous liquid dripped down her wrist, clumping on her skin.

Altair's heart. Ripped from his chest as if he'd worn no armor at all.

Echo's scream pierced the night, and the island screamed with her. Roots burst from the ground; the fractured stone floor of the courtyard heaved; the trunks of trees buckled and their branches cracked like whips. Tanith cried out as the island rejected her, as Echo willed it to reject her. The shadows receded from the darkened corners of the shattered castle walls and a great weight lifted. Echo pushed with all her might, her hands buried wrist-deep in the earth, her blood pumping into the thirsty soil. Tanith flew up and backward, propelled not by her own wasteful expenditure of power, but by a force that flung her away, carelessly, her limbs as limp as a rag doll's. She hit the water with a loud splash and disappeared beneath its surface. The river carried her away, and the island sighed with relief.

Tanith was not dead, Echo knew, but she was gone, and for now, that would have to be enough.

CHAPTER FIFTY-FOUR

Dawn broke across the river, sunlight bathing the ruins of Avalon Castle, scattering across the water's uneven surface. Smoke piped from the angry columns. Morning came, and with it the death toll, reported by the Warhawks who stepped up to fill the power vacuum left by Altair's death and relayed by Avicen in stunned whispers. Twenty-seven dead, two of them children. Most of them Warhawks, asleep in their bunks when the first wall collapsed, buried beneath feet of stone and charred wood. Those lucky enough to be trapped in the wing of the castle opposite Tanith's attack were spared. It took hours for Echo and the surviving Warhawks to clear an opening for the others to emerge. They had stumbled out into the feeble dawn light in various states of shock. Ivy had pushed her way through the crowd to fling her arms around Echo. Rowan hovered behind her, his eyes red with sleepless strain. Echo extracted herself from Ivy's embrace and pulled Rowan to her. Their last fight seemed so small, so petty. She held him as he buried his face in her hair and breathed in the scent of her. Over his shoulder, she saw Dorian and Jasper climb over the maze of debris, whole save for a few bruises. Strangely, none of the Avicen recoiled from Dorian's presence, though the scales at his temples gleamed in the sun.

"He helped us," Rowan explained as he pulled away. "One of the load-bearing walls had started to crack, and he just grabbed people and got them to safety before it collapsed. He saved a lot of lives."

"Where's Quinn?" Echo asked. She was surprised to find that she cared about the warlock's fate. His was a life misspent on the acquisition of magic and power, but it was still a life. He was their prisoner and they were responsible for him. She didn't want one more death on her conscience. It was weighted down enough as it was.

"Save for a few broken bottles, the wine cellar wasn't damaged," said Ivy. "He's shaken, but he'll live." Her expression darkened, almost as though she wished she could trade his life for that of one of the perished Avicen.

Twenty minutes later, the scent of antiseptic stung Echo's nostrils as Ivy dabbed at the scrapes on her face. They were superficial wounds—nothing serious enough to leave a scar—but Ivy insisted on treating them. After finding the one relatively quiet place in all of Avalon, Ivy had shoved Echo into a rusted metal folding chair in the section of the great hall being used to treat the moderately wounded, refusing to accept Echo's protests of "No, really, I'm fine. Please go help someone who needs it."

Rowan stood behind Ivy, watching the proceedings over the Avicen's shoulder. As a healer's assistant, he was useless, but as a sentinel, he was divine. More than one Warhawk had attempted to steal Echo's attention, but he'd sent them all scurrying away with a stony glare. In the wake of Tanith's attack, Echo's status as the firebird—creature of legend, savior of the Avicen—had transformed her into a rallying point. Echo supposed it was one thing for the Avicen to hear about her exploits in the Black Forest, but seeing it with their own eyes was something else entirely. Now everyone wanted her attention. All she wanted was a shower.

"Ivy, honestly, I'm fine," Echo said, pushing at Ivy's fluttering hands. Ivy frowned but relented, ceasing her ministrations and crumpling the gauze in her hands into a tight ball.

"You say that," Ivy argued, "but you don't look fine."

Rowan broke his stony silence at last. "You look like hell."

"Thanks, guys." Echo shifted uncomfortably in her chair, the need to flee like an itch under her skin. Every beat of her heart sent a searing heat through her body, as if she'd swallowed the sun. The voices in her head clamored for attention, but their words were drowned out in a cacophony that didn't feel the least bit human. Or Avicen. Or Drakharin. The presence was alive, but it wasn't a person. If Echo focused, she felt as though she could isolate the facets of sound that crowded her mind. There was the whisper of blades of grass caressing each other in the breeze. The soft slap of water against a pebbled shore. The whistle of wind between the stems of wildflowers. The sigh of the soil against the castle's foundations. The island spoke in its own ways, and Echo could hear it just as clearly as she could hear the murmurings of the firebird's long-dead vessels within her mind. She had tied herself to the island's defenses, and this was the result.

She could feel the pulse of the island with her own heartbeat, a force so wild and inhuman that she felt as though her skin would burst from trying to contain it all.

"What the hell happened out there?" Rowan asked.

Echo worried the skin of her cheek between her teeth before answering. How could she summarize the sensation of tying herself to a piece of land, winding its threads with hers in a messy tangle of magic and humanity and earth? "I'm not sure I understand it myself," she admitted, "but I beefed up the wards the way we wanted to, just . . . better. And faster."

"And Tanith?" Ivy asked. Her white skin was ashen with confusion, worry, and fear. First the Avicen had lost the Nest. Now the sanctity of Avalon had been breached. It was too much, too soon. "Will she come back?"

Echo shook her head. She wasn't sure how, exactly, but she knew one thing for certain: Tanith would never be able to set foot on Avalon again. Not as long as there was breath in Echo's lungs. It was Echo's will that had propelled Tanith from the island, and it was Echo's will that would continue to reject the Dragon Prince's presence. It was old magic, the kind she'd read about in the Ala's books. Magic fueled by blood and sacrifice and a desire so strong that nothing could stand against it. Echo's blood in the soil—no, the *firebird's* blood in the soil—had guaranteed that the island was *hers*. Hers to defend. Hers to protect. "She won't come back. She can't. I made sure of that."

Ivy's shoulders sagged with relief. "I don't get it," she said softly, "but I really needed to hear that." She began to unwind more gauze from the small pile of supplies on the table beside her, her movements sharper now, more precise. Less weighted down with uncertainty.

"But the Dragon Prince isn't dead," Rowan said. Ivy's relief had not been contagious enough to spread to him. It wasn't a question, it was a statement of fact.

"No," Echo said. "She's not. And she'll try something again, eventually, but I hurt her. Bad. I could feel it, like the two of us were connected. She won't be back soon."

"Still, she will be back. And she'll come back stronger." Rowan shook his head, the tendons in his neck rigid with tension. "She'll be regrouping. We have to do the same."

Gods, he sounded old. Old and tired. Echo swallowed back a lump in her throat. The memory of the last time the three of them had been together batted at her heart. There had been laughter and cake in a quaint little pastry shop on a sunny London street. The people they'd been then had no idea what awaited them. She wished, with a fervor that threatened to choke her with its intensity, that she could travel back in time. That she could warn them. That she could stop herself from hunting down the firebird. That she could wrap them all up and keep them safe.

Regret, she thought, was the most nefarious of emotions. It overwhelmed. It strangled. It was utterly useless.

Ivy's hands inched toward Echo once more. She attempted to slide the jacket down Echo's arms, but Echo caught her friend's hands in her own to still them. "Ivy. Stop."

Ivy shook her head. "You fought the Dragon Prince off, Echo. You're hurt. You need me to help you."

The heat in Echo's chest scorched her bones as it pulsed with renewed strength. Ivy was right. Echo was hurt. There was something desperately wrong with her, but she didn't want to let her friends discover what it was. Paranoia coiled its way through Echo's mind. Ivy had all but confessed that she needed Echo to be strong for her now. They all did, even Rowan, who would never admit it. The Avicen needed a hero, and Echo was going to be that for them. She couldn't let them see her bleed. Couldn't bare her vulnerability to their gazes. She would slink off and tend to her wounds on her own. Let them have the fantasy that she was as strong as they needed her to be.

"Stop," Echo said again. "There are people who need you more. I'll be okay." She offered a small smile that she hoped was convincing. "I promise."

Over Ivy's shoulder, Rowan caught Echo's eye. He'd always been sharper than anyone gave him credit for. He saw things with an artist's keen gaze; details that seemed insignificant to others rarely ever escaped his notice. Echo's words seemed to placate Ivy, who began bundling up her supplies to go help the wounded, but Rowan was not so easily fooled. His head tilted to the side in a silent question. Echo kept that same small smile plastered on her lips. He looked like he was about to press the issue, but a savior arrived in the form of a Warhawk. Sage.

Orange eyes flitted between the members of their trio, alight with an acute curiosity. But if the Warhawk had questions, she kept them to herself. "Rowan," she said, "we need you out there. The remaining Warhawks are divvying up recovery tasks." She nodded at Echo once before turning on her heel and leaving without a backward glance, trusting Rowan to follow her. He almost didn't.

"Go," Echo said. "Both of you. The Avicen need your help. I'll be fine."

I'll be fine. It was her new mantra. It was also a raging lie.

But it was enough to make them leave her alone, and for that, Echo was grateful.

Whispers followed Echo through the halls until she reached her bedroom. She locked the door behind her, shutting them out, and let the silence wash over her.

She took stock of her injuries in the claw-foot mirror in the corner of the room. Angry red scars crisscrossed her skin in thin welts. Unlike the last time she'd faced Tanith, she didn't find herself miraculously cured, her wounds stitched together by an unseen cosmic force. Her palms still stung. Violet, who had been knocked unconscious, not killed, had wrapped Echo's hands with strips torn from her own cloak before Ivy had found her. Now time was the only thing that would heal her. Her still-bleeding wounds were a reminder that she wasn't invincible. But then, neither was Tanith.

Echo met her own gaze in the mirror. The wide brown eyes were hers, though if she angled her head just so, she saw shades of other women, other vessels. Rose's eyes had been darker, Samira's lighter. Even the texture of her hair seemed to change in the reflection. It was normally straight and fine, a chocolate-brown undistinguished to the point of plainness when compared with the vibrant feathers of the Avicen. If she closed her eyes, she could imagine the gentle cascade of feathers down her back, long and bold like Rose's. Or a tumble of copper curls belonging to another vessel whom Echo could not name. She was herself and yet she was not. She was all of them. But Rose had walked away from the firebird. Samira's chance to hold its power inside her had been stolen from her with a blade across the throat. Echo was left to carry its unbearable weight. She alone was left to face the darkness that craved her demise. She'd felt its call just as surely as it had felt hers. The firebird and the kuçedra. The light and the dark. Two sides of the same coin. She had warded the island against Tanith, but she knew the writhing shadows of the kuçedra were waiting, biding their time.

Slowly, she disrobed, shedding articles of clothing one by one. The mirror reflected the horrible truth she had felt pulsing under her skin.

On her rib cage, slightly to the right of her heart, a rounded spot had begun to show, darker than a bruise. Blackened veins branched from it, as if the toxic malevolence were being pushed outward by the force of her heartbeat.

No one could touch the kuçedra's power and remain untainted. Not even Echo. Not even the firebird. It had gone to the Nest in search of her. It had ridden Tanith's body to Avalon, eager to sink its claws into Echo, to infect her with its darkness. Its shadow dwelled inside of her like a cancer, and last night's battle would continue to rage beneath her skin. She pulled on a long-sleeved T-shirt, wrinkled from having been rolled into a ball at the bottom of her backpack. She would hide her mark as long as she could, and so long as there was blood in her veins, she would fight.

CHAPTER FIFTY-FIVE

A large four-poster bed awaited Echo in her bedroom—it wasn't really hers, it never could be—but she spent the night curled in a too-soft armchair in the Ala's room, the soft sounds of the river drifting through the open windows, Phineas Ogilvy's *A Compendium of Fairy Tale Creatures* resting on her knees. She had every intention of returning it to Professor Stirling, but she wanted to read it first. She fell asleep before she'd even finished the preface.

The sound of Ivy's voice roused Echo from her slumber.

"We found a cure," Ivy said quietly, her gaze flicking to the Ala's silent form on the bed. "Maybe. We think. We hope."

They had interpreted the page she'd stolen from Caius's library. It was a formula for an elixir, the chief ingredient of which was the bloodweed Echo had found in the heart of the Tian Shan mountains. It was their best chance, Ivy explained, of fighting the infection. It was a long shot, and they had no choice but to take it. Even the Ala, as powerful as she was,

was weakening rapidly. The beat of her heart had slowed, and her breath had grown shallower as her lungs succumbed to the poison coursing through her veins.

"Someone should be in soon to give it to the Ala," Ivy said, running a hand through her matted feathers. She looked like she needed a good meal, a bath, and a five-hundred-hour nap. "I have to get back to work, but I wanted to tell you myself."

The news was enough to make Echo break her vigil. She slipped from the Ala's room to follow Ivy, her steps as quiet as a cat's. Silence had descended on Avalon in the wake of the attack and the halls were empty enough for Echo to slink through them unnoticed. Fifteen paces ahead of her, Ivy walked, shoulders hunched and arms wrapped tightly around herself. Sorrow plucked at Echo's heart. Ivy shouldn't have to carry that weight. No one should.

Ivy disappeared through a door off the great hall that led to a kitchen that hadn't seen culinary action in years. The sounds of hushed voices and spoons clanging against pots floated through the open door. Echo inched forward. Right before the heavy wooden door closed, she caught it with the toe of her boot to keep it from slamming. She ducked inside, keeping to a low crouch to avoid detection. She didn't want anyone to ask why she was here or what she needed. The Avicen needed a hero. Echo needed to be one, no matter the cost. She was supposed to be their savior, but all she'd brought them thus far was ruin.

Small vials of red liquid sat on a nearby countertop, their contents shimmering in the gaslight like rubies. With a flick of her wrist, Echo had one in her hands. The glass was hot to the touch and the vial felt like it was burning a hole in her pocket as she exited the kitchen and made her way back to the Ala's room, silent as a shadow. No one had seen her. No one had to know.

Back in the room, Echo made sure to lock the door behind her before taking the vial out of her pocket. She transferred it from hand to hand, warming her palms against it. If this worked, no one would ever have to know that Echo had not escaped her encounter with Tanith—with the kuçedra—unscathed. The cork slid free with a soft pop and the pungent scent of bloodweed assaulted Echo's senses. She knocked back half of the elixir before the odor could make her gag. The second the liquid touched her tongue, her body rebelled. A wave of nausea more powerful than she'd ever felt before rolled through her so swiftly that she almost didn't make it to the toilet in the adjacent bathroom before vomiting up crimson.

The black patch of skin over her heart throbbed. With a trembling hand, she yanked the collar of her shirt down far enough to look at it and the sight was almost enough to make her retch again. The black spot had grown. Her pulse hammered in her throat. She could feel every thin vein protruding from the infected area as the toxin burned through her veins like acid. This wasn't right. The elixir was supposed to help her. This didn't look remotely helpful.

She tried to choke down the rest of the elixir, but her body rejected it once more. Every swallow brought a growth of the blackness in her veins as if the poison were spreading out of pure spite. Echo heaved into the toilet, one hand resting against the cool porcelain, one hand clutching the vial so tightly she could feel it starting to crack in her grip. The truth sat heavy in her empty stomach. The elixir would not work on her. Perhaps Echo was too different. She was the firebird. Something not human, not Avicen. Not quite mortal. The rules, it would seem, did not apply to her. Her throat burned as the last of the elixir was expelled from her body. Tears threatened to fall, but she would not allow them. With a strangled scream, she threw the vial against the wall, watched it rain shards of glass on the stone floor. She would find no salvation in a magic potion; she was on her own. Like always. Her limbs felt heavy with exhaustion, only made worse by the trauma of purging her body of the elixir, but she cleaned up the evidence of her failed cure as best she could. No one needed to know. She rinsed out her mouth and splashed cold water on her face. If she looked like hell before, she could only imagine what she looked like now.

Silently, she made her way back to the Ala's bedside. There was nothing for her to do but wait. She picked up the compendium she'd dropped in her haste to follow Ivy, but her eyes made no sense of the words on the page. Sleep claimed her soon enough.

At dawn, a gentle hand nudged her shoulder. She jerked awake. One of the healers from the infirmary stood beside her, a bowl of oatmeal in one hand and in the other a tray bearing a needle, a small bottle full of red-brown liquid, and an empty plastic bag with the biohazard symbol.

"I thought you might be hungry," said the healer.

Echo accepted the bowl with murmured thanks. Her stomach felt hollow, but she didn't dare eat. She was a bundle of nerves, and the smell of brown sugar and oats made her insides twist. Silently, she watched the healer prepare the Ala's injection and only half listened to the explanation that an intravenous dosage was being given to those incapable of swallowing. The sight of the needle sliding into the crook of the

Ala's elbow seemed as though it should have been an impossibility. Echo had never seen the Ala bleed. It was unthinkable that something as mundane and fragile as the metal of a needle could ever pierce the Ala's flesh. To Echo, she had been invincible, a Titan among mortals. The healer withdrew the needle, placed it carefully within the plastic bag, and applied a bandage to the Ala's arm. It was the pale peach color sold in the first-aid section of pharmacies, and it stood out against the Ala's dark skin like a fresh wound.

"Will it really help her?" Echo asked.

"We hope so," replied the healer. "Though I can't say how long it'll take for the elixir's effects to take hold on a case as advanced as hers. If they ever do."

"I'll wait," said Echo.

The healer hesitated, pity etched in the lines of her face. She folded her hands, unfolded them, folded them again. "She might not wake up."

"I'll wait."

Biohazard bag in hand, the healer departed, sparing Echo a sympathetic glance as she closed the door.

Echo folded herself into the armchair by the Ala's bed and drew up her knees. She opened *A Compendium of Fairy Tale Creatures.* Its watercolor illustrations were vibrant in the morning sun, in exquisite condition despite their age. Mindful of the book's increasingly fragile spine, she flipped through the folio's pages with care, admiring one meticulous drawing after the other as the hours slowly slipped by. They were done in the style of Audubon's *Birds of America,* but these creatures were fantastical. Unicorns drinking from crystal springs, gryphons sunning their wings on wide flat rocks, dryads emerging from oaken alcoves. A phoenix, its feathers gold and red, rising from a mountain of ash. Beneath each illustration was a brief hand-lettered explanation of the creature's folkloric origins.

The phoenix, Ogilvy wrote, *is a ubiquitous beast, appearing in mythologies the world over. The concept of death and subsequent resurrection is a popular concept and in ancient civilizations is often embodied in the form of a bird. In ancient Egypt, this entity was known as Bennu. The Persians called it Huma. Slavic mythology features a similar creature known as the firebird. Many iterations of the tale share a commonality: the appearance of a phoenix-like figure is often viewed as either a blessing or a curse, or in some cases, paradoxically, both.*

"A curse," Echo read aloud. That was what she was. A plague upon the Avicen house. "Sounds like me."

"I've always found your company quite pleasant," came a weak voice from the bed.

Phineas Ogilvy's *Compendium of Fairy Tale Creatures* slid from Echo's lap, forgotten as she launched herself from the armchair and fell to her knees beside the Ala's bed. A trembling hand reached for Echo. The swelling in the Ala's veins had diminished, and her skin was as smooth as polished jet.

"Ala?" Echo's voice was barely more than a whisper, but the Ala's face cracked into a fragile smile at the sound of it.

"I'm here, little magpie. A little worse for wear, but free of that vile place."

It took every spare ounce of Echo's willpower not to throw herself atop the Ala's chest and weep. The Ala's smile faded, like the sun retreating behind a cloud.

"Help me up," said the Ala. Echo did as she asked, piling pillows behind the Ala's back and testing them for maximum fluff. She settled on the bed, one leg folded beneath her, her hand clutching the Ala's like a lifeline.

"Vile place?" Echo asked. "What do you mean? Where were you if not here?"

A shiver stole across the Ala's body despite the summer heat and the blankets heaped upon her. "Someplace dark," she said. "And cold. A void where nothing good or clean or bright has ever existed. I could feel it there, the kuçedra, hiding where I could not see it." Her eyes were glassy, unfocused, as if she were slipping back into that terrible nothingness. "But I could feel it. A great drain, as if the life was being stolen from me. It was feeding on me, growing stronger as I grew weaker." She shook herself, her strength returning in small pieces. Her gaze rested on Echo, warmth seeping into it like the coming of dawn. "Was it you who freed me?"

"I can't take all the credit," Echo said. She hid a sniffle behind the back of her hand, though she knew the Ala's keen eyes missed nothing. "Ivy did the hard part."

The mention of Ivy's name made the Ala sit up straighter despite the weakness that obviously still plagued her. "Is she all right?"

Echo nodded. "She's fine. She'll be happy to know you're awake."

The Ala canted her head to the side. *Keen eyes,* Echo thought. "And the others?"

"Rowan's okay. He's downstairs, helping the other Warhawks. Dorian and Jasper, too."

The absence of one name was not lost on the Ala. "And Caius?"

Echo looked down at the fraying laces of her boots. They'd

need replacing soon. Outside, a bird warbled a lonely tune, its song carried away by the wind and the river.

"He's gone. Tanith took him," Echo said. "I lost him."

We lost him. Rose's grief was fresh and strong, compounding Echo's own.

"Chin up, my little magpie." With her free hand, the Ala nudged the underside of Echo's jaw. "Nothing is ever lost forever." She patted Echo's knee. "Now, tell me what happened while I was sleeping. I could feel the kuçedra coming closer, but then all of a sudden it retreated, as if something had pushed it back."

"That might have been me," Echo said. "Tanith found us." Echo didn't mention how. The shame of her carelessness burned like a brand. She'd given up the location of the Avicen sanctuary the moment she'd touched Tanith. The kuçedra had looked into her soul and seen all her secrets. The carnage outside was on Echo's conscience. "We fought. I won."

"You did something," the Ala said. "The island feels . . . different. Charged."

"Remember that spell we used to create the wards around my room in the library?" Echo said. "The ones that were bound to me and kept other people out?"

The Ala nodded.

"I found another use for it."

"Clever girl," said the Ala. A cough shook her chest. It was wet, as if she'd been drowning and was now on dry land. She pounded her chest weakly until it subsided. "And our forces? Altair?"

Echo closed her eyes. The sight of Altair's heart, clutched in Tanith's clawed fist, leaking blood onto her porcelain skin, was as fresh as it had been the day before. "He died."

The Ala was silent for several minutes. Echo opened her eyes. The sheen was difficult to see on the Ala's dark skin, but the tears were there, falling silently from raven-black eyes. She didn't brush them away, as Echo would have. She let them fall freely. "We've lost so much, you and I. We will not lose any more."

"But how? I can't fight Tanith like that again," Echo said. The Ala was the one person she didn't need to be tough for. "She's too strong. She has an army. She has the kuçedra." A flash of memory: armor shredded as if it were as flimsy as tissue, blood soaking into blackening soil, the cry of a vulture awaiting its carrion. "She bound it to herself just as the firebird is bound to me. She's its vessel now. How can I beat that?"

"An army does not a victor make," said the Ala. "And power can be overcome. Caius was stolen from you. You know what you have to do."

"What's that?"

"You're a thief, Echo." The Ala squeezed Echo's hand, her grip strong despite her frailty. "Steal him back."

ACKNOWLEDGMENTS

When you're a rookie writer, there's one bit of wisdom you tend to hear a lot: second books are hard. But hearing it and living it are two different things, and nothing quite prepares you for just how hard your second book is going to be to write. Thankfully, I (and *The Shadow Hour*) had a team of amazing people to keep me (relatively) sane when it felt like I wouldn't survive to see the end of this book.

I'm incredibly lucky to have an editor like Krista Marino. There were times during the writing process when I felt completely adrift, and she was always there to reel me back in when I needed it. Krista, thank you so much for your patience and your sage advice and your kind words.

It takes a small army to produce a book, and I'm glad the folks at Delacorte Press and Random House Children's Books are on my side. Aisha Cloud, you are a great publicist and a fantastic person. I loved the cover for *The Girl at Midnight* so much and I wasn't sure how Alison Impey was going to top it, but did she ever. The fact that Jen Wang's gorgeous illustrations are on these covers continues to blow my mind. I'm in love with the work you've all done.

A million thank-yous to my agent, Catherine Drayton, for helping me keep my head on straight when I was feeling most overwhelmed. Between the expected challenges of writing a book and the unexpected challenges of illness and injury striking at the worst possible times, Catherine was there to hold my hand, and I'm so, so, so grateful.

I'm indebted to the early readers of *The Shadow Hour.* The Midnight Society—Amanda, Idil, and Laura: You guys are my true north. When it felt like I had no direction, I reminded myself that I was writing this book for you (mostly because I know you'd straight up murder me if I didn't). And Virginia Boecker, who read a very messy version of this book and managed to find the good in it when I couldn't see it: We survived our Book Twos. Go team.

And to the readers of *The Girl at Midnight:* Thank you. Seriously. Thank you for spending time with Echo and Ivy and Jasper and Dorian and Caius and Rowan and Rose. Thank you for your tweets and your Tumblr messages and your emails. Thank you for caring about the people who live on the page. Thank you.

Turn the page for a special preview of the thrilling conclusion to

THE GIRL AT MIDNIGHT series.

Published by Delacorte Press, an imprint of Random House Children's Books,
a division of Penguin Random House LLC, New York.

PROLOGUE

It had been so hungry for so long.

Hungry and cold, wandering the abyss, alone and unmoored. A solitary shadow lost in a dark sea.

No, It had not been hungry. Hungry was too gentle a word for what It had felt. It had been ravenous. There was a great, yawning chasm inside It that ached to be filled.

But there was nothing with which It could soothe Its hunger, slake Its thirst. There was just the nothing in which It was suspended. Trapped. Caged. It was the only thing that existed, adrift in all that nothing. It, and the bright shining light of Its seal. The bars of Its cage glowed with a warmth upon which It wanted to burn Itself. But try as It might, It could not reach the light. The light remained, like an end to Its long torment, out of Its grasp.

Until one day, the Light went out.

It did not understand where the Light had gone, but It felt a release the moment the Light disappeared. Like air rushing into a vacuum. The Light had departed and the Darkness inched forward, through the void, waiting to be burned. Waiting for the Light to reappear, casting It back into the solace of the shadows, but there was nothing.

Nothing. Except a door, left ajar in the Light's wake.

It rushed through the opening left in the absence of the Light and broke free of the cage It had known for so long that It had forgotten there was anything else in the world.

And, oh, what a world it was.

It had forgotten what it felt like to be free, to be able to soar cross the skies, as unstoppable as a storm. Like a wild beast It fed on the first thing It found, a village filled with life and love. It devoured that place, shrouding it in darkness, but the meal was a small one, which only served to whet Its appetite for more.

There were lights and sounds and people. The people It favored so. Their screams were delicious, coating the insides of Its empty belly, easing the growling ache that had taken up permanent residence there. It had been so empty, but now . . . now, It could feast. It gorged Itself on the things It found, yet still, It felt a tug.

The Light was not gone. Not truly. Not completely. The Light was there, somewhere, in the world—the great, wide world, with its sumptuous offerings and delectable woes—and It realized now what the Light had been. Not solely a cage—though it had been that—but a complement. A companion. They needed one another to exist, though. It had despised the Light. Hated it with every particle of Its being, and that hate had sustained It, but without the Light, there was no counterpoint to Its existence. No balance.

And so, It sought out the Light. Sniffed out where its

presence was strongest. Through this world It floated, drawn to places where that other thing burned brightest. There, It planted Its seeds of sorrow, drank Its fill from the dead and dying. Another feast It had found, this one a familiar taste, so like the little beasts that had locked It away, all those eons ago. It took particular delight in the flavor of the suffering. The pain almost sated the hunger. Almost, but not quite. There was still something missing. Something vital.

But try as It might, It could not tether Itself to the world. It did not belong. It was other, like the Light. But the Light had found a place to call home. A port at which to anchor. It had nothing. Nothing but a vague sense of self-awareness. Of the things that were It and not It. It wandered the world, as lost as a frightened child, until It heard her calling Its name.

It had forgotten that It even had a name.

Her shout was the roar of a dragon, all fire and smoke and ash. It could smell the blood in which she bathed, and It shivered with anticipation. It fed on death and woe, and that was what she brought with her. Across the unfathomable distance of the void, It felt her cry, her longing, and It strained to find her, to reach for the feast she had prepared for it.

It answered her call with one of its own: *Who are you?*

It sensed the moment she heard Its voice, cutting through the sound of the screams of those she betrayed. She paused, her sword dripping with the blood of sacrifice.

I am Tanith, she said. *I am the Dragon Prince.*

That was not the answer It craved. Names were meaningless in the abyss, and titles even more so. Darkness desired no label. It repeated Its query, delivering it with enough force to make her stumble, despite the distance that divided them.

Who are you?

It needed to know. It needed to be sure.

She seemed to understand then. *I am death,* she said, her voice echoing across the distance. *I am destruction. I am yours and you are mine. Come to me, kuçedra. Come to me and give me your strength.*

Her want was so fierce. It knew, with stunning clarity, what she yearned for: power for herself, for her people, enough to remake the world in her image, to destroy everything that wasn't what she wanted. The magnitude of her hunger matched Its own. Her desire was a beacon, and It followed that beacon to shore.

Kuçedra. That was Its name. It was a fine name, a name to be feared. It was this name she called out, allowing herself to find It, for It to find her. Perhaps there was power in names after all.

CHAPTER ONE

The Agora had, in Echo's modest lifetime, never been this empty. On an average day, it was packed to the rafters with a wild assortment of characters selling everything from mismatched tea sets to magic potions of varying efficacy. Most of the shops were owned and operated by Avicen, most of whom had evacuated when their safe haven—the Nest—proved to be less safe than they'd thought.

Echo walked past shuttered storefronts, gravel crunching beneath her boots. Beside her, Rowan kept a watchful eye on the stragglers who had refused to abandon the once-bustling market in the wake of the Nest's fall. His hands were thrust into his pockets; he would have looked like he was out for a casual stroll if not for the tension threaded through his back and the tightness of his jaw. The Agora was not the same as it once was, but then, Echo thought, none of them were.

The gaslights that illuminated the Agora's cavernous

interior cast a greasy yellow glow over the bare tabletops and darkened windows. Gone was the plum-feathered Avicen woman named Crystal who had peddled a bizarre collection of knickknacks culled from all over the globe. If you were looking for buttons to adorn a Victorian-era waistcoat, she was your girl. If you were in the market for a shrunken head—cursed, naturally—pilfered from an obscure cultist tribe in the depths of the Amazon rain forest, she was also your girl. But now, her little kiosk stood empty, bare of its eccentricities and strangely morose in the Agora's gloom. Also gone were the blacksmith—an Avicen by the name of Othello who had a deep and abiding obsession with speaking in iambic pentameter—and the cobbler and the baker. The cobbler had repaired more than one pair of Echo's boots over the years, and the baker would sneak her treats when his wife wasn't looking in exchange for the latest issue of *Spider-Man*. She'd spotted the cobbler in one of the overcrowded rooms in Avalon Castle, where those who'd survived the attack on the Nest had sought refuge, but the baker was listed among the missing. A wall in the castle's foyer had been requisitioned as a board for people to post notices of loved ones unaccounted for, though Echo had let her gaze wander to it only once, and only for a few seconds. It made her stomach feel as though icicles were sprouting inside, spearing her tender organs with their sharp chill. There were too many names on that board she recognized, too many faces she knew. There was nothing she could do for the lost and the dead. At least that's what she told herself.

She wondered if the plum-feathered Avicen woman—Crystal—had survived the attack on the Nest. Echo hadn't seen her photo on the board, but she hadn't pored over every single one. She'd spent a few days raking her eyes over the haunted faces of the refugees at Avalon, but doing so had threatened to drive her mad. It was easier, Echo found, to wonder about the people whose faces she didn't see. She couldn't bear to think of them as dead, and if, by some miracle, they weren't, she couldn't bear to see the accusation she feared would be in their eyes. Not all of the Avicen blamed Echo for the tragedy that had befallen them, but enough of them did to stoke the embers of guilt in Echo's heart to a roaring fire.

Echo and Rowan stuck to the edges of the Agora to avoid the few vendors who had bothered to stay—warlocks, every last one of them, probably selling mummified kittens in jars or something equally horrific. Their pale gazes burned holes in her back. They watched, but they didn't approach. A small part of Echo hoped they were afraid of her. Warlocks were bad—the kind of bad that should exist only in fairy tales where tricksters spirited away firstborns or made princesses spin gold until their fingers fell off. They were as monstrous as humans could make themselves, and if monsters were afraid of Echo, then maybe she stood a chance in the messed-up fairy tale her own life had become.

Her footsteps slowed as she approached her destination: Perrin's Enchanting Essentials.

"Wait outside?" she asked Rowan. She didn't like the look of those warlocks, even if she was newly fearsome. Judging by his terse nod, Rowan didn't like the look of them either.

"Hurry back." He took up a position by the door, looking every inch the strapped Warhawk recruit, despite his civilian clothes. He had changed too, just as much as Echo had. With a small huff, Echo steeled herself and entered the shop.

The door swung open with a weak squeal. The hinges were rusty, something that happened to metal with ease down in the Agora, yet Perrin had been fastidious about maintaining his shop; he'd taken such pride in it. But he wasn't here anymore, not to oil the hinges, nor to wipe down the glass countertops, nor to refill the small bowls of fragrant flowers placed strategically around the room. The flower petals had long since wilted, and the display cases had collected a heavy layer of dust. Handprints cut through the dust in spots, evidence that someone had tampered with the protective charms Perrin had placed on the cases to guard their contents. Those cases stood mostly empty now, ransacked of anything of even moderate value. Shame flooded Echo at the sight. It hadn't occurred to her that no one would be around to tend Perrin's shop after . . . well, after.

If she was completely honest with herself—and she avoided doing that more often than she cared to admit—she had deliberately skirted memories of Perrin. She hadn't wanted to remember him. Not his life. Not his death. Memory was a burden borne by the survivors. Dying, Echo knew now, was easy. It could be painful or frightening or any number of things, but when it was done, it was done. She had died once before. She knew, better than most. It was living that was hard. Moving forward when memory wanted nothing more than to pull you back . . . that was the real challenge. Like Sisyphus pushing his boulder uphill for all eternity, it was a battle that could not be won. But the living kept trying because that was what it meant to be alive. To keep going lest the boulder crush you under its weight. That would be giving up, and giving up was not an option. It hadn't ever been, not for Echo, not since stabbing herself in the heart and tying her life inextricably to the fates of thousands.

Echo walked toward the back room of Perrin's shop, where she knew he kept the stuff too expensive or rare or downright dangerous to display. The skin between her shoulder blades prickled as if she weren't alone. A glance around showed that she was, but the feeling lingered. Ghosts, then. Or guilt. Sometimes it was hard to tell the difference. Even if she didn't want to remember Perrin, it was only a matter of time before memory—fickle, cruel thing it was—caught up with her. She didn't want to remember the first time she'd entered this very shop, hand clutching the Ala's, eyes as wide as saucers, as she took in the utterly disorganized assortment of glittering wares. Didn't want to remember the cookie he'd given her when he caught her eyeing the open box of macarons on the countertop—it had been a raspberry-flavored one, and the cloyingly sweet filling had stuck to the roof of her mouth. She didn't want to remember the first time she'd accepted a job from him; for some reason, he'd wanted a 1961 Mickey Mantle baseball card—"Mint condition or don't bother darkening my doorstep, please"—and so Echo had tracked down a collector, slunk into his office, and swiped the card from his album when he was out to lunch. Perrin had given Echo a six-month supply of shadow dust in exchange, teaching her the ways of the Avicen's barter economy.

And that was how she'd decided she ought to be a thief instead of a mere pickpocket. She'd discovered something about herself: she was good at stealing other people's things, really good. The knowledge that she'd developed such a talent filled her with a confidence she'd never had before.

She didn't want to remember how much the person she was now had been shaped by Perrin's request for a baseball card. And she did not want to remember the last time she had seen him, eerily motionless, either dead or dying, reduced to nothing more than a pile of rags huddled in the corner of a damp dungeon in the belly of Wyvern's Keep. She hadn't said goodbye; she'd been angry at him. He'd told the Drakharin about her—what she did, where to find her—and it hadn't mattered to her then that the information had been tortured out of him or that he'd died scared and alone and in pain.

Regret clawed at Echo's insides like a beast fighting to break free. Her vision blurred as she rifled through the back room, messier than it had been even when Perrin was alive. His records were less of a system and more of a loose constellation of papers strewn about his desk, crammed into drawers, and spilling over densely packed bookshelves. What she was searching for would be hidden, most likely. Perrin had managed to track her for the Drakharin using a bracelet he'd fashioned from braided leather, shiny beads, and his own feathers. Echo had left the bracelet in her cell in Wyvern's Keep, but she knew a tracker was no good without a way to track it. He'd probably used a scrying bowl or a mirror or something like that to locate the bracelet, which he knew had been attached to Echo. The same bracelet Caius and his Drakharin agents had used to find her when she'd been hunting down the objects Rose had scattered around the globe, a scavenger hunt that led straight to the firebird. It was the feathers that made locating it possible. A little biological material, a clever enchantment, and a reflective surface to tie a charm to, *et voilà:* a tracking spell, so easy even a modest shopkeeper could use it. If Perrin had been around for Echo to ask why he'd done it, he probably would have said it was to keep an eye on her. But he wasn't around, so she couldn't ask. She shoved a pile of books off a box, flinching when the noise reverberated through the abandoned shop. The counterpart to the bracelet had to be here somewhere. If it wasn't, then their only lead to find Caius was dead. Dead, dead, dead.

She should have said, "Goodbye."

She should have said, "I'm sorry you got dragged into this mess."

She should have said, "Thank you for the macaron. It was lovely and I was so hungry and you were kind when I had known so little kindness."

But she hadn't said any of those things. She had left his broken body to rot in that dungeon, and now there was no one left to say anything to at all.

Echo stepped over broken glass and collapsed tables, making her way to the office where Perrin kept his account books.

The room itself was modest. Large, heavy tomes, bound in unassuming brown leather, lined the shelves, their spines embossed with golden dates spanning back to the late nineteenth century. The Agora had been around for a long time. When it was established, the island had been a Dutch colony by the name of New Amsterdam, and the market had weathered the years since. Perrin's records were meticulously arranged in chronological order on shelves that covered every inch of wall space. The books' bindings had been worn smooth by age and handling. The business had operated, like most Avicen enterprises, on a complicated bartering system. Echo's involvement with Perrin had been relatively simple. He had requests. She fulfilled them, acquiring goods out in the human world that were difficult for an Avicen to come by, and in return, he kept her in a steady supply of shadow dust.

But she knew from watching him work in the shop that his other arrangements had not always been as simple. The shopkeeper had woven a complex web of favors and debts, and each of these books was a record of every transaction he had performed in the year stamped on its spine. The books had obviously been pulled off the shelves with frequency. There was a scant bit of dust on them from the months of neglect, but they still showed signs of once-common usage. Echo had no doubt that Perrin remembered, with the aid of his detailed record keeping, every favor owed him by the Avicen—and occasional warlock—who passed through his shop. A less discerning eye might not have caught the slight aberration among the books, but Echo, who spent the vast majority of her life surrounded by books in various states of disrepair, noticed it.

A single ledger, almost identical to its neighbors. The year, written in faded golden lettering on its spine: 1961. Echo snatched at a fragment of memory: Perrin, listing the greatest baseball teams in the history of the sport during one of the slow days at his shop, when Echo had come around looking to stock up on shadow dust only to find herself roped into one of his diatribes on sports. She couldn't remember most of what he had said, but she remembered the enthusiasm in his voice as he'd described the virtues of the 1961 Yankees: Victors of that year's World Series after defeating the Cincinnati Reds in five games; home of both Mickey Mantle and Roger Maris, who were famous for racing to beat Babe Ruth's home run record. The memory would probably have remained buried deep in Echo's subconscious if not for the condition of the ledger.

The spine was not cracked.

The leather showed signs of handling, particularly near the top where someone would have pressed their fingers to the book to pull it off the shelf. But unlike every other ledger in the office, it showed no sign of having been opened repeatedly. Echo doubted that Perrin had no reason to ever consult the book to see who, in 1961, owed him either favors or fortune. This book was not for reading. She rested her hand atop it and pulled.

The ledger did not slide off the shelf as it should have. Instead it angled forward like a lever. Echo continued applying gentle pressure to the book until she felt a click. The shelf swung toward her, revealing a shallow alcove set into the wall.

"Jackpot," Echo whispered.

Inside the alcove were the treasures Perrin didn't want found, some more obviously valuable than others. A triptych frame housed three tintypes of Avicen whom Echo had never seen before; the Avicen in the pictures were all short, like Perrin, and one of the younger ones had his deep-set eyes. Family, most likely. If the photos had been tucked away in this secret alcove, they had probably meant a great deal to Perrin. He would never be coming back for them, and it seemed wrong, somehow, to leave them there, forgotten. Echo slung her backpack off her shoulders and unzipped it. She carefully folded up the triptych and wrapped it in a scarf she found wadded up at the bottom of her backpack. Perhaps the Ala would know if Perrin had any surviving relatives who would appreciate the pictures. If not, then Echo would keep them, and even if she did not know the names of the Avicen in them, she would remember them. For Perrin.

On the alcove's uppermost shelf, she found what she was looking for: a silver bowl, decorated with ornate etchings scrolling around its exterior. It was a scrying bowl. The same one Perrin must have used to track the bracelet he had given her. Inside the bowl's basin was a ball made up of multicolored rubber bands. Echo put it aside, extremely doubtful that it was related to the bowl and its use. Perrin's hoarding habits had always skirted toward the peculiar.

The bowl was heavy in her hands, far heavier than it looked. It must have been made out of solid silver, and not merely plated in it. The designs carved into the sides depicted roses, tangled up with vines, and long, willowy branches of blossoming mugwort, with its distinctive thin, sharp leaves. Both flowers were common in divination rituals, and Echo suspected that carving them into the silver had amplified the magic of the bowl. She held it in both hands and breathed deeply. The Ala had been trying to teach her meditation techniques, but so far, Echo had proved to be an atrocious pupil. It was so rare for the wheels in her mind to stop spinning long enough for her to find that calm place the Ala insisted was there. Echo tried it now, pulling in slow, languid breaths, focusing on nothing but the silver bowl. The weight of it. How it felt in her hands.

Her eyes closed. In the silence, she listened for the sound of the blood rushing through her veins, the beating of her heart, the flow of air in her lungs. And then she found it. That calm place. Once she was there, she knew exactly what the Ala had meant during those interminable lectures. She was hyperaware of the nerve endings in her skin. All her senses were heightened. She heard a mouse scuttle across the floor in the main room of the shop, the faint murmur of voices out in the Agora as the warlocks went about their business. The silver bowl was cool against her palms, and the more Echo focused her attention on it, the more she noticed about it. There was magic in it, worked into the metal itself, perhaps by whoever had done the carvings.

No ordinary bowl would hum with that kind of energy.

Echo opened her eyes. The sensation of magic left her in a dizzying wave, like air rushing from her lungs after a punch to the gut. The Ala had mentioned something about disengaging from a meditative state, but Echo hadn't really been listening. Now, she wished she had. She took a moment to steady herself. Her skin felt like it was stretched a little too tight over her skeleton, and the sounds that she had noticed had retreated back into silence, too slight or far away for her to hear them. She made a vow to herself to actually listen when the Ala was imparting wisdom the next time they sat down for a chat. There was so much for Echo to learn, so much that she did not understand. Arming herself with knowledge had always been her way of making herself not feel quite so helpless. Even when she had been a tiny runaway, living off stolen scraps, she'd had the books in her library to ground her. Listening wasn't as easy as reading, at least not for Echo, but she made a silent promise to do better in the future. The Ala needed Echo at her best. All of her friends—her family—did.

Caius did.

And that's what she would give them.

Echo zipped up her backpack and gave the room a final, cursory glance. Maybe the Ala could send someone down here—if there was anyone to spare—to gather Perrin's things. Or maybe even take over the shop. The world would return to normal. Echo would make sure of that. Or die trying. Either way.

She slung her bag over her shoulder and exited Perrin's Enchanting Essentials, possibly for the last time.

Rowan quirked a questioning eyebrow at her as she joined him. "Did you find it?"

She nodded. "Right where I thought it would be."

"Good," said Rowan. "Let's get out of here before those warlocks find the courage to try to catch themselves a firebird."

"You know, I think I liked it better when no one paid me the slightest bit of attention." But those days, Echo mused, were long gone. She was someone now, whether she liked it or not.

Armed with the newfound scrying bowl, Echo made her way out of the Agora, ignoring the curious stares of the warlocks and Rowan's answering glares. She felt lighter as she left, soothed by the fact that she was being productive, that she had purpose. With a skip in her step, she exited the market's secret entrance, in the hot dog restaurant on St. Marks Place, and breathed in some not-so-fresh city air.

Onward and upward, Echo thought. There was work to be done. She had a locator spell to learn and a lost prince to find.